MURDER

ON THE BLUEGRASS
BOURBON TRAIN

D1602577

MURDERS IN BOURBON COUNTRY

SCARLETT DUNN

SCARLETT DUNN BOOKS

ACCLAIM FOR SCARLETT DUNN

"Dunn intersperses enough action and love in this faith-filled inspirational to soften the hardest hearts. Weaknesses are revealed, temptations are strong, tough lessons are learned, and forgiveness is earned. This uplifting novel will keep readers warm all winter."

—*Publishers Weekly* Starred Review
Christmas at Dove Creek

"*Promise* is a brave, resilient heroine of faith...[in] Dunn's subtly inspirational western romance. *Finding Promise* follows *Promises Kept* in Dunn's McBride Brothers series; libraries will want both and those to follow."

—*Booklist* Starred Review

"Dunn gives great visual accounts of the town, with well-developed characters. With fast-paced writing, and many unexpected twists and turns, you will want to keep reading to see the outcome. Like the first installment, this book leads the reader to strong emotions and opinions. Conflict begins right from the start."

—*RT Book Reviews,* 4 Stars
Return to Whispering Pines

"An enjoyable historical romance with charming characters...The storyline is believable and flow smoothly, with nice twists and turns.

Dunn is a talented author who gives fans what they expect in historical romance."

"Fans of both ethical dramas and historical romances will find much to enjoy."

"It is bittersweet when a series ends; questions are answered, readers are reunited with beloved characters. Mary Ann was a favorite; she defied her family and society to explore the Wild West and to prove she could take care of herself. Dunn in a talented author who has brought new and refreshing ideas to the historical romance genre."

"A Textured, uplifting, inspirational love story."

"Marshal Jake McBride is the quintessential romance hero: strong, fiercely loyal to his family and dedicated to justice."

"The banter between these two free-spirited characters had me smiling bigger and bigger as I turned each page. I didn't want it to end!"

"This one swept me off my feet...I didn't want it to end!"

"For those who want a little historical romance and bad boy cowboys, this is the perfect read."

To the beautiful state of Kentucky

PROLOGUE

THE PALE LEMON BENTLEY CONVERTIBLE screeched to a halt at the end of the long driveway. An elegantly groomed platinum blonde sprang from the vehicle, leaving it running as she stormed toward the man casually leaning against a shiny black Mercedes.

"What do you mean you're breaking it off?" she shrieked.

"Calm down, darlin', before you have a heat stroke." K.C. Cleary's deep voice was as smooth as an expensive aged bourbon flowing over ice. He'd chosen the isolated farmhouse to meet Eugenie because he knew she would be in rare form by the time she arrived. Thankfully, no one lived within a twenty-mile radius to hear her rant. But that also meant the miles she'd driven afforded ample time to fuel her anger. He intended to remain calm, no matter the insults she hurled his way.

K.C.'s cool demeanor infuriated her all the more. "Don't *darlin'* me! How dare you text me and say you're breaking it off! I'll tell you when we end this relationship!" She poked his chest with her forefinger, emphasizing each word, while carefully avoiding damage to her perfectly manicured acrylic nail. "And we are *not* ending it now."

Expelling a deep breath, K.C. looked heavenward, silently asking for patience to deal with her histrionics. This was exactly the scene he had intended to avoid. "Eugenie, you're ignoring the fact that I discussed this situation with you last night. Then you send me a text this morning as if we haven't been over this. I agreed to meet you one *last* time to tell you that I'm serious."

He'd tried to end their affair last night in a gentlemanly manner, but he'd obviously made a mistake waiting until she'd had a few shots of bourbon to discuss the matter. He repeated the same carefully crafted words he'd used last night. "We were good together, but we both knew our affair wouldn't last forever."

Stepping away from her, he made a sweeping gesture with his hand as if imitating a game-show model presenting a valuable prize. "Look at you, you're a lovely woman. You certainly won't have any problem replacing me."

Eugenie couldn't argue that point. She knew she looked great. She'd specifically selected her most flattering suit, the color matching her Bentley, to make a point. It was her intention to show K.C. what he was about to lose. Since dating him she'd lost over twenty pounds, and she was so toned she could have starred in an infomercial hawking the latest workout contraption guaranteed to work miracles. Exercise was not something she enjoyed, but her daily routine, plus a fabulous plastic surgeon, made it possible to maintain the appearance of an ageless thirty-nine-year-old. It was a source of pride that she could keep pace with a man twenty-plus years younger. "You're right, we *are* good together, and I'm not ready to call it quits. Considering all I've done for you, I think you should be more grateful."

K.C. bristled at her comment. "I believe I've given as much as I've taken."

Seeing her temper tantrum was not having the desired result, she tried a different approach. Lowering her voice an octave in an effort to sound seductive, she reminded him of the advantages of their relationship. "What other woman could name a Thoroughbred after you? I know you'll want to be in the winner's circle with me when K.C.'s Conquest makes his run for the roses. What about our weekend getaways to the Hamptons and all of the other romantic trips? Do you think you can find another woman who can give you anything you want with no strings attached?"

While Eugenie may not realize it, K.C. thought there were always strings attached. It wasn't necessary for her to remind him of her generosity, he need only glance at the Patek Philippe watch on his wrist. And he had to admit, it was a heady experience to have an expensive Thoroughbred, considered to be a real contender for the Kentucky Derby, named in his honor. But her wealth hadn't been a consideration when he'd started dating her. Her marital status had been upmost in his mind. He'd never dated a married woman, and he'd made that disastrous decision in a moment of weakness, accompanied by an ill-advised fifth shot of Cleary's best bourbon. To Eugenie's credit, she didn't pretend she wanted a divorce from her husband, and he didn't pretend he would marry her if she became a divorcée. Eugenie enjoyed the prestige of being Mrs. Jefferson Grayson, and nothing on earth would tempt her to change her status. For that, he was thankful.

Still, he was determined to end this affair today. He was disappointed in himself for dating a married woman, and he should never have allowed it to get to this point. Not only did he break his own code of ethics, he'd betrayed Eugenie's husband, who happened to be a good, decent man.

"Eugenie, I'm not thinking about finding another woman. I want to be alone for now. I have a lot going on at the distillery and it's taking up most of my time." He thought his explanation sounded sincere, even if it wasn't the entire truth. The part about the distillery was accurate since business was better than ever, but that wasn't the only reason he was making changes. Honey Howell had everything to do with his decision. As soon as he'd found out that Honey was leaving California and coming home to stay, he'd started making plans. He realized a long time ago that Honey was *the one* who got away. He considered himself an intelligent man, and he wasn't one to make the same mistake twice. He knew what he wanted his future to look like, and that future included Honey Howell.

Eugenie eyed him suspiciously. "You don't like being alone, and I know you aren't devoting all your free time to business. I'm not stupid, K.C. Don't you think I've heard about all of the women you date?" She flapped her hand back and forth in the air, dismissing the notion that other women could possibly be competition. "Oh, I knew that you weren't serious about any of them, and you've always been available for me. We both know you'll never settle down with one woman, so why should we break it off?"

He wasn't about to mention the other relationships he'd already ended this week. He was definitely thinning out the herd. For the first time in a long time, he was going to have an entire weekend to himself, doing exactly what he wanted to do without feeling he needed to accommodate one of the women he dated. "Eugenie, you need to find a man who can give you the time you need."

"I haven't asked for more time," Eugenie countered.

He didn't want Eugenie as an enemy, he just wanted to end the relationship without enmity. There was little doubt in his mind that Eugenie really cared whether the relationship was over or not. She simply didn't like the fact that he was the one ending it. "Eugenie, we both knew this wasn't going to last. I had hoped you would understand and we could part friends."

Glaring at him, Eugenie repeated slowly, as if he didn't understand, "I told you, I'll be the one to tell you when it's over."

Though he wanted to avoid being the bad guy, it was obvious she'd made the decision for him—it had to be a scorched-earth approach. He stared at her a moment, trying to decide if there was another way to get his point across. Finally, he threw his hands in the air. "I'm done."

Eugenie narrowed her eyes. "You're going to be sorry over this decision. You can't treat me this way and think I will just walk away."

Frustrated, K.C. didn't know what else to say. Not yet noon, it was already over ninety degrees, and even hotter standing on the asphalt. His shirt was beginning to stick to his skin. He jiggled his keys in his hand, impatient to drive away and leave this sordid affair behind. "I was hoping we could remain friends, but I see that's impossible." He turned to his car.

Eugenie reached for his arm and held on. "Friends! You just wait and see what happens to your distillery when I'm done with you! Cleary's will be out of business in a year. Why do you think Cleary's has been the featured bourbon for every important social event in Kentucky since we've been together?" When he didn't respond, she pointed to herself. "I made it happen."

K.C. blew out a breath of air in irritation. "Don't be a drama queen, Eugenie, it doesn't suit you."

"Drama? I'll show you drama! Remember what I said. I will take pleasure in ruining you. Don't think you can change your mind when your business goes bankrupt."

With her mouth in a sneer, K.C. thought she might physically attack him. He'd never seen a woman so enraged. He jerked his arm free from

4

her grasp and stepped away from her. All he wanted to do was get in his car and drive away.

"The great master distiller! You think you are master of the universe! You will see how mistaken you are!" With that last taunt, she made a sharp half-pirouette in her Louboutin stilettos and marched back to her car. Once inside the Bentley, she slammed the gearshift into drive and turned the steering wheel to the left, pulling away from the Mercedes. Instead of directing the car down the driveway, she pulled thirty feet forward, rammed the gear in reverse and pressed her foot hard on the gas pedal.

K.C. was opening his car door when he heard the squeal of rubber and he turned just in time to see the Bentley's rear bumper closing fast toward him. Hurling his body over the hood of his car, he barely escaped being squashed between the Bentley's bumper and the door of his Mercedes.

Eugenie kept her foot on the pedal until the driver's-side door of his Mercedes was completely crushed to the center console and the Bentley's tires were smoking. Seeing the car wasn't moving, Eugenie shifted into drive and pulled forward.

Thinking Eugenie had completely lost her mind, K.C. expected her to put the car in reverse again and take a second bite of the apple. He ran to the front porch to get out of her way in case she thought about running over him.

Eugenie hesitated for a heartbeat, then whipped the Bentley to the left and roared down the driveway. She didn't bother to stop, or look in the rearview mirror. If she had, she might have seen K.C. in the middle of the driveway shaking his fists in her wake.

CHAPTER ONE

ELVIS STREAKED ACROSS THE ROOM so fast he could have given a racing greyhound some competition as he zeroed in on his target. Instead of a mechanical lure, Elvis's eyes were on his favorite human. Honey Howell was removing books from a large corrugated box when she heard the one-hundred-six-pound canine's nails doing a clickety-click number on the hardwood floor. Problem was, she didn't have time to brace herself before Elvis launched his sturdy body into her outstretched arms. Limbs entwined, they landed unceremoniously inside the box Honey was unpacking. Unable to evade the bloodhound's sloppy kisses, not to mention the stream of drool trickling down her neck, Honey laughed. "Elvis, did you miss me?"

"Can't you tell?" Woodrow Howell held out his hand to help his granddaughter to her feet.

Taking hold of his outstretched hand, Honey attempted to maneuver into an upright position, but Elvis's weight prevented her from wiggling free. With his nose glued to her neck, he was sniffing her as if he'd forgotten her scent.

"I'm happy to see you, Elvis," Honey told him.

Woodrow reached for Elvis's collar with his free hand and gave it a gentle tug. "Let her up, Elvis."

With Woodrow's aid, Honey managed to get to her feet. She wrapped her arms around her grandfather and gave him a hug. "How are you, Gramps?"

"I'm good now that you are back where you belong. I'm sorry I wasn't here to greet you, but my flight was delayed last night. It's good to have you home."

"I'm happy to be home. Mom told me you would be getting home late last night. Thanks for letting me live in the cottage. You know I love this place."

Woodrow glanced around the living room, admiring the progress she'd made in one day. "Nonsense. This place hasn't been used in a long time. It needs someone to look after it. It looks better already."

"There wasn't much to do. I just moved the furniture around. The contractor did a beautiful job with the renovation, and I love the new furnishings." Several walls had been removed, and Honey thought the open floor plan made the fifty-year-old cottage appear much more spacious than before. The newly added arched windows allowed for more natural light, which she preferred.

"My contractor does great work. I think he hired a designer to select the furniture. My only input was to tell him to select sofas with Elvis in mind. I knew he would be sleeping on them at the first opportunity," Woodrow replied.

Elvis nudged Honey's hand, earning him an ear rub. "He's a good boy." Turning toward the kitchen with Elvis on her heels, Honey tore off a sheet of paper towel to wipe the slobber from her neck. "I made some fresh coffee a few minutes ago. Do you have time to sit and chat?"

Woodrow followed Honey to the kitchen and pulled out a chair at the island. "Do you have something sweet to go with that coffee?"

Honey smiled at his question. Her grandfather loved sweets, and she thought it must be a trait passed down the family line, like the gene for green eyes she'd inherited from him. She pointed to the cake stand on the counter. "Mom brought a coffee cake yesterday when she came by."

"Perfect." Noticing a stack of books on the counter, Woodrow leaned over to read the titles. "Brushing up on the bourbon business?"

Honey placed his coffee on the counter. "I have a lot to learn, Gramps." When her grandfather had called saying he wanted her to come home and learn the business, she didn't think twice about leaving her marketing position in California. She worked with a film production company at a job she loved, but she was ready to come home. Years ago, Woodrow had told her she would be the one to inherit the family business founded by their ancestors over two hundred years ago. Bluegrass Bourbon was one of the oldest distilleries in Bardstown, Kentucky, as well as one of the most respected in the industry. It was important for her to prove she could keep the business thriving for future generations.

Thomas Howell, Honey's father and Woodrow's only child, had married the heir to Morning Glory Farms, a successful Thoroughbred breeding and racing facility. Thomas took over the reins of that corporation, and he no longer had an interest in running the distillery. Honey's brother, Preston, had worked with their father for several years, and he was equally obsessed with the horse industry. If Woodrow had been disappointed in her father's decision, he'd never said as much. He understood it was difficult not to let horses get into your blood if you were born and bred in Kentucky. Everyone thought horse racing was a much more glamorous endeavor than owning a distillery.

"Gramps, are you disappointed that Preston didn't change his mind about joining you in the business?" Woodrow had never made her feel she was his second choice to head the business, but she wondered if he had hopes of Preston having a change of heart.

"Not at all. Even if your brother had shown an interest, you are more suited to this business. I think you are both where you were meant to be."

Honey was honored that he had so much faith in her abilities. She leaned over and kissed his cheek. "Thanks for that, Gramps."

"Do you think you will miss the glamorous life in California?"

Though she had enjoyed professional success in California, and she'd made some friends in the industry, she found it difficult to relate to the self-absorbed culture. When Woodrow called to ask if she was ready to come home, she thought of the line from *The Wizard of Oz*: *There's no place like home.* "I was ready to come home."

"Your family is thrilled to have you back. And I'd say judging by a phone call I received a couple of weeks ago, someone else was thrilled you were coming home."

Honey knew he was referring to K.C. Cleary. "K.C. and I have been talking every day since I told him I was coming home. He told me he would be here when I got back, but I haven't seen him yet. He probably tried to call, but I can't even find my cell phone. I'm sure the battery needs charging."

"I know he's excited to see you," Woodrow responded. "Is there a chance you two might start dating again?"

Honey smiled. "We've been good friends for a long time, but I'm not certain it will be more than that." K.C. had dated a lot of women over the years, but the last time they'd spoken, he told her that he thought he was ready to settle down. He'd mentioned that he wanted to start dating her again. Though she had never considered a future with K.C., she wasn't going to rule it out. Not only was K.C. handsome, he was intelligent and a man of good character. Now that they were going to be competitors in the bourbon business, they would be seeing a lot of each other.

"It's time K.C. settled down. He's a fine man, and he's played the field long enough. What he needs is a family. He'd make a great father."

Honey agreed that K.C. would make a fabulous father, but only K.C. could make the decision when he was ready. "What is it you always say? *Don't count your chickens before they hatch.*"

Woodrow laughed. "Touché." He took a drink of his coffee, then leaned back in his chair, ready to talk business, but was distracted when Elvis lurched to his feet and charged toward the front door. A few seconds later, there was a knock on the door.

Honey looked at Woodrow and laughed as she walked around the counter, headed to the door. "I see he still hears things that I don't."

"He's has amazing abilities," Woodrow replied.

Reaching the door, Honey saw the chief of police through the beveled glass sidelight. "It's Hap Nelson." Gripping Elvis's collar, she moved him away from the door so she could pull it open. She gave Hap a wide smile. "This is a surprise."

"How's my girl?" Hap pulled Honey into his arms and gave her one of his legendary spine-crushing bear hugs.

"I'm good, Hap." Honey's gaze shifted to the man looming behind Hap wearing reflective aviator sunglasses. He was a tall, muscular man, with wavy black hair and darkly tanned skin. She watched him lean over and rub Elvis's ears. Elvis eagerly accepted his attention, which told her Elvis had met him before.

The man tapped Hap on the back. "Let her breath, Hap. Her lips are turning blue," he teased.

Hap chuckled and released his hold on Honey. "Woodrow told me you were coming back home to stay." He gave Elvis a pat on the head as he turned to the man accompanying him. "Honey, I'd like you to meet Bardstown's newest detective, Sam Gentry."

Sam removed his sunglasses, and Honey felt her heart skip a beat. The man had the most beautiful blue eyes she'd ever seen. She extended her hand. "Nice to meet you, Sam."

Taking her hand in his, Sam smiled. "A pleasure to meet you."

Sam was the antithesis of the aging, portly Hap. Hap's khaki uniform shirt was straining to cover his bulky midsection, while the detective's light blue shirt emphasized his muscled chest and trim waist. He obviously spent some time in a gym. Honey noted his direct gaze, his firm handshake, and his perfectly erect posture. Everything about him oozed confidence. Even in ninety-degree temperature, there wasn't even a hint of a wrinkle on his crisp starched shirt.

Sam leaned over and scratched Elvis behind his ears again. "How are you doing, Elvis?"

"You've met Elvis?"

"Yes, we've met a couple of times. Did you name him?"

Honey figured he'd met Elvis through Woodrow. "Yes, we're both Elvis fans."

"You mean Elvis likes Elvis's music?"

Honey nodded, and held her arm out in invitation, "Please, come in."

When they reached the kitchen, Honey noticed Elvis was still by Sam's side, nudging his hand with his nose, wanting another ear rub.

Sam chuckled at Elvis's antics, and leaned over to scratch him behind the ears. "You have a fine dog."

"Actually, he's my grandfather's dog," Honey replied as she watched Elvis sniff Sam's neck.

Woodrow walked over to the men and slapped Hap on the shoulder. "Don't believe her, Sam. Elvis is devoted to her and no one else."

Sam shook Woodrow's hand. "Nice to see you again." His eyes slid to Honey. "I can understand Elvis's devotion."

Woodrow laughed. "I'm sure you do." He motioned toward the counter. "Take a seat at the counter. Honey has fresh coffee and coffee cake."

Hap pulled out a chair and sat down. "We stopped at your house and your housekeeper told us you were here."

"And here I thought you came by to welcome me home," Honey teased as her gaze drifted to Sam. Startled to see he was staring at her, she quickly turned to the cabinet and retrieved two more cups.

"Consider us your welcoming committee," Hap replied.

Honey placed the cake stand on the island counter and removed the glass dome. Once she filled the coffee cups, she sliced three huge servings from the coffee cake and slid them in front of the men.

"How long have you been working with Hap?" Honey asked Sam.

"Three months." Sam sat down and looked at the large slice of coffee cake. "This looks delicious."

"If this is the way you treat uninvited guests, you better plan on seeing us every morning," Hap teased. He elbowed Woodrow, and added, "Now I see why you're here so early."

Woodrow laughed. "I came over to make sure my granddaughter is ready to get to work first thing tomorrow morning."

"Are you ready to take over the family business, Honey?' Hap asked.

"Not yet. I have a lot to learn. Gramps knows everything there is to know about the bourbon business, and he's going to keep busy teaching me," Honey replied.

"You'll do fine running the business one day," Woodrow told her. "Your marketing expertise is just what we need." He glanced at the men and added, "I'm afraid we haven't kept up with the times. I wanted Honey to come home and learn what she can from me about bourbon while I'm still kicking."

At seventy-eight years of age, Woodrow had a pragmatic attitude about time catching up to him. He'd been fortunate to work fifteen-hour days most of his life, and he still enjoyed working in the business he loved, but logic told him it was only a matter of time before he'd be forced to slow down.

"You're going to be kicking for many more years," Honey responded.

Woodrow grinned at her. "That won't be good news to my competitors. But never forget, time waits for no man."

Honey smiled, remembering that line was one of his favorite sayings.

"Woodrow, you're going to outlive us all," Hap commented.

Seeing Elvis eyeing the pantry where she had stored some treats, Honey opened the door and pulled out his favorite doggie bones. "I didn't forget you, handsome."

Instead of reaching for the treat, he stood on his hind legs, placed his paws over her shoulders and nuzzled her neck. Honey wrapped her arms around him. "Elvis, you are the only man for me. No one could be as handsome as you, or as loyal."

Elvis let out a contented sigh, as though he was telling her he was in complete agreement.

Woodrow glanced at Sam and saw he was watching the pair. "Elvis loves to dance with her when an Elvis song comes on."

Sam chuckled. "Is he a good dancer?"

"The best," Honey replied.

"I don't know about dancing, but I've never seen a dog with such a nose. Honey, did you know just last month Elvis found a missing child in the next county. The poor boy was lost in the woods for six hours when I called Woodrow to see if Elvis might be able to help us out," Hap told her.

"Mom told me about that." She kissed Elvis on top of his head before she gave him his treats. "You're my hero, Elvis."

"Woodrow, Hap tells me you have a new bourbon," Sam said.

"Yes, and Honey's home just in time to handle the roll-out. Her first priority is to plan an event to introduce the bourbon."

"I heard you hired a new master distiller," Hap said.

Woodrow nodded. "I hired Cullen Harper. He's a sharp young man who worked for a small distillery in New York. He's working as an apprentice under Alan Snyder right now. He's overqualified as an apprentice, but that title seemed to appease Alan—as much as Alan can be appeased. I expected Alan to retire a long time ago, but it hasn't happened yet. Though I think age is catching up with him. He's never been one to interact well with other employees, but lately he's been impossible. I'm thankful Cullen hasn't walked off."

"How long has Alan worked for you?" Sam asked.

"Over forty years," Woodrow responded.

Honey remembered Alan as a quiet, unfriendly man. Alan was her grandfather's age, but not many men were in the same stratosphere as far as health, vigor and personality. She stared into Woodrow's green eyes, thinking they still held a youthful twinkle. As far as she could tell he hadn't aged one day in the last twenty years. He was tall and lithe, with thick white hair that accentuated his darkly tanned face. Woodrow was the embodiment of a distinguished Southern gentleman, and women of all ages were naturally drawn to him. He did two hundred push-ups every morning, rode horses frequently, played golf with his buddies, and enjoyed some bourbon each evening. Honey had often thought if a shot or two of bourbon a day was the secret to Woodrow's youthfulness, she should follow his lead. Woodrow was still in fabulous shape and could outwork any person half his age.

"Maybe Alan doesn't retire because he doesn't have a family to occupy his time. Sometimes the job is all a man has in his life," Hap said thoughtfully.

"You may be right about that, Hap. He's led a solitary life." Woodrow reached over and patted Honey's hand. "He's not as fortunate as some of us."

They chatted about the bourbon industry while they finished their breakfast, and then Hap explained the reason for their visit. "Woodrow, Sam and I have a favor we'd like to ask. But our problem is, we can't tell you right now why we're asking."

Woodrow turned to look at the man he'd known for over thirty years. "It sounds serious. What do you need?"

"We'd like to borrow Elvis," Hap answered.

"Elvis wouldn't be in any danger. As a matter of fact, all he will be doing is going over a car for us. We need to see if he can find something that might help us," Sam explained. "We'll have him back in two hours."

Woodrow realized Hap might need Elvis to search for evidence of human remains, and didn't want to say as much in front of Honey. "As I said, Elvis is basically Honey's dog. He'll be staying with her now that she's back home."

Sam looked at Honey. "What do you think, Honey? Can I take Elvis for a few hours?"

"He will only be searching a car and won't be in danger?"

Sam smiled at her. "You have my word."

"Can you tell me who the car belongs to?" Woodrow asked.

"I'm sorry, Woodrow, but I can't discuss this case right now. I wish I could say more, but I can't," Hap replied.

Woodrow turned to Honey. "What do you think, Honey?"

"If it's okay with Elvis, it's okay with me." She rubbed Elvis's ears. "You want to go with Sam and Hap for two hours."

Elvis walked over to Sam's side and nudged his hand. Sam gave Honey a questioning look as he scratched Elvis behind the ears. "Do you think he understood you?"

Honey arched her brow at him. "Don't you?"

Sam shook his head in disbelief. "He's one special dog."

CHAPTER TWO

WOODROW GREETED HONEY AND ELVIS when they walked in his office the next morning. "I see Hap and Sam retuned Elvis safe and sound."

"Hap returned exactly two hours later. He still didn't tell me anything specific, but he said Elvis was a big help." Honey pulled Elvis's ball filled with treats from her bag and tossed it to him.

"Sam wasn't with Hap?" Woodrow asked.

"No, Hap was alone."

"Hap tells me Sam is the smartest detective he's ever seen. What did you think of him?"

"He seems very capable," Honey answered diplomatically. She wasn't about to tell her grandfather that Sam was one of the most handsome men she'd ever seen. She'd been somewhat disappointed that he didn't bring Elvis home.

"He's single," Woodrow said.

Honey shook her head at him. "You're incorrigible."

Woodrow laughed. "Well, I would like great-grandchildren while I can still play with them."

Honey changed the subject. "When do I get to meet the new apprentice distiller?"

"He had a meeting this morning, but he will be here before noon. You two should get along well together. You're about the same age, and the ladies seem to be crazy about him."

Honey waggled her finger at him. "First, K.C., then the new detective, and now your new apprentice distiller. Stop playing Cupid. Mom has called dibs on that."

Woodrow sighed loudly and threw his hands in the air. "I know all about your mother's shenanigans. She's always trying to pair me up with her lady friends. What would I do with a woman in her fifties? There just aren't enough men to go around here."

Honey shook her head at him. "You'll get no sympathy from me. I get the sons of her friends."

"At your mom's last party, she was kind enough to invite Cullen to welcome him to Bardstown. He was a big hit with the ladies. Your mom told me some of her friends are—what do you young people call it—*tiger* ladies?"

Honey laughed. "Cougars. They are called cougars, Gramps."

Woodrow snapped his fingers. "That's it. Cougars! I don't think a wreath of garlic around Cullen's neck would have discouraged some of those women."

Honey could just imagine her mother's friends fighting over the poor guy. Any time an attractive man arrived in the small town, phones started ringing with the news. "Wait until they meet the new detective."

Woodrow arched his brows at her. "So you think he's handsome?"

"Tsk tsk." Honey waggled her finger at him. She glanced at her watch. "My new assistant will be here soon. I wanted to tell you a little about her."

"How did you have time to hire an assistant?" Woodrow asked.

"I interviewed on Skype."

"Skype?"

"I'll show you how to use Skype if you like."

Woodrow held his hands in the air as if warding off an evil spirit. "Not necessary. That's why I'm hiring you. I don't have time for all of this technical stuff. I know bourbon and that's all I need to know at this point in my life. My blasted cell phone rings enough now as it is."

The look on his face told Honey he'd rather lie on a bed of nails than learn new technology. "At least you are using an iPhone now. Anyway, don't be surprised when you see Georgia."

"Georgia?"

"Her name is Georgia Byrd."

Woodrow gave her a questioning look. "Why do you think I would I be surprised?"

"Let's just say she's a bit unique. But her technical skills are amazing, and that's what we are going to need."

"Is she a local?" Woodrow asked.

"She's from Louisville. She told me she might move closer to avoid the long drive."

Woodrow's secretary peeked inside his open door and told him that Honey's new assistant was in the lobby.

"Please show her in." Woodrow stood and walked around his desk.

Elvis jumped up and ran to the door. Honey followed him to make sure he didn't frighten Georgia her first day on the job. "Hi, Georgia, come in."

"Hi, Honey." Georgia didn't really look at Honey, her eyes were glued on the giant bloodhound standing beside her.

In his usual manner, Elvis wanted to see if he approved of the new employee—he sniffed Georgia's backside.

Honey reached for his collar to pull him away. "This is Elvis. As you can see, he has his own method of introducing himself."

Georgia eyed Elvis warily. "He's really big."

Honey knew Elvis's size intimidated most people. "He's friendly with people he likes." Honey leaned over to look Elvis in the eye. "Elvis, tell Georgia you are happy to meet her."

Elvis nudged Georgia's hand with his head. Georgia relaxed and gave his head a gentle rub. "Hi, Elvis. I want you to like me."

Honey smiled at her comment. "He approves. Come on in and meet my grandfather."

Woodrow extended his hand to Georgia. "Woodrow Howell."

Georgia nervously shoved her thick, blue-streaked hair from her face before she shook his hand. "Georgia Byrd."

Woodrow pointed to a chair. "Please have a seat. Honey was just telling me how talented you are."

Honey had to hand it to her grandfather, he didn't even crack a smile when he glanced at Georgia's hair. She wondered if he'd noticed her combat boots. "I was just telling my grandfather about your excellent technical skills."

Georgia pulled her blue laptop from her camouflage duffle bag before she placed it on the table beside her chair. "I'm so excited to work for you. Even though I know I can do the job, I have been turned down so often I was beginning to think I'd never be accepted into the corporate world." She tapped her laptop. "I've already started working on ideas to update the website. We definitely need a virtual tour of the distillery to show the beautiful grounds."

Honey noticed Georgia's laptop matched the streaks in her hair. No doubt about it, Georgia was unique, but Honey liked her. She understood her need to be accepted for her skills without sacrificing her personality. "I'm so excited to hear you say that. I've already taken some videos that might be helpful."

"Honey says you live in Louisville. Where did you work previously?" Woodrow asked.

"My uncle owns several funeral homes in Kentucky, and I've been working for him for four years. I handled all of his social media accounts, his advertising, and anything else he needed me to do," Georgia replied.

"Should we feel guilty about stealing you away from a family business?" Woodrow asked.

"Oh, no, my uncle knew I would leave when I found the perfect position," Georgia assured him.

"Georgia, one of the first things on our agenda will be planning a social event to introduce the new bourbon." Honey pulled a folder from her briefcase.

"We need to do something special for the occasion. Unfortunately, I'm not giving you two much time to plan," Woodrow added.

"I wanted to talk to you about a formal evening on the dinner train." Honey pulled two brochures from the folder and handed one to Georgia and the other to Woodrow. "The train is totally refurbished and it is absolutely gorgeous. Gramps, I know you've been on the train several times."

Georgia opened the brochure and looked at the photographs of the interior of the dining cars. Tables were covered with white tablecloths, and adorned with place settings of delicate white china embellished with a shimmering gold border of racing thoroughbreds, ornate sterling silver flatware, etched crystal stemware, and napkins folded in the shape of a fleur-de-lis filled the water goblets. At the center of each table, Baccarat vases held perfect red rosebuds. "I've never been on a train. I didn't know they were so beautifully decorated. The photographs we take that night will look fabulous on our website."

Honey smiled at Georgia's enthusiasm. "I thought we would invite the group from California who enjoy coming to our Derby parties. They are already acquainted with many of our friends here. We'd have a bourbon tasting and a fabulous dinner while they enjoy the beautiful countryside."

Woodrow was pleased that Honey had selected a local venue for the occasion. "That sounds like a wonderful plan. It would be the event of the summer. Be sure to invite that nice movie producer who owns that farm in Kentucky."

"Jerry Bruckheimer?"

"That's the fellow! A delightful man. I had the pleasure of meeting him at one of the Derby parties and we had a most interesting conversation."

"I will definitely extend an invitation to him and his wife."

"I love his movies," Georgia admitted. "Do you think I could take a selfie with him?"

"I'm certain he wouldn't object." Honey imagined a lot of people would ask for selfies with the celebrities that night. "Gramps, I'm glad you like the idea. I was worried the dates wouldn't be available if I waited, so I booked the train before I left California. I've already discussed a tentative menu with the chef, and we plan to incorporate some of my bourbon recipes."

"I'm happy you thought to book ahead. They are always busy in the summer."

Honey handed him a piece of paper. "Here's the list of people I thought you would want to invite. If you want some changes, let me know as soon as possible. I'd like to get the invitations out tomorrow."

Woodrow glanced over the list. "This looks good, but I'll take a closer look tonight."

"After the train event, I thought we would schedule several tastings at various local venues for the bourbon debut. We will start planning those dates immediately."

"I see you have everything well in hand." Woodrow stood and

excused himself for another meeting. "Stay here if you like, I'll only be thirty minutes, then I'll give you two a tour and introduce Georgia."

Honey and Georgia continued to discuss their marketing plans when Elvis stood and placed his head on Honey's lap.

Honey stroked his back. "Are you feeling left out, Elvis?"

"He seems quite attached to you," Georgia commented.

"He has been since the first moment we met."

Georgia smiled at Elvis when he nudged Honey's hand when she stopped petting him. "It was a sign."

"A sign?" Honey resumed stroking Elvis's head.

"That love at first sight does exist," Georgia responded.

Honey didn't know if she actually believed there was such a thing as love at first sight. On the other hand, she had fallen in love with Elvis that quickly. "I guess you're right. I fell in love with him at first sight."

After Woodrow gave them a tour of the distillery and introduced Georgia to everyone, they headed back to his office. He stopped when he spotted his new apprentice master distiller walking down the hall. "Here comes the man you need to meet."

With the sunlight streaming in from the windows, all Honey could see was a tall, rather muscular man walking toward them.

"Cullen, I want you to meet my granddaughter and her assistant, Georgia."

"Honey, I've heard all about you," Cullen said.

Honey extended her hand. "My grandfather has been singing your praises."

After shaking Honey's hand, Cullen turned to Georgia and shook her hand. "Woodrow mentioned that Honey found a computer guru."

"That's me." Georgia replied.

Honey noticed Georgia couldn't take her eyes off of the handsome new apprentice. She wondered if Georgia just fell in love at first sight.

Cullen turned to say something to Woodrow, and Georgia leaned close to Honey's ear and whispered, "Mr. Howell saved the best for last."

Honey grinned at her, but she wondered what Georgia would say if she met the town's new detective. In Honey's estimation, Cullen couldn't hold a candle to him.

Woodrow turned toward his office. "Cullen, do you have time to hear the plans for the release of our new bourbon?"

"Certainly." Cullen fell into step beside Honey. "Your grandfather tells me he managed quite a coup, stealing you from Hollywood."

"I don't know about that, but I hope I can live up to his expectations. Georgia and I have plans to improve our social media advertising."

"They told me some of their plans yesterday, and you are going to be impressed, Cullen." Woodrow checked the time on his watch. "Go ahead with your meeting and I'll be there in a few minutes." He glanced at Georgia. "My secretary is going to show you your office and make sure you have everything you need."

Before Woodrow walked away with Georgia, Cullen said, "Woodrow, I'm meeting with the wood chefs at one o'clock, and if you have time, I'd like you to join us."

"Of course," Woodrow responded.

"Wood chefs?" Georgia whispered to Honey.

Cullen overheard Georgia's question. "That's what we call the coopers."

"Coopers?" Georgia had no idea what they were talking about.

"They are the people who make the barrels," Honey explained.

"Why are the barrels so important?" Georgia asked.

"The color of the bourbon, as well as much of the flavor, comes from the barrels," Honey replied.

Woodrow smiled at her. "All of that studying is paying off."

"Remember you said that when I tell you my plans," Honey replied.

Honey and Cullen walked into her office, and Elvis jumped up from his pallet and ran to her. She leaned over and kissed the top of his head. "I wasn't gone that long." When Honey took a seat, Elvis stood beside her and buried his nose in her neck. When she heard Cullen chuckle, she explained Elvis's penchant for neck sniffing. "I think he likes my perfume."

"Bloodhounds have great noses. Maybe he should sniff our bourbons," Cullen teased.

Honey picked up her pen, opened her notebook and wrote something down. "Maybe he should."

Cullen was surprised Honey would take his comment seriously. "Do you think he could differentiate between bourbons?"

"I most certainly do." Honey noticed Elvis didn't really pay attention to Cullen. That told her either Elvis was around him frequently, and he knew Cullen wasn't a *dog person*, or Elvis didn't like him. "Tell me about the new bourbon we will be introducing." Honey had already heard Alan's description, but she wanted to hear Cullen's opinion.

Cullen discussed the important notes to the nose and palate. "You'll notice the caramel and vanilla with a slightly sweet, but spicy finish."

"Do we have a name for the bourbon?" Honey asked.

"The only thing I've heard tossed around is Woodrow's Best Bourbon."

Honey frowned. "That won't do. We need something much more interesting…more tantalizing."

"I like the sound of that," Cullen agreed. "But that's your department. Leave the mash bill to me, and I'll leave the marketing to you." He watched her scribble another note.

"How do you like working with Alan?" When Honey spoke with Alan earlier, she thought she'd rather work with a grizzly bear. Her grandfather hadn't exaggerated when he told her Alan wasn't very communicative. It was an understatement. Alan was curt with his responses, and didn't freely offer any information. She had the feeling he considered her an interloper.

"Alan is an unusual man," Cullen replied diplomatically. "He's quite secretive."

Honey laughed. "I agree with that. I get the impression he doesn't like to play well with others."

Cullen shrugged his shoulders. "As I said, he's an unusual character."

Honey studied Cullen's expression, trying to discern what he was really thinking. "I apologize. I shouldn't ask you a question that would put you in a difficult position." She decided to inquire about his prior experience. "My grandfather tells me you were a master distiller at a smaller distillery before you joined us."

"I worked for Sawyer Distillery in New York. I left there almost two years ago because I wanted to work in Kentucky. I had a non-compete clause in my contract which forced me to stay out of the industry for one year. I wanted to be available when the right opportunity came along."

"Why Kentucky? This is a long way from New York." Honey wondered if a man accustomed to living in New York would be happy living in a small town.

"I wanted to work for the best distillery in the country, and naturally that meant moving to Kentucky. I'd always heard Kentucky is a great place to live and raise a family. I must admit I've never lived in a town as small as Bardstown, but I'm adjusting," Cullen replied. "And of course, your grandfather made me a very attractive offer."

"Probably because he knew you were worth it."

"I'd like to think so."

"And he knew you would have to put up with Alan." Honey wasn't really teasing. She didn't think there would be enough money on earth to put up with Alan's attitude on a daily basis.

Cullen grinned at her. "There is that. Think I should ask for a raise?"

Honey laughed. He'd mentioned family, but Honey remembered Woodrow told her he was single. "You mentioned family. Do you have children?"

"No, I was thinking in terms of the future. I'm not married," Cullen replied.

Honey realized she shouldn't have ventured into a personal conversation with a fellow employee, or at least one who was attractive and single. She needed to keep in mind her future role with the company. Some questions that seemed appropriate in the course of everyday conversation between coworkers would be inappropriate for a boss. Woodrow saved her from an uncomfortable silence when he joined them.

"Has Cullen told you how Pickett's Distillery is cutting into our market?" Woodrow asked.

"I was just about to mention that," Cullen responded.

"I thought you told me Pickett's was nearly bankrupt a few years ago," Honey said.

"They were. When the last member of the family died, it took a while before they found a buyer. Didn't your mom tell you that her friend Bunny and her new husband bought Pickett's?"

Honey remembered her mother mentioned Bunny's fifth marriage. "Mom told me Bunny married again, but she didn't mention the purchase of the distillery. I didn't know Bunny was interested in the bourbon industry."

"Bunny told your mother her new husband was a master distiller somewhere in New York. I asked Cullen if he'd ever heard of him, but he hadn't. They introduced a new bourbon a few months ago that tastes so similar to Bluegrass Select that I'm not certain I can tell the difference."

"I don't think I can tell the difference either," Cullen added.

Honey was surprised by her grandfather's admission. He was widely regarded as man who could distinguish between bourbons with his eyes closed. "You really think his bourbon is that close to Bluegrass Select?"

"Yes, and he's advertising that fact in his marketing campaign. His latest advertisement says something like—*Why pay more for the older bourbon when Pickett's has the same great flavor at half the price? See if you can tell the difference.*" Woodrow shook his head in frustration. "He has that advertisement on a huge billboard on the way to Louisville."

"He must know what he's doing if you can't tell the difference. Is his bourbon really half the price?"

Woodrow nodded. "And he has a nice-looking bottle."

Honey made another note to check out Pickett's bottles and the billboard. "The bourbon was in Pickett's inventory?"

"It must have been included in the sale, and they decided it was ready for distribution," Woodrow replied.

"He's either a good businessman or he got real lucky with that bourbon," Cullen commented.

CHAPTER THREE

"MOM, THIS IS A SURPRISE." Honey gave her mother a hug when she walked through the door. "Georgia and I were just doing a little work."

Lorraine strolled inside the cottage with the confidence of a blonde beauty queen on a red-carpeted runway. "I thought you girls could use some treats after a long day of work at the office. When you told me you'd invited Georgia over tonight, I didn't know you intended to work."

After Honey's introduction, Lorraine smiled at Georgia. "Honey tells me you are a computer wizard. I may need to steal you one day. I'm afraid every time I turn on my blasted laptop, I do something wrong."

"I'd be happy to help anytime." Georgia was immediately charmed by Lorraine's friendly personality.

Elvis walked to Lorraine and nudged her hand.

"How's the big hero?" Lorraine rubbed his head. "I brought you some goodies too, Elvis."

"Go ahead and give him a small treat, but not too much, I don't want to ruin his dinner," Honey said.

Lorraine gave Elvis a large bone she'd purchased at the doggie bakery. "Enough work, girls. Time for some chocolate." She plopped down on the sofa and pulled three boxes of bourbon balls from her oversized designer bag.

Honey glanced at the boxes of bourbon candy. "We haven't had dinner yet. And why are you bringing a competitor's product here?"

Honey grinned at Georgia. "I should warn you, my mother is addicted to bourbon balls."

"Bluegrass Bourbon doesn't make bourbon balls or I would buy them." Lorraine pursed her lips as she tore the plastic off one box. "I wonder why that is? I've never asked Woodrow. Your grandfather has made bourbon balls before and they were delicious."

Honey walked to the kitchen and grabbed her notepad. "Good thought, Mom." On her way back to the living room, she turned on some music for Elvis. Within minutes, Elvis Presley's distinctive rich voice filled the room singing "Can't Help Falling in Love." "That's our song, Elvis."

Leaving his toy behind, Elvis stood on his hind legs and placed his paws over Honey's shoulders.

Honey wrapped her arms around him and they swayed with the music.

"I can't believe Elvis likes Elvis. That's the cutest thing I've ever seen," Georgia said.

"You should hear him howl when he hears 'Hound Dog.'" Lorraine popped a bourbon ball in her mouth, and extended the box to Georgia. "Have one, Georgia. I promise you won't get tipsy."

Georgia pulled a pecan-topped ball from the box. "I've never had these before." When she took the first bite she leaned back on the sofa, closed her eyes and savored the bourbon flavored treat. "Yummy! These are delicious!"

Lorraine tapped the box. "These are my favorites."

Ending their dance, Honey and Elvis walked back to the living room. Honey leaned over her mother's shoulder. "Give me one."

Lorraine passed the box to her. "Weren't you two planning on tasting some bourbon tonight?"

"Yes, I brought home several bottles."

"Let's get started. You don't mind if I join you, do you?" Lorraine asked.

"Of course not." Honey lined the bottles of bourbon on the counter. "Georgia and I are not bourbon drinkers, but we need to learn everything we can about our products. Today Alan and Cullen were talking about the different flavors, so we need to see if we can taste the differences."

Lorraine rubbed her hands together. "Let's get started." Lorraine pointed toward the kitchen. "Did you see the Glencairn glasses I put in the cabinet?"

"Yes, and thank you," Honey replied.

"What are Glencairn glasses?" Georgia asked.

"Gramps says they are the best glasses for tasting bourbon," Honey answered. "I have an assortment of goodies for our tasting." She uncovered the platter filled with aged parmesan, nuts, orange slices and dried cherries. She opened a box of crackers and added some to the plate. "Do you think we should have dinner first?"

Lorraine winked at Georgia. "Bourbon balls are our appetizer."

Honey wasn't sold on the idea of not having dinner before tasting bourbon. "What do you think, Georgia?"

"I'm with your mom. These bourbon balls are wonderful. As far as I'm concerned, they can be our appetizer and dinner." Georgia plucked another piece from the box and shoved it in her mouth.

"I knew I was going to like you, Georgia." Lorraine thought Georgia's T-shirt had the word *chocolate* written on the front. "What does your shirt say?"

Georgia grinned at her. "*Books and chocolate—what more does a girl need?* I guess that tells you where I fall on the subject of chocolate."

Honey grabbed several Glencairn glasses from the cupboard. "Mom, you decide which bourbon we are going to taste first. Just a tiny taste of each one."

Lorraine inspected the bottles Honey had lined up on the counter. "We'll start with the original bourbon. Might as well begin with the one that made Bluegrass Bourbon famous." She followed Honey's instructions and poured a small amount into the three glasses. "This is less than an angel's share."

"Someone mentioned the *angel's share* at the distillery today. What does that mean?" Georgia asked.

"It means…" Honey started to respond, but stopped as she reached for her notepad. After she quickly wrote a note to herself, she continued her explanation. "The angel's share is the amount of alcohol that evaporates during aging. In warmer weather bourbon expands in the barrels, then in the cooler temperatures the bourbon contracts. More or less volume could be lost due to the location of the barrels in the rickhouses. The higher floors are hotter and dryer."

"I have another question," Georgia said. "What does the *mash bill* mean?"

Honey realized Woodrow was right—her studying had paid off. "The mash bill is the mix of grains in the recipe, and you must have at least fifty-one percent corn to be considered bourbon. The distillers can change the taste, texture, and character of the bourbon by changing the grain recipe."

Lorraine picked up the bottles to carry to the coffee table. "Enough of this technical jargon. Let's take this party to the living room and do our tasting in comfort. Honey, bring your tasty morsels with you."

Honey opened the pantry and grabbed another treat for Elvis. She didn't want him to feel left out, or he might be tempted to do some chocolate tasting. Grabbing the platter from the counter, she walked to the living room.

"The first thing you want to do is look at the color of the bourbon." Lorraine held her glass in the air. "This is a nice old bourbon. Remember the older the bourbon, the darker it will be. Next you smell, or nose the bourbon." Lorraine gave a demonstration. "Keep your mouth open to appreciate all of the aromas. Then take a sip and slowly chew before you let it slip over the back of your tongue."

Following Lorraine's instructions, Georgia gasped when she swallowed. "It really burns."

Seeing Georgia's reaction, Honey took a very small sip. "It does burn a bit."

"But what do you girls taste?" Loraine asked.

"I don't know." Georgia reached for another bourbon ball.

"It's difficult to tell, eating the bourbon balls." Honey took another small sip. "I think I taste caramel. Do you think that's because of the bourbon balls?"

Lorraine popped another bourbon ball in her mouth. "It does have a hint of caramel that enhances the flavor of dark chocolate in the bourbon balls."

"I like it with the bourbon balls. The chocolate calms the burn," Georgia said.

Honey laughed. "You two would think poison would taste good with chocolate."

"True. But now eat a cracker to cleanse your palate." As they munched on a cracker, Lorraine poured a small amount of bourbon from a different bottle in clean glasses.

"Mom, you didn't tell me Cullen Harper attended your party."

Lorraine took a sip of her bourbon before she responded. "I didn't?"

"No, you didn't. What did you think of him?"

"I think he's very handsome," Georgia said.

Lorraine agreed with Georgia's assessment. "He is that, and he seems like a very pleasant young man. He's not married, Honey."

"Not relevant." Honey took a sip of the second bourbon.

Georgia reached for another bourbon ball. "I think that's a sign."

Lorraine's eyes bounced from Honey to Georgia. "A sign? What's a sign?"

"A sign of something that is meant to be," Georgia replied.

Lorraine furrowed her brow, still confused. "I'm not following."

"How could someone as handsome as Cullen be tempted to come to a small town if he wasn't meant for Honey?" Georgia flopped her hand in Honey's direction. "I mean, look at her. She's as beautiful as he is handsome. It's destiny."

Honey rolled her eyes. She wondered if her assistant was already getting tipsy on two small sips of bourbon and a few bourbon balls.

Lorraine smiled at Georgia's romantic notions. "I see what you mean. It could be destiny."

"Stop it, you two. There will be no playing Cupid." Honey pointed to the bottle of bourbon. "Focus on the bourbon."

"I like the taste of this bourbon, and it didn't burn on the way down," Georgia remarked.

Lorraine nodded her agreement. "That's Bluegrass Select."

"But I still like the bourbon balls better than bourbon," Georgia admitted.

"The hidden gems of Kentucky. But don't let Woodrow hear you say that they are better than his bourbon," Lorraine teased as she reached for a piece of cheese. "I think this bourbon pairs well with cheese."

"Mom, Gramps said Bunny and her new husband purchased Pickett's

Distillery." Honey explained to Georgia that Bunny Hughes was a longtime friend of her mother's.

"She's Bunny Hughes Spencer now. She bought Pickett's Distillery for Troy—that's her new husband's name. He's another handsome man, muscle on top of muscle, but he's also twenty-five years younger than Bunny," Lorraine said.

Honey thought she detected a note of disapproval in her mother's voice. "Don't you like him, Mom?"

Lorraine leaned back on the sofa and looked at her daughter. "I really don't know what I think about him. But there's something about him that…" She threw her hand in the air. "Oh, I don't know, maybe it's just the age thing. It's probably unfair of me to judge him so harshly."

"Why did Bunny marry a man so much younger than she is?" Honey asked.

Lorraine shrugged. "There's no reasoning with Bunny, she's just very insecure. And I think she just likes to be married."

"Older men marry younger women all the time, so it only seems fair in reverse," Georgia said.

"True. But generally everyone thinks younger men marry older women for their money." Lorraine knew several women who had married younger men and the gossips had not been kind. "Whereas older men are trying to cling to their youth by marrying younger women. I think they are showing off for their contemporaries."

"I can't understand why younger women want to date older men. What do they have in common?" Honey asked.

"I think the only thing Bunny and Troy have in common is money. She has a lot of it and he likes to spend it," Lorraine replied.

"So he's a male sugar baby?" Georgia quipped.

Lorraine laughed. "Something like that."

"Did Bunny date him a long time before they married?" Honey asked.

Lorraine was about to stuff another bourbon ball in her mouth, but her hand stopped in midair. "They'd only dated for a few weeks. All of her friends tried to warn her that he might be marrying her for her money. She was angry with all of us, but we didn't want her to make a huge mistake."

"Is she really that wealthy?" Georgia asked.

"Bunny?" Lorraine raised her perfectly plucked eyebrow. "She's one of the richest women in Kentucky. Her family was quite wealthy, and then her first husband was extremely wealthy. When they divorced, Bunny ended up with fifty percent of his assets."

"Gramps said her new husband must know what he's doing in the bourbon business," Honey told her.

"Really?" Lorraine reached for another bottle of bourbon. "Are you ready to try another one?"

They both nodded, and Lorraine poured from the third bottle. They took a sip at the same time.

"The second was my favorite so far," Georgia said.

"I agree," Honey said.

"Bluegrass Select is also my favorite," Lorraine concurred.

Honey set her glass aside and walked to the kitchen, opened the pantry and pulled out Elvis's food. Once she filled his bowl she turned to the women. "I'm going to order dinner. We need real food."

"The last time I was here I put some menus in the drawer next to the sink," Lorraine told her.

"What would you like, Georgia?" Honey found the menus and read the choices. "Italian, Chinese, Subs?"

"Anything. I like all food," Georgia replied.

"What about pizza?" Lorraine asked.

Once the pizza was delivered, the women sat at the counter, and Honey poured freshly brewed sweet iced tea. "I think we've had enough bourbon for one night."

"I can't believe after all of those bourbon balls I'm still hungry," Lorraine said.

"Mom, you're always hungry." Honey rarely saw her mother when she wasn't eating something. She didn't know how she stayed so trim.

"You're right. When I'm with the girls, we always have salmon. You know how they are about their figures." Lorraine took a big bite of the double-pepperoni slice, closed her eyes and slowly chewed. "This is heavenly."

Georgia pulled a slice from the box. "I eat pizza at least three times a week. I consider it one of the main food groups."

"Georgia, did you remember to bring a change of clothing?" Honey had told her to prepare to stay the night in case they worked late.

"Yes, but I can drive home tonight."

"It's getting late, and my extra bedroom is ready and waiting for a guest. Maybe we can do some work in the morning before we go to the office."

"I know I kept you girls from your work tonight, but this has been fun," Lorraine said.

Honey was happy her mother joined them. "We've enjoyed it, and you taught us how to taste bourbon properly. We wouldn't want to embarrass ourselves in front of the experts."

"And thank you so much for bringing the bourbon balls," Georgia added.

Lorraine leaned over and patted her hand. "A woman after my own heart. There's one box left and I want you to keep it for later."

"Thank you." Georgia hadn't met another human on earth who liked chocolate as much as she did—until Lorraine.

"Honey, I think you should talk Woodrow into making bourbon balls," Lorraine said.

"I think that's a great idea. But I need to work on a recipe."

"I think Woodrow has his great-grandmother's recipe. When your father and I were married, your grandmother made bourbon balls for the reception. I remember Woodrow said it was an old family recipe, and they were the best I've ever had."

"I'll get the recipe and make some for the party were planning to introduce the new bourbon." Honey told her mother about the party they were planning on the train. "I'm inviting some of our Hollywood friends."

Lorraine had hosted large Derby parties for more than twenty years, and many people from Hollywood attended annually. "I think that sounds like the perfect evening. Of course, some of my friends will be looking for Cullen."

"He'll be there." Honey remembered what her grandfather had told her about her mother's friends. "We wouldn't want to keep Cullen from the *tigers*."

"Tigers?" Georgia asked, not following the conversation.

"She means cougars, don't you, Honey?" Lorraine laughed. "Woodrow has been telling secrets."

CHAPTER FOUR

T HE NEXT MORNING HONEY WAS in her office when Woodrow peeked inside. "Honey, can you come to my office for a few minutes?"

Honey glanced up from her computer screen. "Sure thing. I'm just going over my list of things I want to discuss with you."

When they reached Woodrow's office, Cullen was sitting at one end of the long walnut table. Alan was sitting at the opposite end of the table looking surly. Honey chose a chair closer to Cullen, and Elvis settled on the floor beside her.

"We wanted to show you some designs for the new bottle," Woodrow explained as he took his usual seat at the head of the table.

Honey looked over the bottles lined up on the desk. She picked up three bottles, mentally envisioning how their logo would look. "I've been thinking about names for the new bourbon, and last night when I was explaining to Georgia the meaning of angel's share, something came to mind. I thought we should give the devil his due. What do you think about naming the new bourbon Bluegrass Devil's Due Bourbon?"

"I think that sounds great," Cullen said.

Woodrow smiled wide. "I like it." He looked at Alan. "What do you think?"

Alan shrugged. "I still don't understand why our apprentice should be in this meeting."

Woodrow frowned at Alan's comment. "I invited Cullen to sit in."

Honey watched her grandfather stare at Alan a full minute, as if he was daring him to say another word. She'd rarely seen her grandfather angry, but he was now. If there was one thing her grandfather would not abide, it was treating someone rudely. Even in the most heated discussions, Woodrow always conducted himself in a gentlemanly fashion. "You are welcome to leave, Alan."

Alan remained silent as he left his seat and walked out the door.

"I apologize for Alan's offensive behavior, Cullen," Woodrow said.

"Think nothing of it. I understand he feels his position is threatened. Actually that was the most I've heard out of him in days. At least I know he's alive," Cullen responded, trying to lighten the mood.

Honey saw Woodrow smile slightly, but his calm demeanor wasn't fooling her. He was fuming.

"It's good of you to put up with him. Now back to the matter at hand. We need to meet with the label designers and see what we can come up with. Honey, I want you involved in the design. If you like those three bottles, we can have them work up labels and see which one we prefer."

"I'll get with them today." Honey jotted down a reminder in her notebook.

"Did you want to run some of your ideas by us now?" Woodrow asked her.

"I'm ready if you are." She wasn't going to allow Alan's foul mood to ruin the day.

"Cullen, do you have time to stay? I'd like you to hear what Honey has in mind. You are going to be a big part of the future of this company, and we'd value your opinion," Woodrow said.

"Of course. I'm very interested to hear what Honey has planned."

"Good. The floor is yours, Honey."

"First, Mom came by last night and she brought some bourbon balls. She mentioned that you had an old family recipe passed down from your great-grandmother."

Woodrow nodded. "That recipe is over a hundred years old."

"Mom said they were the best bourbon balls she'd ever tasted." Honey glanced Cullen's way. "If anyone knows bourbon balls, it's my mother."

"I think she has a bourbon ball party a month with her friends," Woodrow added.

"I hate to admit this, but I've never had them," Cullen said.

"If you like chocolate and bourbon, you'll like them," Honey said. "Gramps, if you'll give me the recipe, I'll make a batch and we can see what everyone thinks."

"Do you plan on serving them on the dinner train?" Cullen asked.

"I thought we could have bourbon balls on each table. I also think we should make our own brand of bourbon balls to compete in the retail market."

"A box of bourbon balls makes a wonderful gift from Kentucky, and I would love to make them under our label," Woodrow said.

They discussed the pros and cons of pursuing the idea, and all concurred it was worth moving forward.

"The second item I wanted to discuss is hosting daily tours of the distillery."

"I know Cleary's Distillery started give daily tours last year," Woodrow commented.

"I'd like to incorporate tours of the cooperage as well," Honey added.

"Do you really think people would want to tour the cooperage? The visitors would get hot and dusty," Cullen said.

"They might enjoy seeing how the barrels are made, particularly the charring process. They could have a choice of tours, without or without the cooperage. We could also offer a tour of the grounds so people could see the original log cabins on the property." Honey thought the only person who might object to her ideas would be Alan, but she thought he would complain if gold bullions popped out of the barrels. "We have a prime location and a beautiful facility. We could promote group tours as well. We have ample parking space to accommodate large crowds."

"Well, Cleary's doesn't make their barrels, so we will be offering something they can't." Woodrow looked at Honey and smiled. "What else do you have in mind?"

"I think we should add a café to the distillery. Of course, we would start small, and have a limited menu and only be open for lunch initially. The original stone building on the property is a beautiful historic building that is not being used. With minor renovations, it would be the perfect location for a café. That building overlooks the grounds, and we can add a patio. We could use part of the café as a bourbon-tasting area at the end of the tours. A commercial kitchen would be perfect for making bourbon balls instead of hiring another company to make them for us."

"Would we keep the outdoor sandwich shop open?" Cullen asked.

"I think we should for the visitors who prefer something quick," Honey replied.

"You have been giving this a lot of thought." Woodrow was clearly impressed with his granddaughter's ideas. Why don't we walk to the old building and you can show us what you have in mind?"

Feeling encouraged by their interest in her ideas, Honey stood. "Let's go."

When they reached the stone building on the hill, Woodrow opened the door and turned on the lights. "Though we haven't used this building for a few years, we've kept it well-maintained and have it cleaned regularly."

Honey noted the excellent condition of the stone walls, the huge wooden beams, and the old-fashioned sconces throughout the building. "I've always loved this building."

"They don't build them like this anymore. I purchased those sconces from an old theater that was being demolished years ago," Woodrow told them.

"I can see why you think this would make a great restaurant," Cullen said.

"If it is well received, we will start serving dinners on Friday and Saturday nights," Honey replied. "We could add little lights to the trees on the grounds, and when guests are dining on the patio, they would have a lovely view."

"Have you thought about a menu?" Cullen asked.

"Yes. I've been thinking about our menu for the party on the train, and I thought recipes featuring bourbon would be a good idea for that night. I've been going over some of my favorite recipes with bourbon in the ingredients, and we can incorporate them into our menu for the café. I planned on trying out some recipes tonight. If you two want to come by for dinner, you can be my guinea pigs."

"Actual home cooking?" Cullen asked.

"Didn't I mention Honey is a wonderful cook?" Woodrow asked.

"No, you left that part out." Cullen smiled at Honey. "Count me in if I get a home-cooked meal."

"Remember you will be a guinea pig. I can't promise I won't poison you," Honey teased.

"I've eaten takeout nearly every night since I moved here. I'll take my chances," Cullen replied.

Honey pointed to an area at the side of the soon-to-be café. "I think this would make the perfect entryway to the gift shop."

"Another gift shop?" Cullen questioned. "We sell some items in the visitors' center now."

"I think we should have a larger gift shop offering all of the bourbon products I have planned. Naturally, we would include our products on our website to sell online. After the bourbon tasting at the end of the tours, the guides could direct the visitors to the gift shop for purchasing gifts and memorabilia."

"What products do you have in mind?" Woodrow asked.

"There are many items we could add under our label featuring our bourbons in the ingredients: Woodrow's steak sauce, barbecue sauce, honey bourbon—you get the idea. I plan to start working on the recipes right away. I would like to sell accessory items bearing our logo, but I would also like to carry handmade items from local artist. We could even host an event each year on the grounds featuring the work of our local artists."

"That would help many of the locals to have visitors from around the world see their handiwork." Woodrow walked around the space imagining what Honey was planning. He stopped suddenly and faced them. "Honey, I like your ideas. This is exactly what our business needs. Are you thinking of doing all of this at one time?"

"I think it makes sense to do it all at once. While the renovation is going on, I'll work on all of the recipes and we'll be ready to go when the café is finished. Georgia and I are going to do some shopping tomorrow at our competitor's gift shop to see what they carry."

Cullen whistled. "Woodrow said you like to move fast."

"What do you think about this, Cullen?" Woodrow asked.

"I'm impressed. It's a big job to take on all at once, but like Honey says, it makes sense. We're in a great location for locals to dine. When the tourists are on the bourbon trail, we will have a nice place to eat and buy a wide variety of Kentucky products."

"Then let's get started," Woodrow said. "Honey, I asked Chance McComb to stop by the cottage tonight. He's the fellow who did the remodeling, and he's going to renovate the patio area around the pool. We can talk to him about your plans and get a quote on the entire project."

"Invite him to join us for dinner," Honey said.

"I'm certain he'd be grateful for an invitation. Like Cullen, he's single and he'll appreciate a home-cooked meal."

Honey arched her brow at Woodrow, silently warning him not to play Cupid again.

Woodrow winked at her.

"As a single man, I can tell you my mouth is already salivating at the thought of a good meal. It isn't easy to meet people here once they hear my New York accent," Cullen said.

"Small towns can be a bit clannish," Woodrow remarked. "We'll see what we can do about that."

"Georgia will be there, and I'll call my brother and invite him," Honey said.

"I met Preston at your mother's party. I learned a great deal about Thoroughbreds that night," Cullen said.

Honey laughed. "You can be sure at any party you attend in Kentucky, the conversation will inevitably revolve around horses sooner or later."

"I enjoyed our conversation immensely," Cullen replied. "You're certain you don't mind me barging in tonight?"

"Not at all. Feel free to come anytime you want."

"Shall I bring white or red wine?" Cullen asked.

"That's very kind of you. A cabernet would be great."

Honey stopped by the grocery on her way home from the distillery to pick up the items she needed for her impromptu dinner. She loved to cook, and she was excited to test her recipes on her guests. After carrying all of her groceries to the kitchen, she filled Elvis's dog bowl halfway with dry dog food.

Elvis looked up at her with his soulful brown eyes. Using his snout, he nudged her hand holding the humongous scoop, a not-so-subtle hint he wanted more food in his bowl.

"I'm not filling it to the brim, because you are getting a special treat later."

Elvis emitted a low guttural sound, somewhere between a growl and a whine.

"I was going to give you a huge slice of rare tenderloin sans bourbon sauce tonight. But if you don't want it..."

Elvis licked her hand before he buried his nose in his food.

"Good choice." She patted him on the head before she walked inside the pantry to pull out the ingredients she needed for her bourbon marinade. Once she lined up the items on the counter, she wrapped an apron around her waist. After she made the marinade, she poured it over the meat to let it work its magic. She washed the potatoes and popped them in the oven before she washed the greens for her salad. She was in the process of making her bourbon dressing when Elvis ran to the door.

Though she didn't hear the doorbell, Honey followed Elvis to the door and saw Georgia through the side window. Georgia surprised her once again by what she was wearing. Instead of army-surplus-shop chic, Georgia was wearing a lovely floral bohemian-style maxi dress. "You look great," Honey said as soon as she opened the door.

"Thank you, my mom bought the dress for me. It's not really my style, but I thought it was a good time to wear it since your grandfather is going to be here for dinner."

"You don't need to dress differently for my grandfather, but you do look lovely." Honey smiled when she noticed the combat boots peeking beneath the hem of her dress.

"Something smells great," Georgia said, as she leaned down to say hello to Elvis.

"We are having beef tenderloin with bourbon cream sauce, a salad with bourbon dressing, grilled asparagus, baked potatoes, and bread pudding with warm bourbon sauce."

"Sounds wonderful. What can I do to help?" Georgia asked.

"Come to the kitchen and I'll put you to work."

Honey assigned Georgia the task of preparing the asparagus while

41

she prepared the bread pudding. As they worked they discussed the upcoming changes at the distillery, and of course, Cullen Harper.

"All of the women in the office think Cullen is the next best thing to chocolate," Georgia said.

"He is handsome," Honey said, but her thoughts were on a certain detective. She didn't have an opportunity to talk to him much the morning he'd stopped by with Hap. She didn't know anything about him, other than the fact that Woodrow said he was an excellent detective and he was single.

"You mentioned there were going to be three single men here tonight."

Honey wondered if that was another reason Georgia had made more of an effort with her appearance tonight. "Yes, besides Cullen and my brother, my grandfather said the contractor we are going to hire to do the renovations at the distillery is going to be joining us. By the way, I haven't asked if you have a boyfriend, Georgia."

"Not at the moment. I dated a guy for a couple of years, but I realized he wasn't interested in a future together, and I wasn't willing to wait around while he decided if he ever wanted to get serious. What about you? Are you dating anyone?"

"No." Honey thought about K.C. Cleary, wondering why he hadn't called. Several times she'd thought about calling him, but each time she'd picked up her phone she'd been interrupted.

"Is your brother handsome?" Georgia asked.

"I think so. He's two years younger than me, six feet one, blond hair, hazel eyes, and he will talk horses until you fall asleep."

"I've never ridden a horse," Georgia confided.

Honey could hardly imagine someone from Kentucky who had never ridden a horse. "Have you ever wanted to learn?"

"They're so big, they sort of scare me."

"You would get over that fear once you see how much fun it is."

"Does he have a girlfriend?" Georgia asked.

"Who? Cullen?"

"Your brother."

Honey didn't want to sound encouraging since she didn't think

Georgia was her brother's type. "I'm not certain if he's dating anyone in particular."

"I think Cullen will ask you out," Georgia said.

"I don't think coworkers should date." Honey had no intention of dating someone who worked at the distillery.

Elvis took off toward the front door just as someone cracked it open.

Preston reached down to pet Elvis as soon as he walked in. "Hey, Elvis, how's it going, big guy?"

Hearing her brother's voice, Honey called out, "Come on in the kitchen, Preston."

Preston walked to the kitchen and hugged his sister. "I'm glad you're back home."

"It's good to see you. Say hello to Georgia."

"Hi, Georgia. I've already heard all about you from my mother. She tells me you share her chocolate habit."

Georgia smiled at him. "Honey has two chocoholics on her hands now."

Preston held up the bottle of wine he was carrying. "Honey, I know you prefer cabernet."

"I just told Georgia you were my favorite brother." Honey kissed his cheek.

Preston winked at Georgia. "She's right, I am the perfect brother. I'm also her only brother. What can I do to help?"

"We have everything under control. Why don't you go ahead and open the wine? We can have a glass while we finish cooking. Cullen is bringing a bottle for dinner." Honey poured the bread pudding batter into a baking dish and set it aside until she cooked the tenderloin. "Preston, would you turn on some music? Not Elvis though, I don't have time to dance."

Preston chuckled as he picked up the remote on the counter. "Elvis couldn't wait for you to come home so he would have his dancing partner back." He glanced at Georgia, and said, "Have you seen those two nose to nose?"

"They danced last night. It's the cutest thing I've ever seen."

Elvis ran back to the front door just as Woodrow and Cullen walked in. Woodrow stopped to greet Elvis, but Cullen walked to the kitchen and set the two bottles of cabernet he was carrying on the counter.

"Thank you for the wine." Honey noticed he'd ignored Elvis again.

Cullen pointed to the wine glasses on the counter. "I see you've already started."

Preston shook Cullen's hand. "Good to see you again. I brought a bottle to fortify the women while they were cooking, but we'll need more."

"Something smells delicious," Cullen said.

Woodrow greeted Georgia and Preston before he walked over to Honey and kissed her on the cheek. "Cullen is right. Whatever you're cooking smells wonderful."

Honey removed her oven mitts and gave Woodrow a hug before she repeated the menu. She turned to open the oven door to place the pan holding the tenderloin on the middle rack.

Woodrow pulled a piece of paper from his pocket and handed it to her. "Here's my great-grandmother's bourbon-ball recipe."

Honey carefully unfolded the delicate paper yellowed with age and read the recipe. "Your grandmother had beautiful handwriting. I'll scan it and return the original to you."

While everyone chatted, Elvis suddenly ran to the door again. All eyes turned to the door to see who was going to walk in this time. No one opened the door, but a knock came a second later.

"I guess that must be Chance," Woodrow said.

"Relax, Gramps, I'll go."

CHAPTER FIVE

HONEY WAS SURPRISED TO SEE Hap and Sam standing at her door again. After Hap greeted her and Elvis, he walked toward the kitchen, leaving her alone with Sam in the foyer. Sam leaned over to pet Elvis, who was nudging his hand.

"How's my boy?" Sam gave Elvis a brisk rub as Elvis nuzzled his neck.

Honey was surprised Elvis was sniffing Sam's neck again. "I think you have a fan."

"It's mutual. Elvis was a big help the other morning." He straightened and smiled at her. "Is that a requirement?" he asked, his blue eyes glittering.

Honey drew her brows together as she looked up at him. Was he asking her if it was a requirement for Elvis to like him? "Pardon?"

Sam pointed to her apron.

Glancing down, Honey saw she was wearing an apron that said *Kiss the Cook*. "Oh, I didn't realize I was wearing this one."

Sam's mouth tilted in a grin. "And here I was hoping it was an open invitation."

He was so handsome that Honey wished she had the nerve to say it was definitely a requirement.

Honey was still staring at him when she heard Hap say, "Something sure smells good in here." Honey forced her eyes from the handsome man in front of her and turned toward the kitchen. "I hope you haven't had dinner. We'd like you to join us."

"We don't want to intrude," Hap said reluctantly.

"Speak for yourself," Sam teased. "I haven't eaten all day and I do want to intrude."

"Are you on duty, or can you have a bourbon or wine?" Woodrow asked.

While Woodrow was introducing their new guests to Georgia and Cullen, Honey escaped to her bedroom to freshen her makeup. Reaching the master bath, she glanced in the mirror and groaned at her reflection. Not only did she have smudges of flour on her face, she'd totally forgotten that while she was preparing dinner she had haphazardly twisted her hair on top of her head and secured it with a clip. Wiping her face with a wet cloth, she quickly reapplied some light foundation and blush before she picked up her lipstick. As she covered her lips with Kiss Me Pink lipstick, she glanced down at her apron and thought about Sam's comment. *Who wouldn't want to be kissed by him?* She removed the clip and quickly ran a brush though her long hair. Pulling off her apron, she briefly considered changing clothes, but it was almost time to remove the tenderloin from the oven. At least her slim black skirt was flattering, and she was still wearing high heels. She settled on unbuttoning the top button of her white blouse and added a multi-strand turquoise necklace. Glancing in the mirror once last time, she thought the final product looked as good as it was going to get tonight. When she walked back to the kitchen, Elvis ran to the patio door and barked.

"It's Chance," Woodrow said as he slid open the patio door. "I was getting worried about you, Chance."

Chance shook Woodrow's hand. "Sorry, Woodrow, I was held up on my last job. I've been out here for a few minutes looking over the pool area to see what we can do."

"Good. Come in. Honey said dinner is almost ready. You can tell us what you have in mind."

Woodrow introduced Chance to everyone, and Honey wondered how many more attractive men were going to walk through her door tonight. Her kitchen seemed to be raining men—handsome men at that. "Chance, you did a wonderful job renovating the cottage. This kitchen is so wonderfully appointed, I thought you must do a lot of cooking." Honey thought a professional chef couldn't have designed a more functional kitchen.

Chance laughed. "I never cook. Since Woodrow invited me tonight, I've thought of nothing else but having a home-cooked meal."

"We were lucky to have stopped by at the right time tonight. I remember what a good cook you are, Honey," Hap added.

"I was just about to ask what brought two of our town's finest here again so soon," Woodrow said.

"Before you start grilling our guests, why don't you move to the dining room? Dinner is almost ready." While the guests were taking their seats, Honey pulled the tenderloin from the oven and placed it on the counter. She turned around and bumped right into Sam's muscled chest. "Oh, I'm sorry, I didn't know you were standing there."

"I was just going to place my weapon on top of your refrigerator. Is that okay with you?"

"Of course." She watched him remove the holster clipped on his belt.

When he glanced at her, Honey quickly moved to the center island where the salad was waiting to be tossed. After she prepared the salad, she filled the plates and passed them to Georgia, who was standing on the opposite side of the counter. Turning her attention to the tenderloin, she sliced off a huge chunk and cut it into little cubes. By the time she placed it in Elvis's bowl, he was nearly jumping up and down. She leaned down to his ear and whispered, "You get the best slice." She then placed the rest of the tenderloin on a large platter and drizzled the bourbon cream sauce over the top.

Turning around to hand Georgia the platter, she saw it was Sam standing a few feet from her and not Georgia.

"Did you really give him the best slice?" Sam asked in a teasing tone.

Honey glanced at Elvis, who was swallowing his last piece of meat. "He thinks so."

Sam chuckled as he reached for the platter in her hands. "I'll take that."

"Thank you." Honey turned back to the oven, pulled out the baked potatoes, and slid the bread pudding in to bake. After scoring the potatoes, she added butter and sour cream. Once she placed the potatoes on a platter along with the asparagus, she handed it off to Georgia.

Georgia returned to the kitchen as Honey was removing the sourdough bread from the warming oven. "How did we get so lucky?" she whispered.

Honey didn't need to ask what she meant. "I was just thinking the same thing. Did you notice Sam's blue eyes?"

"Wow! Did I ever! Sleeping Beauty blue," Georgia gushed.

Honey scrunched her brow in confusion as she sliced the bread. "What?"

"Don't you ever watch the home-shopping shows late at night?" Without giving Honey a chance to respond, Georgia said, "They are always selling turquoise from a mine somewhere out West, called Sleeping Beauty. The turquoise is a vivid blue, just like your necklace. It's supposed to be rare and in high demand because the mine is closed. Yet every time you turn on the shopping shows, or go online looking for turquoise jewelry, there seems to be an abundance of Sleeping Beauty."

Honey grinned, and glanced Sam's way to make sure he wasn't listening to their conversation. "I like that name—Sleeping Beauty blue."

"Anyway, it's definitely a sign."

"A sign?" Honey thought that she'd never keep up with Georgia's train of thought.

"It's a sign that you noticed his eyes first."

"Why is that a sign? I always notice a person's eyes first. Chance has gray eyes," Honey replied, proving her point.

"You don't notice if a man is wearing a wedding ring first?"

Honey shook her head and glanced at the men standing around her dining table. "No, but I did notice they are all very tall."

"By the way, he isn't."

Honey definitely wasn't following Georgia's conversation. "Who isn't what?"

"Sleeping Beauty blue isn't wearing a wedding band."

Honey rolled her eyes. She placed the bread in a basket alongside a container of garlic butter.

"This is a sign for you not to waste an opportunity with three gorgeous men around. I guess we have to take Cullen off the list, but Sleeping Beauty and Chance are fair game."

Honey had to admit Georgia had a point there. She couldn't remember the last time she'd even noticed one handsome man, much less three. *If K.C. Cleary stops by tonight, then I'll have four handsome men at my table.* Her eyes bounced from Sam to Chance. Chance was attractive, but he didn't make her heart pound like the handsome detective. She glanced Sam's way again, only to find him grinning at her as if he was reading her mind.

Hap reached for the basket of bread just as Honey was about to place it on the table. "Honey, this dinner looks delicious."

"Thank you." Seeing Georgia had taken the seat next to Preston, Honey sat between Cullen and Chance, across from Sam.

As Hap added a couple of slices of tenderloin to his plate, he glanced Woodrow's way. "Woodrow, you were right, Sam and I did stop by tonight for a specific reason."

All eyes went to Hap. Honey though his usual jovial tone now sounded quite serious.

"You know K.C. Cleary," Hap paused, but he didn't wait for a response. "Well, his brother Jack called us a few days ago to tell us K.C. is missing. No one has seen him for at least a week."

Honey thought she hadn't heard Hap right. "Did you say K.C. is missing?"

Hap hadn't considered how Honey might take the news. Knowing she was good friends with K.C, he made an effort to moderate the sound of his concern. "Honey, all we know right now is that no one has heard from K.C. in a week."

Sam watched Honey as she processed the news. "Do you know K.C. well?" He'd had several days to learn a great deal about K.C. Cleary. He was told Honey and K.C. were once good friends, but he didn't know if they were still in contact since she moved to California.

"We've been friends for a long time. He told me he would call when I got back to Bardstown, but I haven't heard from him yet."

"Is that unusual for him—not to call when he said he would?" Sam asked.

Honey didn't have to think about Sam's question. "Very unusual."

"Sam went to K.C.'s home with Jack, but we didn't find anything that would help us locate him. Normally, we wouldn't think much of a man taking off, but since his car is still in the parking lot at Cleary's

Distillery, we're making every effort to locate him. Everyone agrees that this is totally out of character for him. We've called his phone and it goes directly to his voice mail," Hap told them.

"I can't imagine K.C. taking off without informing Jack," Woodrow agreed. He glanced Honey's way, hoping she didn't realize Hap and Sam probably had Elvis check out K.C.'s car the other morning.

One look at Honey's face told Sam that she was very upset by the news. He wished Hap hadn't brought the subject up during dinner. He didn't want to question her about the nature of her relationship with the missing man right now, but that didn't stop his silent speculations. It was no secret in the community that K.C. had an active dating life. A few people he'd interviewed thought K.C. was seeing someone that he was keeping under wraps. In his experience when a man kept a relationship private, it was likely the woman was married or otherwise unavailable. Perhaps K.C. didn't want Honey to know about the woman he was seeing.

Hap wasn't as hesitant to talk about K.C.'s dating life in front of everyone at the table. "We found out that in the last several weeks K.C. had apparently stopped dating. It seems he'd broken off all of his... I don't know if *relationships* is the right word, but he'd taken a sabbatical from dating. Apparently, he'd been seeing someone on the sly before then."

"Why would he need to keep it a secret? Was she married?" Cullen asked.

"That's what we assumed from the comments made to Sam. But even if that was the case, and he planned a vacation with the mystery woman, he would have told Jack he was leaving town." Hap shook his head. "At the moment this whole situation has us baffled."

"K.C. wouldn't date a married woman," Honey blurted out.

"I agree with Honey. K.C. has always dated a lot of women, but he is a man of integrity," Woodrow commented.

Sam thought about their response. While he didn't know Honey, Hap had spoken highly of her. Woodrow was a well-respected man in the community, and his opinion carried some weight. Sam turned his gaze on Honey again. "Do you remember the exact day you last spoke with him?"

Beautiful blue eyes aside, the thought crossed Honey's mind that

Sam's steely-eyed stare, along with his size, would make him an intimidating interrogator. She had a feeling he already knew that she'd also dated K.C. "He called a few days before I left California. I'm not sure of the exact time, but I can check my phone."

"Did he mention taking a trip?" Sam asked.

Honey shook her head. "No. He said he would come by when I got here and bring his tool box." Her eyes met Sam's. "That was an old joke between us. He was always teasing me that every time he came to my house, I found some work for him to do."

Woodrow chuckled. "That sounds like K.C."

Sam smiled slightly. "Did he mention anything worrying him?"

Honey's mind was racing, trying to recall every detail of their latest conversation. "K.C. was always upbeat, he'd never mentioned any problems." She didn't mention that K.C. had asked her to consider dating him again—he'd told her that he wanted a more serious relationship than the last time they'd dated.

Noticing Honey didn't have meat on her plate, Sam held the platter of tenderloin across the table. "Did you speak frequently, or was it unusual for him to call?"

Honey slid a piece of meat to her plate. "We spoke fairly often while I lived in California."

Sam then held the basket of bread to her. "I'm afraid I don't have much to go on. He hasn't used any of his credit cards, and his cell phone hasn't pinged off any towers for a week."

"That sounds rather ominous," Chance said.

Honey glanced from her grandfather to Hap, then back to Sam. "No one would have a reason to hurt K.C."

Sam cocked his head and gave her a thoughtful look. "Why do you think that?"

"K.C. is a wonderful guy. There must be a logical explanation for his absence." Honey told herself there had to be a valid reason he was gone. But what could it be?

"Wonderful guys can get into bad situations," Sam responded softly. "The employees at Cleary's said K.C. had been unusually quiet lately, like something was on his mind."

"Most likely business was on his mind. Cleary's business is booming," Woodrow said.

Sam glanced Cullen's way. "Cullen, have you met K.C.?"

"No, but I've heard all about K.C. Cleary. I guess you could say his reputation precedes him."

Sam was interested in what Cullen had to say. "What do you mean?"

Cullen shrugged. "I've heard Cleary is known as the man with the Midas touch, among other things."

"K.C.'s made quite an impact in the bourbon industry, particularly for someone his age. He's considered to be somewhat of a genius," Woodrow explained.

"What other things have you heard, Cullen?" Sam asked.

Cullen chuckled. "Women are particularly infatuated with him. I heard all he had to do was glance a woman's way and she'd fall at his feet."

Sam looked at Honey to gauge her reaction to Cullen's remark, but she seemed lost in her own thoughts.

"Woodrow, since you and K.C. travel in the same circles, if you get wind of anything, would you let us know?" Hap asked.

"Of course."

"Honey, weren't we planning on going to Cleary's gift shop tomorrow?" Georgia asked.

"Yes." Honey glanced at Sam and explained. "I wanted to see what items they carry in the shop." She'd even thought about visiting K.C. while she was at the distillery.

"If you hear or see anything that might be helpful, would you give me a call?" Sam asked.

"Certainly." Honey thought about the many times she'd met K.C. in the park next door to Cleary's Distillery to have lunch with him. She thought it would be a nice place to take Georgia for lunch and give Elvis a little nature time while they were out.

Sam looked over at Chance. "I haven't asked you, Chance, but do you know K.C.?"

"Of course. I haven't seen him in a while, but I did see his Mercedes at Rick Jarboe's Body Shop a few weeks back. Rick was repairing the Mercedes."

Hap stopped eating and looked at Sam. "I didn't hear about K.C. having a wreck."

This was the first Sam had heard about K.C. being involved in a wreck. "I didn't know anything about a wreck. His car is perfect."

"The driver's side was mangled, pushed all the way into the console," Chance told them.

Sam glanced across the table at Honey. "Did he mention a wreck to you?"

"No." Honey thought she knew K.C. well. *If he'd had an accident, why didn't he tell me?*

"Rick told me that K.C. wasn't in the car at the time it was damaged," Chance said.

Honey looked across the table at Sam. "Is that why you needed Elvis?"

Sam looked into her eyes and nodded. "He didn't find anything."

Honey breathed a little easier knowing if something terrible had happened to K.C. in his car, Elvis would have found something.

The discussion finally centered on Honey's dinner, and she received rave compliments on the tenderloin and the bourbon sauce, as well as the bourbon salad dressing.

Woodrow looked at Honey and winked. "I'd say your recipes are a big hit."

"I think they are an easy crowd to please." She glanced around the table at her guests. "Feel free to stop by anytime this week and be my guinea pigs."

Sam smiled at her. "I'll gladly be your guinea pig if I can eat like this every night."

"Wait until you've had dessert," Preston said. "You'll probably want to move in."

Preston obviously hadn't considered how his comment could be interpreted, but when Honey looked Sam's way again, he arched a dark brow at her. It left no doubt what he was thinking about her brother's comment.

Feeling a blush rising from her neck to her cheeks, Honey jumped to her feet, wanting to escape to the kitchen before her face matched her Kiss Me Pink lipstick. "Would anyone like coffee?"

Honey filled her hands with empty plates as she left the table. Georgia followed her, carrying the remaining plates. When they reached the kitchen, Georgia said, "Your brother is very nice."

"I think so." Honey noticed Preston seemed to be paying a lot of attention to Georgia during dinner.

"What are you two gossiping about?" Preston asked as he placed the empty platters on the counter.

Both women jumped at the sound of his voice.

"We were talking about you," Georgia admitted.

Preston grinned. "Sis, you better be telling her all good things about me."

Georgia didn't give Honey a chance to confirm or deny their conversation. She gave Preston a flirty little smile. "Wouldn't you like to know?"

Honey watched the interaction between her brother and Georgia for a few minutes before she realized she hadn't started the coffee. Once she pushed the buttons on her coffee maker, she pulled on her oven mitts. "Preston, would you grab the dessert bowls on the second shelf?" She pulled the bread pudding from the oven and placed the baking dish on a trivet. While it was cooling, she increased the heat under the bourbon sauce she'd left simmering on the burner.

"Dessert smells as good as the dinner," Sam said.

Honey turned from the stove to see Sam leaning over the counter. She tried to avoid thinking about the look in his eyes moments earlier. *Remain calm*, she told herself. "I hope you like it. Have you had bread pudding with bourbon sauce before?"

"No, but after that meal, I'll try anything you cook."

Honey started scooping the bread pudding into the dessert bowls. She made an effort not to look at Sam, but failed. And when her eyes met his, she felt her cheeks warming again. Georgia was right. His eyes did match her turquoise necklace. The man was too handsome for his own good. She turned away and asked Preston to pour the coffee.

"I'll do it. I ate so much I need to move around, and I want to check out this fancy coffee machine." Sam walked around the counter and looked at the machine.

"It's a great appliance if you are a coffee lover. Would you prefer an espresso?" Honey asked.

Sam started to fill the cups on the counter. "What are you having?"

"Coffee."

"Coffee is good with me. I'll hold you to an expresso another night."

Georgia and Preston returned to the dining room, but Sam stayed in the kitchen with Honey.

"Do you think you will miss California?" Sam asked.

Honey turned back to the stove to stir the bourbon sauce. "No, I love it here. Where are you from?" She'd already noticed he didn't have a Kentucky accent.

"Dallas."

"What made you decide to move to our small town?"

"My grandmother lives here. I'm the only relative she has left, and she's getting up there in age. She needs me close."

Having lived in Bardstown most of her life, Honey was certain she would know his grandmother. "Who is your grandmother?"

"Virginia Gentry."

Honey smiled. "I know her. She owned the only bed-and-breakfast in town for many years."

"She sure did. I stayed with her a few summers during my younger years. I learned all of my handyman skills at that bed-and-breakfast."

"How is she doing?"

"I think she does well for her age. She didn't want to leave Kentucky, so when I heard Hap needed a detective, I applied."

Honey didn't think it would be an easy transition for a detective coming from a large city to a small, quiet town. "Has it been a difficult adjusting to life in a small town? I imagine your professional life was probably much more demanding in Dallas."

Sam leaned against the counter next to her. "Like most places now, crime never stops. We've had a few murders recently, and I've also helped out on some murder cases in Louisville and Lexington. And drugs are a problem in all towns across the country. I keep busy."

Honey looked up at him, thinking how dangerous his job had to be. She wondered if that was the reason he seemed so self-assured.

Sam pointed to the sauce she was stirring and grinned. "How long do you have to stir that?"

Flustered, Honey lowered her eyes to the sauce. "It's ready. I guess I should pour it over the pudding before it evaporates."

"I'd like to take you to dinner Saturday night as a thank-you for tonight."

Glancing up at him again, Honey noticed he'd inched closer to her. Did he feel obligated, or did he want to take her to dinner? "You don't need to thank me. It was a pleasure having you tonight."

He moved his head closer to her ear. "I guess I didn't word that well. I want to take you to dinner Saturday night."

He was so close to her face that if she turned a fraction of an inch her lips would be touching his face. Handsome and charming. A lethal combination, she told herself. She picked up the pan and poured the sauce over the pudding, praying she could form a coherent response. "Okay."

"Is that a yes?" he whispered.

Honey nodded.

Once everyone finished dessert, Hap and Sam had to get back to the station. Honey and Elvis walked them to the door.

Hap gave Honey another hug. "Thanks for feeding two starving cops, and I'm sorry if I caused you to worry about K.C."

"I'm sure K.C. will have a good excuse for being away." Honey tried to sound positive, but she knew she wouldn't sleep tonight for worrying about him. As soon as everyone left, she intended to give him a call.

Sam surprised her when he leaned over and kissed her cheek. "Thank you for dinner. I'll see you Saturday at seven." He pulled a business card from his pocket. "If you need a cop at any time, call me." He leaned close to her ear, and whispered, "By the way, you look beautiful tonight, but I really liked those little red shorts you had on the other day."

The man flustered her. She wished she had the nerve to grab him and give him a kiss he'd remember until the next century.

Sam turned his attention on Elvis and gave him a good-bye rub. "Nice to see you, Elvis."

That one move scored major points with Honey. It must have made an impression on Elvis too, since he followed Sam out the door.

"Come back here, Elvis, you aren't going with them." When Elvis walked back to her, she grabbed his collar. They watched them drive away, and when they were out of sight, Elvis started whining.

Honey scratched his ears, thinking she understood how he felt. She'd never met a man who took her breath away—until now. "Come on, let's go back to the kitchen."

After plans were made to meet Chance at the distillery the next morning to discuss the renovations, Woodrow, Cullen and Chance left the cottage at the same time. By every measure, Honey thought the night was a success. Everyone enjoyed her bourbon recipes, and she had a dinner date with a very attractive man planned for Saturday night. She should be floating on air. Problem was, she couldn't stop thinking about K.C. *Where could he be?* She glanced down at Elvis and thought about him searching K.C.'s car. It was good news that he didn't find anything, so she held onto that fact. "Come on Elvis, let's go clean up."

Georgia was rinsing off the plates and Preston was filling the dishwasher when Honey and Elvis walked back to the kitchen.

"We've got this, sis. You and Elvis relax for a while," Preston said.

Honey had a feeling Preston's sudden interest in domestic work was due to Georgia. "You two are my guests. I'll do the cleaning."

"We'll be done in no time," Georgia said.

"Preston, what do you think about K.C. missing?" Honey asked.

"I know K.C. well enough to know he wouldn't walk away from his business."

"He always calls when he says he will. I'm really worried about him."

Preston pulled her into his arms and kissed the top of her head. "I know you are. But I'm sure there's some reasonable explanation. Now go relax with Elvis and let us finish up in here."

"Thanks for helping." She opened the pantry and pulled out the bloodhound-shaped cookie jar filled with Elvis's treats. As soon as she tilted the dog-head lid back, *"You ain't nothin' but a hound dog"* erupted from the canister. Elvis started to howl.

CHAPTER SIX

EARLY THE NEXT MORNING HONEY gave Chance a tour of the proposed location for the new café and gift shop. "How many people do you think we could seat?"

"A room this size could easily accommodate about seventy-five people with comfortable space between tables." He pointed to the wall across the room, and added, "We can go through that wall and add the outdoor patio. It offers the prettiest view of the land." He quickly sketched out a rough layout of the kitchen and dining area. He handed his drawing to Honey. "Is this what you have in mind?"

After looking over his drawing, Honey knew Chance was the right man for the job. "I think you must be a mind reader. This is exactly what I was imagining. I would like to keep as much of the exposed stone as possible."

"Sounds good. This is a beautiful old building and you want to show it off. Now let's talk about the gift shop."

They spent two hours together going over the details of the renovations. "If Woodrow approves the costs, when could you fit this into your schedule?"

"Woodrow said you wanted to move fast, so we could start right away."

"Really? Woodrow said your schedule is always full. I thought we might have to wait a few weeks."

"I have a couple of crews. I keep myself available, along with a small crew to work on emergency projects. I'll work on this project and your patio at the same time."

"Wonderful." Honey was excited everything was falling into place so quickly.

As they left the building, Chance said, "If you don't have plans Friday night, I'd like to take you to dinner."

Honey had already invited her family to dinner Friday night. "I'm sorry, I planned on cooking Friday, but you are welcome to stop by. As I told you, I need guinea pigs."

Chance had heard her accept a date with Sam for Saturday, so he didn't press. "I'll be there working on your patio, so count me in."

When Honey returned to her office, she grabbed her bag and Elvis's leash and hurried to Georgia's office. "Are you ready to go?"

As they walked toward the front door, they heard someone yelling, "You're going to be sorry you hired him." Alan stalked past them and hurried out the door. Honey assumed he was giving Woodrow grief over Cullen again.

Georgia looked at Honey and raised her eyebrows. "Seems like someone is unhappy."

Honey shook her head. "That man is impossible."

Twenty minutes later, Honey pulled into the parking lot at Cleary's Distillery. She parked under a big oak tree across from the gift shop entry so Elvis would have some shade and a nice breeze while they were in the gift shop.

"Without being obvious, we need to take note of the products on their shelves. See what you like about their displays, and what we think we can improve upon," Honey said.

"You want me to take photos with my phone?" Georgia asked.

"I don't think we should." She didn't think K.C. would mind if they took photos, but she didn't feel right about it without asking him first. Honey had tried to call K.C. last night after she climbed into bed, but just like Hap said, her call went to his voice mail.

Honey lowered the windows for Elvis. "Be good, we won't be gone long."

Although Elvis wasn't happy he couldn't go with them, he dutifully sat in the driver's seat and watched the women walk away.

The entryway to the gift shop was rather boring in Honey's opinion. "They should make the exterior more appealing."

"It's a sign," Georgia said.

Honey smiled at Georgia. "What kind of sign is a boring entryway?"

"It's a sign that our gift shop will be much more successful. I know we will make the place so nice that visitors will want to come inside and shop."

Heaven help her, she was beginning to agree with Georgia and her signs. She would make certain the exterior of their gift shop was as beautiful as the interior. She envisioned large urns filled with colorful flowers flanking each side of the wide double doors of their building.

While in Cleary's shop, Honey and Georgia roamed the aisles without once being asked by the two clerks, who were busy talking to each other, if they needed assistance. Honey slowly made her way near the two women to see if they would acknowledge her presence. Not once did they even look at her. The women were discussing K.C. Cleary's disappearance.

"I heard Jack has no idea where K.C. took off to," one woman said.

The other woman harrumphed loudly. "He probably took off with that married woman he's been dating."

"I don't know if those rumors are true. That's not like K.C. to date a married woman," the other woman replied.

"Well, he may not be dating a married woman, but everyone knew he was seeing that bleached blonde floozy in the office. You know the one with the store-bought boobs."

"That's Gloria. You have to admit, she's really pretty," the woman responded.

Honey stood at the end of one aisle and listened to the women gossip for several minutes. They were totally unaware of her presence. It irritated her that they were discussing K.C.'s personal business without a care who might be listening.

Honey and Georgia didn't make a purchase. They walked out the door without one word from the two clerks.

"Do you think they even knew we were in the store?" Georgia asked.

Honey shook her head. "I can't see how they would ever sell anything with those two women working. Remember what they look like in the event they ever apply for a job at our shop."

When they reached the Jeep, Honey said, "Oh no!"

"What?"

Honey pointed to the driver's-side window. "Look at Elvis."

Elvis was sitting in the driver's seat with an open bag of Cheetos in his mouth, and the telltale sign of orange Cheetos dust on his snout.

"I guess he couldn't get to his treats." Honey had packed his doggie treats in a plastic bowl.

"Guess again." Georgia opened the passenger-side door and picked up the open plastic bowl on the front seat sans the lid. "Not a doggie treat in sight."

"Elvis, you should be ashamed." Honey shooed him out of the driver's seat.

Elvis quickly jumped in the back seat without relinquishing the bag of Cheetos.

Honey leaned around her seat back and yanked the bag from his mouth. "No you don't. You aren't going to finish that bag."

Elvis howled.

Georgia gave his head a rub. "Don't be mad at him, I shouldn't have left my bag in the car to tempt him with all of the goodies I had in there."

Honey expelled a loud, dramatic sigh as she looked at Elvis. "I thought he'd outgrown the stage where he eats everything in sight. When he was a puppy he was always stealing my Cheetos."

Elvis groaned in response.

"My mom's dog is ten years old and he still likes to eat my shoes," Georgia said.

Honey put her key in the ignition. "I guess I should be thankful Elvis hasn't developed that habit." She turned around and shook her finger at him. "You'd better not eat my shoes, buster."

Elvis stretched out, put his head on the seat and covered his eyes with his paws.

Honey eyed him suspiciously. "You know you aren't sorry."

Elvis whined and turned his head away from her.

"Now he's pouting." Honey started the Jeep and drove to the entrance of the park next door where they planned to have lunch. "He didn't eat our sandwiches, did he?"

Georgia held up the plastic container holding the sandwiches. "He didn't find the combination to this bowl."

Finding a parking spot near the pathway, Honey turned off the Jeep and reached for Elvis's leash. "There are some picnic tables along the path. I hope we can find one close to the lake."

After attaching Elvis's leash, they jumped from the Jeep. "If he gets a whiff of something interesting we may never find him. Now that he knows he's in the doghouse, he'll probably listen to me for a few minutes."

They walked almost halfway around the lake before they found a vacant table. While they ate their sandwiches they discussed the inventory at Cleary's gift shop.

Honey told Georgia about the conversation she'd overheard between the two clerks. "They weren't even concerned that a customer might hear them."

"I guess you should call Detective Gorgeous."

Honey laughed at Georgia's new nickname for Sam. "Detective Gorgeous? You mean Hap?"

Georgia laughed. "Very funny. Hap's very nice, but I wouldn't call him gorgeous. I'm referring to the detective who is so handsome he could be a movie star. The same detective who made certain Cullen and Chance heard him invite you to dinner before he left the other night."

"He did no such thing," Honey protested.

Georgia rolled her eyes. "Anyway, Detective Gorgeous told you to call if you saw or heard anything of interest."

Honey frowned at her. "I don't think he meant I should call if I heard idle gossip."

"Of course he did. That's how detectives get their leads. Actually, I think he just wanted you to call him." Georgia reached into her bag, pulled out two bottles of water and handed one to Honey.

Honey ignored Georgia's suggestion to call Sam. She opened the bottle of water and poured some into the empty plastic bowl for Elvis to drink. He quickly lapped up the water and stretched out on his back in the grass. After they finished their sandwiches, they decided to walk the rest of the way around the lake. Elvis wasn't happy he was on a leash, but Honey wouldn't relent. "Sorry, buddy, but this is for both of us."

After a few minutes of walking, Georgia was nearly breathless. "How long is it around this lake?"

"Two miles. Are you getting tired?"

"Yes, but I need to work off all of the food I've been eating. I've already finished the box of bourbon balls your mom gave me."

"You better watch out, you'll become addicted," Honey said, smiling.

"You can't get tipsy on those things, can you? I mean, I can still drive, can't I?"

Honey laughed. "There's not much bourbon in them. By law, it can't exceed a certain percentage. But I don't know about eating a whole box at one time."

Suddenly, Elvis took off running with his nose to the ground, dragging Honey along behind him.

"Elvis! Slow down!" Honey commanded.

Elvis paid no heed. Whether Honey wanted to go with him or not, Elvis was on a scent. And she knew from experience there was nothing as determined as a bloodhound on the trail of something he wanted to find. Elvis pulled her off the path into the trees.

Georgia was running to keep up with them. "What's wrong with him?"

"He probably smells a raccoon, or some other critter we don't want to find," Honey grumbled, refusing to drop his leash.

Halting abruptly, Elvis furiously sniffed the ground. Honey slid to a halt at Elvis's backside, and Georgia ran into Honey's back.

Honey tugged at Elvis's leash, trying to urge him away from whatever he was sniffing. "Come on, Elvis, let's go back to the pathway."

Ignoring Honey's order, Elvis took off again, pulling her deeper into the woods. Honey used both hands to pull on his leash to stop him, but she wasn't strong enough to hold him back. He was on a mission.

"Elvis, if you are on the trail of a bear, you won't get treats for a month," Honey threatened as he pulled her along behind him.

Georgia came to an abrupt halt. "You mean there are bears here?"

Honey couldn't stop to reassure her. "I don't think so. Elvis is a very smart dog and he wouldn't really go chasing after a bear." She hoped she sounded convincing, but truth was, Elvis could be on the trail of any animal. When Georgia didn't respond, Honey glanced over her shoulder to see if she was still behind her.

Elvis chose that moment to come to a dead stop. Unfortunately, Honey had her head turned looking for Georgia and she slammed into Elvis's big body. Losing her balance, she tumbled forward and fell over Elvis's back. Bracing her hands in an effort to cushion her fall, she dropped Elvis's leash. Instead of making contact with the earth, her palms landed on a hard mound that was covered with debris. Shoving her hair from her face, she looked down to see what was beneath her hands. It took her a few moments to comprehend what she was seeing. "What in the world is…" Before she finished her thought, she realized she was staring at two eyes peeking from layers of leaves and brush. Lifeless human eyes. In a panic, she scrambled backward. "Oh no! Oh no!"

Georgia hurried to Honey's side. "Are you hurt?"

Honey pointed to the mound rising from the earth. "Eyes…there are eyes."

Georgia slowly moved forward, and saw the eyes that had Honey in a panic. Her gaze swept the length of the form beneath the brush. "Yeah, they're eyes. And they are attached to a body."

Honey forced herself to look again, and that's when she saw a knife handle sticking out of what was possibly the person's torso.

"He's definitely dead." Georgia pointed to the knife. "Do you know who it is?"

Honey had only seen the eyes for a split second, and she had no desire to take a second look. "I only saw eyes."

Georgia leaned over and brushed the debris from the face. "It's a man."

"Don't touch him, Georgia." Honey couldn't bring herself to look at him, because lurking in the back of her mind was the thought that it could be K.C. She couldn't allow herself to go there.

Georgia closely studied the part of the man's face she'd uncovered. "Number twenty-one won't even help this guy."

Honey stared at Georgia, wondering if she was in shock. "What are you talking about?"

"Number twenty-one is the makeup I use on the deceased. Believe me, it makes everyone look great," Georgia replied nonchalantly.

Georgia was definitely in shock. "Georgia, are you okay?"

"I told you my uncle owns funeral homes," Georgia said, as if that explained her nonsensical conversation.

Honey nodded, wondering if Georgia thought she had found a new client for her uncle's services.

"Sometimes I make up the deceased when there are too many people for his regular lady to handle. Sally is an excellent makeup artist, and she can replicate any hairstyle from a photograph. Anyway, Sally taught me how to do makeup, and the foundation we use is numbered. Number twenty-one is my favorite. If we don't have time to mix colors to get an exact match, number twenty-one always works." Georgia leaned closer to study the man's face. "I'd say this is a good reason to call Detective Gorgeous. It's a si—"

Honey stuck her hand in the air before Georgia could finish the word. "Don't say it!" What kind of sign was finding a dead body anyway? She fumbled in her purse for Sam's business card.

The phone rang once and Sam answered. "This is a surprise."

"Sam, this is Honey Howell."

Sam chuckled. "I know. I called your brother earlier and asked him for your cell number. I already added it to my phone."

Honey didn't think to ask why he wanted her number. "I think you need to come to the park."

Hearing Honey's serious tone, Sam knew something was wrong. "Are you there now?"

"Yes, Georgia and I went to Cleary's today to see their gift shop. Then we had lunch in the park next door…" She was rambling because she was nervous. She took a deep breath, trying to calm down and focus. "We found, well…Elvis found…a body."

"A body? You mean—a deceased person?"

"Georgia says it's a man. He was stabbed."

Sam jumped to his feet, pulled his keys from his pocket and headed to the door. "How do you know he was stabbed?"

"There's a knife sticking out of his chest." Honey told him their location off the path as best she could recall.

Sam wanted to make certain Elvis didn't take off. Bloodhounds often had a one track mind when they followed a scent. "Is Elvis still with you?"

"Yes." She glanced around and saw Elvis sniffing the area around the body. "Elvis, come here."

"Keep him with you, don't touch anything, and walk back out to the pathway. I'll be there in fifteen minutes." Sam clicked off as he ran from the building and jumped in his car.

Nine minutes later, flying gravel and dust trailed Sam's black sedan as he raced down the path toward Honey. His eyes were on her face as he threw his car into park. She looked pale, like she'd just seen a dead body. Before he could open the door, Elvis ran around the front of the car to greet him. Sam rubbed Elvis's ears as he hurried to the women. "Good boy."

Once he reached Honey, he placed his hands on her shoulders, lowered his head so he could see her eyes. "You okay?"

Honey nodded. She pointed to his car. "I don't think you are supposed to drive on the pathway."

Sam smiled. "I'm a detective. I can drive on the pathway." He glanced at Georgia, who was sitting on a large duffel bag. "Are you okay, Georgia?"

"I'm okay. I wasn't the one who fell over the dead body," Georgia quipped.

Sam's eyes slid to Honey. "You fell over him?"

Honey nodded.

"How far away is he?"

Honey turned to point to the area, but she realized she had no clue how far away the body was. "Elvis will take you."

Sam handed Honey his car keys. "You two sit in the car. There's bottles of water in the cooler on the back seat." He picked up Elvis's leash. "Why is his nose orange?"

"Cheetos," Honey said.

"What?"

"He opened a bag of Cheetos. It's Cheetos dust," Honey clarified.

Sam shook his head. "Let's go, boy."

"You have anything chocolate in your car?" Georgia called after him.

Sam didn't hear her question. Elvis had taken off through the trees and Sam was jogging to keep up. A few minutes later, Sam and Elvis walked back to the car. After Sam called Hap to tell him what was going on, he jumped in the car with Elvis. He pulled out his notepad and started questioning Honey and Georgia. "As soon as the men get here, I'll drive you back to your car."

"We can walk back." Honey pulled a wet wipe out of her purse and cleaned Elvis's nose.

"I'm driving you back," Sam insisted.

"I told Honey he's been dead for a while and that number twenty-one won't work on that guy," Georgia commented.

Sam turned in his seat to look at Georgia. "Number twenty-one?"

"Don't ask," Honey warned. She dreaded asking the question she needed to ask. While she didn't really look at the man, she had a nagging suspicion those eyes belonged to K.C. "Do you know who he is?"

"It's K.C. Cleary." Sam wanted to ask some questions, but knowing Honey and K.C. were friends, he hesitated. When he saw tears drop over her cheeks, he pulled his handkerchief from his back pocket and handed it to her.

Giving Honey a moment to collect herself, he turned to Georgia. "How did Elvis find him?"

"He just pulled Honey into the woods. I guess he smelled something."

Honey dabbed at the tears that she couldn't seem to contain. "I put him on a leash because I didn't want him to take off in the woods if he caught a scent of some animal. He was sniffing the pathway and he dragged me into the woods."

"I'm sure he remembered the scent from the other day. Did you touch the body?"

"I turned to talk to Georgia and Elvis stopped suddenly. I ran into him, lost my balance and then fell on..." She swallowed and whispered, "K.C.'s body."

Sam nodded and jotted down that information in the event her DNA was found on the body.

Georgia put her hand on Honey's shoulder. Preston had told her Honey and K.C. were very good friends. "I'm sorry, Honey. I know he was your friend."

"I've known him a long time. No matter what anyone says, K.C. was a good person," Honey replied.

Georgia glanced at Sam. "How long do you think he's been there?"

"Not long. He didn't die here." Sam had seen enough murder scenes to know what to look for.

"Why do you say that?" Honey asked.

"Not enough..." He stopped, not wanting to upset her even more. Discussing dead bodies could sound gruesome, even to the most hardened professionals. He reached over and placed his hand over Honey's and gave it a gentle squeeze. "I'm sorry about your friend."

"Honey, I think you should tell Sam what you heard in the gift shop," Georgia urged.

Honey related the conversation between the clerks. "They were so busy gossiping that they didn't even speak to us."

Sam wrote down the information. "It may be nothing more than gossip, but it's worth checking out. I already spoke to the people in Cleary's office, and I remember the blonde." Seeing a police cruiser pulling up behind them, Sam jumped from the car.

Georgia leaned to Honey's ear and whispered, "You think he remembers her store-bought boobs?"

CHAPTER SEVEN

O N THEIR WAY BACK TO the distillery, Honey called Woodrow to tell him about finding K.C.'s body. When they arrived at the distillery, Woodrow insisted they go home for the remainder of the day. Honey didn't argue, she knew she needed some time alone. No matter Georgia's cool demeanor, Honey thought she probably needed some time to process what she'd seen today.

When Honey arrived home, she filled Elvis's bowl with fresh water and gave him a treat before jumping in the shower. Leaning against the cool tile, she closed her eyes and cried. It saddened her to know K.C. had died in such a horrible way. No matter what was said about him, she knew he was a good man.

She thought she heard the phone ringing, but she ignored it. Woodrow had probably called her mother and father, but she couldn't bring herself to talk right now. She'd have time to answer their questions later. The only time she'd seen a dead body was at a funeral home, and seeing K.C's blank stare was a sight she would never forget. By the time she was all cried out, her sadness turned to anger. She wanted to know who killed K.C. and why. Making a promise to herself to do everything she could to find out why he was murdered turned her grief into purpose. She knew if the situation were reversed, K.C. would do the same thing for her.

While drying her hair, she tried to stop thinking about K.C. and focus on what she was going to prepare for dinner. She had a few extra hours before Woodrow would be there for dinner, so she decided to make some bourbon balls.

Once the bourbon balls were made, she started on dinner. She was placing bourbon-glazed pears on the grill when Elvis ran to the door to greet Woodrow.

Woodrow walked to the kitchen and put his arm over her shoulders and hugged her. "Are you okay?"

"I'm fine. I talked to Mom and Dad earlier."

"I know finding him like that had to be a shock. How did Georgia handle it?"

"Surprisingly well." Honey told him about Georgia's work at her uncle's funeral homes. "I guess that explains why she handled the whole thing much better than I would have expected."

"Where is she tonight?"

"She's spending the night with her parents. Is Cullen going to be here?"

Woodrow walked to the patio door to see if Chance had been there working. "Cullen said he couldn't make it tonight. Did you know Chance was out here working on the patio?"

Honey turned around and looked out the door. "No. Maybe he came when I was in the shower."

Woodrow glanced at Elvis. "It would be unusual for Elvis not to bark. I guess he recognized him. He's been around Chance several times."

"I think he did bark when I was in the shower, but I ignored him." Honey realized Elvis had been lying in front of the patio door the entire time she'd been cooking. "I'm glad Chance is here because I have a huge piece of salmon, and I made some bourbon balls earlier. Mom was right, your great-grandmother's recipe is delicious." Honey inclined her head toward the refrigerator. "Why don't you try one and tell me what you think."

Woodrow opened the refrigerator and lifted a bourbon ball from the tray. "These are beautiful. It's an art to make them by hand and keep them uniform in size. They are all made by machines these days." He popped the chocolate ball in his mouth. "Honey, you better not let your mom taste these, or you'll be making them every day. They are as delicious as they look."

Honey smiled. "I'll be making some more for Mom and her friends to try. These are for anyone who shows up tonight. That's dessert." Honey thought if she hadn't been so upset earlier, she might have thought to ask Sam to stop by tonight.

Woodrow headed toward the patio door. "When will dinner be ready? I'll run out and tell Chance to wrap up what he's doing."

"Fifteen minutes. The grill is hot, and I'll start the salmon in a minute." While Woodrow was outside, Honey filled Elvis's bowl with dry dog food. "Sorry, buddy, no steak tonight."

Elvis was about to attack his food when he cocked his head toward the front door. A second later, he ran to the door. Honey knew someone was going to knock, so she headed to the door. When she pulled it open, Sam was casually leaning against one of the columns. Honey thought he looked tired, but even the dark circles under his eyes did not detract from his handsome face.

"I didn't even knock." Sam smiled and leaned over to scratch Elvis behind the ears. "He's a great dog."

"He's the best." Honey stepped to the side and motioned him inside. "You're in time for dinner. I was just going to put the salmon on the grill. Gramps is on the patio with Chance."

Sam was disappointed he wasn't going to be alone with her. Not only did he want to spend some time with her, but he was hoping to learn more about her relationship with K.C. Cleary. "I didn't come to intrude on another dinner. I just wanted to see how you were doing."

"I hope you can join us." Honey led him to the kitchen. She picked up the basting brush to coat her salmon with the bourbon glaze.

"I can't think of a better way to spend an evening." He walked around the counter to the grill and stood beside her. "Let me do the grilling. I haven't done much on an inside grill, but I can hold my own on an outdoor grill."

Honey finished brushing the glaze on the salmon and handed him the platter. "Be my guest. I need to check the vegetables in the oven."

Just like the night before, Sam removed his gun and placed it on the top of her refrigerator. After he washed his hands, he put the salmon on the grill. While the salmon was cooking, he turned to watch Honey move around the kitchen. "You didn't tell me how you are."

"I'm okay. I really don't want to think about it anymore today." She appreciated he was kind enough to stop by to see how she was handling the day's events, but she needed to stop thinking about it. Before she started mixing her dressing, she looked at him. "It was thoughtful of you to check on me, but I just can't talk about it."

He nodded. "Will you answer one question before I let the subject drop?"

Honey gave him a tentative smile. She had a feeling she knew what he was going to ask. "Number twenty-one?"

Sam arched his brows and grinned. "Exactly. I thought she was in shock."

"I thought the same thing at first." Honey told him about Georgia working for her uncle, and how she assisted with applying makeup to the deceased.

Sam chuckled. "I was really worried about her. She's probably seen more...things than I have." He caught himself before he said *dead bodies*.

"I was trying to remain calm for her sake, but she was as cool as a cucumber."

Sam pointed to the pears with grill marks on the platter next to the grill. "So tell me what the pears are for."

Honey was happy to change the subject from murder and dead bodies. "We are having grilled bourbon-glazed pears on arugula, with goat cheese and walnuts."

"Sounds delicious. What's for dessert?" His mouth was already watering.

"I made some bourbon balls earlier."

"It's been a long time since I had a bourbon ball. Actually I don't eat many sweets, but after I tasted your bread pudding, I may become addicted."

"Gramps gave me an old family recipe and I made a few changes." She opened the refrigerator and pulled one ball off of the tray. "You can try one before dinner if you like."

Sam took a couple of steps toward her and opened his mouth.

Honey placed the candy to his lips and Sam took the whole thing in his mouth along with the tips of her fingers. He stared into her eyes as he slowly released her fingers. "Hmm."

The man made her heart do flip-flops with little effort. Georgia was right on target giving him the nickname Detective Gorgeous. Honey had to remind herself to speak and resist the urge to look into his Sleeping Beauty blues like a lovesick calf. "What do you think?"

"I think I could have these for dinner."

"Now you're beginning to sound like my mother."

"Is that a good thing?" Sam asked.

"My mother is addicted to bourbon balls."

"I can see why." Sam reached for the refrigerator door handle. "I think I'll have one more if you don't mind."

Teasing him, Honey slapped her hand over his, preventing him from opening the door. "No you don't. I don't want you to spoil your appetite. I'll need your opinion on the rest of the dinner before you have more."

Sam relinquished his grip on the handle, turned his hand over and linked his fingers through hers. "Aw, come on, that's no way to treat your guest."

Honey thought she would just about give him anything he asked. "Well, maybe one more." She slowly pulled her hand from his and turned her attention to her dressing. He had her so flustered she couldn't remember if she'd added the bourbon.

Sam moved close beside her and braced one arm on the counter. "I'll be good and wait until after dinner." He watched her work for a moment, then said, "There's one thing I can't figure out and I'm a good detective."

Honey pulled a spoon from a drawer and stuck it in her dressing. "What can't you figure out?"

"Why some man hasn't snapped you up by now." He wondered if K.C. Cleary had intentions of doing just that.

She didn't dare say she'd wondered the same thing many times. While she thought of an appropriate response, she dipped the spoon into her dressing and held it to his mouth. "Tell me if you taste bourbon."

Sam tasted the dressing. "I don't think so. Am I supposed to?"

"I think I forgot to add it." She picked up the bottle of bourbon and measured out a few teaspoons to the mix.

Sam hadn't forgotten his question. "Why aren't you married, or involved, or whatever people call it these days?"

"Why aren't you?" Honey countered.

"I've been told my profession interferes with serious relationships," he replied honestly. "Your turn." He wanted to specifically ask her about K.C., but now that she was smiling he didn't want to ruin the mood.

Honey hesitated to tell him that she'd never really been in love. She'd dated several men, some for many months, but she never felt more than friendship with any of them. "I guess I can't find a man I love more than Elvis."

Before Sam could ask another question, Woodrow and Chance walked through the patio door. Sam greeted the men, then returned to the grill and flipped the salmon.

By the time Sam removed the salmon from the grill, Honey had the salad and vegetables on the table.

Woodrow and Chance complimented the salmon, causing Honey to smile at Sam. "I can't take credit for the salmon. It seems our detective is a master griller."

"Mine doesn't taste this good at home. Your marinade is the secret ingredient," Sam said.

When they finished dinner, Sam helped Honey clear the table. "Can we have the bourbon balls now?"

Honey laughed at his expectant look and nodded. She retrieved the bourbon balls from the refrigerator and passed them around as Woodrow poured the bourbon he'd selected.

Chance reached for a second handful of bourbon balls. "Honey, I've had a lot of bourbon balls and these are the best ones I've ever eaten."

"Are you going to sell these in the gift shop?" Sam asked.

"That's our plan if everyone likes them as much as you do."

"Let me know when the first box is ready. I'm buying it." Sam shoved another one in his mouth. "If Hap finds out that I had dinner here again tonight and didn't call him, I may be looking for a new job." Popping another bourbon ball in his mouth, he said, "Maybe I'll buy the first dozen boxes."

Woodrow laughed at him. "I thought Honey's mother could eat more bourbon balls than anyone I ever saw, but I think you have her beat."

"He'll have stiff competition from Georgia," Honey said.

"I'll take them both on. But I'll have to add five miles onto my morning run," Sam replied.

Honey groaned. "I need to do the same thing. I haven't been jogging in weeks. I planned to start in the morning."

"Would you like to run with me? I feel it's only fair to warn you that I run at five in the morning."

Judging by his physique, there was no question he was in great shape. She doubted she could keep up with him. "Where do you run?"

Sam hesitated a moment since he didn't want to bring up what happened earlier in the day. "The park."

The park was the last place Honey wanted to go. "I think I will stick to the trail here."

"I'm the only one who uses your trail these days," Woodrow said. He looked at Sam and added, "Sam, you should come here and run Honey's trail. It winds around the whole property. Years ago Honey planted wild flowers, added statuary and benches along the trail. I didn't understand why she was going to all of that trouble. But now when I ride or take a walk, I know why she worked so hard designing every detail. It makes my walk so much nicer seeing all of the flowers in bloom. There's always something pretty to see."

Sam's gaze met Honey's. "Would you mind sharing your trail with me?"

"Not at all. I'll see you outside at five in the morning. Although I may not be able to keep pace with you." Honey didn't relish the idea of running at five in the morning, but she'd learned a long time ago, it was necessary to keep to a routine, or it was too easy to find an excuse not to exercise. With all of her projects moving into high gear, five in the morning was about the only time she could schedule to run. She just hoped she wasn't so out of shape that she would embarrass herself in front of Sam.

Before Sam and Chance left, Woodrow asked them to walk outside so Sam could see the work being done on the patio. Honey had a feeling they were discussing K.C.'s death. While they were on the patio, she packaged some bourbon balls for them to take home.

When they returned to the cottage, Chance said, "Honey, if you have time in the morning, I'll need to get with you on the appliances for the kitchen. We need to get them ordered as soon as possible."

"I'll meet you at eight. I'm meeting with the train's chef at nine."

The dinner train event was less than thirty days away. If everything worked out according to her plan, she would advertise the opening of the café on the train by showcasing some of the food they would be serving. She planned to schedule the grand opening of the café a week after the dinner train event.

Honey walked them to the door, and she watched Sam rub Elvis's ears as he had done the night before. The man was scoring points left and right. Not only had he cooked the salmon to perfection, he'd helped her clean the kitchen after dinner, and two nights in a row he'd taken the time to say goodbye to Elvis.

Sam leaned over and kissed her near her ear. "Thanks for the great dinner. Get some rest. I'll see you at five."

"Sam, the gate will be closed in the morning, so you can use this code." Woodrow handed Sam a business card with the code to the entry gate written on the back.

"Do you usually keep the gate closed?" Sam asked.

"Not through the day, but I do at night. We have alarms on all of the buildings, including the stable," Woodrow replied.

"I noticed some well-placed cameras on your property, but I think it would be a good idea to keep the gate closed twenty-four-seven. We've had an increase in burglaries."

Woodrow nodded. "You're the expert."

After Sam and Chance left, Honey and Elvis walked Woodrow halfway to his house.

They walked slowly, giving Elvis plenty of time to check out the territory.

"I think Sam is taken with you. What do you think of him?" Woodrow asked.

Honey expected Woodrow would get around to asking if she had an interest in Sam. "What do you think of him?"

"I like him. Hap says he's the smartest man he's ever worked with. He thinks Sam will be the one to replace him if he wants to stay in Bardstown. Hap's opinion goes a long way with me. He's a fine man himself." Woodrow put his arm around Honey's shoulder. "But I ask again—what do you think of him?"

Honey didn't hesitate to discuss her thoughts about Sam. "I like him.

I'll admit I'm often hesitant about dating men as handsome as Sam. They usually have a long line of women clamoring for their attention. I'm certain he could have a different date every night of the week. But there's something about him that makes me feel he's not even aware how handsome he is."

"Hap told me women are always asking him if Sam is single. Not many men would move to a small town just to be close to their grandmother in her waning years. He could have opted to move her to Texas, which would have certainly been more convenient for him. I'd say that speaks to his character."

"Just wait until he meets Mom's friends. They won't be able to keep their hands off of him. Just like…"

Woodrow looked at her. "K.C.?"

Honey nodded. Her heart felt like someone was ripping it from her chest. "I can't believe he's gone."

"I know." Woodrow pulled her closer. "You weren't in love with K.C., were you?"

"No. I loved K.C. as my friend. He was a wonderful person, and I can't believe what people are saying about him."

Woodrow leaned over and kissed her on the cheek. "You just remember all of K.C.'s good qualities, and don't listen to the gossips. Now go on back to the cottage and get some rest. I think Elvis has sniffed around enough."

Reaching the cottage, Honey decided to sit outside in a lounge chair by the pool while Elvis continued his investigation. As much as she tried to avoid thinking about K.C., her thoughts drifted that way. Who could have despised him so much that they would stab him? She didn't understand that kind of hate. No one deserved to die that way. Certainly not K.C. As if sensing her gloomy thoughts, Elvis jumped on the chair beside her and dropped his head on her lap.

Honey absently stroked his head as her thoughts shifted to Sam. Not only was the man unbelievably attractive, he was good to Elvis, and he was very considerate of her feelings. To think he'd stopped by just to see how she was handling what she saw today was surprisingly thoughtful. She didn't know how he could handle seeing dead bodies on a regular basis. Ruffling Elvis's fur, she said, "Elvis, I don't envy Sam's job."

CHAPTER EIGHT

A T TEN MINUTES TO FIVE, Honey was outside stretching when Sam pulled up. Elvis was meandering around the yard, sniffing everything in sight, but when he heard Sam's car, he came running. When Sam opened his car door, Elvis put his front paws on Sam's thighs and licked his face. Laughing, Sam ruffled his fur.

"Are you running with us this morning, Elvis?"

Honey approached his car. "He's not happy if he doesn't go where I go."

"Smart dog." Sam got out the car and stared at her. "How tall are you?"

"Five feet."

"Really? I thought you were taller."

Honey couldn't stop herself from gazing at his long, long muscled legs. He was wearing black running shorts and a blue T-shirt with the Marine Corps emblem across the chest. Just as she had expected, he was in great shape from head to toe. The man was all muscle. She doubted he had more than one percent body fat. "How tall are you?"

"Six three."

Her eyes were glued to his chest. "A marine, huh?"

Sam gave her a mock salute. "Yes, ma'am."

If she had known he was a marine she would never have agreed to run with him. She'd made the mistake of running with a marine before, and even though the man was ten years older, he could run forever. And Sam was in much better shape than that man. Not only that, but Sam was more than twelve inches taller, which meant she would be taking two steps for each one of his. Great.

As if he read her mind, Sam said, "My stride will be much longer, so you set the pace."

"Okay. I may not talk much, I'll be the one gasping for air."

Sam flashed her a mischievous grin. "I know how to do mouth to mouth."

Honey felt a blush rising from her neck. She couldn't think of a response, so she started jogging on the trail and Sam fell into step beside her. Elvis happily trotted along with them, stopping occasionally to satisfy his curiosity before catching up to them again.

Honey tried to lengthen her stride, but she still took two steps to his one. "You have very long legs."

Sam chuckled. "I'd look pretty funny at six three with short legs."

They talked sporadically, and Honey was surprised when she saw the mile marker. The run was so enjoyable, she hated to turn around, but she needed to get in better shape before she ran more than two miles with him. She pointed to the three-foot turtle statue on the side of the path. "That's the mile marker where I'll turn around. I'm going to need some energy for the rest of my day. The two-mile marker is a buffalo statue, and the three-mile marker is a horse."

"Great markers. I'll run for a while before I turn around." Sam waved at her before kicking into another gear.

Honey was sitting on the porch when Sam and Elvis returned. She noticed neither one was breathing hard.

"That's a great trail. Woodrow was right, every mile is more scenic than the last."

"You're welcome to run here anytime you want. I don't have to be here. I imagine you were bored running at my speed." Honey opened the door to the cottage and Elvis ran to his water bowl.

Sam followed her inside. "I enjoyed running with you. I haven't had a running companion since I was in the marines."

"I'm afraid I'm not in that league, but it was fun." She pointed to a chair. "Please, have a seat. Would you like some water?"

Sam spread his arms and looked down at his wet clothes. "I'm sweating so much you may not want me to sit on your chairs."

"They're leather and I have towels. I always have towels on hand for Elvis's drool."

Sam grinned. "I thought you were going to say for my drool."

Honey laughed and pointed to the refrigerator as she turned toward the bathroom. "There's some bottled water in the refrigerator."

Returning to the kitchen, Honey handed him a towel, and Sam gave her a bottle of water he'd opened for her.

"Would you like coffee? I can whip up some eggs for breakfast," Honey offered.

"I don't want you to think I just come over here to mooch food off of you."

Honey had another thought for a bourbon recipe. "How about some French toast with bourbon syrup?"

"You know you're spoiling me, don't you?" Sam took a big gulp of his water.

"You're turning out to be a great guinea pig." She walked to the pantry and pulled out the brown sugar, cinnamon, and vanilla, along with a bottle of bourbon. "It will only take me a minute."

"What can I do to help? I know you have an early meeting." He'd heard Chance tell her he'd meet her this morning. He had a feeling Chance wanted an opportunity to get to know her better, just like he did.

"We have time. Would you grab the milk, butter, and eggs from the refrigerator?" She placed a mixing bowl on the counter along with a loaf of brioche she'd purchased at the market.

Sam saw a plastic bag full of bourbon balls in the refrigerator. He picked it up and held it in the air. "You aren't taking these to Chance, are you?"

Honey glanced his way to see him holding the bourbon balls. "They're for Georgia. I gave Chance some last night."

Sam frowned. "I know. I think you gave him more than me."

Honey laughed. "I most certainly did not. You each received one dozen."

Sam put the requested items on the counter beside her. Spying the bourbon bottle, he picked it up. "Am I driving you to drink so early in the morning?"

Shaking her head at him, Honey said, "It's for the recipe. Remember, I'm testing my bourbon recipes on you."

"If Hap smells bourbon on me, he'll swear I was drinking this morning."

"Tell him you were with me."

Sam arched his brows at her. "If I tell the guys at the station I was with you at five in the morning and had breakfast, they might jump to the wrong conclusion."

Feeling her face getting warm, Honey pushed the bread toward him. "Would you mind slicing..." She glanced up at him. "How many pieces can you eat?"

"I think this guinea pig can eat about six pieces."

"Slice eight, and make them one inch thick." Honey pointed to the knives on the magnetic strip.

As he sliced the bread, he watched her mix all of the ingredients together. She then picked up a mason jar and poured the contents into a pan to warm.

"What's that?"

"Syrup with bourbon." She pointed to the pantry. "Would you get the griddle and put it on the range at medium-high heat? Add a few pats of butter."

"Yes ma'am."

Sam leaned over and said his good-byes to Elvis at the door. When he straightened, he looked at Honey, and reached out to tuck a strand of hair behind her ear. "Thank you again for sharing your trail and for breakfast." His fingers lingered on her cheek. "That was the best breakfast I've had in a long time. But don't tell my grandmother I said that. She often makes me breakfast on Saturdays."

Honey smiled up at him. "Your secret is safe with me."

Sam held her gaze, and the intensity of his beautiful blue eyes had her heart pounding. She thought he was going to kiss her, but he leaned over and whispered in her ear, "Have a good day. Be sure to tell Chance about our run this morning."

She shivered to her toes. The man definitely took her breath away. She tried to remain calm and concentrate on what he said about Chance, even though it didn't make sense why he thought Chance would be interested in their run. "Okay. Be safe."

Pulling into the parking lot at the distillery, Honey saw three news vans near the front door. Before she left the Jeep, she attached Elvis's leash to his collar. As soon as she opened her door and stepped to the pavement, three reporters converged on her, shoving microphones in her face. The reporters were screaming over each other, and Honey had no clue what they were saying. Elvis started howling. Chance seemed to appear out of thin air and shielded her from the reporters as he escorted her inside. Once they walked through the door, Chance turned the lock. "Are you okay?"

"What in the world is going on?"

"It was hard to hear above Elvis's howling, but I did hear K.C. Cleary's name. I guess word got out that you were the one who found him yesterday," Chance replied.

"Thanks for your help. I was totally ambushed." Honey glanced at the reporters knocking on the glass doors. She took Elvis's leash from Chance's hand. "Let's go to my office. Maybe they will give up and leave."

"Should I leave the door locked?"

"Yes. Employees have a key, and I'll ask Woodrow's assistant if anyone is expecting guests."

While Chance was in Honey's office, Georgia stuck her head inside the door. "Did those reporters ask you questions?"

"They tried, but Chance saved me. I was afraid Elvis was going to eat one of their microphones. He was not happy."

"I told them we weren't free to discuss the case. It's already so hot and humid out there that they'll probably get tired and leave," Georgia replied.

"I hope so. I have an appointment at nine and will have to face them again." She tore three pages from her notebook and handed them to Georgia. "These are items you can order for the kitchen and the gift shop today. Chance says he will be finished in thirty days, and we'll plan on opening the café one week after the dinner train party."

"Will do."

Before Georgia walked away, Honey said, "Wait a minute, Georgia." She opened her handbag and pulled out the plastic bag filled with bourbon balls. "I made these last night, and since I think you are now an expert, tell me your honest opinion."

Georgia reached for the bag and clutched it to her chest. "Thank you! I forgot my chocolate goodies this morning. You saved my life."

"I had some last night and they are delicious," Chance said.

"What about Detective Gorgeous, did he like them?" Georgia asked.

Chance snorted at Georgia's nickname for Sam. "Why do you call him that?"

"Duh. Isn't it obvious?" Georgia retorted.

Honey smiled at Georgia's response. "He loved them." Glancing back at Chance, Honey said, "Sam told me to tell you about our run this morning. Had he asked you to join us?"

"No. Did you have a good run?"

"The man wasn't even breathing hard after a few miles. I told him he's out of my league. You should run with him, Chance. I'm certain you'd make a better showing." Honey glanced up and saw Georgia was still standing there, grinning from ear to ear. "What?"

Georgia just smiled as she turned to leave. "See you later."

After their meeting ended, Chance walked to Woodrow's office, and Honey and Elvis left the building. She hadn't reached the parking lot when she spotted the reporters waiting under the shade trees, ready to pounce. More reporters than before were running toward them from all directions, converging on her like locusts. Elvis started to howl again. They were still some distance from her Jeep when a car screeched to a halt near them, causing the reporters to scatter.

Sam jumped out of his car, took Elvis's leash from Honey and guided them to her Jeep. He opened the driver's-side door, and Elvis jumped inside, landing on the passenger seat. Sam held the reporters back as Honey climbed in. Once Sam closed the door, he turned to face the reporters. "Miss Howell is not at liberty to speak about an ongoing investigation. We will be giving you an update and answer your questions outside the department at one o'clock this afternoon."

Questions were shouted, but Sam held his hands in the air. "As I said, there will be no comment until we hold our press conference at one o'clock. Now I don't want to have to escort you off private property, but I will if you don't leave immediately."

The reporters were grumbling, but Sam held his ground, forcing them to get in their vans and leave the premises.

Honey was impressed with his air of authority. The man demanded respect, and obviously the reports didn't challenge him. Honey started the Jeep so she could turn the air conditioner on for Elvis. The reporters had him so worked up he was slobbering all over the seat. She reached for her towel in the back seat and wiped the drool streaming from his jowls.

When she turned back to Sam she saw Chance approaching the Jeep, so she opened her window.

"How did you know those reporters were here?" Chance asked Sam.

"Someone called and said they were in the parking lot."

"You've had a busy morning. Honey said you had a good run," Chance said.

Sam could tell Chance thought he was going to have Honey all to himself this morning. He was tempted to tell him Honey was off limits. But that wasn't his call—at least not yet. But as his grandmother always said, there were more ways than one to get your point across. "The run was great, and she also cooked me breakfast."

Elvis climbed on Honey's lap so he could stick his head out the window. "Thank you, Sam. I didn't know what I should say to them, if anything."

Sam leaned over, braced his arm on her door and rubbed Elvis's ears. "I didn't think they would come here to harass you, or I would have been here earlier."

"I should have thought they might show up here. It's a small town and a murder is big news. I'm certain you have better things to do than shoo away reporters," Honey told him.

"Honey, after the breakfast you made me, the least I can do is keep reporters away." Sam hoped Chance was listening to every word.

Honey didn't want Chance to feel like she wasn't appreciative of his help. "Chance helped me out earlier with those reporters." She glanced his way. "Thank you, again."

Chance smiled at her. "Anytime. I'll see you at home tonight." He gave Sam a smug smile, nodded and walked away.

Sam frowned as he watched Chance walk to his black Hummer. He turned back to Honey. "Is he coming to dinner tonight?"

"I'm not cooking tonight because I will be late getting home. He said he would be working on the patio."

"Why is he doing the work when he has several crews?"

Honey shrugged. "I guess because he's friends with Woodrow."

"Uh-huh."

Elvis nudged Sam's hand, encouraging him to keep rubbing his ears. "Take care of her, Elvis." He leaned in and planted a brief kiss on Honey's lips. "See you later, honey."

Honey watched him until he got in his car. While it wasn't a long or intimate kiss, it still left her speechless. She certainly hadn't expected a kiss at that moment. *And did he call me honey or was he saying my name?* Sometimes her name created confusion in such situations. And what was going on between Chance and Sam? She sensed some tension between them. Yet that didn't make sense. They seemed to get along well last night during dinner. She glanced at Elvis, who was sitting with his nose glued to the vent. The blowing air was making his big droopy jowls flop. "Men are a puzzle, Elvis."

Elvis groaned.

Honey put the gear in reverse. "Not you, you're perfect."

Her phone rang just as she was about to leave the parking lot. Glancing down at the screen, she saw it was her mother. "Hi, Mom."

"Honey, I wanted to let you know that I'm having a rather impromptu party a week from Saturday. I'm inviting some of the people that you plan to include on the train event. I'm also inviting Cullen so the girls won't get mad at me."

Honey smiled to herself. Naturally, all the women would want Cullen to attend. "I can invite Georgia."

"Oh, Preston is inviting her. Apparently they hit it off very well."

"I didn't think Georgia was Preston's type, but he seems to really like her."

"I'm not sure Preston has a type. Why don't you invite that new detective to the party? His name is Sam, isn't it?"

"Yes. Sam Gentry."

"I haven't met him, but I hear you have a date with him Saturday night. Someone told me he's also very attractive." When Honey didn't comment, Lorraine said, "Well, is he?"

"Yes, he is." She wasn't about to tell her mother that Sam was more handsome than Cullen.

"How did you meet?"

"He came to the cottage with Hap."

"Well, please invite him to the soiree. Your father and I would like to meet him since you're dating."

Honey exhaled loudly. "We aren't dating, Mom. He invited me to dinner to repay me for the dinner at the cottage."

"Still, we would like to meet him. Of course, I will see you before then. Maybe he'll be at the cottage one night when I come by."

Honey wanted to change the subject, and she knew what would change her mother's focus. "I made some bourbon balls yesterday and I set aside a dozen for you."

"Are they in your refrigerator?" Lorraine asked.

"Yes, why?"

"I'm driving over there right now to get them. I'm starving."

Honey was still laughing as her mother disconnected. "That was too easy, Elvis."

Before she could stick her phone in her purse, it rang again. "Hi, Georgia."

"I saw Detective Gorgeous handle those reporters."

"He's very efficient," Honey replied.

"Did he tell you if he has any leads on K.C.'s murder?"

"I think it's too early for that, and I'm not sure Sam would tell me."

"You know most of the people in this town. Do you have any idea who could be a murderer?" Georgia asked.

"I've been thinking about that. I can't think of anyone who could do such a terrible thing. I wonder if K.C. just happened onto some sort of crime in progress." Just like small towns everywhere, there were always secrets.

"Maybe he saw some sort of drug buy, or something like that. There are drug problems in many small towns now. I think we need to go back to that gift shop and see what we can find out from those two chatty women."

"I guess it wouldn't hurt to ask what they know," Honey agreed.

"The first people the police suspect are the ones who find the body. We don't want to be under suspicion and have negative press when we are going to have a big social event."

Honey wasn't worried about bad press. She'd made a promise to K.C. to find his murderer, and she intended to keep that promise.

CHAPTER NINE

S AM ARRIVED AT HONEY'S COTTAGE a few minutes early Saturday night. When she answered the door, he stood there staring at her without uttering a word.

"Hi," Honey said.

"You look beautiful."

"Thank you." Honey had changed clothes five times. He hadn't mentioned where they would be dining, and she didn't want to be overdressed. She finally settled on a flirty little black-and-white silk dress and red high heels. "I wasn't certain what to wear tonight."

"I should have told you what I had in mind, but you would look great in a burlap bag."

Honey could say the same thing about him. He looked even more handsome than normal in his dark jacket, white shirt, and red tie. It looked as though they had planned their wardrobe. She hadn't seen him for a few days, and she was excited to see him tonight. "You look very handsome."

He leaned over, kissed her cheek and said, "Your red high heels are a distraction. I should get a medal if I can concentrate on driving tonight."

Honey laughed. "You are an officer of the law. I think you can handle a little thing like red stilettos."

"Every man has a weakness." He'd been so sidetracked by her figure-hugging dress that he hadn't realized until that moment that Elvis wasn't by her side. "Where's Elvis?"

"He's with Woodrow." Honey was worried about Elvis. He was

becoming so attached to her that he didn't want to leave her side. She thought it would be good for him to spend some time away from her.

"Are you ready to go?"

"Yes." Honey reached for her bag on the table in the foyer and walked out the door. Sam turned the lock and pulled the door closed.

"You don't have to lock the door."

"You don't lock your door?"

Honey shook her head.

"Do you have your key?"

"Yes."

"Good. I would be happier if you had a deadbolt."

Honey thought he was being overly cautious. "We've never had any problems here."

"Times have changed." Sam didn't want to frighten her needlessly, but a good thief could avoid their cameras and breach their security. "I hope you aren't starving, because we are driving to Louisville."

"It's a nice night for a drive." Honey couldn't wait to see what restaurant he'd chosen. Her mother always said that you could tell a lot about a man by the restaurant he chose on a first date. She didn't ask where they were going, she wanted to be surprised.

After he opened the car door, he held her hand as she slid inside. Once he was behind the wheel, he asked, "Has the press bothered you since I saw you last?" He'd been so busy at work that he hadn't had time to call her.

"No. I think your press conference answered a lot of their questions." She'd seen Sam on the local news that night, and he had the press eating out of his hand.

Sam had wondered if she'd spent time with Chance since the last time he saw her at the distillery. He was still irritated that Chance rubbed it in that he was going to see Honey that night. "How's the patio coming along?"

"It's looking great. Chance has worked late the last two nights."

So, Chance was at the cottage every night. Sam didn't want to appear like a jealous suitor, but he was curious if she'd cooked dinner for him. He reminded himself he was a good detective, he should be able to think of a way to ask a question without yielding to the green-eyed monster.

"He'll probably stretch out this job just so he can eat your wonderful cooking."

Not picking up on Sam's subtle inquiry, Honey laughed. "That's what he said. Of course, that was before I ordered pizza the other night for dinner. But he'd worked until nine o'clock, so I imagine he would have eaten anything. I was busy working on the interior design of the café, and time got away from me."

Bingo. That was easy. "Chance is single, so I guess he can work late in the evenings." He'd bet a month's wage that Chance was working so late because he was interested in her.

"Woodrow says he is a very hard worker. He's very fond of him."

Sam really wanted to ask if she was very fond of Chance. "I'm certain Woodrow is a good judge of character."

"Yes, he is. He speaks highly of you."

Sam grinned. "Then I'd say he's an excellent judge of character."

They discussed the bourbon business, and Sam's profession as they drove. Honey saw a huge billboard advertising Pickett's Distillery, and she silently read the caption. *Why pay more for the same great taste at half the price of the most expensive bourbon.* Sam asked her a question, and she forgot all about the billboard.

When they reached their destination, Honey was pleased by Sam's choice of restaurants. The historic Brown Hotel was a favorite of her family. Every time she walked inside the lobby it was like walking back in time. The hotel's rich past seemed to seep through the walls, reminding those who entered that this was a place where elegance and genteel manners still reigned.

Sam escorted her to the English Grill where they followed their host to a secluded table. From the oak paneled walls to the equestrian paintings, the room not only had a storied history, but it provided a very romantic setting for an intimate dinner. Holding her chair, Sam said, "I've been here a few times and the food is always excellent. We can hear each other talk without raising our voices."

"I haven't been here in a long time. It's a great choice."

After a fabulous dinner, Sam decided to take the back roads on the drive home, avoiding the expressways. Honey found him to be an excellent conversationalist, and a man with varied interests. He loved to sail, and when she told him she'd never been sailing, he offered to take her out on his boat.

"Do you ride?" Honey asked him.

"Did you forget, I'm from Texas? I worked on my granddad's ranch until I left for college."

"When you were running on the trail, did you notice how the trail splits off at the third mile?"

"Yes, I meant to ask you about that. I wasn't quite sure I was headed in the right direction."

"I forgot to tell you about that. Our riding trail is to the right and it also covers the entire property. You don't have to worry about where you step on the running trail. Gramps and I are riding tomorrow if you would like to join us."

When they arrived at Honey's cottage, Sam walked her to the front door. Honey decided against inviting him inside for coffee. She was tired, and she had to get Elvis from Woodrow's house. "I almost forgot I was supposed to extend an invitation to you. Mom and Dad are hosting a small party next Saturday and she wanted me to invite you."

Sam leaned against the column and looked at her thoughtfully. "Your mom is inviting me to a party?"

Honey didn't want him to think she'd been talking to her mother about him. "Preston mentioned seeing you at dinner the other night."

"Your mom is inviting me, but you aren't?" Sam was teasing her, but he did want to know if she wanted him to go to the party.

"She told me to invite you, but yes, I'm also inviting you. If you would prefer to go alone, or with…" She hesitated when he took a step closer.

He lowered his head to look into her eyes. "If you're about to suggest I would want to go with someone other than you—don't." He brushed his lips over hers, and quickly pulled back a few inches. "If you are inviting me, then I'd say..." He hesitated—his eyes remained on her lips. Without another word, he pressed his lips against hers and pulled her into his embrace.

When he pulled away, Honey wanted to drag him back to her.

"I'd say..." He couldn't remember what he wanted to say, so he kissed her again. This time he didn't pull away, and Honey wrapped her arms around his neck. The kiss was long and mind-numbing.

Sam dragged his lips from hers and rested his forehead against hers. "I'd say if you are my date, the answer is yes."

Honey didn't say anything; she was still reeling from his kiss.

"Do you have a western saddle?"

Still rattled, Honey gave him a puzzled look. "What?"

"I wanted to know if I need to bring my own saddle tomorrow."

"Oh. We have western saddles and we also have a couple of quarter horses in the stable."

"Good. I'll see you tomorrow." At least he knew she hadn't made plans with Chance on Sunday, or next Saturday night. After that kiss there was no way he was going to give Chance the opportunity to get his foot in the door. He held his hand out, palm up.

Honey looked at his hand and she realized he was asking for her key. She opened her clutch, pulled out the key and handed it to him.

He opened the door, flipped on the inside light, and out of habit, he glanced around the room. He reached for her hand, and once he put the key in her palm, he raised her hand to his lips and brushed a kiss over her fingers.

Honey thought that was one sexy move. "Thank you for a wonderful evening."

He held her hand as he gazed into her eyes. "You're trouble with a capital T, Honey Howell. Go inside while I'm still behaving like a gentleman." Whistling his way back to his car, he turned to her before he opened the car door. "I miss Elvis greeting me. Tell him hello for me. And lock your door." Once he started his car, he waited until she closed her door before he drove away.

She was just getting ready to change her shoes to walk to Woodrow's when there was a knock on her door. Through the sidelight she saw Elvis and Woodrow standing there.

When she opened the door, she said, "I was just getting ready to walk to the house."

"I think Elvis saw Sam leave. He wasn't happy that he wasn't invited on your date," Woodrow told her. "He's paced all night."

Elvis whined and nudged against her as if he hadn't seen her in weeks. Honey leaned over and kissed his snout. "Sam said he missed your greeting."

"You look lovely. I bet you knocked Sam's socks off."

Honey motioned for him to come inside. "We had a nice evening at the English Grill. Could I get you something?"

"No, it's too late for me. I'm not staying, I just wanted to bring Elvis home before he drove me crazy."

"Sam is coming over tomorrow to ride the trail with us."

"He might think I'm a third wheel."

Honey kissed him on the cheek. "You'd never be a third wheel, and Sam likes you."

The first few days had been a flurry of activity, and Wednesday was no different. It was nearly five o'clock when Honey checked her calendar to make certain she'd accomplished everything she'd planned for the day. She glanced at the note she'd written for that evening—*dinner with Chance*. She'd completely forgotten she'd accepted his dinner invitation.

Georgia stuck her head in the doorway. "I'm going home. Do you need anything before I leave?"

Honey was throwing her notebook inside her purse. "No, I'm headed out too. I forgot I have dinner plans with Chance."

"Chance? What about Sam?" Georgia asked.

"Chance has asked me a couple of times. He wanted to thank me for the meals I've provided since he's been working on the patio."

"That's not the reason he's asking you out. He's interested in dating you."

"He's just being nice," Honey countered.

"He'd better watch it, or Detective Gorgeous might arrest him for something," Georgia teased.

Honey shook her head. "Contrary to what you think, not every man is interested in dating me. And dinner with Chance is not a date."

"Does Sam know you are going out with Chance?"

"I had no reason to mention it. Besides, I haven't talked to Sam since we went horseback riding with Woodrow." She thought they'd had a great time on their ride, and she was surprised she hadn't heard from Sam.

"You mean he hasn't called you?" Without waiting for Honey's response, she said, "That's a sign."

"What kind of sign?" Honey turned out the lights to her office, and Elvis jumped up and followed her out.

"It's a sign he is very interested. He doesn't want you to know, so he's playing it cool."

"Or, it could be a sign that he dates lots of women, and I'm just one of many." Honey didn't want to say after that kiss they'd shared, she thought he was interested. But he hadn't called.

"If he dates so many women, why did he want to see you the very next day after he took you to dinner?"

"Maybe he was just filling up his calendar."

"No way. He seriously likes you. I can tell by the way he looks at you. He's probably really busy with the murder investigation."

Honey wanted to change the subject. "Are you looking forward to Saturday night?"

"Sort of."

Honey didn't think that sounded like the response of someone excited to go to a dinner party with a guy she was obviously interested in. "Is something wrong?"

Georgia groaned. "I don't have a dress for a fancy party."

"Georgia, it's not fancy. You will be fine with whatever you want to wear," Honey assured her.

"There's going to be a lot of, well, you know—important people there. I don't want to embarrass you or Preston."

Honey was tempted to ask if she was getting serious with her brother, but that was a conversation for another day. "You would never embarrass either one of us. But if you'd like to rummage through my closet and see if you can find something you like, you are more than welcome."

"You're a lot smaller than me," Georgia said.

"I have some loose summer maxi dresses that I'm certain would work. Come over tomorrow after work, and you can see if there's anything you like."

"I haven't been to this diner in years." Honey was relieved Chance had chosen the local diner instead of driving to Louisville for dinner. She had a lot of work left to do tonight and she didn't want to be out late.

"It may not be as fancy as some places, but they have good food," Chance replied.

While they waited for their drinks and salads, they discussed the work Chance was doing at the distillery. Before the main course was served, Honey saw Sam and Hap walk through the door. One of the waitresses hurried to the door and greeted them warmly. The waitress walked beside Sam as she directed them toward a booth. She linked her arm through his, and smiled up at him like he was a delectable dessert.

Sam appeared to be interested in what the waitress was saying, but he was also covertly surveying the room. When his gaze landed on Honey, he disentangled himself from the eager waitress and headed in her direction. Once he reached her table, his eyes shifted to the opposite seat. If he was surprised to see Chance sitting there, his expression didn't give it away.

"How are you two doing?" Sam extended his hand to Chance.

Chance smiled wide. "Great. We're enjoying a night out for a change. Honey is always working and so am I, so we thought we'd take a break tonight."

Honey thought Chance made it sound like they were a couple making decisions together, trying to coordinate their schedules.

Irritated by Chance's response, Sam leaned over and kissed Honey on the cheek. "How are you doing, honey?"

There it was again. Was he calling her by name, or was he calling her honey? "I'm fine." She wanted to ask why she hadn't heard from him since their horseback ride. "How are you?"

"I hate to admit it, but I was stiff for two days after our ride." He glanced at Chance and explained his comment. "Woodrow, Honey, and

I rode the trail Sunday. I've been out of the saddle too long and I paid the price."

"Honey, I'll have to take you to my farm if you want to do some riding." Chance turned his eyes on Sam. "Have you found K.C. Cleary's murderer yet?"

If Chance wanted to yank his chain, Sam thought it was time to show him who yanked harder. "Getting closer every day." His gaze slid to Honey. "Honey, I've been so busy this week I haven't had time to think." It was a little white lie. He'd picked up his phone a dozen times to call her, but he'd talked himself out of it each time. When he wasn't thinking about solving murders, he was thinking about her, but he didn't want to come on too strong. "I'm looking forward to this Saturday. What time should I pick you up for the party?"

Honey felt the tension between the two men again. "Seven would be good."

"See you then." He nodded in Chance's direction, and walked back to the table where Hap was sitting.

Honey knew Sam told Hap she was in the diner, because he turned around and waved. Sam was facing her direction, so she couldn't avoid looking at him. As she ate dinner, she tried to focus on Chance's conversation, all the while discreetly observing what was happening at Sam's table. The waitress spent more time by Sam's side than she did any other table. Sam didn't look toward her table one time.

CHAPTER TEN

"I'M SO HAPPY TO FINALLY meet you, Sam," Lorraine said, linking her arm through his. "Come with me, I want you to meet Honey's father." After the introduction, Lorraine left the two men discussing the latest crimes in town. She joined Honey, who was talking to Georgia and Preston.

"He's so handsome, Honey," Lorraine whispered in her daughter's ear. "Could he be *the one*?"

"Mom, don't start. We're friends, nothing more." She hadn't seen Sam since the night she was dining with Chance, nor had he called all week.

Lorraine watched Sam and she noticed how he would glance Honey's way every few seconds. "I don't know about that. The way he looks at you says he's very interested."

"I don't mean to butt in, but I agree. Detective Gorgeous likes her a lot," Georgia added.

Lorraine looked Georgia's way and laughed. "Good name for him. Honey shouldn't let this one get away."

"I'm right here. I can hear you two," Honey reminded them.

"Well then, what do you think of him?" Lorraine asked.

"I like him."

"Where did he take you to dinner?"

"The Brown. We had a wonderful dinner."

Lorraine gave an approving smile. "Obviously he's a man of taste and one who appreciates tradition."

Honey rolled her eyes. Thankfully, she was saved from answering more questions when Woodrow joined them. A second later Sam walked up and shook hands with Woodrow. Lorraine took hold of Sam's arm again. "I want to introduce you to some of the other guests you haven't met."

Sam placed his hand at Honey's waist and whispered in her ear. "You're coming with me."

They approached an attractive couple and Lorraine said, "Sam, I'd like you to meet Eugenie and Jefferson Grayson."

Sam shook hands with Jefferson Grayson before turning his attention on his wife. He was well aware they were the town's most prominent citizens. "I tried to see you the other day, Mrs. Grayson."

Eugenie took a small sip of her bourbon and water as she looked Sam up and down. "Why on earth did you want to see me?"

"I have a few questions about K.C. Cleary." Sam felt Honey staring at him, but he kept his eyes on Eugenie.

Eugenie lifted her chin in the air and arched her brows at Sam. "What kind of questions could I possibly answer about Mr. Cleary?"

Eugenie tried to appear unruffled, but Sam had questioned many people, and he was adept at recognizing the signs when he'd hit a nerve. He had already spent hours investigating, and he knew K.C. Cleary had been seen on more than one occasion with Eugenie Grayson. It was just a matter of time before he found out how serious their relationship was. He'd interviewed many prominent people in the past, and Eugenie might think she could intimidate him, but she was mistaken. Her icy demeanor and superior attitude didn't faze him. "I understand—"

Jefferson Grayson interrupted him, saying in his smooth Southern drawl, "I'm sorry, Detective, but my wife and I didn't know K.C. very well. We would see him at social functions, but we're not in the bourbon business. I'm afraid our paths didn't cross often."

Sam stared at Jefferson, trying to get a measure of the man. "That's not what I've—"

This time it was Lorraine who interrupted him by taking hold of his arm. She pointed across the room. "There's Marge and Cliff Horton, Sam. I know they wanted to meet you." She glanced at Eugenie and Jefferson. "You'll excuse us, won't you? Cliff specifically told me he wanted to discuss something with Sam." Without waiting for their response, Lorraine deftly maneuvered Sam across the room. Honey was nearly running to keep pace with them. Not stopping until they reached an area behind a huge elephant ear plant, Lorraine turned to face Sam and Honey. "Sam, I don't know if you are aware, but Jefferson and Eugenie Grayson are very influential people. I didn't want you to get off on the wrong foot with them."

"Thank you, Lorraine, but I know who they are," Sam replied.

"You do?" Lorraine was clearly surprised by his admission. "Why on earth would you question Eugenie about K.C.?"

Honey placed her hand on her mother's arm. "Mom, Sam may not wish to share information about his investigation."

Sam smiled at Honey. "I can share a few things. Let's just say a woman matching Eugenie Grayson's appearance was seen with K.C. several times over the last year. I did go to the Grayson estate to interview her, but was turned away at the gate. Tonight may be the only opportunity I'll have to let her know I intend to question her, and I wasn't going to let it pass. I apologize if I have created a problem for you."

"I just hope you didn't create a problem for yourself. Jefferson Grayson can make a formidable enemy, and I bet he will be on the phone with Hap before the night is over."

"I'm not concerned about that. I have a job to do."

"I just can't imagine why Eugenie would be seen with K.C. As Jefferson said, they are not in the bourbon industry. I'm sorry if I interfered with your investigation," Lorraine responded.

"Don't worry about it. I'll find a way to question her." After seeing Eugenie's reaction, Sam had no doubt she knew K.C. better than her husband admitted. He just wondered if Jefferson Grayson was aware of his wife's relationship with the late K.C. Cleary.

Lorraine saw her friend Bunny approaching with a glass of bourbon in her hand. "Bunny, I want to introduce you to Sam Gentry. Sam, this is my friend Bunny Spencer."

Bunny extended her hand to Sam and gave him a wide smile. "So you are our newest detective."

"Yes, ma'am." Sam politely shook her hand.

Bunny spared a quick glance at Honey. "Hi, Honey."

Honey didn't think Bunny had aged a day in the last ten years. Maybe she should ask her for the name of her plastic surgeon. "Nice to see you again."

An attractive, tall, blond man walked to Bunny's side. "I'd like you to meet my husband, Troy Spencer." She held her hand in Honey's direction. "Troy, this is Lorraine's daughter, Honey, and her date is the new detective we've heard so much about, Sam Gentry."

Sam extended his hand to Troy. "I hear you own Pickett's Distillery."

"Yes, my wife and I purchased Pickett's after we were married." Troy wrapped his arm around his wife's waist.

Honey recalled that her mother had described Troy as attractive and charming. She was accurate in her assessment, if one found the muscled playboy type appealing. Even though Bunny had gone to great lengths to deny the passing of time, she still looked much older than her new husband. "My grandfather tells me you are making great progress with Pickett's."

"That's quite a compliment coming from one as knowledgeable as Woodrow Howell. I'm amazed he's taken note of our little distillery," Troy replied.

"My grandfather likes to see everyone in this business succeed."

"From what I hear, your date has quite a successful reputation in his profession." Bunny smiled again at Sam. "Why don't you tell us about some of your exploits in Texas?"

"I doubt my stories would be of interest to anyone," Sam replied evasively.

"Attractive and humble. How alluring—and rare." Bunny took a sip of her bourbon, her eyes never leaving Sam.

Troy reached for the glass in her hand and tossed back what little bourbon remained. Bunny turned and stopped a passing waiter, instructing him to bring her another drink. When she turned back to the group, she said, "Come now, Sam, do tell us about your heroics in Texas."

Sam didn't know how she came by her information. "Sorry to disappoint, but I've never considered myself heroic."

The waiter appeared at Bunny's side and she lifted her drink from his tray. "I heard you single-handedly captured the head of a drug cartel in Texas. Not only that, but you were shot in the process."

Honey looked up at Sam. He hadn't mentioned he'd been shot. "When did this happen?"

"Just before he came to our quaint little town," Bunny answered for him.

"The retelling sounds more dramatic than reality." Sam preferred not to discuss the incident. He glanced at Troy. The man was obviously annoyed with his wife's drinking, or perhaps he didn't care for the attention she was giving him. Either way, Sam wanted to change the subject and he knew the perfect way to do it. "Troy, did you happen to know K.C. Cleary?"

Sam noticed Lorraine glance Bunny's way. Bunny didn't notice because she was still staring at him. Judging by her glassy eyes, Sam figured she'd had one drink too many.

"I believe I met him at some function a few months ago. Troy glanced at his wife, and seeing her eyes were fixed on Sam, he gave her a not a not-so-gentle squeeze. "Isn't that right, sugar?"

Irritation crossed Bunny's taut features. "I believe you met him at the bourbon festival. Of course, I knew K.C. for a long time, like everyone else in town."

Sam glanced at Honey to see her reaction to Bunny's odd behavior. Honey arched her brow at his silent question. Sam winked at her. He decided to ask some questions to get Bunny's mind on something else. "Did you happen to know if K.C. dated anyone in particular?" He'd already uncovered names of several women K.C. dated, but he wanted to know if this group had different information.

Bunny took another drink of bourbon before she responded. "I really can't say who he was dating. K.C. was known for being a prolific womanizer."

"It's a shame what happened to him. I can't imagine why anyone in our small community would kill K.C.," Lorraine said.

Sam felt Honey shiver at her mother's comment. No doubt she was thinking of what she saw in the park that day. He placed his arm around her waist and pulled her closer to him. He regretted discussing K.C.'s murder in front of her tonight.

Troy gave Sam a subtle grin. "Maybe he was seeing the wrong

woman. A jilted lover or husband could have allowed jealousy to get the best of him."

"Was he known to date unavailable women?" As soon as Sam asked the question he saw Lorraine's eyes shift to Bunny.

"I wouldn't know," Bunny responded.

Sam wondered why Lorraine kept looking at Bunny. "Did you keep up with him, Lorraine?"

"I knew him quite well. Honey was a friend of his, so I saw him often before Honey left for California. Not so much after that, other than at parties. He dated the owner of the salon where I go, but that was some time ago."

Lorraine and Bunny discussed the hairdresser, and Sam committed to memory the hairdresser's name and the name of her salon.

"I thought Bunny would never stop staring at you," Honey said, once they were in Sam's car.

Sam grinned. "You think she liked me?"

"I think she liked you a lot more than Troy liked her drooling over you. And did you see the look on his face when she invited you to join them on their yacht?"

Sam had caught Troy eyeing Honey a couple of times. "I also heard him invite you to come along."

"I'm afraid Bunny would snatch me bald," Honey countered.

"I'm not going without you."

Honey laughed. "Don't tell me the big bad detective needs a protector?"

"Around her? You bet I do!" Sam turned the ignition in the car. Before he put the car into gear, he turned to her. "Was Bunny really drooling? Why don't you drool over me?"

"Isn't one woman drooling enough for you?" Honey teased.

"Depends on the woman." He stared at her for a few seconds before he drove down the winding driveway. "Bunny doesn't seem like the kind of woman your mother would have as a friend."

"They went to high school together. Mom said she's really changed over the last few years. She obviously drinks too much, and she been married several times."

"Your mother is a loyal friend," Sam replied. "Your brother seems to be attracted to Georgia."

"I'm very surprised at that attraction," Honey admitted.

"Do you object to their relationship?"

"Not at all. Georgia is a great person. She's not like other women Preston has dated, but I think she's good for him." Honey couldn't get over the fact that Preston was, by every measure, quite conventional. It was fairly shocking to see he was attracted to a woman who thought combat boots were a fashion must.

"Sometimes there's no explaining animal attraction, and they say opposites attract."

Honey finally asked the question that had been on her mind. "Why didn't you mention that you were shot?"

Sam glanced her way. "I don't know, it just never came up. It wasn't the first time."

His matter-of-fact statement stunned her. She wondered what it would be like to be married to a man whose profession was so dangerous. Would she worry every time he left home that he might not return? "How many times?"

"Twice." Sam didn't want to talk about it now. "Do you think Bunny dated K.C. Cleary?"

"I know what you're thinking. I saw the way Mom and Bunny looked at each other when you asked your questions. Mom will tell me what's going on when Bunny's not around."

Sam laughed. "I love the female mind."

Honey knew something was up by the way her mother kept looking at Bunny. "Sam, I want you to know K.C. really was a good man. The K.C. I knew wouldn't date a married woman."

Sam could hear the affection she felt for K.C., and he wondered if she was capable of being objective now that he was deceased. "How can you be certain?"

"I had known him a long time. He always dated a lot of different women, but he never dated a married woman."

Sam hesitated, but he knew he was going to eventually ask her questions, so he might as well do it now. "Were you one of the women he dated?"

"K.C. and I started dating for a few months before I left for California. We hadn't really dated before—as a couple."

"Why did you start dating?"

Honey thought about his question. "He just asked me to dinner one night. We kept it light and continued to date other people. When I received the offer in California, we remained friends."

"Would you have stayed in Kentucky had he asked?"

"No. As I said, we kept our relationship light. I understood K.C., and I didn't think he would ever be ready to settle down."

Sam was relieved that her relationship with K.C. hadn't been serious. Everyone had praised K.C. for his intellect, but in Sam's opinion, a smart man would have figured out Honey was one great catch. He would never have let her leave without him. "Do you think he thought you two might pick up where you left off?"

"I know he was interested in dating again."

Sam waited to see if she would say if she was interested in dating K.C. again, but she didn't offer that information.

"From what you said earlier, I have a feeling you must think K.C. was dating Eugenie Grayson."

"I think she knew him better than she admitted tonight," Sam replied.

"Those two women in the gift shop said K.C. was dating that blonde who works in Cleary's office, and she was angry with him for dating other women."

"Gloria? She was very upset to hear of his death. She told me K.C. wasn't dating other women. She said they were in a serious relationship."

So he was on a first-name basis with Gloria. The women in the gift shop said she was really pretty. "What do you think about her?"

Sam glanced her way, wondering if he heard a hint of jealousy. "What do you mean?"

"I know K.C. was not in a serious relationship with her. Is she the type of woman who would kill him if she found out he was dating other women and not serious about her?"

"I've often been surprised by people who commit murder, but I don't think she was involved in any way. I'm not sure she was aware he was dating other women, or at least one other woman."

"I'll ask around to see what I can find out." Honey thought someone in the small town would tell her who K.C. was dating.

"Honey, asking questions could be dangerous when murder is involved. Leave the investigation to me."

Instead of telling him what he wanted to hear, Honey asked, "Do you know when the medical examiner will release his body?"

"Tomorrow morning." Sam pulled into Woodrow's estate and punched in the code on the gate. Reaching Honey's cottage, he turned off the ignition, unbuckled his seat belt and turned to face her. "His parents said the funeral would be Tuesday."

Honey nodded. She looked out the window as she thought about K.C. "This has to be hard on his mother. She was very close to K.C."

Sam watched her for a moment without commenting.

Honey removed her seatbelt and turned to him. "K.C's parents divorced when he was twelve. He was very close to his father, but after the divorce, K.C. rarely saw him. That's when he stopped believing in the family unit. I always thought that was the reason he never wanted to settle down."

Sam nodded. "That's a tough age for a kid to go through something like that. I see so many kids messed up after a divorce."

Later that night Honey was about to jump into bed when her phone rang. Seeing it was Georgia, she quickly answered.

"Did Detective Gorgeous fill you in on his investigation?" Georgia asked.

"He basically said he had a few leads, but he didn't reveal anything important."

"I heard some people at the party talking about K.C. tonight. I got the feeling everyone thought he was dating one of the women at the party. No one mentioned names, but the people in their little cliques knew who they were talking about."

"Yeah. Bunny wasn't anxious to talk about K.C. tonight. Of course, her husband was standing right there, so that may have been the reason."

"She had no problem staring a hole through Detective Gorgeous all night with her husband standing right beside her."

"I think she likes Sam."

Georgia snorted. "Ya think? I don't think her husband approved of her drinking, or her flirting."

"I think she must have started drinking before the party. She seemed pretty intoxicated." Before they left the party, Honey saw her mother steer Bunny toward the master bedroom, followed by a waitress carrying a carafe of coffee.

"I wonder why she spent so much time flirting with Detective Gorgeous. Her husband is a good-looking guy."

In Honey's opinion, Troy was attractive, but he couldn't hold a candle to Detective Gorgeous. "I don't know. Maybe she just likes the attention."

"Why don't we go over to that gift shop again and see if we can get the women to talk to us about what they've heard?"

Before Honey responded, she thought about Sam telling her to leave the detective work to him. She knew he was looking out for her welfare, yet she was confident she could find out things he couldn't. Locals knew her and her family, and that went a long way in a small town when asking questions. "Let's give it a try. K.C. was my friend, and I want to know who murdered him."

CHAPTER ELEVEN

"I SAW YOU TWO ON THE news. You found K.C.'s body in the park," the woman at the gift shop said.

"Yes, we did." Honey recognized the clerk as one of the two women who had been working the day they had visited. Honey hoped the woman was as chatty today. Discreetly glancing at her name tag, Honey said, "Dottie, I'm sure hearing of K.C.'s death must be upsetting since you knew him."

Dottie leaned over the counter and lowered her voice, even though they were the only people in the shop. "It's the saddest thing I've ever heard. But K.C. loved to chase women. I bet one of the women he jilted did him in."

"Do you really think a woman would kill him over being dumped?" Georgia asked.

"I think it's possible. Did you hear the rumor that he was dating a married women? I guess if that's true, then maybe the husband got wind K.C. was dating his wife and offed him," Dottie theorized.

"Did anyone ever mention a particular woman?" Honey asked.

Dottie shook her head. "Not by name. But I heard she was a very rich older woman."

Honey glanced at Georgia. "I wish we could find out the identity of that woman."

"To tell you the truth, I wouldn't put it past Gloria to kill him. She was mad enough to kill him when she found out he was dating other women at the same time he was dating her," Dottie told them.

Honey didn't let on she knew who Gloria was. "Gloria?"

Dottie inclined her head toward the distillery. "She works in the office. Bleached blonde hair, big boobs—and she didn't have them two years ago, if you know what I mean. She's not the brightest bulb in the socket. She was telling everyone K.C. was serious about her and that he was going to propose. When one of the other girls in the office told her that K.C. was dating other women, she threw a hissy fit right in the distillery."

"Had they dated a long time?" Georgia asked.

"I think about three months off and on," Dottie replied.

"If a woman thought she was in a serious relationship, she might get pretty angry to find out her man was seeing another woman," Georgia said, encouraging Dottie to keep talking.

"Yeah, but every woman in this town knew K.C. wasn't a marrying kind of man. Gloria had to know, but she was interested in landing a rich husband. She's thrown herself at every man in the office, or at least every man with a big enough bank account. I really don't know what K.C. saw in her." Dottie drew her mouth in a frown. "She's looks cheap and acts cheaper."

Honey thought Dottie's expression said it all—she did not like Gloria one little bit. But Sam seemed to like her, Honey reminded herself. He didn't think Gloria had anything to do with K.C.'s murder. "Did you like K.C.?"

"I didn't know him well, but he was always polite and professional to me. In my opinion, he was too good for the likes of Gloria."

"Gloria must really be something special. I'd like to see what she looks like," Georgia said.

Honey was curious to see what she looked like too.

"She's not as special as she thinks. My mom called women like her floozies." Dottie glanced at her watch. "If you want to see her, just wait here a few minutes." She pointed to the window. "She'll be passing that window on her way to lunch. She always leaves the building for lunch about this time." Dottie walked around the counter and headed to the window. "I think she probably meets men during her lunch hour."

A few minutes later, Dottie saw Gloria walking from the main building. "There she is."

Honey and Georgia joined Dottie at the window to watch Gloria walk down the sidewalk toward the gift shop. Honey's first thought was Gloria's attire was inappropriate for the office. Her blouse was so revealing it left little to the imagination, and her skirt was so tight Honey wondered how she could sit. Despite her outrageous wardrobe choices, Honey thought Gloria was an attractive woman.

"Would you just look at that low-cut blouse! You can even see her push-up bra. She really likes to show off those store-bought boobs." Dottie pursed her lips in disapproval.

"She got her money's worth," Georgia retorted, trying to stifle a laugh.

"I'm amazed she doesn't throw her back out the way she swings those hips," Dottie muttered.

Gloria stopped directly in front of the window where they were standing on the opposite side. Looking at her reflection, Gloria fluffed her hair, smoothed her skintight skirt and pulled her blouse lower.

Honey was so focused on Gloria that she didn't notice the car pulling up to the curb. When Gloria turned from the window and gave an enthusiastic wave to the person in the car, the three women shifted their attention to the car. Honey thought the car look similar to Sam's. When the door opened and Sam jumped out, Honey took a step back from the window.

"That's Detect—" Georgia stopped when she heard Honey softly say, "I know."

"Who is he?" Dottie asked, craning her neck to see the man. "Oh, I know him. He's that handsome detective who was in here asking questions."

Sam removed his sunglasses, and even through the window the impact of his megawatt smile and those blue eyes hit Honey full bore. Honey's gaze bounced back to Gloria to gauge her reaction to Sam. It didn't surprise her to see a wide smile plastered on Gloria's face. When Sam approached her, Gloria stood on her tiptoes and bushed her lips over his cheek. This certainly wasn't a chance meeting.

The women watched in stunned silence as Sam opened the passenger-side door and Gloria slid inside his car.

"Wonder what he's doing with her?" Dottie asked.

Honey thought the answer was fairly obvious. Sam was getting to know Gloria better. But was it for business or pleasure?

Honey started the Jeep and clicked the air on full speed. Her thoughts were moving at the speed of light. When Sam had walked her to her door Saturday night, instead of kissing her like he did after their dinner date, he gave her a peck on the cheek and thanked her for a lovely evening. She hadn't heard from him since then.

Georgia couldn't handle Honey's silence. "I bet he's taking her to lunch. You know this town. Where would they go? We should follow them."

Honey turned to Georgia and shrugged. "Why?"

"I know you like him. Don't you want to know if there's something going on between them?"

"Sam and I have been on two dates. It's not serious. It's really none of my business." Honey thought about the way Sam had smiled at Gloria. He seemed to be laying on the charm, just as he had done with her.

"I bet he thinks you're dating Chance since he saw you two having dinner together."

"He knows Chance is working on the patio and the café. There's no way he thinks we're dating," Honey countered.

"That doesn't mean he doesn't think you're interested in Chance." No matter how cool Honey was acting, Georgia knew it upset her to see Sam with Gloria. "Since Elvis is with Woodrow, why don't we go to lunch?"

Honey reluctantly agreed and drove to the nearest restaurant. As they walked inside, Georgia brought up their conversation with Dottie. "Do you think Dottie might be on to something?"

Honey was thankful the conversation was no longer about Sam. "What do you mean?"

"I know you don't believe it, but what if K.C. was dating a married woman? If the woman's husband found out, he could have followed them and killed K.C. in a moment of passion."

"I would think in a moment of passion, the husband would be more likely to kill his wife. Anyway, according to Dottie, there could be a few suspects—Gloria being one of them."

They followed the hostess to their table, and as soon as they started to sit down, Georgia elbowed Honey. When Honey glanced her way, she saw Georgia was staring at a nearby table. Sam was sitting in a booth facing them, but he hadn't seen them yet. He was leaning forward, totally engrossed in whatever Gloria was saying. Honey thought about the night they'd dined together. Sam was very observant of his surroundings, and she had no doubt he would notice them eventually.

"Maybe we should leave," Honey whispered.

"Not on your life. Be cool." Georgia slid into the booth first, forcing Honey to sit facing Sam.

Quickly taking a seat, Honey picked up the menu and made an effort to concentrate on what she was going to order. As much as she tried not to look Sam's way, she found herself glancing at him over the top of her menu. Food was on the table in front of him, but he wasn't eating. His full attention was on the woman across from him. The way Gloria was leaning over, Honey imagined Sam was enjoying the view.

"What are they doing?" Georgia asked as she pretended interest in her own menu.

"Gloria is still talking, and Sam is thoroughly enamored. He's probably thinking about dessert. She certainly doesn't look like the type of woman K.C. would have dated." Honey lowered her menu and when she looked at Sam again, he glanced her way. He leaned back in the booth and stared at her.

"He just saw me." Honey placed her menu on the table and focused on Georgia.

Georgia smiled. "Good. Did he looked surprised?"

"Not really. He'll probably think we followed him. I wish we had left."

Georgia shook her head at Honey. "Not on your life. As a matter of fact, tonight I want you to cook at home and invite Chance to have dinner with you. I have a feeling Detective Gorgeous will stop by. If he does, it will serve him right to see you entertaining Chance."

"You make it sound like I should use Chance to make Sam jealous."

Georgia shrugged. "And your problem with that would be?"

Honey didn't respond because the waitress placed a basket full of warm cornbread muffins on the table.

Snatching a muffin from the basket, Georgia slathered on some butter. "I think this is a sign."

Honey rolled her eyes. "You think everything is a sign."

"How many places could you have chosen to go to lunch?" She didn't give Honey time to respond. "Detective Gorgeous needs a reminder that you have more than one fish in the sea. As a matter of fact, I think you should invite Cullen over one night."

"I can't date someone I work with." Honey's gaze slid Sam's way again. "Maybe Sam's just not interested."

"Oh, he's interested. I've seen the way he looks at you. Of course, this could be a very innocent meeting. He could be questioning Gloria about K.C.'s death."

"I would think his questioning would be done at the police station," Honey replied dryly.

"Only if you're a suspect. He's probably pumping her for information, and it would have taken longer to take her to the station." Georgia was trying to make Honey feel better about the situation even though she thought Sam made a huge mistake taking Gloria to lunch.

The waitress reappeared and they placed their order. Honey surreptitiously glanced Sam's way several more times, but not once did she catch him looking her way.

After the waitress delivered their meal, Honey changed the subject. "How are things going with Preston?"

"Great. He's my date to the dinner train party. You don't mind, do you?"

"Of course not. I think that's perfect." Glancing over Georgia's head, Honey saw Sam stand. "I think Sam is leaving with her."

"That was a quick lunch. They have to pass this way, so don't acknowledge him," Georgia whispered.

Honey kept her eyes on her salad as Sam and Gloria approached. Thankfully, Georgia asked her a question and she managed to avoid looking at the couple as they reached their table.

Gloria passed by their table, but Sam stopped and said, "Hello."

"Hi," Honey and Georgia replied in unison.

"What are you two doing here?" Sam asked.

Honey avoided looking directly at him. "We happened to be in the area and decided to stop for lunch."

"What are you doing here?" Georgia asked bluntly.

"I was interviewing one of K.C. Cleary's friends," Sam replied.

"Do you always interview suspects over lunch?" Georgia asked sweetly.

Sam chuckled. "I didn't say she was a suspect." Sam's eyes slid to Honey and added, "She says K.C. was going to propose marriage."

"And you believe her?" Honey didn't attempt to keep the sarcasm from her voice. "She's the only one saying that."

Sam didn't have to be a detective to pick up on Honey's chilly reception. He wondered if seeing one of the women K.C. dated upset her. "Do you have a reason to believe she—" Sam was interrupted when Gloria latched onto his arm.

"I turned around and you weren't behind me, honey," Gloria cooed as she wrapped her hand around Sam's bicep. She turned her gaze on Honey and Georgia, and her eyes widened in recognition. "I saw you two on the news. You found poor K.C." Still clinging to Sam's arm, she snuggled closer to him. "Is that how you know them, honey?" Without waiting for a reply, she informed Honey and Georgia about her relationship with K.C. "K.C. and I were about to be engaged. His death came as quite a shock. I can't imagine why anyone would want to kill him."

When there was a lull in Gloria's one-sided conversation, Sam was finally able to introduce them. He didn't know what he expected, but Honey and Georgia's reception was not particularly friendly.

"It must have been terrible finding K.C.'s body. I don't think I could have handled finding him like that. I'm so glad we have a detective as smart as Sam on the case. I know he will find the person responsible," Gloria gushed.

"I'm certain the detective has been *very* helpful." Knowing Gloria was lying about her relationship with K.C., Honey said, "I spoke to K.C. not long ago and he didn't mention you."

Gloria lifted her chin and shrugged. "I guess he didn't know you well enough to discuss our relationship."

"Quite the contrary. K.C. and I had been friends since we were children. He told me everything," Honey retorted.

Sam thought Honey's voice was no longer cool—it was freezing. While he was tempted to hear what the women had to say to each other, he was more worried that a catfight might break out in the middle of the restaurant. He thought the wiser course was to put some distance between the two women. Wrenching his arm from Gloria's grasp, he pulled his car key from his pocket. "I need to drive you back to work."

Gloria smiled up at Sam. "It was so nice of you to take me to lunch. I haven't been out since K.C.'s death."

Honey thought Gloria looked at Sam much the same way Elvis looked at him—with adoring eyes.

"You must really be grieving," Georgia muttered.

"I am. That's why I appreciate Sam so much. He's been so kind to me," Gloria cooed in response.

Sam saw Honey arch her brow at Georgia, and being a good detective, he realized Gloria was digging him a very deep hole. "I'll see you two later." He quickly escorted Gloria from the restaurant.

Georgia watched them walk out the door. "I don't know how you remained civil to that woman."

"I wanted to snatch her bald. She's lying about her relationship with K.C." Honey didn't know if she was angry over what Gloria said about K.C., or the way she was hanging on to Sam.

"Dottie certainly has her pegged. I think the word *floozy* describes her and her store-bought boobs perfectly." Georgia stuffed another muffin in her mouth.

Despite her frustration over the encounter with Gloria, Honey couldn't stop laughing.

CHAPTER TWELVE

U NABLE TO GET SAM OFF of her mind, Honey was in an irritable mood when she arrived home after work. She took Elvis out for a walk along her trail, hoping time to think things through might clear her mind. They walked a mile before they turned back to the cottage. Honey lingered on the patio where Chance was wrapping up his work for the day. "It's looking beautiful out here."

Chance smiled at her compliment. "Thanks. I'll be done in a couple of days."

"How have you done so much work in such a short amount of time?"

"My men help me during the day. They have families, so they leave at a reasonable hour. I don't mind putting in longer hours," Chance replied.

Honey started to ask him if he would like a steak, but she hesitated when she remembered what Georgia said about Sam thinking she was interested in Chance. Why should she care what Sam thought? There was no reason she shouldn't ask Chance if he would like a steak, since she planned to cook one for herself. "Would you like a steak? I was planning to grill tonight."

"That sounds great. I'm starving. Can I help with anything?"

Honey pointed to the grill on the patio. "If you don't mind, you can fire up the grill. It's a nice night to cook outside."

"I'll get things cleaned up out here and get the grill going." After Chance stored his tools, he started the grill before he headed inside to wash his hands. "I can grill the steaks if you have other things to do."

Honey opened the refrigerator and pulled out the steaks. "Here you go. I'll get the salad ready." She followed him to the patio and lit the candles on the tables. While Chance manned the grill, Honey tossed the salad with the bourbon dressing she'd made. She didn't have time to make a dessert, but she had everything she needed to make banana splits after dinner. She added a bottle of wine along with the dinnerware on her tray and carried it to the patio.

After dinner, Chance carried the tray filled with empty plates to the kitchen. Honey handed him a knife and two bananas. "You can split the bananas."

Chance flipped the knife in his hand like a professional chef. "I think I can do that much."

Honey placed the bananas in vintage banana-split dishes, added the ice cream, toppings, and crowned the concoction with whipped cream and maraschino cherries. Once she pulled some treats from the pantry for Elvis, they walked back to the patio to enjoy their dessert.

Chance scooped up a big bite. "I haven't had one of these in years. I feel like a kid."

"I remember when I was a child, Gramps would take me to get ice cream every Sunday."

Chance was reminiscing about visiting the same ice cream shop when Elvis jumped up and ran to the side of the cottage. Honey yelled for him, but when he didn't return she sat her banana split on the table. "I better go get him, or he may end up five miles away."

"I'll go." Before Chance stood, Elvis walked around the corner of the house with Sam beside him.

Seeing Chance was there wasn't a surprise to Sam since his Hummer was in the driveway. But what he didn't expect was the romantic scene on the patio. Honey and Chance were sitting side by side, with candles burning on every table. He also noticed the bottle of wine along with two empty glasses sitting on the table. "Sorry to intrude, but I did knock on the front door. I guess Elvis heard me."

At the mention of his name, Elvis nosed Sam's hand. Sam rubbed his ears as they walked.

That's okay. Won't you sit down?" Honey asked. "Would you like a banana split?"

"No, thanks."

Chance held a spoonful of ice cream in the air, and gave Sam a smug smile. "You really should have one, it's delicious. Honey and I were just saying how young we feel."

Sam ignored him. He wanted to see Honey tonight to explain the reason he'd been with Gloria this afternoon. After the way Gloria was clinging to him, he was worried Honey got the wrong impression. But seeing her with Chance made him think he'd been concerned when there was no reason to be. Every time he turned around, Chance was with her. He didn't like it. He'd tried not to come on too strong and scare her off, but maybe he'd played it wrong and gave Chance an opening. He needed a new tactic. "I stopped by to ask you some questions. Could I have a few minutes of your time?"

Honey had to hand it to Georgia. She'd said Sam would stop by tonight. Unfortunately he didn't come by for the reason Georgia thought. He only wanted to ask questions about K.C. "Of course." She glanced at Chance. "Would you like some coffee or espresso? I'll make some while I answer Sam's questions."

"Coffee would be nice," Chance replied.

Sam, with Elvis by his side, followed Honey inside. Honey walked to the counter and pushed some buttons on the coffeemaker. "Would you like coffee, or something else?"

"Coffee sounds good." With her back to him, Sam checked out what she was wearing. Her little white shorts and snug red T-shirt certainly complimented her figure. He thought about the first time he saw her. She was wearing red shorts and a white T-shirt. She looked so delectable he could hardly form a thought. He wondered how Chance ate dinner with his tongue hanging out.

"What did you want to ask?" Honey opened the refrigerator, pulled out a pitcher of cream and sat it on the counter beside a container of sugar.

"I don't take cream or sugar," Sam reminded her, and he'd noticed she drank her coffee black.

"Chance does."

Sam ground his teeth together. "Figures," he mumbled. *He looks like one of those guys who would like foo-foo drinks.* "You seem to be spending a lot of time with Chance."

Was Georgia right after all? Is he jealous? "We are doing a lot of work together. He's here every night, so it's only natural that we're together." Why was he questioning her about Chance when he was having lunch with Gloria?

"It looks like a real romantic setting out there with the candles." Sam didn't want to admit he was jealous, but he was.

Honey wasn't about to tell him they were citronella candles. "How was *your* lunch today?"

Sam frowned as he pulled away from the counter and crossed his arms over his chest. "Something interesting happened today. When I drove Gloria back to the distillery, I stopped in the gift shop."

Honey arched her brow. "And?"

"Dottie is a fount of information. Like Gloria, every thought in her head spills out."

Though she wasn't a detective, Honey knew what was coming. She turned toward the cupboard and pulled out three cups. "Thoughts aren't the only things spilling out of Gloria."

If Sam had been in a better mood, he would have laughed at her remark. He'd noticed Gloria's assets, but he didn't take the bait. He ignored Honey's comment, knowing there was no way he would win that exchange. Besides, Honey was every bit as well-endowed as Gloria—he'd noticed. She just didn't expose her figure in scanty clothing.

"You wouldn't happen to know anything about two women in the gift shop asking questions this morning, would you?" Before she replied, he held his hand in the air, level with the top of her head. "One woman was about this tall, blonde"—Sam looked her up and down—"petite, with a nice curvy figure." That last part was his observation, not Dottie's. "The other woman had blue hair." He brought his hand to his jaw and scratched his dark fourteen-hour stubble. "I know I'm just a bungling small-town detective, and I realize there are several blonde women in this town, but I can only remember seeing one person with blue hair."

Honey wasn't going to deny she was at the gift shop. Just because he'd complimented her figure didn't mean he wasn't a jerk for taking Gloria to lunch. "Your point?"

Leaning down, Sam looked her in the eye. "I thought I told you not to play detective."

Placing her hands on her hips, Honey remained defiant. "K.C. and I were friends. I want to know who killed him."

The muscle in Sam's jaw twitched. "Don't you think I want to know the same thing?"

"Some people might say things to me they wouldn't say to you," Honey countered.

Sam gave her a thoughtful look. "Maybe I should look at you and Georgia as suspects. Why were you at that gift shop on the very day that you happened on K.C.'s body?"

Honey returned his scowl. "I told you, we were checking out our competition."

"I find it odd that despite the fact the park was crowded that day, no one else happened on the body." Sam wasn't serious, but he was trying to make a point.

"We wouldn't have found him either if not for Elvis."

At the mention of his name, Elvis nudged his way between them. His eyes darted from Honey to Sam, who were ignoring him but were shooting daggers at each other. He nosed Sam's hand.

Sam tore his gaze from Honey and rubbed Elvis's ears. "Hey, buddy, I don't consider you a suspect."

"Are you insinuating I am?" Honey snapped.

"Since you ignored me when I told you and Georgia to leave the detective work to me, I think I should put you at the top of my list. I guess I could always arrest you for interfering in my investigation."

"I'm not interfering, I was trying to help." She filled three cups with the freshly brewed coffee and added cream and sugar to one. "Unless you have more questions, I really need to get back to my guest. Of course, you could take me to lunch and interrogate me." She picked up two cups and headed toward the patio door. As far as she was concerned, he could carry his own coffee. She was no longer in the mood to be a polite hostess.

Sam looked at the lone cup of coffee left on the counter. He debated his options. He could walk outside, drink his coffee with them and interrupt their little romantic evening. Or, he could walk out the front door and try to put Honey out of his mind. If he walked back out on the patio and Chance gave him another smirk, he might forget he was an officer of the law. He liked Chance—he just didn't like him with Honey. He looked down at Elvis, who had stayed by his side. "That's the second time I've seen them together. I've always heard there's no education in the second kick of a mule." He leaned over and stroked Elvis's back. "I'm not giving up, I'm just reassessing my tactics. See you later, buddy."

After Honey handed Chance his coffee, she turned back toward the open patio door. She waited, but Sam and Elvis didn't walk through the door. She walked back to the door and looked inside the kitchen, but Sam wasn't there. The full cup of coffee was on the counter. When she didn't see Elvis, she walked to the living room and saw him sitting by the front door. "What are you doing, Elvis?"

Elvis looked at her and whimpered. Honey walked around the corner to see if Sam was in the bathroom. The bathroom door was open and the light was off. She crossed the room, took hold of Elvis's collar, and opened the door to see if Sam's car was in the driveway. It wasn't.

"He didn't even say good-bye," she said to Elvis. "Come on, I'll get you a treat."

Frustrated that she couldn't sleep, Honey decided to get out of bed and go to the office early. She hoped work would take her mind off of Sam. After dressing and giving Elvis some dog food that he didn't eat, they climbed into the Jeep. Honey stopped at Randy's drive-thru to buy a breakfast sandwich and a cup of coffee for herself, along with a hamburger for Elvis. Being the third car in line, she turned to say something to Elvis when two cars in an adjoining parking lot caught her attention. One of the cars looked familiar. It was a dark midsized coupe, rather nondescript, but then she read the license plate—MASTER. It was Alan Snyder's car. She'd noticed that particular license plate in the parking lot at the distillery, and when she'd asked Woodrow who owned the car, he told her it was Alan's. She didn't see anyone sitting in Alan's car, but there were two people sitting in the silver Jaguar parked next to his. The car in front of her moved ahead in the drive-thru line, and she forgot about the Jaguar as she searched for her wallet.

Later that morning, Georgia stopped in Honey's office with a fresh cup of coffee and a treat for Elvis.

Honey was grateful for the interruption, particularly since she was bearing hot coffee. "Thank you. I was just going to get another cup."

Georgia sat in a chair and gave Elvis his treat. Elvis nabbed the peanut-butter-flavored offering between his teeth, but instead of eating it, he placed it next to his bowl that still held the hamburger Honey had bought him that morning. Georgia looked at Honey and frowned. "Are you two sick? Elvis isn't eating and you look terrible."

Honey leaned back in her chair and took a sip of her coffee. "I didn't get much sleep last night and Elvis is upset. I even bought him a burger from his favorite drive-thru this morning, but it didn't help."

"It's still in his bowl. Why is he upset?"

Honey told Georgia about Sam's visit last night while she was having dinner with Chance.

Georgia smiled wide. "I told you he would come by. It serves him right to think you are interested in Chance."

"He came by because Dottie told him about our visit and he was angry with me. He left without saying good-bye and Elvis is still depressed."

"Sam used Dottie as an excuse to come by. What did he say when he saw you with Chance?"

Honey thought about Sam's reaction last night. "He did say something about the candles and the *romantic scene*."

"See, it's a sign."

Honey sighed loudly as she rolled her eyes at Georgia. "Oh no, not another sign."

"Yeah, the universe is telling Sam that he needs to step up his game if he's going to hold your interest."

Honey shook her head. "I'm not certain Sam cares about keeping my interest."

Georgia stood. "Let's go."

"Go where?" Honey asked.

"You and Elvis need some fresh air. It's almost lunchtime and we'll see if we can entice Elvis with another hamburger."

Honey looked down at her desk covered with papers. "I have so much I need to get done today. Our dinner is going to be here before we know it and we both need to buy a dress."

"We'll buy dresses tomorrow." Georgia pointed to Elvis. "You know he needs cheering up."

Honey stood and looked at Elvis, who was lying with his head resting on his paws. His big brown eyes followed her every move. "You want another hamburger?"

Elvis groaned.

Pulling her handbag from a drawer, Honey walked around her desk. "I guess if you don't want a hamburger, Georgia and I will go alone."

The women were about to walk out the door when Elvis lifted his head. Honey looked back at him. "Are you sure you don't want a hamburger?"

Slowly, Elvis stood and walked to her at a snail's pace.

Honey laughed and pulled his ear. "You'll suffer through, right?"

They were almost to Honey's Jeep when she noticed Alan's car was parked next to hers. She was just about to tell Georgia about what she saw at the drive-thru that morning when Alan approached his car.

"Hi, Alan. You were certainly out early this morning," Honey said.

Alan stopped and looked at her. "What are you talking about?"

"I was going through Randy's Drive-In this morning and I saw you in the parking lot next door."

Alan unlocked his car and opened the door. "You must be mistaken, you didn't see me."

Honey was about to tell him there couldn't be two personalized license plates exactly alike, but she didn't have a chance. Alan jumped behind the wheel, started his car and quickly pulled away.

Honey watched him drive out of the parking lot. "It was your car, you jerk," she muttered.

"What was that about?" Georgia asked.

"Did you see his license plate?"

"I noticed it the other day when I was pulling out of the parking lot behind him. Why?"

"Well, that license plate was in a parking lot next to Randy's this morning at five o'clock. I didn't see Alan, but his car was parked beside a silver Jaguar with two people inside. There were only two cars in the parking lot."

"Maybe he had an early morning date that he didn't want anyone to know about."

Honey couldn't fathom anyone dating Alan. She arched her brow at Georgia. "Alan?"

Georgia laughed. "Yeah, I guess that is pretty unlikely."

CHAPTER THIRTEEN

K.C. CLEARY'S FUNERAL DREW SUCH A huge crowd that the church doors were opened, allowing the service to be heard outside. Honey thought the family would find some comfort to see how many people considered K.C. a friend. Everyone knew K.C. was the kind of person you could call at any time and he would be there if you needed help. He was the friend everyone turned to for advice. Not only was he intelligent, he had a great sense of humor and was fun to be around. His friends would miss him. As much as Honey tried to maintain her composure, she couldn't stop her tears from the moment she sat down.

Woodrow, Honey's parents, and her brother slid into the pew beside her. Woodrow put his arm around her shoulders. "Are you okay?"

Honey nodded. "It's hard to believe he's gone."

After the solemn service, Honey attended the final good-bye at the gravesite. As she listened to the pastor's parting words, she searched the faces of the people surrounding the gravesite. According to Georgia, people who committed murders often attended the funerals of their victims. Honey didn't know if that was true, but Georgia watched all of the true crime shows and she considered herself an expert on the subject. Was the murderer there among them, pretending to be grieving? Honey thought it took a whole different kind of crazy for a murderer to attend the funeral of the person they'd killed.

Her gaze landed on Bunny Spencer and Eugenie Grayson side by side on the opposite side of the coffin. Generally only family and close friends attended the closing service at the cemetery. Both women had told Sam they didn't know K.C. well. As she watched the women she heard the pastor say, "Sometimes there's no understanding why someone is taken too soon, but we can all rejoice that we will be together again one day." She couldn't disagree with his statement. She didn't understand why anyone would kill K.C. Her eyes traveled from the women to the men in attendance. She didn't see Troy Spencer or Jefferson Grayson. Looking past the group, she saw the lone man standing some distance away from the other mourners. The aviator sunglasses gave him away. Sam. Was he here to gauge the reaction of those in attendance? Did he expect the murderer to attend K.C.'s funeral? Even at a distance she could sense the intensity of his stare.

Walking back to her Jeep, Honey made a detour when she saw an old friend, Rick Jarboe, who was also a good friend of K.C.'s. If anyone in town knew what was going on with K.C., it was Rick. They had been best friends for many years, and she recalled that Chance said K.C's car had been in Jarboe's Body Shop for repair.

Rick was getting into his car when Honey approached. "Hi, Rick."

Rick turned and smiled at her. "Honey, how are you doing?"

Honey shrugged. "Ask me tomorrow."

"Yeah. It's a sad day."

"Yes, it is." Honey thought she was all cried out, but she found herself tearing up again.

"I know K.C. was really looking forward to you coming home. You know he was crazy about you, Honey."

Honey felt a huge lump in her throat. When she could finally speak, she said, "Rick, I want to ask you something."

Rick braced his arm on top of his car and waited for her question. "What is it?"

"Chance McComb mentioned he saw K.C.'s car in your shop. I spoke to K.C. just before I left California and he didn't tell me he'd had a wreck."

"That new detective asked me the same thing when he came by the shop."

"He was at your shop?" Honey didn't know why she was so surprised, since Hap mentioned several times that Sam was a great detective.

"Yep." Rick pointed to the row of cars on the road parked near the gravesite. "There he is, standing by that black sedan. I can't remember his name, but I got the feeling he's a tough one. I wouldn't want to be on his bad side."

Honey turned to see Sam leaning against his car with his arms crossed over his chest. He was staring directly at them. "Sam Gentry is his name."

"Well, he was asking if K.C. wrecked his Mercedes. I guess Chance told the cops what he saw."

"Chance said the damage was bad."

"The driver's-side door was crushed nearly to the center console. But K.C. wasn't in the car at the time, if that's what you're thinking," Rick told her.

Honey frowned. "Was someone else driving his car?"

"No one was driving. According to K.C., it was parked at the time. I asked him what happened and he said someone was mad at him." Rick shook his head and smiled. "He was actually laughing about it. He told me he was really angry when it happened, but in hindsight he thought it was pretty funny. He also said something I thought was odd at the time."

"What was that?"

"He said, '*It was well worth getting rid of the problem.*'"

"You mean someone intentionally did that to his car?"

Rick shrugged. "That's what he said."

Honey thought someone had to be very angry to do something like that. "Did he say who it was?"

"He wouldn't tell me. You know K.C. wouldn't say anything bad about anyone. All I know for sure was the color of the car who hit him—it was yellow. I kept a part of the car door that I replaced. It's streaked with paint from the other car."

"Would you show it to me?"

Rick didn't ask why she wanted to see a wrecked car door. He simply told her to follow him to his shop.

They arrived at Rick's shop ten minutes later. Once Honey walked inside his garage, Rick picked up a piece of crumpled black metal from a table and held it out to her. "I cut off a small piece and gave it to the detective."

Honey saw light yellow paint fused with black on the slice of metal. She had a feeling Rick knew the person who was driving the other car. Rick loved cars, and he always knew what everyone in town drove. There couldn't be that many locals who owned yellow cars. "You know who owns the car that did this, don't you?"

"I can make an educated guess." He placed the metal back on the table. "I kept this in case K.C. wanted to file a claim against her. If someone intentionally did that to my car, they'd for darn sure pay for it."

"Her?"

Rick realized his blunder and grinned. "Yeah."

"Wouldn't there be black paint on the yellow car?"

Rick nodded. "You can bet that car was repaired the next day."

"So you didn't do the repairs on that car?"

"Nope. If I'm right about the owner of this particular car, they wouldn't darken the door of a small-town body shop."

"You must think it was a local woman who everyone would know," Honey guessed.

Rick winked at her. "You were always a smart one. Let's just say it was a woman who was very upset over something. Angry enough that she wasn't concerned about damaging an eighty-five-thousand-dollar car."

"Angry enough to want K.C. dead?"

"Honey, you should be careful. If my hunch is right, this is not someone you'd want for an enemy. This person wouldn't have murdered K.C., but they would have paid to have it done if they were involved at all. Jealousy can make people do some stupid things."

"And you didn't tell the detective who you thought may have been involved?"

"I have no proof, but I gave him names of people who drive yellow cars."

"Can you give me those names?"

Rick looked at her a long moment before answering. "I could, but I won't. I don't think it's a good idea for you to go snooping around. It could be dangerous. I don't have to remind you that K.C. is dead. It may or may not be related, but there's no sense in taking foolish chances."

"Don't you want to know who did this to K.C.?"

"You know I do. But we're not just talking about damage to K.C.'s car—we're talking murder. You need to leave this to that detective to find the person responsible."

Honey released a deep breath. "I'm sorry, I shouldn't have said that. I know you were close friends."

Rick put his arm around her shoulders. "That's okay. I understand how you feel, but we need to leave this to the professionals. That detective seems like a sharp one, and I'm sure he can defend himself if necessary."

"Rick, if K.C.'s car was damaged so badly, how did he get it to your shop?"

"I drove my tow truck out to get it."

"To his home?"

"No. He was out on Old Honeysuckle Road, at that old farm. You remember the old Tucker place where all of us would go swimming when we were kids?"

"Of course, I remember. They had a fabulous pool. Is the Tucker farm still vacant?"

"Yeah, I think it has been empty for years."

"Why was K.C. out there?"

"He said he had a meeting out there that morning. We both know K.C. would never do anything illegal, and he wasn't a man who would kiss and tell. I just assumed he'd met a woman out there for some reason."

"You're right. K.C. wouldn't do anything illegal."

"Honey, K.C. did say one thing you might want to know. He told me when he saw the old Tucker place again it brought back a lot of good memories. He told me you always loved that farm, and he was going to approach the owner about buying it. I think he was making plans for the future."

As Honey was pulling out of Rick's garage, she spotted a black car on the other side of the street. Sam. *Of all the nerve!* He had followed her. She expected him to pull out behind her, possibly turn his lights on and pull her over. Every few seconds she checked her rearview mirror until she was well over a mile away, but no one was behind her.

On her way home, Honey replayed her conversation with Rick. He said a woman was responsible for damaging K.C.'s car. But murder?

K.C. was stabbed in the chest. She was confident a woman couldn't overpower a man K.C.'s size, unless he was incapacitated in some way. She knew an autopsy had been performed on K.C. Now all she needed to do was find out what the coroner's report said.

Lorraine met Honey at the front door of the cottage. "I was beginning to wonder if you were ever going to make it home. I tried calling you but you didn't answer."

Honey hugged Elvis before she tossed her handbag and keys on the counter. "Sorry, Mom. I turned off my phone before the funeral and forgot to turn it back on. You didn't mention you'd be stopping by."

"Come and sit down," Lorraine instructed. "I brought Chinese food with me. I thought you might not feel like cooking." Once in the kitchen, Lorraine punched the timer on the microwave. "I just need to warm it up." She poured two glasses of iced tea and handed one to Honey.

Honey took a seat at the counter. "Thanks for bringing dinner. I'm glad you came because I have something I wanted to ask you."

"I think I know what it is." Lorraine pulled the food from the microwave and placed it on the counter in front of Honey. She filled both of their plates with rice, kung pao chicken, and several pieces of crab rangoon.

"Okay, then spill." Honey picked up her chopsticks and plucked a piece of chicken from her plate.

"At the party I couldn't say anything in front of Troy, but I think Sam should know that Bunny was always flirting with K.C."

Honey couldn't say she was surprised by that news. "Was it as obvious as the way she was flirting with Sam?"

"Outrageously so, I'm afraid. She was always hanging on to him at parties. And you know K.C. was too much of a gentleman to be rude. He'd be polite to Bunny, but it was clear he wasn't interested. If Sam is under the impression that K.C. was dating Bunny, then he's wrong."

Honey thought if Bunny flirted with K.C. more than she did Sam, then her husband would have to be blind not to notice. "Was this before she married Troy?"

"Before and after. She'd flirt with K.C. in front of Troy. I think she tries to make Troy jealous."

Honey nibbled on a piece of crab rangoon. "Why would she want to make her husband jealous?"

"She said she didn't want Troy to take her for granted. She told me she's worried he'll find someone younger. In her own messed-up reasoning, she thinks it keeps him on his toes if he thinks other men are interested in her."

It was impossible for Honey to understand why a woman would marry someone they didn't trust. "Mom, why are you friends with that woman?"

"She wasn't always like she is today. I've known her since we were children, she was a wonderful person, but she changed after her first divorce. After twenty years of marriage, her husband left her for a younger woman. Bunny always wanted to have a child, but her husband didn't want children. When his younger girlfriend became pregnant, he was thrilled. He divorced Bunny and married her. Oh, Bunny received a bundle of money, but she was never the same. She started drinking and became a bitter woman. None of her subsequent marriages have lasted more than a year. I couldn't let go of an old friend because she is going through a difficult period. I wouldn't be much of a friend, would I?"

Honey couldn't fault her mother for being loyal to Bunny. She wasn't particularly fond of Bunny, but she felt sympathy for her. "I wonder what K.C. thought of her."

"He never said a word to me about her one way or the other. I think you should know K.C. changed when you told him you were coming home."

Honey cocked her head toward her mother. "How so?"

"I don't think K.C. had been happy since you moved to California. He dated a lot of different women, but not the same one for any length of time. Once he found out you were coming home he stopped dating. I'd still see him at parties, but he was always alone. His mother told me K.C. couldn't wait for you to move home. She thought he was in always in love with you."

"Mom, do you think K.C. dated a married woman?"

"I've heard the gossip about K.C. and a married woman, but I didn't believe that story. As I said, it wasn't Bunny. For one thing, Bunny can't keep a secret, particularly if she's drinking."

"Any other women come to mind?" Honey asked.

"Other than Bunny, I can't imagine another married woman I know who would be so foolish."

"Let's say you're wrong, and Bunny was dating K.C. If he tried to break it off, do you think she's capable of murder?"

Lorraine stirred the food on her plate with her chopsticks for a few moments before she answered. "I would hate to think that Bunny could murder anyone."

"That's not a *no*."

"No," Lorraine said emphatically. I seriously can't imagine anyone I know committing murder. Don't you think it could simply be a matter of K.C. being in the wrong place at the wrong time and murdered by a stranger?"

"I think he knew his killer. Sam said K.C. was killed somewhere else and moved to the park. According to Georgia, who is a self-proclaimed expert on murder, a woman is most likely the perpetrator since K.C. was killed with a knife."

"Could a woman kill a man with a knife?" Lorraine asked.

"That's what I've struggled with. I don't think it's possible unless the man, particularly K. C., was asleep or otherwise in a weakened condition."

Lorraine's eyes widened. "You're right. K.C. was in fabulous shape. Maybe he was asleep, drugged, or possibly drunk?"

Honey nodded.

Lorraine shivered. "Honey, this is not a topic for dinner."

"I guess not. But I want to find the person who killed him."

They ate in silence for a few minutes, and then Lorraine swiveled in her chair to face Honey. "I can't remember even seeing K.C. tipsy, much less drunk. Can you?"

Honey had been to countless parties with K.C. over the years, and he rarely had more than one drink. "Never."

Honey sipped her iced tea as she thought about her conversation with Rick. "Mom, did anyone ever buy the Tucker farm on Old Honeysuckle Road?"

"I have no idea. Why on earth are you thinking about that place right now?"

Honey told her about her conversation with Rick Jarboe. "Rick picked him and his car up on Old Honeysuckle Road."

"I can't see why K.C. would meet someone out there."

"It's a very isolated place. I guess he didn't want anyone to see him. I know Sam thinks he was meeting a woman."

"Makes sense, particularly if he was having a rendezvous with a married woman."

"Mom, what color is Bunny's car?"

"Silver."

CHAPTER FOURTEEN

EARLY THE NEXT MORNING, HONEY and Georgia wrapped up the details for the dinner train party before driving to Louisville to shop. After two hours of searching for the perfect gowns, they found what they were looking for. By the time they returned to Bardstown it was midafternoon. Instead of driving home, Honey parked in front of a century-old two-story redbrick building.

Georgia read the quaint wooden sign suspended on chains above the entryway. "Why are we stopping at the coroner's office?"

"I went to high school with Mitch, the medical examiner. I want to ask him some questions about K.C."

Georgia unfastened her seat belt. "Don't we know how K.C. died? I mean, there was a knife in his chest."

Honey reached for her purse in the back seat. "We think we know how he died. I want to know if Mitch found something that hasn't been made public."

Georgia grabbed her camouflage bag. "Have you found out something you haven't told me?"

"You said the murder weapon indicates a woman killed him. If that's true, do you think a woman could stab K.C. in the chest without some defensive wounds?"

"Good point."

"Maybe he was drugged or asleep? I want to find out what Mitch knows."

Once inside, they told the receptionist they were there to see Mitch.

Within minutes, Mitch arrived in the lobby and greeted Honey warmly. Honey introduced Georgia, and Mitch invited them to his office where they could speak in private. He pointed to some chairs in front of his desk. "Please have a seat." He glanced from Honey to Georgia. "What brings you here to see me?"

Honey took a seat and got straight to the point. "I wanted to talk to you about K.C."

Mitch leaned forward, placed his arms on his desk and gave Honey a sympathetic look. "I heard you found him. I'm sorry you had to see him that way."

"It was terrible." Honey couldn't think about seeing K.C.'s body without becoming emotional, but she forced herself to take a deep breath and continue. "I can't understand why anyone would kill him."

"I feel the same way. K.C. was a fine person," Mitch agreed.

"Mitch, I don't know what you are allowed to tell me, but I was wondering if K.C. was drugged."

Mitch arched his brows, indicating his surprise at the question. "Why would you ask that?"

Honey glanced at Georgia. "We think a woman murdered him. But unless he was incapacitated in some way, we can't see how a woman could have overpowered him. K.C. was a large man and he was in great shape."

Mitch folded his hands together. "I wish I could tell you more than was disclosed publicly, but that new detective has asked me to keep some details private for the time being."

"Is it true that more women use a knife as a weapon than men?" Georgia asked.

Mitch looked at Georgia and nodded. "That's my understanding, but that doesn't necessarily mean a woman committed this crime."

"Rick Jarboe told me K.C. had some problems with a woman. Do you know who it was?" Honey asked.

Mitch shook his head. "I've only heard rumors."

"Did K.C. have defensive wounds?"

"Honey, losing a friend is difficult, and I know everyone has a lot of questions. I'm confident they will all be answered in due time."

"Mitch, is there anything you can tell me? Anything at all?" Honey implored.

Mitch glanced at his open door, then lowered his voice so his secretary wouldn't hear what he had to say. "Honey, I'm not supposed to say anything that has not been made public."

"You have our word that we will not mention our conversation to anyone," Honey assured him.

Mitch hesitated, and just when Honey thought he might not say more he whispered, "I will tell you that there were no defensive wounds on K.C.'s body."

Honey glanced at Georgia. "We promise not to mention this conversation to anyone."

Georgia bobbed her head up and down in agreement.

"Good. Now promise me that you two will leave the investigation to the police. K.C. was murdered and this is dangerous business. Our new detective seems to be a very thorough man."

Without agreeing to his request, Honey and Georgia thanked him and left his office. As soon as they were out the door, Georgia whispered, "I think we are on the right track."

"I agree."

"Where to now?"

"Back to the office. I want you to do me a favor." Honey told Georgia to find out if the county clerk's office could tell her how many yellow cars were registered in their county. "The lady that runs the office is Vivian Hartley. Tell her I said hello."

"Is there anyone in this town you don't know?" Georgia asked.

Honey smiled. "Just the people who arrived in the last couple of years."

Honey pulled up to the distillery's door to let Georgia out. "Would you get Elvis? I'll take him with me."

Georgia opened the door to the office, whistled for Elvis, and he came running. Once he was through the door, he leaped inside the Jeep.

Georgia laughed. "I guess he was ready to go." She leaned around Elvis, who had already planted himself in the passenger seat, to ask Honey where she was going.

"Old Honeysuckle Road. I want to see the farm where K.C.'s car was wrecked."

"Have you thought about what will happen if Detective Gorgeous finds out we're still snooping around?"

It wasn't her intention to upset Sam, but since he'd left the cottage without saying good-bye the other night, she hadn't heard from him. "I don't care if he finds out. We aren't doing anything illegal."

"Okay, but call me so I know you're safe. I'm not sure you should go out there alone."

Honey stroked Elvis's back. "I'm not alone. I have the best protector around."

It had been a long time since Honey had driven the scenic rural road leading to Tucker's farm. The lush green countryside hadn't changed, and the scent of honeysuckle lining the two-lane road filled the air for miles. She glanced at Elvis, who had his head hanging out the window, his jowls flapping in the wind. Elvis was in his happy place. "Do you smell the honeysuckle, Elvis?"

She'd driven for nearly thirty minutes and hadn't seen another car. *This is the perfect place to meet someone in secret.* "I think we are getting close, Elvis." The farm was several hundred acres, and she couldn't remember the exact location of the driveway. In the distance, she saw a car pulling out on the road. She squinted, trying to determine the color of the car. Yellow or cream? The sun was too bright and she was too far away to be certain. As she approached the area when the car had pulled out, she slowed down. Though the driveway was hidden by the dense brush, she saw a sliver of asphalt peeking through the greenery. If only she'd been a minute earlier she might have been able to see the driver of that car. The driveway was at least five hundred feet long, ending at the old antebellum-style mansion. She looked for a sign to see if the property was for sale, but if there was one, it had succumbed to the unkempt foliage.

At the end of the driveway, Honey turned off the engine. "Let's look around, Elvis." She reached in her purse, pulled out her phone, and shoved it in her pocket. As soon she grasped the door latch, Elvis was crawling over her to jump out first. "Hang on, you're squashing me."

Once the door was opened, Elvis leaped to the ground and started sniffing the driveway. Honey walked up the stairs to the columned porch and looked through the door's sidelight. In the massive circular foyer she saw a huge crystal chandelier suspended over a large round marble table. Beyond the wide arch of the foyer she could see furniture and large paintings lining the walls. Everything looked neat and orderly. She found it odd that a home everyone thought had been vacant for years had such expensive furnishings inside. She knocked on the door, but didn't really expect anyone to answer.

Elvis joined her on the porch and Honey scratched his long floppy ears. "Let's walk to the back, Elvis." When they reached the back of the house, she stopped to look through the back door glass, but Elvis continued on, sniffing his way to one of the large outbuildings.

Honey followed Elvis to the building that looked more like a large warehouse than the barn she remembered. With nose to the ground, Elvis walked the length of the metal sliding door. Honey thought about peeking inside the building, but the door was padlocked. She couldn't imagine why someone would build such a costly structure on property that was vacant. Pulling her phone out of her pocket, she checked for a signal. Unable to make a call, she walked halfway around the building before she found a spot where she had service. She called Georgia's number, but her call went to voice mail. After she left Georgia a message, she turned to look for Elvis.

Elvis was making his way toward her with his nose still to the ground, sniffing footprints in the dirt. She wondered if they were K.C.'s footprints. Elvis sniffed his way around the building, and then suddenly stopped to investigate something lying in the dirt.

"What did you find?" Honey walked over to him and picked up a piece of a broken bottle. While it wasn't intact, and had no identifying label, she could smell the familiar scent of bourbon on the glass.

At that moment, her phone rang and she nearly jumped out of her shoes. She pulled her phone out of her pocket and without a glance at the screen, she said, "I just left you a message."

"Really? What did you say?"

She hadn't expected to hear Sam's voice. "Oh, I thought you were Georgia."

"It's Sam."

"Hi."

"What are you doing?"

"Right now?" Honey asked.

"Yeah."

"I'm hanging out with Elvis at the moment."

"Really? Where are you?"

"I doubt you know the place. I used to come here when I was in high school," Honey replied.

"You might be surprised at all of the places I've been lately. I know the area pretty well."

Honey thought she should change the subject. "Did you have a reason for your call?"

"Do I need a reason to call?" Sam asked.

Elvis caught Honey's attention when he stopped sniffing, cocked his head in the air and focused on the tall grass. As if he heard or caught the scent of something interesting, he took off like a rocket, running through the grass. Losing sight of him, Honey raced after him, forgetting about Sam's question. "Hold on a minute, Elvis took off." Just as she reached the area where Elvis disappeared, he came trotting out of the brush with Sam by his side.

"Look who I found." Sam shoved his phone in his pocket.

Though it was a steamy day with the temperatures in the nineties and high humidity, Sam looked as handsome and cool as usual in his white shirt, blue silk tie, and his aviator sunglasses. But he was not smiling. Honey clicked off her phone.

"What are you two doing out here?" Sam asked.

"Just looking around," Honey replied. "What are you doing out here?"

Sam pointed to the piece of glass she was holding. "What do you have there?"

She'd forgotten all about the sliver of glass in her hand. She held it out to him. "Elvis found it. A piece of a broken bottle."

Sam smelled the shard. "A bottle of bourbon?"

"Smells like bourbon to me."

"Where did he find it?"

Honey pointed to the huge warehouse structure. "Right over there."

Sam started walking toward the building, and Elvis stayed by his side. "What are you looking for out here, Honey? Are you in the market for property?"

Honey tried to keep pace with his long strides. "You know why I'm here. K.C. had been out here and I wanted to know why. I haven't been here since I was in high school and I was curious about the place."

Sam stopped walking and turned to look at her. "Have your forgotten K.C. ended up dead?"

"How could I forget? I want to know why."

Removing his sunglasses, Sam squeezed the bridge of his nose. "Honey, I've asked you to stop running around town asking questions. I don't want to worry about something happening to you."

The dark circles under his eyes indicated he'd probably been working long hours without a lot of rest. "You don't need to worry about me. I can take care of myself."

"If you have questions, why don't you ask me?" Sam asked.

"Okay. Why was K.C. out here?"

"He was meeting someone," Sam responded.

Placing her hand on her hips, Honey glared at him. "I figured that much out by myself. Who and why?"

"I can't say."

"You can't say, or you don't know?"

"I know."

"Did he meet Gloria here? Is that why you won't tell me?"

"Gloria? Is that why you are so interested in K.C.'s murder? Are you upset with K.C. for dating *her*?" He couldn't imagine a woman as beautiful as Honey being jealous of Gloria, or any other woman.

"I don't care if K.C. dated Gloria. I know she was lying about being in a serious relationship with him. He wasn't in a serious relationship with any of the women he dated. But I do care if she murdered him."

"He didn't meet Gloria here. How do you know he wasn't interested in any particular woman?"

"He would have told me."

"Were you and K.C. in a relationship or not?" He knew he wasn't asking as a detective, but because he wanted to know.

"I've answered that question before."

Sam considered her response. She'd told him they dated, but he didn't know the extent of their relationship. "How do you know he would have told you about every woman he dated?"

"I'll answer your question if you answer one for me."

Sam stared at her. "What's your question?"

"What color of car does Gloria drive?"

He knew the reason she was asking the question. "Blue."

Honey didn't hesitate to answer his question. "K.C. and I were close friends. I told you the truth when I said we weren't in a serious relationship. He told me he wanted to date again when I moved back to Bardstown. I think he was beginning to consider settling down. And to answer your other question, K.C. always told me about the women he dated. He didn't keep secrets."

"But he didn't mention dating a married woman."

"Do you know for certain he did?" Honey countered.

Sam didn't answer her question. "I don't think you knew him as well as you think. Now, show me where Elvis found the bottle."

Honey remained quiet as she walked to the back of the building and pointed out the exact spot. As Sam walked along the perimeter of the building, she thought about what he'd said about her not knowing K.C. Was it possible she didn't know K.C. as well as she thought?

When Sam made his way back to her, he tapped the back of the warehouse. "This is a new building."

"There was a big old barn here," Honey replied. "Do you know who owns this property?"

"Yes."

Since Sam didn't elaborate, Honey figured he wasn't going to tell her.

Sam hooked his thumb on his holster. "I guess if I don't tell you, you'll be at the courthouse as soon as you leave here."

Honey glanced at her watch to check the time. She could make it to the courthouse before it closed. "Most likely."

"Eugenie Grayson bought this place almost a year ago." Sam had much more information than he was willing to share. Many of the people in this town were closely connected, and he wasn't taking a chance something might be said that should have been held in confidence.

"Eugenie?" Honey couldn't imagine why Eugenie wanted this place. She owned several hundred acres, which included a gorgeous horse farm that was one of the most beautiful places Honey had ever seen. "I wonder why she wanted to buy this place. It's so far away from everything."

Sam leveled his eyes on her. "Probably to meet someone."

CHAPTER FIFTEEN

H ONEY'S PHONE RANG AS SOON as she pulled out on Old Honeysuckle Road. "Hi, Georgia."

"I have the names of ten people who drive yellow cars registered in this county. Doesn't seem like yellow is a real popular color here. I ruled out six names since they are all young, and probably aren't our suspects."

"Who are the other four?"

"Jay Young, Nora Clark, and I think the last two names are going to interest you the most. Jefferson Grayson and Troy Spencer."

"Very interesting." Two of the four people certainly knew K.C. Honey had never heard of Jay Young. There was absolutely no way Jefferson Grayson would do something as outrageous as intentionally damaging K.C.'s car. *What about Eugenie Grayson?* Could Eugenie be the one who rammed K.C.'s car? She couldn't imagine Eugenie would do something so beneath her dignity. But Sam had just told her that the Graysons purchased the Tucker property a year ago. And Rick Jarboe towed K.C.'s car from that property weeks ago. Suddenly, she realized Sam didn't actually say Jefferson and Eugenie purchased the property, he said Eugenie Grayson. At her mother's party, Eugenie said she only knew K.C. socially. She couldn't possibly be the married woman K.C. was dating on the sly.

Could Troy Spencer be involved? He didn't really know K.C., so what possible motive would he have to kill him? It was possible Bunny could have been driving Troy's car. That made more sense to her even though her mother didn't think Bunny was involved romantically with K.C.

"Georgia, what was the name of the woman who owns a yellow car?"

"Nora Clark. Do you know her?"

"I don't, but I think Mom has mentioned someone named Nora before. Call Wild Horses Salon and ask for her." Honey remembered her mother said K.C. dated a woman who owned a salon.

"And if she answers, what do you want me to say?"

"Make appointments to get our hair done for the party," Honey told her. "Get the works— nails, pedicures—everything they have to offer."

After making a few more stops, Honey was tired by the time she arrived home. When she drove up to the cottage she saw her father's car, along with Woodrow's golf cart he drove around the property. "Elvis, it looks like we have company. Did I offer to cook tonight? I don't remember."

Elvis's tail was wagging in response.

"You'll have to help entertain them. I'm not in the mood for company." All she wanted to do was feed Elvis, jump into a bath filled with lavender scented bubbles, and relax for at least an hour. She sighed loudly and turned off the engine. "Let's go see what they want to eat."

Honey and Elvis walked inside to see Woodrow, her mother, and her father sitting in the living room. She dropped her purse on the table in the foyer. "I didn't know you guys were coming over. Are you hungry?"

"We came over to talk to you, dear," Lorraine replied.

"About the party?" Honey walked to one of the sofas and sat beside Woodrow.

Woodrow shook his head. "No, it's not about the party. I'm sure you have that under control. Honey, your father and I had a call today that concerned us."

The seriousness in his tone got her attention. "From whom?"

"Hap," Thomas replied. "Honey, I'm not in the habit of telling you how to run your life unless you come to me for advice, but your mom and I have discussed this with your grandfather, and we all agreed we should talk to you."

Her eyes skipped from her parents to her grandfather. "What's going on?"

"Hap voiced his concern about you running around town asking too many questions about K.C.'s murder. He thinks it's dangerous, not to mention interfering with their murder investigation," Lorraine responded.

"That's nonsense. Sam's just offended because he thinks I don't trust him to find out who killed K.C." Honey jumped up and walked to the pantry to get Elvis's food.

"Sam's not offended, he's worried, Honey. How many murders do you think we've had here in ten years?" Woodrow asked. "I don't know why K.C. was murdered, but he most likely was at the wrong place at the wrong time."

Her father stood and started pacing the floor, as was his habit when he was worried. "I agree with Woodrow. I don't think K.C. was involved with anything illegal, but I do think it's possible he saw something that resulted in his death. That, or some man had an ax to grind."

Honey walked from the pantry and stared at them. "So all of you think K.C. was dating a married woman?"

Everyone looked at each other before Lorraine finally spoke up. "We have to consider it's a possibility."

Honey threw her hands in the air. "Then who was it?"

"There you go again, asking questions you shouldn't be asking. Leave this up to the police, Honey," her father repeated. "Whatever happened, the result was murder. And I don't want you jeopardizing your safety by asking questions."

"Dad, if it was your friend who was murdered, you'd want to know what happened," Honey countered, as she filled Elvis's bowl.

"True enough, but I would give the police an opportunity to find out what happened. Sam seems competent, and Hap says he couldn't ask for a better detective."

"Hap said Sam's been working night and day on this case. They are catching a lot of grief just for questioning some of our more prominent citizens. Sam is experienced and certainly knows how to handle an investigation. Why aren't you giving him a chance? Do you think you are being fair to him by asking questions behind his back?" Woodrow asked.

Honey had no reasonable answer to his questions. Patience had never been one of her virtues. She was angry someone murdered K.C., and each day his murder seemed to preoccupy her thoughts. But she couldn't argue with Woodrow. She probably wasn't being fair to Sam, though she was reluctant to concede that point just now. It was a lowdown dirty trick for him to have Hap call her family. Hap knew all he had to do was call Woodrow and she would do anything he asked. She felt like calling Sam and giving him a piece of her mind.

"Can I get you something to drink?" They asked for iced tea and Honey opened the cabinet and pulled out the glasses.

Lorraine walked to the kitchen to help her. "Sweetheart, I know you cared about K.C., but you really need to leave this to the police. They know you talked to Rick, and that you've been out on Old Honeysuckle Road. Hap said Sam mentioned you had Georgia call the county clerk for information. And I also know you have an appointment with Nora."

"Word does get around fast," Honey mumbled. "Is she the woman you were talking about who dated K.C.?"

"Yes," Lorraine whispered.

"How did Sam know about that already?" She hadn't even talked to Georgia until she'd left Sam at Old Honeysuckle Road.

"Hap didn't mention that, but you need to stay out of Sam's investigation." Lorraine spoke loudly so Woodrow and Thomas could hear what she was saying, but she whispered in Honey's ear, "I'll make an appointment at the same time. Nora knows me well and will tell us what she knows. I just don't want you to endanger yourself. And if Sam thinks that's possible, then you must promise me you'll be careful."

Honey gave her mother a grateful smile. She could always count on her to understand. "Thanks, Mom. I'll be very careful."

"I'll call you later and find out what you want to know from Nora." Lorraine turned back to the men. "We're ordering pizza. Honey's had a full day and we need something easy."

The men nodded their agreement, calling out the toppings they wanted as they walked outside to see the work Chance had completed.

As soon as her father pulled the sliding door closed, Honey told Lorraine why she wanted to speak with Nora. "Mom, I want to know the last time Nora saw K.C., and if he mentioned anything troubling him. I also want to know if she knew other women he was dating."

"She'll tell me. She's been my hairdresser for a long time and she can't keep a secret."

Honey glanced through the patio door and saw Woodrow and her father walking around the pool. "Did you know Eugenie owns the Tucker property on Old Honeysuckle Road?"

"I don't believe she ever mentioned that to me. Lorraine pulled the pitcher of iced tea from the refrigerator and filled the glasses. "What did you think you would find out there?"

Honey shrugged, and held up one finger as she punched in the number to the local pizza parlor on her cell phone. While she waited for someone to answer, she leaned against the counter. "I didn't know what I would find. I just wanted to see if I could figure out why K.C. was out there. The grass is really high, but someone has some expensive furnishings inside the house. And a large warehouse like structure was built where an old barn used to be."

"What was inside the warehouse?" Lorraine asked.

Holding up her finger again, Honey gave her pizza order to the person on the phone. When she hung up, she answered her mother's question. "That building had padlocks on the doors. Maybe some kids have been out there partying, because Elvis found a broken bourbon bottle."

"I wouldn't be surprised," Lorraine responded.

"Can you think of anyone who drives a yellow car?"

"Nora drives a yellow car." Lorraine turned and looked at Honey, and added, "Troy Spencer also drives a yellow car. Why?"

"I told you about Rick Jarboe repairing K.C.'s car. The car that hit K.C.'s was yellow."

"That's why you called the county clerk's office?"

Honey nodded. "Do the Grayson's have a yellow car?"

"Oh, I forgot all about Eugenie's Bentley. It's a gorgeous car. But it's not the same color of yellow as Nora's." Lorraine arched her brow. "You don't really think Eugenie Grayson would be involved in something like this?"

"No, I can't imagine that. But do you think her husband could have been jealous of K.C. for any reason?"

"Heavens no. You saw Jefferson at the party. He's a very attractive and charming man. He would never have a reason to be jealous. Not to mention the man is so well-known that I'm surprised he can take a bath without it making the news. The press is always nearby. Eugenie has told me many times that they have a fabulous relationship. They certainly appear to be very devoted to each other."

Honey thought about what her mother said about the varying colors of yellow. "Mom, can you describe the exact color of Nora's car?"

"Nora's car is what I would call a bright sunflower yellow. Beautiful flower, but a bit gaudy on a car. Eugenie's Bentley is more of a lemon chiffon. An elegant color, as one would expect."

Honey smiled at her mother's description of colors. "What about Troy's?"

"It's closer in color to Eugenie's rather than the sunflower yellow."

The paint on K.C.'s black car had to be lemon chiffon. "When will you be seeing Eugenie?"

"I'm meeting Bunny and Eugenie for lunch tomorrow. Do you want me to look over Eugenie's car to see if I can tell if it has been repaired?"

Honey couldn't help but smile at her mother's willingness to play detective. "No. But would you mind including me in your lunch party? I'll find a way to ask about the property on Old Honeysuckle Road."

"Great idea. You'll make a welcome addition. I'll pick you up at the distillery and we can go together."

"Sounds like a plan."

Honey and Lorraine were already seated in the restaurant when Eugenie and Bunny arrived.

Eugenie sat in the chair across from Honey. "Honey, what a nice surprise to see you here."

"Mom was nice enough to invite me. I hope you don't mind."

"Not at all."

Honey noticed Bunny didn't comment about her presence. The women talked about the dinner train party, and Eugenie seemed particularly interested in the invitation list.

"Has everyone RSVP'd?" Eugenie asked.

Honey waited for the waitress to take their drink order before she responded. "Yes, everyone is coming. It's going to be a fun evening."

"Are you bringing that handsome detective, Honey?" Bunny asked.

"No, the guests list was prepared before I met Sam. Seating is limited, and I couldn't squeeze in another person unless someone couldn't attend."

Bunny sighed loudly. "That's too bad. He's a very handsome man, and obviously a very brave one."

"I'm tired of his questions about K.C. Cleary. He's being a nuisance, and Jefferson told Hap in no uncertain terms that he'd better put a leash on that tall Texan," Eugenie grumbled.

Honey felt she needed to defend Sam. "I can't see why anyone would object to helping with a murder investigation. Having to answer a few questions is hardly a reason to be upset with Sam or Hap. We all want to know who killed K.C."

Eugenie pursed her lips in disapproval. "I do suppose there are many people who have nothing better to do with their time than involve themselves in these tawdry affairs."

"I would hardly call a man being murdered a tawdry affair, Eugenie. K.C. was a member of our community and everyone adored him," Lorraine said.

Honey felt like hugging her mother for supporting her. "Mom's right. We should all want to know if there is a murderer among us."

The pained expression on Eugenie's face indicated she obviously disagreed. "I didn't know K.C. well. The police should question the people who interacted daily with him."

Honey refused to remain quiet. "I have no problem being questioned. Sometimes people see or hear something that they may not think is important, but it could be invaluable information to the police."

Eugenie put her hand to her chest. "Why on earth would that detective think I would know anything about K.C.'s murder?"

"You attended his funeral," Honey reminded her.

Eugenie was in the process of uttering a retort when their conversation was interrupted by the waiter.

Once the waiter left with their orders, Bunny changed the conversation. "Honey, how did you happened to meet that handsome detective?"

Honey was tempted to tell Bunny it wasn't any of her business, but she wanted information from these women. "Hap stopped by to see Woodrow, and Sam was with him."

"That was a stroke of luck for you. Too bad he won't be coming to the party. We need all the handsome men we can get in this town to attend our boring parties. It makes the evenings so much more interesting." Bunny took a sip of her bourbon the waiter delivered.

That was the second time Bunny mentioned her disappointment that Sam wouldn't be at the party. Before she had too many bourbons, Honey needed some answers. "The dinner train route passes behind the old Tucker place before crossing over the lake. I drove the route on Old Honeysuckle Road, and I pulled into the Tucker farm. Unfortunately the grass was so high I couldn't see the lake. I hope the scenery is still as beautiful as it once was."

"We used to take Honey and Preston out there swimming when they were young," Lorraine added in an effort to keep the conversation going.

"Funny you should mention the Tucker place. That detective was asking me about it the other day," Eugenie said.

"Why would he talk to you about that place?" Lorraine asked.

"Because I owned it until a couple of weeks ago." Eugenie looked across the table at Honey. "I'm sure Honey already knew that."

Honey wasn't going to admit she was aware Eugenie purchased the place. "How would I know that?"

"Doesn't your detective keep you informed on his investigation? It could be fascinating pillow talk," Eugenie retorted.

"He's not *my* detective. We've had a few dates, but it's nothing serious. And Sam is too professional to discuss his investigations."

Bunny took another drink of her bourbon as she stared at Honey. "Someone told me they saw Sam with some gorgeous blonde who works at Cleary's."

Lorraine smoothly transitioned back to the topic that she knew Honey wanted to discuss. "Eugenie, why on earth would you want the Tucker property? The home must be in terrible condition."

"It was, but I renovated the place." Eugenie went on to say something about having tax write-offs.

Honey was confident Eugenie's purpose for purchasing that property had little to do with finances, but it might be a plausible story to a detective.

"Troy and I just bought that property from Eugenie," Bunny told them. "Troy needs more acreage for growing corn and warehousing."

Honey thought that made more sense than Eugenie's explanation. As much as she didn't want to believe K.C. was dating a married woman, her intuition was telling her it was true. Eugenie had bought that place to meet K.C. And Sam knew it was true.

Leaving the restaurant, Honey noticed a light yellow car, or as her mother would say, a lemon chiffon car, parked next to them. Eugenie walked to the driver's door.

Honey stopped beside Eugenie's car. "I think I just missed you when I was near the old Tucker place. I noticed a car this color pulling out of that driveway."

"Well, it wasn't me," Eugenie opened the door and gave them a little wave. "I'll see you on the train."

"Is that the color of the car that hit K.C.'s?" Lorraine asked as they watched Eugenie drive away.

"I think so."

"Well, Troy's is almost the same color. If it was Eugenie, do you think it might have been an accident and they didn't want to report it to the police?"

"No, K.C. admitted to Rick Jarboe that it was intentional."

"I guess Bunny could have been driving Troy's car," Lorraine replied.

Honey had already thought of that possibility. She thought all she had to do was figure out which woman was so angry with K.C. that she would ram his car. *But is that person also a murderer?*

CHAPTER SIXTEEN

A WEEK PASSED AND HONEY HAD not heard from Sam since the day he found her at the Tucker farm. She'd been so busy preparing for the dinner train event that she had little time to think about anything else. When she did think about Sam, she thought about calling him to apologize for interfering with his investigation. But she was still upset that he'd had Hap call Woodrow to apply pressure on her. This past week she hadn't had the time to run around town asking questions, but she did manage to call a few of K.C.'s friends to see if they knew anything about the married woman he was *supposedly* dating. She figured Sam must not have heard about that, or Hap would have made another phone call.

Georgia stuck her head inside Honey's office before she left. "Are you sure you don't want me to help you make bourbon balls tonight?"

"Thanks, but I'm leaving early to get them done. Besides, don't you have a date with my brother?"

"Yes, but I'm sure he wouldn't mind helping you out tonight," Georgia said.

Honey switched off the light on her desk. "You've been working so hard, you deserve a night to relax. Tomorrow is going to be a long day. We need to get beautified, and we won't be home until very late after the party."

Georgia smiled as she flipped off the overhead lights. "I'm really looking forward to it. I can't wait to wear my new dress. I've never been to a function like this before."

"You look gorgeous in that dress. Preston will flip over it." Honey looked at Elvis. "Ready to go, big guy?"

Elvis lurched to his feet and wagged his tail.

Honey figured he thought they were going someplace fun. "Sorry, buddy, we are just going home to work."

Arriving home, Honey changed clothes and prepared to make the bourbon balls for the party. It was a time-consuming process, but if they were going to be served at the party, she had to get them done. She'd waited until the last minute to make them so they would be fresh for the guests on the train. Four hours later, she'd made so many bourbon balls that she had to take some to Woodrow's house and store them in his extra refrigerator.

After she showered, she decided to relax on the patio while Elvis enjoyed nature. Chance wasn't working on the patio tonight, and she was grateful to have some quiet time with Elvis. She sipped iced tea as she watched Elvis sniff the territory as if he hadn't smelled it hundreds of times. It didn't take long for her thoughts to drift to Sam. He'd looked completely exhausted when she saw him at the old Tucker farm. She wondered if he hadn't called because he was so busy with his investigation, or if he was still upset with her for snooping around. Hopefully, it was his work, and not *someone* else, that was keeping him busy.

Seeing Elvis sniff something on a table on the other side of the pool, she said, "What is it, Elvis?" When he sat down beside the table and barked, she realized he wanted her attention. She walked around the pool, and when she reached the table she saw a piece of paper tucked beneath the candle. Carefully unfolding the small piece of paper, she read the printed note. *STOP ASKING QUESTIONS OR YOU'LL END UP LIKE K.C. CLEARY.* She read the note again. Was this some sort of joke? How did someone get back here and leave a note without anyone seeing them? She glanced around the patio, suddenly feeling very isolated in the one place where she'd always found solace. Dark shadows lurking at every corner of the property did little to alleviate her fear. "Let's go inside, Elvis." She hurried toward the patio door, but Elvis wasn't beside her. She turned to see him sniffing the dense foliage twenty feet beyond the pool. "Elvis, come here."

Elvis's attention was on his quest and he didn't listen to her command. Instead, he cocked his head and stared at the brush.

"Don't go through those bushes," Honey yelled more forcefully.

Elvis ignored her and disappeared through the brush. "Elvis!" She waited a beat, then said in a louder voice, "Come here this minute!" She heard what sounded like a twig breaking, but when Elvis didn't appear, her pulse started racing. Her thoughts were going in every direction, and most of them were frightening. The person who placed the note under the candle could still be around. She thought about going inside and getting the pistol she kept in the closet, but she was worried someone might try to hurt Elvis if she walked away. She couldn't leave him out here alone. She raced around the pool, and when she reached the bushes, she yelled, "Elvis!" Her heart was pounding in her chest when Elvis popped from the bushes right beside her. At her shriek, Elvis started howling. If someone was lurking in the brush, there was no way Honey would hear them above the racket he was making. Clutching his collar, she nearly dragged him to the patio door. Once inside, she locked all of the doors and pulled the drapes.

"We need to call Sam." Grabbing her phone off the counter, she told herself to calm down before she called. She tried to think logically. *The note could be a cruel joke and not a threat. If it is a real warning and I call Sam, he will probably say, I told you so. But what about Georgia? Could I be putting her at risk by asking questions around town?* She quickly scrolled to Georgia's number.

Georgia answered on the second ring and Honey told her about the note.

"This is a sign."

Here we go again, Honey thought. "Georgia, this could be serious."

"It's a sign that we are asking the right questions, and someone is afraid we are going to find out who killed K.C. I was watching this true crime story the other night, and two women were trying to find out who killed their friend. As soon as they started asking questions they were threatened."

Honey didn't know if Georgia was trying to make her feel better or worse. "I could be putting you in danger. I want you to stay with me, or at your parents' home until Sam solves this murder."

"I doubt anyone knows where I live," Georgia replied.

"Still, I don't want you to stay alone." Honey thought she heard someone in the background talking. "Is someone with you?"

"Preston is here. He wants to talk to you. I'm putting you on speaker."

Once Honey read the note to Preston, he said, "It doesn't sound like a prank to me. It would take us too long to get there from Louisville. I'll stay with Georgia, but I want you to call Sam right now. You need to take this serious, Sis. Make sure your pistol is loaded and keep it close. You still know how to use it, don't you?"

"I know how."

"Good. Is Elvis with you?"

"He's right beside me."

"Now go get your pistol while I'm on the phone," Preston instructed.

Honey ran to the bedroom and pulled her pistol from the closet. "Got it." They said good-bye and Honey called Sam.

"Yeah?" Sam barked into his phone.

"Sam?" Honey was surprised by his curt greeting.

"Sorry, Honey. I didn't look at the screen. I thought it was the office calling." The ringing phone had awakened him from a dead sleep. When he'd walked in his door earlier he'd showered, changed clothes, and sat down on his sofa to relax a few minutes before he made himself a sandwich. But he was so exhausted he'd fallen asleep and the ringing phone jarred him awake. After hearing why Honey was calling, he reached for his pistol, grabbed his keys and headed out the door. "I'll be there in ten minutes. Keep your doors locked."

Honey and Elvis were waiting by the front door when Sam knocked. One look at his disheveled hair told her he was probably sleeping when she'd called. Casually dressed in a black T-shirt and jeans, she noticed his pistol clipped to his belt.

"I'm sorry I called you so late, but Preston said I should."

Once inside, Sam closed and locked the door. He reached for the pistol Honey was holding. "You weren't going to call me before you talked to Preston?"

"I thought it might be a prank." She turned and walked to the kitchen.

Sam rubbed Elvis's ears before he followed Honey to the kitchen. He saw the note when he placed Honey's pistol on the counter. Once he read it, he said, "Do you know someone who would think this is funny?"

"No."

"Where's Chance tonight? Did he see anything?"

"He wasn't here when I came home."

"Have you seen anyone hanging around the property recently?"

"I've been at the office late every day this week, but I don't remember seeing anyone."

Sam walked to the patio door and slid it open. "Show me where you found the note."

Honey led Sam to the table, and Elvis was already on the trail of a scent by the bushes again. "Actually, Elvis found the note and he went through the bushes where he is right now."

"The gate was closed when I came through. Was it closed earlier when you came home?"

"Yes, but I can't remember if I saw it close after I drove through."

Sam pulled a flashlight from the back pocket of his jeans. "Would you get me a leash for Elvis? We'll have a look around."

Honey ran inside and grabbed Elvis's leash from a hook at the back door. She hurried back to the patio and clipped the leash to Elvis's collar. "Be careful."

Sam took Elvis's leash from her. "Go back inside and lock the door. Do you know how to use that pistol?"

"Gramps taught me a long time ago."

"Is it loaded?"

"Yes."

"Good. Don't pick up the note again. It's evidence. Call me if you hear anything that doesn't sound right." Thinking some areas may not have good cell reception, he added, "If I don't answer, call the station."

Honey looked out the patio door every few minutes, getting more worried by the second. Before she drove herself crazy, she occupied herself by making fresh coffee. Two hours passed before she saw them walking through the bushes.

"Elvis caught a scent and he tracked it to the back side of the property. In the morning I'll drive around there to see what I can find."

She thought he looked exhausted. "Would you like some coffee?"

"I thought I smelled coffee. Sounds good."

Honey poured him a cup. "What about something to eat? Did you have dinner?"

"I can wait until breakfast."

"Nonsense. We're awake and you need to eat something. Make yourself comfortable on the sofa and I'll make some sandwiches." After she grilled ham and cheese sandwiches, she carried them to the living room. Sam's coffee cup was empty, and he was leaning back with his eyes closed. Elvis was stretched out on the sofa beside him with his head on his thigh.

Sam's eyes snapped opened when he heard her set the plate on the coffee table. "I can eat in the kitchen."

"Sit still, the sofa's comfortable." Honey poured him another cup of coffee before she lured Elvis from the sofa with some treats.

"Did you call Chance?" Sam asked as he took a big bite of his first sandwich.

Honey took a seat on the sofa across from him. "Why would I call Chance?"

"Wouldn't he want to know about the note?"

His question puzzled her. "I can't see why he would be interested."

"Any man who cares about you should be interested."

Honey realized Georgia was right. Sam did think she had something going with Chance. "I see no reason to involve him in this." She saw an opportunity to find out if he was interested in Gloria. "Would you call Gloria to tell her about your day?"

"Who?" Sam's brows drew together as he tried to make sense of her question. He was so tired he wasn't operating on all cylinders. It took him several seconds to realize who she was talking about. "Oh, you mean Gloria Barnes." After another bite of his sandwich, he picked up his coffee and took a sip. Instead of answering her question, he asked one. "So, are you aren't romantically involved with Chance?"

Honey noticed he hadn't answered her question. "No. I told you that before. Do you have a difficult time trusting people?"

Sam grinned at her. "I guess you could say it's an occupational hazard. I've learned in my profession it's not always what people say, but their actions that usually tell the true story." He finished his sandwich, stood and walked around the table and sat next to her. "Why the candlelight dinner that night?"

Honey rolled her eyes at him. She couldn't believe he'd interpreted that night as a romantic interlude. "They were citronella."

He cocked his head at her. "What?"

"You know—the candles that repel mosquitos. Not exactly an enticing fragrance for romance."

Sam smiled when he realized what she was talking about. He slid his arm along the back of the sofa behind her. "I can see how you would mistake Chance for a big mosquito." He didn't say he intended to squash him like an insect if he didn't keep his mitts off of her.

Honey shook her head at him, but she was smiling. "Very funny. And what about Gloria?" If he wanted more answers, he'd better be prepared to give her some.

Sam moved his arm from the sofa to her shoulders, urging her closer to him. When she looked up at him with the question lingering in her eyes, he said, "There's nothing going on between me and Gloria. It saved me time to talk to her over lunch rather than take her to the station. That's all there was to it."

"Oh, I thought by the way she was hanging on to you that..."

Sam leaned over and brushed his lips over hers. His lips found her ear and he whispered, "Don't think."

And she didn't. She wrapped her arms around his neck just as his lips to return to hers.

Elvis chose that moment to jump on the sofa and flop his big body across their laps. When they pulled apart, Sam stroked Elvis's head. "I've missed you two."

"Elvis missed you. He's been depressed not seeing you."

Elvis looked up at Sam with big brown adoring eyes.

As Sam rubbed Elvis's ears, he glanced at Honey. "What about you? Did you miss me?"

"I missed you a little," Honey admitted.

"This investigation is taking up a lot of my time." Now that he believed she wasn't involved with Chance, he planned to call her every day, even if he got home at midnight.

Honey dropped her head to his shoulder. "I'm sorry if I caused you trouble by asking questions and interfering with your investigation. You know that wasn't my intention."

Sam kissed the top of her head. "You haven't created problems for me. I was worried about you asking questions with a murderer on the loose. Honey, you never know what a desperate person will do."

"Woodrow said Jefferson Grayson was complaining to Hap that you were being a nuisance." She told him about her conversation at lunch with Eugenie and Bunny.

Sam thought of the verbal abuse poor Hap was receiving from the prominent citizens in town. "Yeah, I've created a hornet's nest for Hap. It seems some of our residents don't like answering questions."

"Hap can deal with them. He's had years of experience," Honey assured him. She didn't ask him questions about the investigation, knowing he needed rest more than anything. "You look tired."

"I am, but I don't want to leave you alone tonight. You want to go to Woodrow's?"

"It's late and I'm not going to disturb him. I'll be fine." She didn't want him to leave, but she felt guilty asking him to stay.

"If someone is watching you, it might be good if they know I'm here." He eyed the sofa. All he wanted to do was stretch out for a minute and close his burning eyes.

"You could stay here tonight if you don't want to drive home."

Sam wasn't too tired to tease her. "That's some invitation. I think you read my mind."

She pushed Elvis off of her lap and stood. "I have an extra bedroom. I'll go check to make sure you have everything you need in there." Before she walked to the bedroom, she made a detour to the refrigerator and grabbed six bourbon balls. When she handed them to him, she said, "This is for having the right answers."

Sam smiled. "I always tell the truth." He popped a bourbon ball in his mouth, and added, "This proves honesty is the best policy. If this is my reward, I'll never tell a lie."

"Boy scout," she quipped before turning toward the bedroom.

"I think I like Detective Gorgeous better."

Honey stopped and turned back to him. "How did you know Georgia calls you that?"

"Didn't you know I'm a great detective?"

Honey laughed as she walked toward the bedroom. She turned down the bed, checked to make sure there were towels in the adjoining bathroom, and placed some toiletries on the counter. When she returned to the living room she saw Sam stretched out on the sofa with his eyes closed and his feet hanging off the end of the sofa. Elvis was cuddled up next to him. She gently touched his shoulder. "Sam," she whispered. When he didn't respond, she walked back to the bedroom for a pillow and blanket. After she removed his shoes, she placed the pillow by his head and covered him with the blanket.

She felt safer being in close proximity to Sam and Elvis, so she retrieved her pillow and blanket from her bedroom. She picked up her pistol from the counter and placed it on the coffee table. When she stretched out on the sofa across from Sam, Elvis opened his eyes and looked at her. "Stay where you are, don't wake him," she whispered. Honey watched Sam sleep a long time before she finally drifted off.

A few hours later, Sam awoke hot and sweating. The pendant lights in the kitchen provided enough light so he could see the reason he was roasting. Elvis was sprawled half on top of him, snoring loudly, and a blanket was wrapped around his legs. He didn't know if Honey put the pillow on the sofa for him or for Elvis, but Elvis was the one drooling on it at the moment. He glanced at the sofa across from him where Honey was sleeping peacefully. Seeing her pistol on the table, he wondered if she was afraid to sleep in her bedroom. That thought made him angry. He wasn't going to allow anyone to terrorize her.

His pistol was digging into his waist, so he climbed over Elvis and stood to remove his holster. Elvis opened his eyes, and Sam whispered, "Stay there, buddy." After he gently placed his holster on the coffee table, Sam walked to the bathroom and splashed cold water on his face to cool off. Returning to the living room, he lay down on top of the blanket beside Honey and wrapped his arm around her.

Without waking, Honey turned and rested her head on his shoulder. Seconds later, Elvis climbed on the sofa, wedging his body between their legs. Sam rubbed his ears, thinking how much he'd missed both of them. He couldn't explain how it happened so quickly, but he was crazy about both of them.

CHAPTER SEVENTEEN

THE DAY OF THE DINNER train event arrived with an unprecedented record-busting heatwave. After Honey delivered the bourbon balls to the chef early that morning, she met her mother and Georgia at Wild Horses Salon. While the women were having their hair styled, Lorraine broached the subject of K.C.'s murder with the salon owner, Nora. Nora told them she hadn't seen K.C. in several months before his murder. Not only that, but Nora said K.C. had only asked her out a few times and it was never a serious relationship.

Despite the lack of useful information from Nora, Honey and Georgia were delighted to have a few hours of pampering. To Honey's surprise, Georgia left the salon with red highlights in her hair, replacing the blue.

By three o'clock that afternoon Honey returned home, and the thermometer on her patio was registering one hundred eight degrees. The train was scheduled to depart the station at seven o'clock, and Honey prayed the temperature, as well as the humidity, would drop by several degrees. If not, at least the train would be comfortable once the guests boarded. The day she'd toured the train she noticed the dining cars were almost too cold. But she felt certain no guest would complain tonight. She was just thankful she'd chosen an indoor venue for the party.

As she dressed, she thought she'd selected the perfect gown. She would look cool in the icy-blue silk gown even if she was having a heat stroke. She'd made the decision to have her hair styled in an old-fashioned French twist. Appraising her appearance in the floor-length mirror one last time, she wished Sam could see her in the gown. Unfortunately Sam was working tonight, although he'd told her he would call later. His hours were long and erratic, but she didn't care what time he called. It was more important to her to know he was safe. She didn't know where their relationship was going, but given their last conversation, there was no question they wanted it to go forward. Considering the dangers of his profession, she knew she would always worry about him if she didn't hear from him each night. She glanced at Elvis, who had been watching her dress. She twirled around to give him a good view of her dress. "What do you think?"

Elvis barked his approval.

"Thank you. I think it looks pretty good." She leaned over until she was nose to nose with him. "You be a good boy while I'm gone and when Sam calls later, I'll let you talk to him."

Honey greeted Georgia and Preston when they boarded the train. Georgia's new pale pink gown was perfect with the red highlights in her hair. "Georgia, you look beautiful."

"Thank you. And it's too bad Detective Gorgeous won't be here tonight to see you. On the other hand, he'd probably have to use his gun to keep the men off of you."

"Georgia's right, you look wonderful, Sis. You remind me of a '50s movie star with your hair like that," Preston told her.

"Thank you. And you are looking very handsome tonight. I haven't seen you in a tux in a long time."

"Be thankful it's cold in here. I was about to strip to my boxers just walking from the parking lot to the train," Preston teased.

"The limos will drop the guests off just a few feet from the platform. They won't have to suffer with this heat," Honey replied.

"Great idea," Georgia said.

Preston pointed to the platform. "I see the photographers are already out there waiting to pounce on the Hollywood crowd."

"Yes, I saw them staking out their territory. I'm afraid even this heat won't keep them at bay. I was just going through the cars to make sure all of the tables are ready," Honey replied.

Georgia held out the items she was carrying. "I have the seating chart, the personalized place cards, and the menus. Can Preston and I sit at Jerry Bruckheimer's table? I'd love to talk to him about his movies."

Honey smiled at Georgia's enthusiasm. "Sure. You might suggest putting our new bourbon in a scene in one of his movies," Honey joked as she led them through the cars.

"Maybe I could be eating your bourbon balls in a scene." Georgia looked around at the décor. "The table settings are beautiful, and the bourbon balls look great on those tiered stands."

After they added the place cards and the menus to the tables, they walked to the kitchen car to speak to the chef and the bartender. Seeing everything was going according to plan, they walked back to the boarding area and prepared to greet the guests. Woodrow and Honey's parents were the first to arrive, followed by Cullen.

"The limos will be here in two minutes," Cullen announced.

"Did all of the out-of-town guests make it?" Lorraine asked.

"Yes, and everyone is staying at The Brown. The limo service is transporting them to the train, then back to The Brown later tonight," Honey replied.

"Have you seen Alan?" Woodrow asked.

Honey had almost forgotten about Alan. "Not yet. But the bartender has everything set up for him."

Woodrow glanced out one of the windows. "His car is in the parking lot."

"I'm sure he'll be here soon," Honey replied.

"Once the train departs the station, and the guests have time to order some drinks, I'll say a few words of welcome in the first dining car and then make my way to the other three. After that, Alan can follow me from car to car to discuss our new bourbon and start the tasting," Woodrow said.

"Perfect. After Alan's presentation, the bartenders will take it from there. We can all mingle, answer any questions and listen to the comments about Devil's Due Bourbon before dinner is served," Honey added.

Lorraine lifted a bourbon ball from the serving dish on a table next to her. "I'll already be stuffed on bourbon balls. They look delicious, Honey."

"Just save some for the guests," Honey teased, and everyone laughed.

Cullen glanced out the window and saw the limos pulling up. "Here they come."

As the guests made their way toward the train, they graciously stopped and answered questions from the reporters while the photographers competed for the best shots. Two attendants discreetly checked the names of the guests off the list before they were greeted by Woodrow and Honey when they boarded. Several minutes later, with all of the guests on board, the train slowly pulled away from the station. Many of the guests had met before at parties they'd attended in Kentucky, and they freely moved between cars getting reacquainted.

Honey realized she still hadn't seen Alan, so she was making her way through the first car when she spotted Cullen. "Have you seen Alan?"

"I've been looking for him, but no luck yet."

"I got so busy with the guests that I forgot all about him until the train had already left the station. I'll go through the other cars if you'll tell Woodrow to go ahead and welcome everyone, but wait before he announces the tasting until I find Alan."

"Sure thing." Cullen started to make his way through the throng of people when he saw Woodrow talking with the Bruckheimers.

Georgia and Preston caught up with Honey as she was leaving the first car. "Honey, have you noticed it seems hotter in here now?"

"I thought it was just me."

"No, it's definitely getting warmer in here," Preston agreed.

Honey glanced around the car. She noticed a few of the women were fanning themselves with the menus. "The guests must be feeling the temperature change. I wonder if the other cars are as warm."

"I'll look for an attendant and find out if there is a problem with the air conditioner," Preston offered and walked away.

"Georgia, we need to find Alan. No one has seen him."

Cullen caught up with Honey and Georgia in the second car. "Woodrow is going to wait for your signal to announce the tasting. He's positive Alan's car was at the station when he arrived."

Looking over the faces in the car, Honey muttered, "He must be here somewhere."

Cullen moved closer to Honey and lowered his voice. "Honey, I didn't want to say anything before, but I think Alan has a drinking problem. Maybe he had one too many before the party and is somewhere sleeping it off."

"What makes you think he has a drinking problem?" Honey thought Woodrow would have told her if he suspected Alan had a problem.

"I've found him in one of the rickhouses a few times and he seemed to be...well, I don't know, he acted so odd that I just thought he must be drinking and trying to hide it. Maybe I shouldn't have mentioned it since I have no actual proof," Cullen replied.

"Alan always seems odd," Georgia quipped.

Cullen smiled. "I know. Hard to believe, huh?"

"This conversation stays between the three of us." Honey wasn't going to jump to conclusions about Alan without proof. "Let's just hope he's ready to give his speech when we find him. Just in case he isn't in good condition, would you be prepared to take his place introducing the bourbon, Cullen?"

"Of course."

"Okay. Then let's go through the other cars. The supplies are in the last car past the kitchen. Maybe he's back there for some reason." Honey led the way to the next car.

Just as they were leaving the next car, Preston reached them. "The attendant says they are working on the air conditioning problem. It's getting warmer in all of the cars."

Honey groaned. "That's one problem we don't need tonight. It's probably still over a hundred degrees outside. Preston, would you stay here and make sure they get the air working? We're looking for Alan. He seems to have disappeared."

"Sure thing."

It was slow going since all of the guests stopped Honey to talk. Honey introduced Georgia and Cullen to everyone, and as they conversed they also scanned the car in hopes of spotting Alan.

"Everyone seems genuinely pleased to have been invited," Cullen said.

"I just hope it doesn't get any warmer, or they may not be as happy by the time we return. Although, we could always stop at the lake and jump in," Honey teased. She glanced out a window to see if they were near the lake.

"We can always ply our guests with more bourbon so they don't notice the heat," Georgia suggested.

"We'll keep that in mind," Cullen replied, removing his tux jacket.

"That's not fair. I wish I could take off this dress," Georgia muttered.

Cullen smiled at her. "That would make everyone forget the temperatures."

Georgia frowned at him. "Funny guy."

They walked through the kitchen where Honey described Alan to the chef and the kitchen staff, but no one had seen him. They started checking the small compartments in the last car where all of the supplies were stored. As soon as Honey opened the last door, she saw Alan leaning back on the bench next to the wall. His eyes were closed, and a half-empty bottle of bourbon was sitting on the bench next to him.

"I found him," she yelled to Georgia and Cullen, who were checking the other compartments. "Alan!" When he didn't move, Honey walked inside and tapped him on his shoulder. "Alan, wake up!"

Cullen walked to the doorway, and Honey turned and shrugged her shoulders. "You were right. I think he's passed out. It looks like he vomited."

Cullen walked inside, gripped Alan's arm and gave him a good shake. "Alan, time to get going." Alan didn't respond, and Cullen's eyes slid to Honey. "I think he's dead."

At first, Honey thought Cullen was teasing. But one look at Cullen's face told her he wasn't kidding. "He can't be dead!"

Cullen placed two fingers on Alan's neck. "I'm afraid he is."

Hearing what Cullen said, Georgia walked inside the compartment and closed the door behind her. "Are you sure?"

Cullen shook his head. "No pulse."

Georgia groaned. "Not again."

All three stared at Alan in disbelief.

"I don't see any injuries. I guess he had a heart attack, or judging by the vomit on his mouth, he may have drank too much and choked to death," Cullen speculated.

"Great. Of all nights to drink himself to death, he had to pick this one. I have makeup with me. Maybe I could fix him up and make him look—well, give him more color, like he's sleeping," Georgia offered.

Honey couldn't believe how Georgia remained so calm whenever they found a dead body. "You *are not* putting makeup on him. I need to call Sam." Honey pulled her phone from her purse and called his number, but when nothing happened, she realized there was no cell service. "I don't have a signal." She glanced at Georgia. "See if you have service."

Georgia pulled her phone out. "Nope."

Cullen fished his phone from his pocket. "Afraid not."

"I'm sure the conductor has a way to contact the police in the event of an emergency." Honey turned to leave the compartment.

Georgia grabbed her arm. "Honey, wait. I think this is a sign we should wait until we get back to the station to call Sam. There's nothing we can do for Alan, and there's no sense ruining the evening for everyone by turning back now."

"Georgia's right. Cullen agreed. "Going back to the station now will not benefit anyone. We have a lot of important people on this train who traveled a long way for this event. Think about what the publicity would do to Woodrow and the distillery."

Honey looked down at Alan. Georgia and Cullen had a point—they could do nothing for him now. Yet, she didn't think it was wise not to let anyone know about his demise. "I don't know…"

Georgia interrupted her. "It's only a few hours until we get back. Dead is dead. We're not going to bring him back to life."

"If we hadn't found him, he would still be here in four hours," Cullen added.

Honey felt like she might pass out. The room was stifling hot. She looked at the window to see if it had been opened, allowing the hot air inside. "It's so hot in here."

"It is hotter in here than in the other cars," Georgia agreed.

"It's too hot to leave him in this compartment for hours. I don't know how long it takes for dead bodies to smell, but if they don't get the air going, there could be a serious odor if it gets any hotter," Cullen told them.

"I don't feel right about leaving him like this for hours," Honey said.

"I have an idea." Georgia turned and opened the compartment door. "I'll be back in a minute."

When Georgia returned to the compartment she was followed by two train attendants carrying an extra-large aluminum cooler. Once they deposited the cooler by the door and walked away, she knocked on the compartment door. "Cullen, open the door."

Pulling the door open, Cullen glanced at the cooler. "What's this?"

"A cooler. And they are bringing us another cooler full of ice. I told him we needed to ice down some of our alcohol. We can use it to ice Alan down."

Honey's eyes darted from Georgia to Cullen. "You are not suggesting we put Alan in that cooler?"

Cullen pulled the cooler inside the compartment. "It's a brilliant idea. That way we don't have to worry about someone walking in and seeing Alan like this."

Honey's eyes widened. "You two can't be serious."

"Hang on. I think I hear someone walking down the companionway." Cullen slid the door open and stepped out. After he tipped the men who brought the ice, he walked to another compartment where he'd seen a stacks of fresh tablecloths on shelves. Grabbing two of them, he hurried back to the compartment. Once inside, he covered Alan's body with one of the tablecloths. "We need to hurry. We've already been gone too long."

Honey held her hands in the air. "Wait. Wait. Wait. He won't fit in that cooler."

"Of course he will. Alan is a small man and this is a large cooler." Cullen opened the lid of the cooler, walked to the bench, scooped Alan up in his arms and deposited him inside. He turned to Honey to say *I told you so*, but he saw the look of horror on her face. "It'll be okay, Honey. He's not feeling anything."

Unable to formulate a word, Honey pointed to Alan's body.

Georgia said, "Cullen, look at Alan."

Cullen looked down at Alan's body and saw the reason for Honey's terrified expression. The handle of a knife was sticking out of Alan's back. "I guess he didn't die of a heart attack."

"Cullen, you may want to rethink being a master distiller. I'd say this is a sign that it doesn't appear to be a very safe profession," Georgia said.

Honey's eyes met Cullen's. It hadn't occurred to her there could be a link to K.C.'s murder until Georgia's offhand comment. *What are the chances two men in the same industry, both master distillers, would be murdered in the same town? Probably a hundred million to one. There must be a connection.* "I need to call Sam."

"We need to wait until we get back," Georgia urged again. "We've already moved the body. We're going to be in trouble anyway—now or later. Why should we ruin the evening?"

Cullen placed the second tablecloth over Alan's body, covering the knife handle. "I agree with Georgia. Let's call Sam on our way back to the station. We've already messed this up, so we might as well wait as long as possible." He opened the door and pulled the cooler full of ice inside.

Honey agreed with them on one point—it was going to be bad no matter what they did. They had a famous Hollywood producer on board, and she could already envision the movie trailer. No doubt their characters would be played by fine Hollywood actors, and knowing the talented producer, the movie would be a big hit. She closed her eyes and rubbed her temples, trying to figure out what she should do. "But someone on this train could have been the one who murdered Alan."

"That's possible, and maybe we'll find out who did it before we get back to the station. We can mingle and listen in on conversations. We might get lucky and hear something that would help solve Alan's murder." Cullen used the large scoop inside the ice cooler and started shoveling chunks of ice over Alan's body.

Honey gave him a skeptical look. "I don't think anyone will come out and admit to murdering Alan."

Georgia helped scoop ice with her hands. "Someone may slip up and say something, or do something that will give them away. If we find the murderer, Sam would forget about how long it took us to contact the police. All of the guests will still be on board, and Sam can question everyone when we return to the station."

Cullen stopped scooping and looked at Honey. "Just think, if we hear something to help Sam, it would be a point in our favor."

Honey wasn't sold on their logic or lack thereof. "I know I don't watch crime shows like you do, Georgia, but aren't we disturbing a crime scene?"

"We didn't know we were dealing with a crime scene when I moved him. If someone left their DNA behind, it will still be on him." Cullen opened the door and peeked down the companionway. "No one is coming, so I think we should move the cooler."

"Good idea, Cullen. If someone walks in this compartment, they might get curious," Georgia replied.

"Honey, you need to go on back and tell Woodrow to start. Georgia and I will be there in a minute," Cullen said.

"I'm not going to leave you two here alone to handle this," Honey replied.

"Cullen is right. Someone is going to start looking for us," Georgia said.

"Then let's hurry." Honey wasn't totally behind the plan, but she didn't have a better one.

Cullen glanced from Honey to Georgia. "We can push the cooler out on the back platform. The door is kept closed, and no one will see it unless they walk onto the platform. I don't think anyone will go outside in this heat."

Honey closed her eyes and shook her head. "You think being out on the platform is safer than leaving him in this compartment?"

"I don't think the guests would walk through the kitchen to get there." Cullen closed the lid to the cooler.

Honey didn't know how she would make it through the evening knowing Alan was on board—dead. "I feel terrible doing this to Alan."

"Look at it this way, he's a lot cooler now. It has to be ninety degrees in this compartment," Georgia quipped.

"If Alan found me like this, he'd just toss my body off the train into that lake you were talking about," Cullen added lightly.

Honey didn't smile. She couldn't help but think of all the things that were going wrong on this outing. "Sam is going to be very angry with me."

"I think he will understand. We can't have the guests on the train knowing we have a dead body back here. Everyone would freak out," Georgia stated.

"Everyone but the murderer." Honey didn't think Sam would be very understanding, but it wasn't like they didn't intend to contact him. They just weren't going to call him right away. The guests would be inconvenienced at the station when they returned, but that couldn't be avoided. She thought of Eugenie and Jefferson Grayson. They'd most likely have a coronary if they were detained for questioning. "I think we should leave the cooler in the room." Honey's eyes darted from Cullen to Georgia. "That way we won't be doing more damage to a crime scene than we've already done."

Cullen and Georgia reluctantly agreed. When they left the room, they moved the empty ice cooler several compartments down.

"When will we cross the bridge?" Cullen asked.

Honey glanced out the window before she looked at her watch. She'd lost track of the time. "I think in about twenty minutes."

"Is that the bridge they call Bootlegger Bridge?" Cullen asked.

"It's not the official name, but the locals call it that. The old-time bootleggers used to meet customers at the shore under that bridge to sell moonshine. People would come by boat to buy their booze, trying to avoid the law."

On their way back through the car, Honey saw a compartment door opening near the front of the car. She stopped, turned to Georgia and Cullen, and placed her fingers to her lips. "Shhh." She waited to see who was coming out of the compartment. Troy Spencer walked out and closed the door behind him. He stood there for a moment glaring at the door. Raking his fingers though his hair in frustration, he quickly walked toward the adjoining car, unaware of the threesome watching him.

Once Troy was out of sight, Honey started moving. When she passed the compartment Troy exited, she noticed the door wasn't closed the entire way. While she couldn't see the person in the compartment, she recognized the lavender gown. Once again, Honey turned around to face Georgia and Cullen, holding her finger to her lips as she pointed to the compartment.

When they finally reached the first dining car, the waiters were serving a fresh round of drinks to the guests. Honey didn't think all of the bourbon on the train would help her forget that knife sticking out of Alan's back.

As if he read her thoughts, Cullen stopped a waiter and lifted three drinks from his tray. He handed one to Honey and one to Georgia before he gulped the contents of the third glass.

Before Honey had a chance to take a drink, Georgia yanked it from her hand and exchanged it for a handful of bourbon balls. "She needs chocolate, not alcohol."

Honey popped a bourbon ball in her mouth. "Cullen, go ahead with the tasting." Her gaze slid around the car until she spotted Woodrow. "I'll tell Woodrow you are handling everything."

Before she walked away, Georgia pulled her to a halt. "Honey, remember to smile, you know, look like you are having a good time."

Honey ate another bourbon ball. "You're right." She took a deep breath and attempted to smile. "I'm okay. You go find Preston and mingle while I tell Gramps that Cullen has everything under control."

"Do you think I should tell Preston about Alan?" Georgia whispered.

"No. The fewer people who know about this, the better."

After Cullen's presentation, the guests raved over Woodrow's Devil's Due Bourbon. And once the dinner came to an end, Honey realized that if it had been a normal night, she would have been glowing from all of the compliments from the guests. As it was, she was a nervous wreck and couldn't eat a bite. Georgia and Cullen were handling the situation much better than she was. The one thing she was thankful for was the air conditioning. The temperature remained fairly comfortable in the dining cars throughout dinner. The guests didn't seem to notice it wasn't as cool as when they started the ride. Perhaps they were enjoying their bourbon too much to notice the heat. By all accounts, the evening was a success, and everyone expressed their regrets that it had to come to an end.

When Honey was alone, Georgia and Cullen joined her. "I haven't heard a word that would incriminate anyone on this train," Georgia whispered.

Honey was disappointed that they had no information to aid Sam in his investigation. "I know. I've eavesdropped on a lot of conversations, but heard nothing that would help us. And I haven't seen one person who appears to be the least bit nervous."

"You're the only one who hasn't been smiling," Georgia told her. "But then I know you aren't the murderer."

Cullen gazed over the guests milling about. "If the killer is on this train, he or she is a very cool number."

Georgia leaned over a nearby table and snatched a bourbon ball from the serving tray. "At least the new bourbon and your bourbon balls are a great hit."

Honey thought that was little comfort knowing she was going to have to call Sam. Instead of having some clues to the identity of the murderer, all she had was one more dead body to report, and a lot of explaining to do.

"I know you're worried Sam is going to be mad at us, but I think he will understand," Georgia told her again.

"From your mouth to Sam's ears." Honey was dreading her phone call to Sam.

Georgia nudged Honey. "Shhh. Here comes your mother."

Lorraine smiled at Georgia and Cullen before she clutched Honey's arm. "Please excuse us a moment." She pulled Honey to a spot where they could talk without being overheard. "Honey, I know something is wrong. Out with it."

"Mom, believe me, it's best if I don't tell you," Honey replied.

"But this night has been such a success and I haven't seen you smile once."

Honey saw Woodrow walking their way, and she wanted to jump off the train. She'd never been good at keeping secrets from her family.

Woodrow gave them a wide smile. "It's been a wonderful evening, Honey. You planned the perfect event. I wonder why Alan missed the train."

Honey looked at her watch. They were less than thirty minutes from the station. She might as well tell them the truth, because it was time she contacted Sam. She looked around to see if anyone was close by that could overhear what she had to say. "Alan's dead."

"What? Why would you say something like that?" Woodrow asked.

"Oh no." Lorraine put her arm around Honey's shoulders. "You found another body, didn't you? That's why you've looked like you lost your last friend all evening."

Honey shook her head. "Afraid so."

"Oh, my poor dear," Lorraine whispered sympathetically.

"Are you saying you found Alan deceased on this train?" Woodrow asked.

"Yes. I need to call Sam."

"When did you find him? What happened to him?" Woodrow asked.

Honey explained what happened and Woodrow looked stunned. "Honey, you should have contacted the authorities right away."

"We didn't have cell service, and can you imagine what would have happened if we had to go back to the station to report a murder? The negative press would be horrendous."

Woodrow grimaced. "Honey, I'm not certain I understand your reasoning. And I can assure you, Hap is certainly not going to understand."

Honey felt like crying. It was the first time in her life that Woodrow sounded disappointed in her. "If I have cell service, I'll call Sam now. Honey pulled her cell phone from her small satin clutch. "This is my mess, and I'll take care of it."

CHAPTER EIGHTEEN

A S THE TRAIN APPROACHED THE station, Honey peered out the window and immediately spotted Sam and Hap standing on the platform. She thought Sam appeared cool and calm as he stood there with his hands in his pockets with the sleeves of his light blue shirt pushed up over his muscled forearms. *Appearances can be deceiving*, she reminded herself when she saw the set of his jaw. She thought once Mr. Bruckheimer got a look at Sam, he'd be on the phone trying to cast Tom Cruise as the handsome detective in his movie. Her eyes darted to the throng of people standing behind Sam. Reporters. They were surprisingly silent as they watched the train come to a halt. No doubt Sam had already been forced to deal with them.

Taking a deep breath, she felt like she was preparing to face a firing squad. Without offering an explanation, she'd asked the guests to remain seated when they arrived at the station. They would certainly be upset by the inconvenience, but considering what had happened to Alan, answering a few questions from the police seemed insignificant.

As if timed perfectly, the trained stopped right in front of Sam. Even though she expected him to be angry, she couldn't help but feel relieved to see him looking as competent as ever. It was exhausting trying to maintain a calm façade when she was worried there was a murderer on board the train over the entire evening. She'd welcome Sam taking control of the situation. Standing by the door when it opened, Sam was the first to jump on board.

"Did you tell everyone what happened?" he whispered in her ear.

"No, I just told everyone to stay seated when we arrived at the station." She had already told Sam on the phone what time they had found Alan. While he didn't comment about her delay in calling him right away, she knew he was angry.

Turning to face the people in the car, Sam politely apologized for the delay, explaining the police had some questions for them before they departed. Not once did he mention a dead body on the train. The reporters were shouting questions, but Hap was standing at the door preventing them from boarding the train. Sam asked Honey to follow him to each car as he gave the same explanation to all of the guests. Honey didn't know if it was his air of authority, but not one person voiced an objection. Sam stood directly in front of Eugenie and Jefferson when he told everyone to remain seated, as if he was daring them to say something contrary. When another officer took Hap's place keeping the reporters at bay, he boarded the train and started interviewing guests in the first car.

Once Sam and Honey reached the kitchen area, Sam told the train personnel not to leave the train. Turning to face Honey, he said, "Now show me where you found the body."

Honey led him to the small compartment in the last car. She opened the door, but before she could walk inside, Sam reached for her arm and held her back. "Stay here." He stuck his head inside and glanced around the tiny space. He turned to face her. "Wrong compartment."

Honey looked up and down the companionway. "No, this is the right compartment."

He opened the door the entire way and stepped inside. "Then where is he?"

Honey looked inside the compartment and to her surprise, it was empty—no cooler—no Alan. She pointed to the floor in front of the bench. "He was right there inside the cooler."

Sam shook his head as if he hadn't heard her correctly. "In what?"

"The cooler. We put him in a cooler." Honey hadn't mentioned that part on the phone.

Narrowing his eyes at her, Sam thought she might be in shock. "A cooler?"

Uncomfortable under his glare, Honey took a deep breath and nodded. "We talked about moving him, but we didn't."

"What in the devil do you mean, you talked about moving him?"

Honey stiffened her spine. "Don't yell at me."

This time it was Sam who took a deep breath, as he reminded himself not to lose his temper. "I'm not yelling at you. It must be over one hundred degrees in this car. I'm hot, I'm tired, it's late, and I'm not in the mood for games."

"This isn't a game. When we found him we didn't have cell service. The compartment was already hotter than blue blazes, and we thought we needed to do something. We thought he'd had a heart attack until we put him inside the cooler."

"You picked up a dead body and put him in a cooler?" Sam spoke louder than he intended.

"Don't yell." Honey had to admit now that she'd told him what they did with Alan, it sounded crazy to her. She couldn't blame Sam for being upset.

Sam braced his arm against the wall and rubbed his hand over his day-old stubble. "I guess you better start at the beginning."

Honey gave him the details from the time she boarded the train right up to the moment she called him. "That's what happened."

Sam hung his head, shaking it back and forth. "I can't believe it. Let me get this straight. You found a dead body, but instead of calling me, you put him inside a cooler, iced him down, discussed moving him, and you didn't worry about securing a crime scene, not to mention disturbing one?" He stared at her in disbelief. "Does that about cover it?"

"It wasn't the best decision I ever made," Honey admitted.

"That's the understatement of the year." He stared at her so long that Honey thought he didn't believe her. "Have you been drinking?" he finally asked.

"What? No. Well, yes. But I wasn't when we found Alan."

Sam rested his hand on his holster. "So three seemingly intelligent individuals made this decision stone-cold sober?" He didn't wait for her response. "Where did you discuss moving him?"

Honey pointed to the door at the back of the train. "We discussed pulling the cooler to the back platform."

"Of course you did. Let me see if I have this right. This compartment was getting too hot, but outside, with temps soaring well over one hundred degrees, a metal platform was going to be a lot cooler. Makes perfect sense to me."

"We did put him on ice," Honey mumbled.

"This just gets better and better." Sam turned, stalked from the compartment and walked down the corridor to the back of the car. Once he pulled the door open leading to the platform, he stood there for a moment trying to figure out if he was having some sort of a bad dream.

Honey walked up behind him. "Is he out there?"

Whipping around, he narrowed his eyes at her. "Honey, I don't know what's going on, but I don't have time for games."

"What are you talking about? I'm not playing a game!"

"Then where is this cooler that you supposedly stuffed Alan inside?"

Honey moved in front of him and looked at the empty platform. She turned back around to face Sam. "I don't know what happened to him. What would someone do with a cooler?"

"This is your story, you tell me."

"I don't know. Maybe Cullen or Georgia moved him for some reason."

Sam raised his brows in disbelief. "Uh-huh."

"I'm serious, Sam." She pointed to the compartment. "He was right there over three hours ago."

As much as he didn't want to believe her, he did. But believing her was only part of his problem. "Let's go."

"Go where?"

Sam took her by the elbow and escorted her to the front car, where Hap was interviewing Jefferson Grayson. He whispered something in Hap's ear, and Hap excused himself, telling Jefferson he would be back in a few minutes.

At Sam's signal, Hap followed him and Honey off the train so they could speak in private. Sam was grateful Officer Reed had the presence of mind to push the reporters back twenty feet from the platform. Once Sam briefed Hap on Honey's complete story, Hap stared at her with the same astonished expression Woodrow had given her. "Honey, what in the world have you done?"

Honey didn't have a response. She was exhausted from worrying, and all she wanted to do was go home, curl up with Elvis and have a good cry.

Sam inclined his head toward Honey. "Keep an eye on her, Hap. I'm going to get Georgia and Cullen, to see if they are telling the same story." Sam stepped back on the train. Spotting Georgia and Cullen, he motioned for them to come to the front of the train. They joined Hap and Honey on the platform. Sam gave them each a stern look. "Don't say one word."

Seeing no one was going to argue with him, he glanced at Hap. "Hap, I'm not in the mood to stand out here in the heat. If you want to go back and finish with those folks on the train, I'll put Honey in my car, Cullen in yours, and Georgia in Officer Reed's car. They won't be able to talk to each other, and we can finish the interviews on the train, where it's cooler, and get these people out of here."

Hap tossed him his keys. "Sounds good. Are we going to take these three to the station?" He hoped his question scared the daylights out of Honey.

"Yep. They can wait until we're finished here." Sam turned and reached for Honey's elbow. He was a step too late to stop one of the reporters from scurrying forward and shoving a microphone in his face. His photographer was snapping shots as fast as he could.

"Is it true there was another murder? Was he or she killed on the train?" the reporter shouted.

"No comment," Sam responded, putting his hand out to shield Honey from the photographer.

"We've heard rumors this has something to do with the Bluegrass mafia," the reporter stated. "Is there any truth to that?"

Sam kept walking, his jaw set like granite. When they made it to Sam's car, he opened the passenger door. "Because it's so hot, I'll leave it running. But I suggest you don't drive away. I'll post an officer out here so the reporters can't bother you."

"How did they hear about the murder so fast?" Honey asked.

"They monitor police scanner frequencies." Sam closed the door and walked back to the platform to get Cullen.

"This isn't Honey's fault. It was my idea," Cullen told him.

"Where did you leave Alan's body?" Sam asked.

"Didn't Honey tell you?"

Sam gave him a look that told him not to mess with him.

"We put him in a cooler and left him in the compartment."

Sam just shook his head. After he put Cullen in the back seat of Hap's cruiser, he started the engine, turned on the air, slammed the door, and walked away without another word.

Once Sam got Officer Reed's keys, he walked Georgia to his vehicle. Sam asked her the same question he'd ask Cullen. "What did you do with Alan's body?"

"We put him in the cooler, covered him with ice and left him in the compartment."

"You didn't go back with Cullen and move him?" Sam asked.

"No. We left him in the compartment." Georgia confirmed exactly what Honey and Cullen told him.

As crazy as their story sounded, Sam believed them. He walked back and boarded the train where Hap was waiting for him.

"Sam, I've called in three additional officers to help us out so we won't be here all night. Do you think we should tell the out-of-town folks not to leave town?"

"No, I'm certain the murderer is local. Let's just find out if any of them saw anything useful." Sam told Hap that Cullen and Georgia confirmed Honey's story about where they left Alan's body. "So now we have a missing victim."

"I have a feeling this is going to be one strange case," Hap groaned.

"You mind if I interview Eugenie Grayson?" Sam asked.

Hap slapped him on the back. "Nope. Have at her. Whether you interview her or not, she'll find something else to raise a ruckus about. Jefferson is already as mad as a wet rooster, so we might as well keep it in the family."

"I knew I liked you." For the first time tonight Sam found something to smile about.

The additional officers pulled up to the train fifteen minutes later, and Sam directed one man to the back car. "Don't let anyone on that platform, or in that last car." He then sent the other officers to find Alan's car in the parking lot. "Block off the entire lot. No reporters or photographers allowed."

By the time Sam finished with Eugenie Grayson, she was ready to chew through his badge, make sharp daggers from the metal and spit them at him. If she wasn't the one who killed two men, she was an excellent suspect considering her temper. After spending fifteen minutes with her, Sam was pleased with himself for not slapping handcuffs on her and dragging her to his car. It would have served Honey right to have to deal with an irate Eugenie.

After he allowed Eugenie to disembark, he moved on to interview Bunny Spencer. Problem was, no one realized Bunny had finished off a bottle of bourbon. She was so inebriated by the time Sam started asking questions he knew that it was a waste of his time trying to get information from her. He spent most of his time ignoring her flirting. Thankfully, she hadn't eaten the bourbon balls on her table, and Sam managed to eat them all. Since he hadn't had dinner, it filled the void. Ending Bunny's interview, he moved on to her husband.

After the interviews were complete, they released everyone on the train. Sam watched the passengers walk to their waiting limousines. Microphones and cameras were stuck in their faces as questions were shouted at them from the reporters who'd waited around. He figured the California guests were used to the attention because it didn't seem to faze them.

He learned from the interviews that no one had seen Alan at any time, either before or during the train ride. Only three people saw Alan that night, and he was already dead by then. Woodrow said that he had seen Alan's car in the parking lot when he arrived, but he hadn't seen Alan. Sam walked down the corridor searching for any clues as to the location of Alan's body. He entered the small compartment where Alan was supposedly killed. He saw nothing to indicate there had been a struggle in the limited space. Sam examined the bench closely, and he saw what he thought could be a drop of blood. He wondered if this murder had more in common with K.C.'s murder than a knife.

Fortunately for Honey and her partners in crime, the attendants who carried the coolers corroborated part of their story. Two hours later, Sam, Hap, and Officer Reed made it back to their vehicles to take the occupants to the station for questioning. Honey had reclined her seat and was sound asleep. She'd turned off the engine and opened the windows. Sam figured she was probably worried he would run out of gas since he'd been gone so long. Sam watched her for a minute before he started his car.

When he'd boarded the train tonight he'd seen the anxiety on her face, but she still looked beautiful in her blue gown and her long blonde hair pulled up in some sort of twist. He thought she was the most beautiful woman he'd ever seen. He didn't know what he was going to do. It was imperative for him to remain objective, and he couldn't allow his personal feelings to taint his investigation. Many times he'd seen attractive women who turned out to be murderers. After all, it was Honey who had found two bodies and she was connected to both men. He didn't think she was involved, but he had to work the facts, no matter his personal feelings. He'd told Woodrow he was taking Honey to the station and asked him to care for Elvis. Woodrow asked if he was going to arrest Honey and Sam was truthful. He hadn't made up his mind.

Having led Honey to an interrogation room, Sam left her there with a cup of coffee while he interviewed Georgia in another room. It was past two in the morning, and he wanted to go home, have something to eat, and get some much needed shut-eye. Or even better, he would turn the clock back twenty-four hours, and he would be holding Honey as she slept.

Having completed his interview with Georgia, he walked back to the room where Honey was waiting.

"Could I call Gramps and ask him to take care of Elvis?" Honey asked when Sam entered the room.

"Already taken care of."

"Thank you." Honey wanted to apologize for her terrible decisions tonight, but she didn't know where to begin. Plus, Sam didn't look like he was in a mood to listen.

"I need you to go over exactly what happened one more time," Sam instructed.

Honey took a deep breath before she repeated the events of the entire evening for the second time. "I swear to you, we left Alan in that compartment."

Sam still couldn't believe the decision she'd made to hide Alan. "Can you tell me exactly where you were when you found Alan?"

Honey looked puzzled. "We were on the train."

"But where? How long had you been traveling? Did you notice any landmarks? Can you tell me the exact time?"

"Oh." Honey was so tired that her thought processes seemed to be in slow motion. "I did notice that we hadn't reached the lake. We had probably been traveling about twenty minutes, or a little longer."

"Honey, did it occur to you that there could be a connection between K.C.'s and Alan's murders?"

"It did tonight when Georgia told Cullen being a master distiller didn't seem like a safe profession."

"Did you consider the possibility that Cullen was the one with something to gain if Alan was not in the picture? Didn't you tell me earlier that he handled Alan's presentation tonight?"

"Yes, but I certainly don't think Cullen is involved in either murder. He didn't even know K.C."

Sam stood. "I'm going to speak with Cullen now."

Honey wanted to ask him how much longer she would have to stay at the station, but considering his mood, she was afraid he might decide to keep her there indefinitely.

"I told you it was my idea to hide Alan. Why don't you let Honey and Georgia go home?" Cullen asked.

Sam wondered why Cullen was willing to take the blame for the multitude of bad decisions the three of them made together. Honey and Georgia had already told him that they discussed what to do with Alan. Sam decided it was time for *good cop–bad cop*. The mood he was in, there was no question which one he'd play. He'd send Hap in later to be the *good* cop. "I thought you were a smart guy, Cullen. Why would you make such a stupid mistake? Was it your intention to contaminate the crime scene since you were involved with the murder?"

"What?" Cullen leaned forward in his chair. "You think I was involved in Alan's murder?"

Sam leaned back in his chair and stared at Cullen. "Think about it from my perspective. You are now the master distiller of a major distillery. Even I know that's a coveted position to those in your industry."

"I see what you're saying, but I was going to have Alan's position anyway. The man wasn't quite right. I don't know if he had a drinking problem, but he was one miserable human being, and he was making everyone around him just as miserable. He'd had words with Woodrow, and I didn't think Woodrow was going to put up with him much longer. When we found Alan, the only thing I could think about was all of the long hours of planning Honey had put in to host the perfect evening. There was nothing we could do for Alan, and the bad press would have been terrible for her family and the distillery." He shrugged, sat back in his chair and crossed his arms over his chest. "It seemed like the best decision at the time. I thought Alan had a heart attack, and I would do the same thing again. Alan was a pain in the butt anyway. No one is going to miss that jerk."

"You think he deserved what he got?"

"Yeah, I do. In my opinion, whoever killed him did the world a favor."

Sam didn't know if it was intentional, but Cullen seemed to want to be at the top of his list of suspects. *Is he doing it for Honey?* "Why would you risk your freedom for Honey?" Sam immediately wished he could withdraw that question. It was personal.

"If you're asking if I would do just about anything to protect Honey, the answer is yes. She a great gal, and I owe Woodrow for giving me a chance to work for him." He met Sam's eyes, then added, "I know you two have dated, but that doesn't mean I wouldn't jump at the chance if she showed the least bit of interest."

Sam appreciated Cullen's honesty. His gut told him Cullen wasn't involved in murder, but that didn't mean he could ignore that the three of them had broken several laws. "Why do you think Alan was a drinker?"

"The man's mood was all over the place. He would just up and leave the distillery during working hours, not say when he was returning, or if he was going to return. He snapped at everyone over the slightest thing.

He didn't even want workers going into the warehouses without him to do their jobs. Considering his position, he was very unprofessional. Something was definitely going on with him."

"Do you know of anyone who had a problem with Alan?"

Cullen shrugged. "Take your choice. No one liked him. He may have been good at his job at some point in time, but that time had long past."

"Can you be more specific? Besides you, who had a problem with Alan?"

"Woodrow for one. Everyone in the office heard Alan yelling at him. He left Woodrow's office one day in a huff and said something along the lines of, 'You're going to regret this.'"

This was news to Sam. "Did Woodrow say what the argument was about?"

"No, but I didn't ask. Alan had never forgiven Woodrow for hiring me. I just figured he was still complaining over that."

This was the first tidbit of information Sam hadn't heard. "So Alan disagreed with Woodrow over hiring you?"

"Alan let everyone know he didn't want me there. He made a few nasty comments to me and I put up with it for a few weeks. When I finally told him to face me like a man and stop acting like a whining little girl, he shut up. At least he stopped making snide comments to me. But I imagine he continued to complain to Woodrow."

"Why was he so angry you were hired? Wasn't he past retirement age?" Sam asked.

Cullen shook his head and shrugged. "That's what I didn't understand. He was Woodrow's age, and Woodrow is in much better shape—mentally and physically. Alan obviously wasn't happy working, so it didn't make sense that he didn't just retire."

"Did you go back into that compartment and move that cooler?"

Cullen remained silent for a few minutes.

Sam asked the question again.

"What if I told you I did? Would you let Honey and Georgia go home?"

Sam stared hard at him for a minute. "I'd think about it, but I'm not making promises. I want the truth."

"Okay. Yeah, I did. While Honey was talking to Woodrow, I hurried back to the cabin and moved him to the platform."

"Why?"

"I didn't want anyone to find him, and the back platform seemed like the best place to hide him."

Sam wasn't sure he believed him. But, then again, who would make up this story? He stood and walked to the door. "You're free to go."

"What about Honey and Georgia?"

Sam liked the fact that Cullen wasn't the kind of guy who only worried about his own hide. "I've released Georgia. I think she's still here waiting on Honey."

"Are you going to release Honey?"

"I still have a few more questions for her." Sam opened the door, motioning for Cullen to precede him. "I'm not saying charges won't be pressed against the three of you for obstructing an investigation. I don't need to tell you not to leave town."

"I've no intention of leaving Kentucky. I'm going to wait with Georgia until Honey can leave."

"That might be a while."

"I'll wait," Cullen replied and walked away.

CHAPTER NINETEEN

O PENING THE DOOR TO THE interrogation room, Sam thought Honey looked miserable. The room was so cold that she was shivering. Instead of walking inside, he went to his office and grabbed his jacket. When he returned to the room, he placed his jacket around her shoulders.

Honey gave him a slight smile as she burrowed in the warmth of his jacket, noticing it smelled good, like the man who wore it. "Thank you."

Sam took a seat across from her. "Why didn't you tell me Alan didn't want Cullen around?"

"I didn't think about it. Alan was protective of his position."

"Cullen says Alan was very upset with Woodrow for hiring him."

"Yes, he was. But Alan's mood was the same everyday—rotten. I heard him yelling at Woodrow one day."

"Was it about Cullen?"

"I don't know, but I assumed it was. When I first moved back, Gramps said Alan was always complaining about something."

"Why did Woodrow put up with him?"

"He'd known Alan a long time, and he was hoping he would retire soon. Gramps is a loyal person."

Sam made a few notes, but he was actually buying time to decide what he was going to do with her. He decided he would talk to Hap and ask him what he thought they should do with the three of them. He stepped toward the door, but he made the mistake of looking into Honey's big green eyes.

"Are you going to arrest me?" she asked.

"I'm thinking about it." He leaned his hip against the table next to her. "What would you do if you were me?"

"I don't know. Thankfully, I'm not you. I don't like this murder business. I understand you need to do what's right."

That was one of the many things Sam liked about her. She was honest. He leaned over, cupped her chin and kissed her. When he pulled back, he said, "I don't think I'm an objective interviewer." He stood and opened the door, and that's when he heard a loud, mournful howl.

He turned back to Honey and they both said simultaneously, "Elvis?"

Sam stepped from the interview room to see Elvis charging full speed down the hallway. He zoomed past Sam and didn't stop until he had two paws and his big head resting on top of Honey's lap. Woodrow was scurrying down the hallway trying to keep up with the determined bloodhound.

"Sam, I'm sorry, but I had to bring him down here. He wouldn't settle down at home, and I couldn't take the howling anymore." Both men watched from the doorway as Honey assured Elvis that she was fine. "I can't explain it Sam, but Elvis has always been very protective of her."

Touched by the bond between Honey and Elvis, Sam couldn't fault Woodrow for bringing him to the station. "No problem. I want to ask you a few questions anyway." Sam led Woodrow to the room Cullen had vacated. "Wait for me in here." Sam walked away and straight into Hap's office. After he explained his conflict of interest when it came to Honey, he said, "You need to make this decision."

Hap chuckled. "I think you got it bad, son." He jumped to his feet. "In all fairness, the three of them truly believed Alan died of a heart attack before they moved him. You go talk to Woodrow and I'll talk to Honey. I heard Elvis wailing, and I was thinking if Honey wants to assist in this investigation, she might lend us that dog. We might be more forgiving of any misdeeds on her part if Elvis helps us find Alan's body."

"I was thinking about asking her if I could take Elvis with me to search for Alan tomorrow." Sam looked at his watch. "I mean this morning. All three of them said they'd been on the train about twenty minutes before they found Alan. I have a hunch someone pushed that cooler off the train somewhere over the lake."

Hap whistled. "That's some dense territory and dangerous cliffs out there."

"I know, I've already looked around out there one day when I was at the Tucker farm," Sam replied.

"Elvis would be a big help, and I'll see if I can get the state police to lend us a hand if we need it. Let's get this show on the road so we can all get some sleep tonight."

Woodrow answered all of Sam's questions before asking one of his own. "What are you going to do with Honey?"

"I'm leaving that up to Hap. I don't think I can be neutral when it comes to Honey. What they did was wrong, but if I can solve this crime, and they stay out of my way in the future, it'd be a big help."

"I understand. They certainly didn't use good judgment. I know Honey didn't want to ruin the evening for me, but that shouldn't have been her first consideration."

"Honey did make an attempt to call me, but she didn't have cell service. Cullen and Georgia suggested they wait to call until after the train returned to the station."

"She went along with them." Woodrow couldn't hide the disappointment in his voice.

Hap walked into the room and asked Sam to step outside. He told Sam he'd had a talk with Honey and he made the decision to release her. "I don't think she'll do anything else to involve herself in this investigation."

"Thanks, Hap." Sam opened the door, and told Woodrow that Hap wasn't pressing any charges. "Woodrow, go on home. I'll drive the threesome to get their cars at the train station."

"Thanks, Sam, but Preston is waiting out front to take Georgia home. I can drive Honey and Cullen to their cars."

"I appreciate that, but I'm going to take Honey home to have a look around. I didn't like that note left on her patio, and I want to make sure no one is on the property."

Woodrow shook his hand. "Thank you for looking out for my granddaughter."

Honey sat quietly in the front seat beside Sam, with Elvis in the back seat. Preston had offered to take Cullen to his car and Sam agreed. He didn't want to drive Honey all the way to the train station. "It's been a long night, and I thought we'd pick your car up in the morning."

Honey didn't object and they drove to the cottage in silence. When they arrived, Sam opened the door for her and turned on the lights. She was tired, but she didn't want to be alone just yet. "Would you like some coffee?"

"I'm going to have a look around outside first. Come on, Elvis, you can go with me." They walked around the cottage and Sam watched Elvis do a lot of investigating before he did his business. When Elvis ran to Sam's side, he gave him a pat on his back. "Ready to go inside?"

Honey handed Sam a cup of coffee and Elvis a treat when they walked through the door. "I'm really sorry, Sam."

Sam set his cup on the counter and pulled her into his arms. "I know." He leaned down and kissed her.

When the kiss ended, Honey rested her head on his chest. "Sam, what did that reporter mean about the Bluegrass mafia?"

Sam chuckled. "I have no idea. I guess they think these murders are drug related."

"Drugs? I don't know about Alan, but K.C. wouldn't have been involved with drugs."

"It's not about drugs."

Honey looked up at him and thought he looked too exhausted to talk more tonight. "You're welcome to stay here tonight."

"Thanks, I was planning to ask you if I could stay." He gave her an irreverent grin. "Does that mean I can sleep in your bedroom?"

Honey laughed. "And here I thought you were too tired to talk."

"Who said anything about talking?"

Honey left his arms and smiled at him as she walked away. "The toothbrush you used the other morning is in the first drawer on the left in the bathroom—the bathroom in the extra bedroom. The disposable razors are in the second drawer on the left."

Sam looked at Elvis and shrugged. "Buddy, I guess that's a *no*."

A few hours later, Sam heard someone knocking on the front door. Still groggy, he jumped from bed, but it took him a moment to remember he was sleeping in Honey's extra bedroom. He pulled on his pants, tossed his T-shirt over his shoulder, and automatically reached for his pistol on the nightstand before he headed to the front door. Hurrying through the door, he collided with Honey in the hallway. He reached out and clutched her shoulders to keep her from hitting the wall. He thought she must be as groggy as he was, because she looked surprised to see him in her house. His gaze swept over her from head to toe, and he grinned when he saw what she was wearing. "Morning."

The persistent knocking came again, and Sam forced his eyes from her tiny, silky pink robe and dropped his hands from her shoulders. "I'll get it."

Honey followed closely behind Sam and when they reached the foyer, Elvis was sitting by the door patiently waiting for them. Since he wasn't barking, Sam figured he knew the person on the other side. When Sam pulled the door open, he came face to face with Woodrow and Lorraine. Their eyes darted from Sam to Honey without saying a word.

Sam realized how the scene must look to them. There he was in Honey's home early in the morning, wearing nothing but his jeans, and he hadn't even buttoned them. He was just thankful he'd hadn't answered the door in his boxers. To make matters worse, Honey was standing beside him wearing her sexy little number. A real cozy little scene. Sam's next thought was he wished it was Chance on the other side of that door. It would do his heart good for Chance to see him barefoot and shirtless standing beside Honey in her nightclothes. On second thought, that would mean Chance would see Honey looking so delectable. No way.

"Come on in." Honey motioned them inside and Sam closed the door. She glanced Sam's way and he rolled his eyes. Honey's gaze drifted to his chest, his extremely hard, muscled chest, and she momentarily forgot to move. But it wasn't his muscles that held her attention, it was the scar on his chest. He'd been shot. Moments ticked by before she realized no one had moved, and her mother was glaring at her. Quickly coming to her senses, she turned toward the kitchen. "Come on in the kitchen. I'll make us some coffee."

Woodrow was carrying a folded newspaper, which he slapped against Sam's bare midsection as he passed him. "You might find this interesting."

Lorraine gave Sam the evil eye when she walked past him, but didn't say a word.

"This isn't what it looks like," Sam mumbled. "I spent the night in Honey's *extra* bedroom."

Woodrow didn't crack a smile. "Just so you know, we still fight duels in Kentucky."

"Really?" Sam clutched the newspaper and trailed Woodrow to the kitchen, trying to decide if he was teasing. "Dueling is illegal in most states."

"Plenty of places in Kentucky to hide the evidence. We have twenty-six million acres and less than four and a half million people in the entire state. Do the math," Woodrow countered somberly.

Sam was mentally calculating how many acres per person. Coming up with the answer, he understood why some victims were never found. "But I slept in the other bedroom," he repeated.

Lorraine finally turned to him and smiled. "I'm glad to hear that you slept in the extra bedroom. If not, you weren't going to get any coffee cake." She placed the box she was carrying on the counter. When she opened the lid, Sam leaned over her shoulder to see some sort of gooey confection.

"Hmm. That looks really good," Sam told her, and placed the forgotten newspaper on the counter.

"Coffee will be ready in a minute." Honey glanced at Sam, who was leaning over the counter with his back to her. She saw another scar near his shoulder. He'd told her he'd been shot more than once.

Sam turned around and placed his gun on top of the refrigerator. After he pulled on his T-shirt, he reached for some coffee cups from the cabinet. He leaned over and whispered in Honey's ear. "Morning, Honey."

"Good morning. How did you sleep?" She said it loudly enough so there would be no question Sam had slept in the extra bedroom. After the night she'd had, the last thing she needed was for her family to see a half-naked Sam walking around the cottage first thing this morning.

First, finding dead bodies at every turn, and now the investigating officer was sleeping in her home. They probably thought she was a lost cause.

"That's the best two hours of sleep I've had in days," Sam responded, covertly checking out her itsy-bitsy robe that barely covered her rear end. He needed to stop thinking about her legs, so he walked to the patio door and let Elvis out for his morning sniffathon. While Elvis was outside, Sam pulled his canister of food from the pantry, filled his bowl to the brim, and put fresh water in his water bowl.

"Thank you." Honey liked the way he thought about Elvis first. Although she imagined her family thought Sam looked very comfortable performing the morning tasks, as if he'd done it many times before.

While the coffee brewed, Honey handed her mother a knife and set some plates on the counter. "What brings you two here so early?" As if she didn't know. She had a feeling they were there to voice their opinion about her actions last night.

Woodrow unfolded the newspaper on the counter and slid it toward her. "I thought you might want to see this."

Side by side, Honey and Sam leaned over the counter and looked at the front page. Sam and Honey's photograph covered the entire page. There was no question the photograph was taken last night when the train returned to the station. Honey was in her blue gown and Sam was escorting her to his car. From the angle the photographer had captured them, it looked as though Sam was pulling her along unwillingly. The headline read: *Murder On The Bluegrass Bourbon Train: Bourbon Heir Beauty Hauled to the Slammer.* The article mentioned that it was Honey who had found both bodies. The writer went on to hypothesize that she had to be the number-one suspect of renowned detective Sam Gentry. And it didn't end there. He went on to say the town's newest detective had a conflict of interest when it came to beautiful Honey Howell. *But what this reporter finds strange and out of bounds of professional behavior for the police department is that said lead detective handling the investigation, Sam Gentry, didn't arrest her, but took her home. And as of early this morning, that same detective had not departed Woodrow Howell's estate.*

"Great," Honey mumbled morosely. "Now everyone will think I'm a murderer and a loose woman."

"Nonsense. Anyone who knows you will know this reporter is nuts," Woodrow contended.

Sam looked at Woodrow. "I see they've quoted Eugenie and Jefferson Grayson. When they left the train, they didn't even know a murder had been committed, unless they were the ones who killed Alan. I didn't tell anyone why I was questioning them."

"The fellow who wrote the article is their nephew," Lorraine explained.

"What is Hap going to say about this?" Honey was concerned about Sam's career.

"Hap and I have already discussed our relationship." Sam walked to the coffeepot, picked up the carafe and filled their cups.

Honey stared at him. He'd talked to Hap about her. Under different circumstances, she might have smiled. "What did you say to Hap?"

Sam turned his glittering blue eyes on her. "I told him I was biased when it came to you." He took a sip of his coffee and stared at her over the rim of his cup, wishing he was alone with her. He envisioned backing her to the counter and kissing her lips, her neck, anywhere he found skin. He shook his head to clear his thoughts. He was a goner and he knew it. He finally turned toward Lorraine. "Now, can I have some of that coffee cake?"

"With an answer like that, you deserve a big slice." Lorraine placed a huge piece of the coffee cake on a plate and handed it to him. "Thank you for not arresting my daughter."

Sam grinned at her. "It was a close call." He thought he needed to explain his overnight stay to Honey's mother. "I didn't want Honey to stay alone since she found that note on her patio. She was kind enough to offer me the extra bedroom."

"You are welcome to stay in her *extra* bedroom until you find the person responsible for these murders," Lorraine told him.

"Yes, ma'am." Sam was pleased he had her approval to do what he was going to do anyway.

This time it was Honey who rolled her eyes. She thought both her mother and Woodrow were treating her like a teenager.

"Sam, what do you think happened to Alan's body?" Woodrow asked.

"I think someone pushed that cooler off the back of the train. I was going to ask Honey if I could take Elvis today. I expect I'm going to be searching a large area." Sam wolfed down his cake and held out his plate to Lorraine for a second slice.

Honey noticed how much he was eating. "Sam, did you have dinner last night? Would you like some eggs?"

"I don't have time. I need to get on the road. I did have some delicious bourbon balls on the train last night while I wasted my time interviewing Bunny."

"Bunny drank a whole bottle of bourbon last night," Lorraine said.

"I noticed," Sam replied. He cocked his head at Honey. "Today is Sunday, isn't it?"

Honey nodded.

"Good. I guess you'll be hanging around here all day."

Honey wondered if he was telling her to stay home so she would stay out of trouble. "Are you telling me not to leave town?"

"Nope. I'm telling you not to leave your house," Sam responded, but he was grinning.

"I wasn't planning on it. I'm through investigating, if that's your next question. And you're welcome to take Elvis with you."

Lorraine patted Sam on the arm. "Rest easy, Sam. I don't think she'll want to go anywhere since reporters are at the front gate ready to pounce on her. Georgia is at our house with Preston, so I'll be spending the day here."

Honey groaned. "I can't believe reporters are at the gate." She glanced at Sam. "Can't you arrest them for something?"

"I'd like to arrest them for being a nuisance," Sam retorted.

"I need to get my Jeep sometime today," Honey said.

"We'll wait until the reporters leave and I'll drive you," Lorraine responded.

"Is there anything we can help you with, Sam?" Woodrow asked.

"If we don't find Alan's body in a couple of days, I might be asking for everyone's help." Sam left the kitchen to finish dressing with Elvis by his side.

Honey refilled Sam's coffee cup and carried it to his bedroom. She stuck her head inside the open door and she heard his voice coming from the bathroom. She thought Elvis must be in the bathroom with him.

"Sam, I brought you a fresh cup of coffee," she called out.

"Come on in the bathroom," Sam replied. "Ouch!"

When she walked to the bathroom door, she almost laughed aloud at the scene in front of her. Sam was standing in front of the mirror, shirtless again, his face covered in shaving cream, and a pink disposable razor was in his hand. A bright red spot was slowly making a trail down his frothy white cheek. Elvis was sitting next to him watching intently.

Seeing her in the mirror, Sam held the razor in the air. "How do women use these? My beard is laughing at this thing."

Honey shook her head at him. "Who's winning?"

"Not me," he grumbled.

"Here's some fresh coffee for you. I think you're going to need it." Honey set the cup on the counter in front of him. When she turned to leave the room, he reached for her.

Sam laid his razor on the counter, pulled her to him, and wrapped his arms around her. He didn't say a word, he just lowered his lips to hers. Feeling that silky robe under his hands nearly drove him to distraction. He pulled his lips from hers and whispered in her ear. "Do you always wear pretty stuff like this to bed?"

Honey smiled up at him. "Sometimes I wear a T-shirt."

"You can wear my T-shirt anytime."

"Before or after you wash off your shaving cream?"

Sam grinned, picked up a towel and wiped the shaving cream from her face.

After Sam said good-bye to Lorraine and Woodrow, Honey walked him and Elvis to the door. He leaned close to her ear and nibbled. "We'll see you later. I don't know what time it will be."

"If you're late, I'll keep dinner warm for you." She thought that was the least she could do after what she'd put him through last night. If not for her bad judgment, he might have had a good night's sleep.

"A promise like that will make me get back as early as possible." If she hadn't changed out of that little robe, he might not have left in the first place.

Honey handed him a small plastic bag filled with treats. "These are for Elvis. He likes to be rewarded when he's done a good job. And don't forget to make sure he has water. He drinks a lot."

Sam nodded. "I won't forget." Hearing a car coming up the driveway, Sam recognized Chance's black Hummer. He pulled Honey to him and kissed her. He made certain the kiss was long so Chance would get a good look.

When he released her, she whispered breathlessly, "I think you made your point."

Sam winked at her. "Mission accomplished. See you later, darlin'." He glanced down at Elvis. "Let's go to work, buddy."

Elvis looked at Honey.

"I'll be okay. Mom and Gramps will be here with me. Go with Sam." Honey kissed the top of Elvis's head. "Go show them how smart you are." She glanced back up at Sam. "You might want to remove the tissue from your face so you look more intimidating."

Sam laughed, but he pulled the tissue from the razor cuts on his face. Instead of walking to his car, he waited for Chance to get out of his vehicle. "I've been wanting to talk to you."

"What about?" Chance asked.

Sam told him about the note on Honey's patio, and asked if he'd seen anything suspicious while he was working. Chance hadn't seen anything unusual that he could recall, but he'd left early that day because he had a call that was urgent.

"Mind telling me who called you?" Sam asked.

Chance didn't hesitate to tell him. "It was Bunny Spencer. She was insistent that I install a gate on her property immediately. I met some of my men out there to get started on it."

CHAPTER TWENTY

S AM AND ELVIS WERE ON the way to Alan's home when his cell phone rang. "Yeah?"

"Sam, you need to come to Alan's home," Hap told him.

"Elvis and I are on the way right now. I wanted to get one of Alan's shirts to give Elvis a good scent."

"Good. You're not going to believe what we found."

"We're around the corner now." Sam clicked off and seconds later, he stopped in front of Alan's house. They walked inside and found Hap and Officer Reed searching the home.

"Follow me." Hap led the way to the bedroom at the back of the house.

Reaching the master bedroom, Hap pointed to the bed. "Take a look at that."

The top of the bed was covered with open briefcases with stacks of money in each one. Sam walked to a briefcase and looked at the bills inside. "Looks like Alan was involved in something nefarious."

Hap shook his head. "It does give one that impression, unless Alan had an aversion to banks. Money is stashed all over the place. So far, we've counted a little over three hundred thousand."

"You're kidding. And the man didn't want to retire?"

Hap shrugged and picked up a stack of bills. "We need to find out where all of this money came from."

"More in here, Chief," Reed called out from another bedroom.

Hap, Sam, and Elvis walked to the bedroom where Reed was pulling briefcases from beneath the bed. They found more cash inside six briefcases.

Hap glanced at Sam. "If Alan was an accountant, I would say he was embezzling."

"He won't be spending all of this cash now. What exactly do we know about Alan Snyder?" Sam asked.

"He's lived here all his life, and he worked for Woodrow forever. Never married as far as I know. He wasn't a friendly guy. Can't say I know more than that," Hap replied.

"I guess we better start looking into his background. But right now Elvis and I are going to look for his body." Sam walked back to the master bedroom and found one of Alan's shirts thrown over a chair.

"I'm going to follow you out there. I've asked the conductor if he can take us out to the spot where you think we should start looking," Hap said.

"Great idea. That might save us some walking. I don't know about you, but Elvis and I didn't get much sleep last night."

Hap followed Sam out the door. "Yeah, I understand you were at Honey's all night."

Sam shook his head. "Do you believe everything you read in the papers?"

Hap chuckled. "In this instance, I might."

"Did you see that photograph on the front page? It looked like I was dragging Honey across the parking lot." Sam didn't like the way the photo made it appear as though he was manhandling a citizen.

Hap shook his head in disgust. "I saw it. I'd like to strangle that little twerp reporter, but I'd just give him more to talk about."

"They want murders solved, but if we interview certain wealthy citizens, then we are accused of harassing the public. If we don't do anything, then we aren't doing our job," Sam muttered.

"Don't worry about it. I learned a long time ago the general public understands what's going on. People with nothing to worry about don't mind being interviewed."

"Woodrow brought the paper to Honey's this morning. I'm not certain, but I think he was about to challenge me to a duel," Sam said.

Hap jabbed Sam on the shoulder before he jumped in his cruiser. "I doubt it was that photograph that bothered Woodrow. But I can guarantee you that no man has stayed in that cottage with Honey before."

Sam arched his brow. "Really?"

"I'd bet my life on it. Everyone in a small town knows everyone's business."

Sam found himself smiling. It was nice to know that no man had spent the night with Honey—not even in her extra bedroom.

"Before you go getting a big head, you should know that I've shot skeet with Woodrow and he's a fine shot."

"Duels are illegal in Kentucky, aren't they?" Sam asked.

Sam and Hap pulled their hiking boots out of their trunks when they reached the train station. The conductor told Sam they would reach the lake in forty-five minutes. Sam and Hap made plans to disembark before they reached the bridge. Once the train started rolling, Sam removed Elvis's leash and held Alan's shirt to him. Elvis buried his nose in the cloth, then sniffed the air.

"I've been told bloodhounds can pick up scents in the air as good as they can on the ground," Hap told Sam.

"Honey told me Elvis has been trained in tracking, trailing, human remains detection, and evidence identification. He led me through Woodrow's property the other night and it was all I could do to keep up with him."

"Yeah, Elvis is one special dog."

Nose to the floor of the train, Elvis moved through the car without stopping until he made it to the last car and the exact compartment where Honey said they found Alan. Elvis sat in front of the doorway, alerting Sam. Sam ruffled his ears when he reached him. "Good boy." Sam opened the compartment door to let Elvis inside.

"I need to put him on the payroll," Hap joked.

After sniffing every inch of the compartment, Elvis walked out the door and headed to the end of the car. Before Sam opened the door to the platform, he attached Elvis's leash to his collar. Once they walked onto the platform, Elvis sniffed around and sat down.

Sam stroked Elvis's head and reached in his pocket for the bag of treats Honey had given him. He held a treat to Elvis and praised him by saying, "I'm keeping you as my partner, Elvis."

Joining them on the platform, Hap glanced at his watch. "I guess we have some time before we reach the lake."

"Yeah. Honey told me after they found Alan, she thought they reached the lake about twenty minutes later. She remembered looking at her watch when the bridge came into view because she wanted to point it out to some guests who had expressed an interest in seeing it."

"Yeah, Bootleggers Bridge was a real hot spot in the old days." Hap looked over the landscape. "Well, it's a nice morning for a train ride, but we're going to be facing some steep cliffs as we get closer to the bridge."

"Hopefully, Elvis will catch a scent and that will be our signal to stop the train."

Standing on the platform looking over the steep terrain, they discussed the money found in Alan's home. All they could do was speculate on the reasons Alan had so much cash, since they didn't see anything in the home to indicate he was involved in drugs or some other illegal activity. Sam knew he had a lot more hours of investigating to do before he had all of the answers.

"I haven't put all of the pieces together, but with Alan's murder, I'm convinced this has something to do with the distillery business," Sam theorized.

"Is it possible someone wants us to think they are related? Maybe by killing two people in the same industry, the murderer is making an effort to throw us off the scent, so to speak. Maybe Adam was murdered to cover up the real reason for the first murder."

"I don't think so," Sam replied.

"Is Cleary Distillery doing well financially? Who benefited from K.C.'s death?"

Sam had spent several hours investigating Cleary's Distillery. "Their business is booming, and very healthy financially. K.C. and his brother seemed to excel in business. K.C.'s mother was his beneficiary and she inherited his half of the distillery."

"Hmm." Hap considered all of the reasons people committed murder. "And no problems between brothers?"

"None that I've uncovered. I know K.C. was ten years younger than his brother, but from all accounts they got along well."

"So if there's nothing to suggest it has something to do with Cleary's Distillery, what's your theory?" Hap asked.

"I know what you're thinking. The three possible motives at the heart of every murder: financial, sexual or power."

Hap nodded. "That's been my experience."

"Agree. Well, I'm confident Eugenie Grayson was having an affair with K.C."

Hap let out a low whistle. "That would make for some interesting headlines if it became public. Do you think she killed him, or had something to do with his murder?"

"I think they had an affair for a while, but were fairly discreet. I've interviewed two people who saw K.C. and Eugenie together out of town, which contradicts Eugenie's portrayal of her relationship with K.C. Once I checked into their travel schedules, I found that they were out of town at the same time on too many occasions for it to be a coincidence."

Hap looked at him expectantly. "Always the same destinations?"

"Yep."

"And?" Hap asked, knowing Sam was too good a detective not to have more information.

"And, I think K.C. wanted to break it off with Eugenie because of Honey."

Hap frowned. "What does this have to do with Honey?"

"K.C.'s mother thinks he was serious about Honey, and when he found out she was moving back, he started breaking off his relationships with every woman he was dating. I think he met Eugenie out at the Tucker farm to end their affair. I doubt that conversation went well with Eugenie. I think she became enraged that he was breaking it off and she rammed his car. Having spoken to Eugenie a few times, I'd say it's a good bet she probably threatened K.C. in some way." Sam hesitated a minute, then added, "But I don't believe she killed him."

"Why do you think he wanted to meet her at the Tucker farm?" Hap asked.

"I think that's where they met for their sexual encounters, and K.C. wanted to make certain they would have complete privacy. You know how Eugenie gets angry if something isn't going her way. I bet K.C. thought she'd create a scene if he met her in a restaurant."

Hap laughed at the thought. "You pegged her right. Eugenie doesn't like to be told *no*. Are you sure she was the one who hit his car?"

"I'm sure."

Hap asked the all-important question. "Can you prove it?"

"Yes, I can."

"I reckon a woman with that kind of anger could commit murder, and you've just provided the reason to put her at the top of our suspect list. Sexual. Yet you don't think she killed K.C."

"Eugenie Grayson likes to be treated like a queen. She wouldn't do anything to jeopardize the lifestyle she loves. But let's say she did kill K.C. in a rage. Why would she kill Alan?" Sam asked.

"That would lead us back to a murderer trying to throw us off the scent. Could be a cover-up murder, or maybe the murders aren't related." Hap grew quiet for a moment, then asked, "What if her husband found out about their affair?"

Sam looked at Hap and grinned. "You think Jefferson Grayson would commit murder?"

Hap shrugged. "Not under normal circumstances, but even a man with Jefferson's wealth and status could do things out of his nature if he found out he was being cuckolded."

"I can't argue that point." Sam had often been surprised by people who committed murder. He could never figure out why they didn't just walk away. Anger mixed with pride made men do some really stupid things. "Did you know Jefferson and Eugenie own a racehorse named K.C.'s Conquest? I guess Jefferson could have figured out his wife was messing around with K. C.—the man, not the horse," he clarified.

Hap chuckled. "You're kidding? They actually own a racehorse named for K.C.?"

"I guess you don't keep up with horse racing, but that horse is expected to be a Derby contender."

Hap raised his wrinkled brow. "Interesting."

The train slowed, telling Sam they were getting close to the bridge. Pulling his cell phone out, he checked to see if he had service.

"I hope Elvis is on the scent because we need to stop now unless we want to jump off a cliff." Hap pointed to the bridge. "There's Bootlegger's Bridge coming into view."

Sam glanced down at the landscape surrounding the train, he could see the cliffs ahead. If they didn't stop soon, Sam worried they'd be forced to rappel down to the lake.

Suddenly, Elvis lurched to his feet, sniffed the air and let out a bark.

Sam smiled. "I guess this is where we get off."

Hap had instructed Office Reed to have a boat at the shore by the bridge. "The boat should be below the bridge soon." Hap radioed the conductor to stop the train.

Sam jumped off first, followed by Elvis, then Hap.

Elvis was on the scent as soon as his paws hit the ground. Elvis backtracked several minutes before he turned to the cliffs. They slowly made their way toward the cliffs with Sam keeping a tight hold on Elvis's leash. On the way down the steep incline they looked for anything out of place on the landscape.

"Before Elvis backtracked, I noticed an area where we could get down to the shore easier," Hap suggested.

Sam nodded. "That's where Elvis is headed, so let's take the easy way."

They made it to the area Hap indicated and slowly made their way to the lake's edge. They walked along the bank until they were beneath the tracks where the train crossed the lake. Elvis turned around to look down the lake.

Sam and Hap turned to see what held Elvis's attention. A boat came around the bend carrying three officers in diving gear. Hap waved them to the bank, where they boarded and rode under the bridge, headed across the lake. Nearly halfway across, Elvis walked to the starboard side of the boat and barked.

Sam was watching Elvis and when he reacted, he rubbed his back. "Good boy." He looked overhead at the bridge. "I guess this is where they pushed Alan off."

Hap looked up. "Easy enough to do. It's an old track without any barriers on the sides."

"They put Alan in a long aluminum cooler with a latch. At the height of that bridge, I doubt it's still intact. What do you think?" Sam asked.

"Yeah. I'd say it opened when it hit the water, if not before, and the current could have carried the body and the cooler some distance," Hap replied.

One of the divers sat down beside Sam and Hap. "Are you sure this dog can pick up scents under water?"

"Yes, he can. I've seen him do it," Hap answered.

The divers went into the water. To Sam and Hap it seemed as if the they were under water a long time before they surfaced. When they did return to the boat they said the water was so murky that visibility was nonexistent. They spent several more hours on the lake, but without success. The last time the divers returned, they said they couldn't see a foot in front of their faces. The plan was to return early the next morning if the lake conditions improved.

Reaching his car, Sam decided he was going to call it a day. He'd been putting in long hours and he was tired. And he thought Elvis was ready to go home and see Honey. "I'm going to call our girl," he told Elvis, pulling out his cell phone.

Honey answered, and Sam said, "Elvis and I are calling it a day. He wanted me to call you and tell you to forget about cooking. We decided we'd pick you up and take you out to that old-fashioned drive-in that the guys at the station have told me about. You know, the one in Lexington. I even saw it featured on one of those food shows late one night. What does burgers and fries sound like to you? Elvis is giving it a paws-up."

Honey laughed. She didn't know what surprised her the most—that Sam watched a food show, or that he actually admitted watching. "You haven't been to Parkette's yet? It will take about an hour to get there."

"It's a nice day for a drive. This might be the only night I will knock off early for a while. You wouldn't disappoint two starving men, would you?" Sam teased.

"I just thought you two might be tired."

"We are tired, but we want to take you out. I know it's not a big night out, but Elvis can go with us. He needs to be rewarded for his hard work today." Sam proceeded to tell her about their day and what a great job

Elvis did. "I'm going to stop by my house for some clean clothes. What do you say? Are you ready for a drive?"

"It sounds fun. The burgers are delicious." She lowered her voice and added, "That means I can send Mom and Gramps home."

"Yeah. Then I can be alone with you tonight." Sam was already envisioning her little pink robe.

CHAPTER TWENTY-ONE

"**I** THINK THIS IS THE BEST burger I've ever had." Sam reached over to claim another onion ring from Honey's basket.

"Aren't they delicious? But next time you need to try their fried chicken." Honey watched in amazement as Sam ate two double cheeseburgers and a large plate of fries, not to mention half of her onion rings.

Sam turned to look at Elvis, who was chomping on his second plain burger. "Elvis loves them."

"If he throws up in the middle of the night, you get to clean it up." Elvis was eating so much she was worried he was going to get sick.

Sam didn't think now would be the right time to mention the bologna sandwich Elvis ate on the boat earlier. "He won't get sick. He's having a good time and he earned it."

Honey took a sip of her milkshake and Elvis nosed her straw. "I don't think you need this."

"I would give you a sip of mine, buddy, but I've already finished it," Sam said sympathetically.

Honey handed Sam her milkshake. "Finish mine. It's chocolate and dogs shouldn't have chocolate."

Sam smiled at her. "I know." He took a big sip of her shake. "Can I order him a vanilla shake?"

"No. I'm going inside to the restroom, and I'll get more water for him." Honey opened the car door and handed Sam the remainder of her onion rings. "Finish these. Do you want another burger, dessert, shake or something?" She didn't know where he was putting all of the food he'd consumed.

Sam winked at her. "You're reading my mind. Do you have bourbon balls at home?"

"I think there are still a few in the refrigerator."

"Good. I'll wait on dessert." Sam watched her walk away. He picked up one of his fries and held it to Elvis. "I like your master, Elvis."

Elvis gobbled his fry and licked Sam's cheek.

"You better not get sick tonight and make me look bad," Sam told him. "She won't let you go out with me again."

Elvis sniffed the milkshake in Sam's hand. "Are you trying to blackmail me? You know Honey said you couldn't have this. But when we get home, I'll give you a treat."

Elvis jumped to the front seat, stuck his nose out the open window and sniffed the air. Within seconds, he tried to open the door handle with his paw.

Sam thought he might need to find some grass. "You need to do your business?"

Elvis clutched the door handle between his teeth and Sam got the message. "Okay, let's find some green." He attached Elvis's leash when he got out of the car. Instead of heading toward the grass, like Sam expected, Elvis pulled him around the restaurant to the front door. Sam saw Honey standing outside the restaurant talking to Bunny and Troy Spencer.

Elvis charged ahead, pulling Sam along until he reached Honey. He maneuvered his big body to stand in front of Honey, forcing her to take a few steps back. Staring up at the couple in front of Honey, Elvis emitted a low, menacing growl.

Honey had never seen Elvis act in such an aggressive manner. In an effort to calm him down, she put her hand on his head and spoke to him in a soft voice.

Elvis's volume decreased, but he was still making a threatening sound Honey had never heard before. Sam tried to move him away from the group, but he wouldn't budge.

"You need to do something about that dog. He's dangerous." Troy took a step back and pulled Bunny with him.

"Have you two ever seen Elvis before?" Sam asked, trying to figure out why Elvis seemed ready to attack. Elvis was the most laid-back dog he'd ever seen.

"I've never been around him," Bunny responded.

"Nor have I, but he definitely needs some social training," Troy added.

"Elvis is the friendliest dog in the world. He's just had a long day." Honey couldn't explain his behavior. She leaned down to Elvis and whispered to him again.

Elvis stopped growling, but he still refused to move away from her.

"What are you doing here *together*?" Bunny asked, staring directly at Sam.

"Having dinner," Sam replied.

Bunny glanced Honey's way. "The last time I saw you, Sam was taking you to jail. Instead of the famous people being on the front pages promoting your event, you made the front page. I doubt that was good for your business."

Even at a distance Sam smelled bourbon on her breath. "I didn't take Honey to jail. She was kind enough to come with us to answer our questions without an audience." Sam saw Elvis sniffing the air separating Honey and the Spencers. He wondered if Elvis had picked up their scent from Tucker's farm.

Ignoring Sam's comment, Bunny stared at Honey. "Since you've moved back, a lot has happened in our peaceful little town. Seems like you brought trouble with you."

"No wonder people in town are talking. It's easy to understand why they think you had to have something to do with the murders," Troy added. "Of course, we would never think such a thing."

Honey arched her brows at him. "Of course not."

"It's ridiculous for anyone to think Honey is a suspect. To set the record straight, she didn't actually find K.C., Elvis did. Elvis has a remarkable ability to remember individual scents. If he's met you, you can bet he will remember your scent, particularly if you were at a crime scene." Sam didn't know if Elvis could remember everyone's scent, but he wanted them to believe it was possible.

Troy focused on Elvis. "I've never heard of a dog with that talent."

"Well, I hope you find out who murdered K.C. and Alan." Bunny reached for her husband's arm. "I guess we better be going. We just stopped in for a milkshake on our way to the open air concert tonight." Her eyes drifted back to Sam. "By the way, Sam, I guess you know by now that Eugenie Grayson was having an affair with K.C."

Sam was immediately suspicious of what she had to say. "Why are you telling me this now? You've had other opportunities to give me this information."

"Troy said I should do what I can to assist in the investigation. I'm sure you can understand, Eugenie is my friend. I've known her for years and I didn't want to betray a confidence. I'm not saying she had anything to do with his murder, but she should want to help you. After all, she cared enough about him to betray Jefferson. Don't you think she would want to know who murdered him?"

Sam didn't know why Bunny was talking now, but he wasn't going to let the opportunity to ask questions pass him by. "Was she seeing him when he was killed?"

"Apparently he'd broken it off with her not long before his death. And she didn't take it well."

"Was she thinking of leaving her husband for K.C.?" Sam asked.

Bunny laughed. "Heavens no. Eugenie would never consider leaving Jefferson. She was just having a little fling."

"Then why was she upset when he broke it off?" Sam asked.

"Because he did it first. She would have ended it eventually, particularly if she thought Jefferson might hear the gossip. If you knew Eugenie as well as I do, then you would know she likes to be in control of everything."

Sam focused on Bunny's eyes when he asked his next question. "Do you think she was angry enough to kill him?"

Bunny didn't immediately reply, but Troy spoke up. "You've seen for yourself how contentious Eugenie can be with little provocation."

Sam turned his focus on Troy. "How well do you know Eugenie?"

"I've seen her socially, with Bunny of course," Troy replied, running his fingers through his hair. "I've seen her temper."

Troy's gesture triggered Honey's memory of the night on the train when he walked from one of the compartments. She remembered thinking

Troy looked aggravated or angry about something. With everything that happened that night, she hadn't given the incident another thought. She also remembered the dress the woman was wearing in that compartment. It wasn't Bunny's dress.

"So you think she could commit murder?" Sam asked.

"No one would believe Eugenie could murder anyone," Bunny responded. She turned to leave, but glanced over her shoulder and looked at Honey. "Honey, try not to find more dead bodies."

Honey had a retort on the tip of her tongue, but she refrained from saying it aloud.

"I know what you're thinking," Sam teased.

"Are you going to arrest me?"

Sam put his arm around her shoulders. "Lucky for you I can't arrest people for their thoughts. Although if you wear that little silky robe tonight, you might want to put the handcuffs on me."

Honey laughed. "I'll keep that in mind."

Sam looked down at Elvis, who was still watching Bunny and Troy as they walked to their car. "What's going on with Elvis?"

"I have no idea. I've never seen him like that. I'm worried about him."

Sam stroked Elvis's neck. "He seems fine. Maybe he just didn't like Bunny or Troy."

"I told you he is a smart dog," Honey retorted.

Reaching the car, Honey poured the bottle of water into Elvis's bowl. "We'd better take him for a walk before we head back."

"That's what I was doing when he dragged me to the front of the building."

After Elvis slurped up the water, they led him to a grassy area.

"Sam, have you noticed Troy's habit of raking his hand through his hair?" Honey asked.

"Yeah, I've seen him do that a couple of times. Why do you ask?"

"When he did that tonight I remembered something I saw on the train. It may not be important, but I thought you should know."

"What's that?"

"After we found Alan's body on the train, Cullen, Georgia and I were walking back through the car, and we saw Troy walking from a compartment. He didn't see us watching him. He closed the door to the compartment and he just stood there for a moment, raked his hand through his hair and—well, I remember thinking he looked angry. Once he walked into the next car, we passed the compartment he'd left. He didn't close the door completely and I could see someone else was in the compartment."

"Who was it?"

"Well, I didn't actually see her, but I saw her gown. He was with Eugenie."

Sam stopped walking and looked at her. "He was alone with Eugenie in a compartment?"

Honey nodded. "I didn't see anyone else."

"Was her dress on or off?" Sam asked.

Honey thought he was teasing, but when she looked at him, she realized he was serious. She hadn't really thought about the situation he was suggesting. She thought it was possible that the gown could have been lying on the seat in the compartment. "I couldn't really say. I just saw a dress."

"Could two women have been wearing the same color?" Sam asked.

"No, Eugenie was the only one wearing lavender. I have photographs," Honey replied.

Sam considered the scenario Honey described. "Do you think it's possible they were having a romantic encounter?"

"So much was on my mind that night, but I didn't even consider that possibility."

"Maybe they had a lovers' quarrel," Sam suggested.

"I guess it's possible, but I don't think Eugenie would be attracted to Troy. He's not exactly polished or sophisticated."

"Do you think she would be attracted to K.C.?" Sam asked.

"Oh yes. K.C. was exactly the kind of man Eugenie would find attractive. A self-made man, handsome, intelligent, and interesting. K.C. was a very charismatic man."

Sam felt the sting of jealousy when Honey voiced her praises of K.C., but he reminded himself that she told him she wasn't in a relationship with him. "What did Georgia think of Eugenie and Troy together that night?"

"We never discussed it. I'm not sure she saw the gown as she passed the compartment. And to be honest, we were focused on trying to find Alan's murderer," Honey answered.

"Was Troy wearing his jacket when he stepped from the compartment?" Sam thought if man had a romantic encounter in a confined space, it would make sense he would remove his jacket.

"Yes, he was wearing a white dinner jacket."

"Do you think your mother noticed anything between them?"

"She didn't mention anything to me. But I'll ask her tomorrow."

"Let me know what she says."

Honey thought of something else she'd forgotten to tell Sam. "There's another thing I didn't mention before. One morning on my way to work I drove to Randy's drive-thru, and I saw Alan's car in the parking lot next door. It was five in the morning, and the only other car in the lot was right next to his. It was a silver Jaguar."

Sam knew Bunny Spencer drove a silver Jag. "Are you saying Alan was meeting Bunny Spencer? Why didn't you tell me before?"

"I'd forgotten all about it, and I didn't know it was important. That morning it was still dark outside, but I thought I could make out two people sitting in the Jaguar. I guess it could have been Troy driving the car."

"Did you notice the license number on the Jaguar?"

"No. I mentioned to Alan that I saw him that morning at Randy's, but he denied it was him. I did notice his license plate. It was him."

"You're positive it was Alan?"

Honey nodded. "Do you remember telling me Eugenie owned that property on Old Honeysuckle Road?

"Yes."

"When Mom and I had lunch with Eugenie and Bunny, we discussed that property, and Bunny told us she'd purchased the place from Eugenie a couple of weeks ago."

Sam found it odd that the sale hadn't been recorded at the courthouse. "Did she say why she wanted that property?"

"According to Bunny, Troy wanted more acreage to grow corn, and he needed more warehouse space."

When they reached the cottage, Honey made coffee while Sam raided the refrigerator for bourbon balls.

"I don't see them."

Honey turned to see half of the contents from her refrigerator sitting on the counter, and Sam's upper body was inside her refrigerator. "They are in a blue plastic container."

"I see them." Sam pulled the bowl out and opened the lid. "How did you keep these from your mother today?"

Honey smiled when he popped two in his mouth at once. "She finished off the coffee cake after you left."

"Good. More for me." He held one out to her. "I could be convinced to share one with you since you're making coffee."

"They're all yours."

Seeing Elvis sitting there looking at him with expectant eyes, Sam remembered he'd promised him a treat. When he pulled out the hound dog canister and opened the lid, the music erupted and Elvis began howling. "Does he think he's singing?"

"I don't know, but he does the same thing every time he hears that song, even if he hears it in the car."

After pouring their coffee, they moved to the sofa. As he did before, Elvis jumped up beside Honey and stretched his large body across their laps.

Sam scratched him behind the ears. "He's really protective tonight. What did you whisper to him earlier when he was growling at Bunny and Troy? Whatever you said to him worked like a charm."

"I told him that he couldn't go with you again if he didn't behave himself," Honey replied, stroking Elvis's back.

"Really? That's downright mean." Sam leaned close to Elvis's ear. "She didn't mean it, buddy."

"Will you need Elvis tomorrow?"

Sam knew she was talking about finding Alan. "No. He pinpointed the area for us, and I'm confident if the conditions improve on the lake tomorrow, we'll find him."

CHAPTER TWENTY-TWO

S AM WAS SITTING AT THE lake early the next morning watching the sun break the horizon in a magnificent array of pinks and yellows. The morning light cast a silvery glow over the surface of the water, and for a moment he'd forgotten what was waiting in the depths. He'd been thinking about his case, but his thoughts drifted to Honey. He wished he was enjoying the beautiful daybreak with her and Elvis. If he wasn't thinking about his investigations, he was thinking about them. Once he solved these murders, he planned on spending a lot more time with them.

The divers arrived minutes later, and they were confident their chances of finding Alan's body were greatly improved. Their confidence paid off when they found Alan's body two hours into the dive. Once his body was taken to the medical examiner's office, Sam told Hap he was going to see the Spencers and the Graysons for follow-up interviews.

"Are you telling me I need to be unavailable when the angry phone calls come?" Hap asked.

"Yep."

Troy Spencer gestured toward a chair when Sam entered his office. "What can I do for you, Detective?"

Sam took a seat across from Troy. "I wanted to ask you a few more questions about the night of the party."

"I told you everything that night. I'm afraid the only thing I can remember with any clarity is I had one heck of a hangover the next morning."

Sam didn't smile. "What about what happened before the party started?"

Troy hesitated. "What do you mean?"

"What time did you board the train?"

"I'm not certain of the exact time, but I was talking to that famous producer as we boarded," Troy answered. "The reporters were so loud that it was difficult to have a conversation."

"Did you and your wife arrive at the same time?"

Troy appeared surprised by his question. "Yes, why do you ask?"

"I was curious if your wife was with you when you met Eugenie Grayson in that compartment in the last car."

"I don't know what you're talking about."

Sam felt like laughing. It was obvious Troy hadn't expected that question. He hesitated a heartbeat too long, and his muscled neck, bulging over his tight collar, turned a nice shade of red. He definitely wasn't good at bluffing. *I'd love to play poker with him.* "I think you know exactly what I'm talking about." Before Troy could continue with a denial, Sam upped the ante. "What if I told you that the last car on the train is where supplies are stored, and each compartment has a camera to discourage theft?"

Troy looked at him for a few moments, then threw his hands in the air. "All right, all right. I met with Eugenie in that compartment." He gave Sam a conspiratorial grin. "I'm sure I don't need to tell you why."

"Yes, you do," Sam countered.

Troy exhaled loudly. "Look, I've been seeing Eugenie on the sly for a few weeks. I didn't tell you about it earlier because I didn't want it to get back to my wife."

"Were you seeing Eugenie at the same time she was seeing K.C. Cleary?" Sam hoped Troy didn't go silent and tell him to go pound sand.

"I didn't know Eugenie was seeing K.C. Cleary until recently," Troy replied.

Another lie, Sam thought. "But your wife knew. She didn't tell you?"

"No, she didn't tell me until recently. Of course, I'd heard the gossip. But I don't put much stock in gossip. People around here have nothing better to do than make up stories about Eugenie. She's a wealthy woman and she has enemies."

"Why would she have enemies?" Sam could think of several reasons, judging by the way she'd interacted with him.

"Eugenie can be somewhat unpleasant when she doesn't get her way."

"Has she been *unpleasant* with you?"

Troy leaned forward and rested his elbows on his desk. "She's never been angry with me. I make her happy, if you know what I mean."

Sam wished he could arrest him for arrogance. He didn't believe a word out of his mouth, but he'd played along. "What do you think would happen if you tried to end the relationship?"

"I don't think it would be a problem. We're married, and neither one of us wants more than what it is. We both know it's not the first time Eugenie had a fling. Since I've been in this backwater town, a lot of women have approached me looking for...attention."

Sam had met men with inflated egos before, but Troy took the prize. "What time did you meet Eugenie in that compartment?"

Troy smiled. "I wasn't paying attention to the time. I had other things on my mind." He glanced at Sam and saw he wasn't smiling, and added, "I guess it was about fifteen minutes after the train departed."

"How did you slip away from your wife?"

"Just told her I was going to mingle. She had her bourbon."

The more Troy talked, Sam thought he could understand Bunny's penchant for bourbon. "Did you know Eugenie met K.C. out on Old Honeysuckle Road for their liaisons?"

"Really? They met at the Tucker farm? I wasn't aware of that."

Sam didn't mention the Tucker farm specifically. But he thought Troy was surprised that he'd uncovered Eugenie's and K.C.'s love nest. He had no doubt Troy knew about the relationship between K.C. and Eugenie longer than he was professing.

"If you're looking for a killer, I would think you'd be looking at Cullen Harper. He's the one who had something to gain by Alan's death. I didn't have anything to gain, nor did Eugenie."

Sam stood. "I'm investigating everyone. But now that you mentioned it, who had something to gain by K.C.'s death?"

Troy turned his palms up. "Maybe the two murders aren't related."

Sam tossed his business card on Troy's desk. "Let me know if you think of anything else."

Troy stood and followed Sam to the door. "Where's your four-legged companion today?"

"He's Honey's dog."

Troy chuckled. "Honey is a gorgeous woman. It'd be worth putting up with that dog for her."

Sam didn't comment on his relationship with Honey. "Elvis is a great dog."

"Can that dog really remember every person he smells?"

"That's what they tell me. He's has amazing abilities. Haven't you heard he's somewhat of a local hero?"

"I think I did hear something about him finding a missing child. Maybe he can help you solve these murders," Troy suggested.

"I'm counting on it."

The housekeeper led Sam to the study at Bunny Spencer's home. Within minutes, another woman entered the room carrying a silver tray bearing a coffee service and some fancy little cakes. "Mrs. Spencer will be with you in a few minutes."

Sam hoped Bunny was in better shape than the last time he saw her. He glanced at his watch and saw that it was almost noon. Hopefully, the bourbon hadn't started flowing. He poured himself a cup of coffee and walked around the room. Stopping at the bar, he noticed there were only two bottles of bourbon: Pickett's Reserve and a bottle of Woodrow's Bluegrass Select. He found it interesting there were no bottles from any other competitor. Seeing one bottle with no label, he opened the top and smelled the contents. Definitely bourbon. He remembered hearing a conversation between Cullen and Woodrow the night he had dinner at Honey's. Woodrow said Troy Spencer must be an excellent bourbon man.

Setting his cup of coffee aside, Sam reached for a glass from the overhead shelf, then opened the bottle of Pickett's Reserve. He poured a small amount of Pickett's in the glass, sniffed the bourbon before he took a sip, and rolled the liquid over his tongue. Swallowing slowly, he felt the heat on the back of his throat. He waited a few minutes, then repeated the process with Woodrow's Bluegrass Select. When he finished, he started to pick up his coffee, but instead he decided to taste the unlabeled bottle of bourbon.

"It's so good to see you again, Detective." Bunny walked to the tray the housekeeper left behind and picked up the coffeepot. "Coffee?"

Sam walked to a chair and held his cup in the air. "Already helped myself."

Picking up the plate of cakes, Bunny held it out to him and gave him a flirtatious smile. "Can I tempt you?"

"No, thank you." Sam took a seat in the leather wingback chair.

Bunny sat in a chair next to Sam's and leaned toward him. "What can I do for you today?"

"I want to ask a few more questions about the night of the party."

Bunny laughed. "I don't remember much about that night, but ask away."

"I'd like to know if you were with your husband the entire time."

Arching her brows, Bunny asked, "What do you mean? We were on the same train."

"Yes, but did you two stay together, or did you go your own way?" The night of Lorraine's party, he'd noticed Bunny and Troy didn't seem to spend much time side by side.

"I guess we did a little of both. If Troy doesn't know some of the other guests attending, I will see that he's introduced before I move on. He enjoys talking bourbon and sports. I tend to talk fashion with the women, unless a nice-looking man catches my eye."

Sam ignored her innuendo. He hadn't forgotten the way she'd flirted with him at Lorraine's party. "Was there any time that night that you didn't see Troy?"

Bunny sipped her coffee and stared at him. "I don't see what this has to do with the murders."

Sam chose not to explain. "Can you answer the question?"

Bunny glanced at her watch. "Time for a drink." She set her coffee cup on the table and walked to the bar. "Can I get you one?"

Sam thought she was buying time to think of her answer. He didn't press. "Coffee is fine." Sam heard ice clinking into a glass on the bar. He also heard her muttering something about the housekeeper leaving dirty glasses on the bar. He didn't admit to sampling the bourbon. After she poured herself a double bourbon on ice, she picked up the bottle and walked back to her chair. "Now what were we discussing?"

When she placed the bottle on the table, Sam noticed she was drinking Woodrow's Bluegrass Bourbon Select. "I asked if you saw your husband the entire night."

"I hadn't really thought about it. I guess I can't swear I saw him the whole time," she replied.

"Did you go to any of the other cars?"

"I remember going to the second car before dinner was served. Some of my friends were in that car."

"Was Troy in the second car?"

Bunny shrugged. "I wasn't looking for Troy."

"How well do Troy and Eugenie Grayson get along?" Sam could tell his question surprised her.

"I'm not certain I understand the question."

"It seems they spent some time together on the train. I'm curious how well they know each other."

"Are you suggesting something inappropriate was going on?" Bunny asked.

"I'm not suggesting anything. I'm asking a question." Sam watched her closely. "Since Eugenie is not involved in the bourbon industry, I'm interested to know what they would have to discuss in private."

Bunny stared at him. "How could a private conversation have taken place on a train with so many guests aboard?"

"Your husband and Eugenie were seen coming from a compartment in the last car."

Bunny looked down at her glass and swirled the contents. "I have no idea what they would discuss. You'll have to ask Troy."

"I already did."

"And?"

"I'll let him tell you." Sam stood and handed her his card. "I'll see myself out."

"I'm sorry, sir, but Mrs. Grayson is unavailable," the maid at the Grayson estate told Sam when she opened the door. Sam was surprised he'd made it to the front door, but the gate had been left unattended. He saw no reason not to open the gate himself.

Sam wrote something on the back of his business card and handed it to the woman. "Would you give her this, and tell her I'll wait exactly three minutes." Sam figured it would take her that long to walk to the door if she was at the other side of the house. He didn't like to be hard-nosed with a woman, but he'd make an exception in Eugenie Grayson's case.

Two minutes later, the maid returned and asked Sam to follow her to the office.

Eugenie must have taken him at his word, because she walked in the office before he sat down. She threw his business card on the desk before she turned to face him with her arms crossed over her chest. "What do you mean you want to see me about my meeting with Troy on the train?"

"I think you know what I mean, or you wouldn't have let me in the door."

Eugenie leaned against the desk and glared at him. "Do you have a question, or am I supposed to guess?"

"Tell me about your relationship with Troy." Sam expected Troy had called Eugenie as soon as he left his office.

"Troy and I have been seeing each other for a few months."

"Who knows about this relationship?"

Eugenie shrugged. "No one, as far as I know. We try to be discreet. Of course, now you know. If we hear gossip, we will know where it originated."

Sam was having the same feeling he had when he spoke to Troy earlier. Something about her story sounded as false as Troy's. "Were you seeing Troy at the same time you were seeing K.C.?"

"I told you I didn't know K.C. well."

Sam stared at her long enough to make her uncomfortable. "I thought you might want to tell me the truth this time."

Eugenie glared at him. "I told you the truth."

Sam nodded. "If that's the way you want to play it. But we have a problem."

Eugenie smiled smugly. "Really? And what might that be?"

"You see, I know about the damage to K.C.'s car. I also know about the repairs made on your car. Seems like the two accidents happened at the same time. What's even more of an odd coincidence is the fact that the paint on K.C.'s car came from your car." Sam watched her face, and while he had to hand it to her for keeping her cool, her smile slowly faded.

"I often lend my car to my nieces and nephews."

Sam clapped his hands together as he stood. "Okay, that explains it. I guess you're saying your nieces or nephews meet their lovers out at the Tucker farm on Old Honeysuckle Road. I'd like their names and phone numbers."

Eugenie straightened and walked toward the door. "I suggest you contact my attorney for that information, but don't expect to get it."

Sam followed her to the front door. Before she pulled it open, he took a step closer and looked into her cold eyes. "If you are involved in these murders, I'm going to find out. You might want to talk to me now."

She opened the door. "Don't get in over your head, Detective."

Sam smiled at her before he walked away. If she was issuing a challenge, she was going to be on the losing end. He was confident she was involved, at least in K.C.'s murder. And she was arrogant enough to think there was nothing he could do about it.

Honey answered her phone on the first ring. "I heard you found Alan."

Sam was exhausted, but hearing her voice energized him. "Yeah. The conditions were better today. It didn't take the search team long to locate him."

"Tough day?" Honey thought he probably had a lot of bad days, considering his profession.

"It's better now. I'm stopping by my house for some clean clothes. Do you want me to pick up dinner?"

"Elvis and I are cooking dinner."

"Even better. I know it will be delicious." His stomach was already growling at the thought. He'd been too busy to stop for lunch.

"Actually, Georgia and Preston are on the patio getting the grill ready for steaks. Elvis and I are making twice-baked potatoes and a salad."

He liked Preston and Georgia, but he wanted to be alone with Honey. He'd looked forward to it all day. "That's sounds great. I'll be there within the hour. I need to stop by the liquor store."

"I have wine."

"I need to pick up something else." Since he couldn't be alone with Honey, he altered his plan for the evening.

After dinner, Sam asked Honey to join him in the kitchen. "I found out something interesting today, and I want to see what you guys think. I'll need twelve Glencairn glasses and a tray."

"Twelve? Are we expecting more people?" Honey asked.

Sam grinned at her. "No, and I'll wash tonight."

Honey placed the requested items on the counter. "What is this about?"

"You'll see. Now go on out to the patio. Elvis and I will be right out," Sam instructed.

Honey grabbed a box of crackers from the pantry. "We'll use these to cleanse our palates between tastings."

"Great." Once Sam gave Elvis a treat, he opened his overnight bag and pulled out the two bottles of bourbon he'd purchased at the liquor store. He also pulled out the unlabeled bottle of bourbon he'd taken from Bunny's home. After pouring a shot of Pickett's Reserve in four glasses, he lined them up on the tray. He then poured Bluegrass Select in four glasses and positioned them on the opposite side of the tray. Between the filled glasses, he added a row of empty glasses. Tucking the unlabeled bottle under his arm, he carried the tray to the patio.

"I want each of you to take a glass from the left row," Sam instructed.

Preston was the first one to reach for a glass. "Sam, I didn't know you had such an interest in bourbon tastings."

"This is not going to be a usual tasting." Sam held the tray to Honey and Georgia.

"What do you mean?" Honey asked.

"I want you to tell me if this is one of Woodrow's bourbons." Sam picked up the last glass and tasted the bourbon.

After everyone tasted the first glass of bourbon, Sam looked at them. "What do you think?"

Preston smiled. "That's easy. It's Woodrow's Bluegrass Select."

Honey placed her empty glass back on the tray. "I'm certainly not as experienced drinking bourbon as my brother, but I believe he's right."

"I agree," Georgia responded.

They looked at Sam, waiting for him to confirm their decision. When Sam didn't comment, Preston asked, "Are we right? Is this Bluegrass Select?"

"You'll have to wait a minute to find out. Now have a cracker before we try the second one." Once everyone ate a cracker, Sam held the tray out to them again.

After everyone tasted the second bourbon, Preston frowned at Sam. "What are you trying to pull, Sam? This is also Woodrow's Bluegrass Select."

"Yes, I think it is," Georgia commented.

"It is the same one," Honey agreed. "Did you make a mistake and pour from the same bottle?"

"No, I didn't make a mistake. Now have another cracker." Sam filled the remaining four empty glasses with the unlabeled bourbon.

They tasted the final bourbon from the unmarked bottle. Preston held his glass for Sam to pour him another shot. After Preston swallowed the bourbon, he was confident he was drinking Woodrow's new bourbon. "I wasn't positive at first, but this is Woodrow's Devil's Due Bourbon. Did he give you a bottle?"

Sam looked at Honey and Georgia before he responded. "What do you two think?"

"I think Preston is right," Honey agreed.

Georgia nodded her agreement. "Definitely. I had this on the train, and that was the only bourbon I drank that night."

Honey had a feeling this tasting had something to do with his investigation. "Sam, what's going on? Why do you have us tasting bourbon?"

"I'm working on a theory," Sam answered evasively. "Let's go inside, I want to show you something." They followed Sam to the kitchen, where Sam showed them the bottles he'd purchased.

"Are you certain you poured from the different bottles? I was positive the first two were both Woodrow's." Preston held up both bottles to see if one was full. Seeing both bottles had nearly the same amount of bourbon missing, Preston shook his head. "This is strange."

"Are you up to trying them again?" Sam asked.

"Sure." Preston walked away while Sam poured the bourbons. Honey and Georgia watched Sam fill glasses from each bottle.

Preston tasted both bourbons, and again he couldn't tell the difference. "I'm amazed."

"Gramps mentioned to me that Pickett's tasted very similar to ours. I meant to taste them to compare, but I've been so busy, I forgot all about it," Honey told them.

"There's a significant price difference," Preston added.

"That's what Gramps told me," Honey replied.

"The third bourbon we tasted was Devil's Due Bourbon, right?" Preston asked.

Sam turned the small unlabeled bottle on the counter for them to see. "I don't know."

Honey studied the bottle. "Where did you get this?"

Sam smiled at her. "Let's just say I ran across this today. I'd rather you not know where I found it. It's not something I could use as evidence."

Honey arched her brow at him. "Sam, you didn't do something illegal, did you?"

"I fully intend to return what is left in that bottle," Sam answered. "If I hadn't taken it when I did, I was afraid nothing would be left."

"Why don't we see if Elvis can tell the difference between Pickett's and Bluegrass Select?" Honey suggested.

Sam smiled at her. "That was my next test."

Preston nodded his agreement. "Great idea."

"Let's pour a little of each bourbon in two glasses and put them on opposite sides of the room. I'll take Elvis to the living room and let him sniff the bottle of Bluegrass Select," Honey suggested.

"Honey, go ahead and take Elvis out of the room before Sam pours from the bottles. I'll bring the bottle to you," Preston said.

After Sam poured bourbon in two glasses from each bottle, Preston took the bottle of Bluegrass Select to the living room. As soon as Elvis sniffed the bottle, he trotted back to the kitchen. Sam had placed the glasses on the floor, and Elvis walked to the first glass and sat down. Turning his head toward the second glass, he stuck his nose in the air. He jumped up and walked to second glass and sat down. He looked across the room at the first glass. Finally he stood, walked to an area between the glasses, sat down, and turning his big brown eyes on Honey, he let out a bark.

Honey watched Elvis closely. "He can't tell them apart."

"That's amazing," Georgia commented.

"What about that third bourbon? Honey, do you have a bottle of Devil's Due Bourbon?" Preston asked.

"No, but Gramps does." Honey opened the pantry to give Elvis a treat.

"Is it too late to call Woodrow?" Sam asked.

"I think he needs to see this." Honey picked up her phone and called Woodrow.

When Woodrow arrived, Sam conducted the same tasting experiment on him.

"These are both Woodrow's Bluegrass Select, Sam." Woodrow felt confident he was tasting his own bourbon.

Sam grinned, and held up the two bottles Woodrow tasted.

Woodrow stared at the bottles and shook his head. "I thought all along that Pickett's Reserve was very similar to my bourbon. It's like they have our mash bill."

"Gramps, when we first discussed Pickett's, you told me you might have trouble telling them apart," Honey reminded him. "We want to show you what Elvis did."

They repeated the test with Elvis, and again, Elvis sat between the bourbons.

Woodrow glanced from Honey to Sam. "He's alerting us to both glasses."

Sam nodded. "Yes, he is."

"Why did you want a bottle of Devil's Due?" Woodrow asked.

"You'll see," Sam replied.

Sam made everyone leave the room as he poured bourbon in two small glasses. Once he placed them on the floor, he walked to the living room and handed Honey the unlabeled bottle for Elvis to sniff. Elvis walked to the kitchen and immediately alerted them to both glasses.

"Was that the bourbon in the unlabeled bottle?" Woodrow asked.

Sam shook his head. "No. I poured both glasses from the bottle of Bluegrass Devil's Due Bourbon you brought with you. Elvis sniffed the unlabeled bottle."

Woodrow tasted bourbon from the unlabeled bottle and from the bottle that he'd brought with him. "What the devil is going on? These are both Bluegrass Devil's Due Bourbon." He looked at Sam quizzically. "Where did you find that unlabeled bottle?"

"I can't tell you right now, but I will soon."

CHAPTER TWENTY-THREE

AFTER WOODROW LEFT THE COTTAGE, Preston and Georgia decided they were going to spend the night at Honey's. Georgia was sleeping in the second bedroom, which meant Preston would be sleeping on one sofa, and Sam on the other sofa.

Honey and Sam were washing the glasses when Honey recalled a conversation she'd had with Cullen. "Sam, I just remembered a comment Cullen made when we first met. Elvis was sniffing my neck, and I told Cullen that he likes to smell my perfume. Cullen asked me if I thought Elvis could tell the differences in bourbons. Seeing what Elvis did tonight made me think of that conversation."

Sam found it curious that Cullen would ask that question. Cullen and Troy were both in good shape, and Sam figured either one could have been strong enough to toss Alan's body into the lake. But he didn't share that thought aloud. "Are you suspicious of Cullen?"

"Not really. I can't see him murdering anyone."

While Honey was adding sheets and blankets on the sofas, Sam took Elvis outside for his nightly ritual. As Elvis smelled his way around the perimeter of the patio, Sam was thinking about his next move in the investigation. He thought about Cullen's interest in Elvis's abilities. Did the murders have something to do with Woodrow's distillery? Was Cullen involved? As improbable as it sounded, he thought Bunny and Troy Spencer, along with Eugenie Grayson, were involved in both murders. If the locals heard him say those thoughts aloud, he'd probably be committed. He'd thought all along the murders were related to the bourbon industry, but he couldn't figure out Eugenie Grayson's involvement. Something kept nagging at him about his interviews with Troy and Eugenie. Troy easily admitted to the affair with Eugenie. Too easily? Eugenie confirmed they were having an affair. In his estimation, Eugenie's response seemed rehearsed. Honey didn't believe Troy was Eugenie's type. Was she right? Why would they both admit to an affair that wasn't happening? And was Cullen involved with them in some way?

Hearing Elvis emit a low growl, Sam looked up to see him several yards away staring into the dense brush at the back of the yard. Sam thought he saw movement in the brush, and he didn't want Elvis running after an animal and coming back with briars from head to paws. "Come here, boy."

Elvis ran back to Sam, but his eyes remained fixed on the brush. Sam could tell by the way Elvis was acting that there was something in the brush. Limbs were definitely moving. Most likely a deer, or—before he finished his thought, he heard the familiar sound of a hammer being cocked. Reacting quickly, he dove on top of Elvis as a shot rang out. Lying prone with Elvis's large body beneath him, Sam reached for his pistol at his waist. Not finding it attached to his belt, he remembered it was on top of Honey's refrigerator. He remained still and whispered to Elvis to do the same.

Hearing what she thought was a gunshot, Honey ran out the patio door with Georgia on her heels. Preston had the presence of mind to grab Sam's pistol before he raced outside.

Seeing Sam on the ground, Honey bolted to him. "Sam!"

Sam rolled to his feet and Elvis jumped up beside him. "Honey, get back inside and call Hap."

Honey didn't move. "Are you two hurt?"

"No. Please go back inside and take Elvis."

Preston handed Sam his pistol. Sam heard the snapping of limbs in the distance indicating someone was running through the trees, but his first priority was to keep everyone safe.

Honey and Georgia struggled with Elvis to get him inside the cottage.

Elvis was uncooperative, equally determined to stay outside with Sam. Worried Elvis might jump through the patio door to get to Sam, Honey told Georgia to get Hap on the phone while she held him.

Seeing a stain on Sam's shirt, Preston asked, "Is that dirt or have you been shot?"

"It's just a graze. I don't think they were shooting at me. I think the shot was meant for Elvis," Sam replied. "I'm going to follow him."

"I'll get Honey's pistol and a flashlight. I'm going with you."

"Just get me a flashlight. You need to stay with Honey and Georgia. Hap will be here in a few minutes to lend a hand."

Preston ran inside and returned seconds later with a flashlight.

"Thanks, Preston." He hesitated before running through the brush. "I can't explain right now, but I need you to do something for me."

"Name it."

"Would you make a call to the Spencer home and ask for Troy? I want to know where he is. Use any excuse you can think of to call, but use your cell phone, not Honey's."

Preston didn't hesitate to agree. "No problem."

"Thanks, Preston." Sam took off through the brush. He knew he'd have backup soon if Hap was anywhere near Woodrow's property. He hoped Hap thought to send a unit to the back of the property, if another officer was available in the area. In a rural community, officers understood that they had a vast territory to cover. Without Elvis leading the way, Sam had to rely on his flashlight and his memory from the night Elvis had led him through the property. Sam wished the shooter made his escape on the trail, because there was no doubt he would easily catch him. He wasn't that lucky.

Honey picked up her cell phone to call Woodrow at the same time someone knocked on the front door. Preston looked out the sidelight and saw Woodrow standing there with shotgun in hand.

Honey hustled him inside. "I was just going to call you."

"I heard a shot. What's going on?"

Honey locked the door, and led the way back to the kitchen. "You shouldn't have left your house. What if the person is still lurking around?"

Woodrow propped his shotgun against the patio door. "Where's Sam?"

Preston filled him in on the events, but he didn't mention Sam had been shot.

Woodrow leaned down and petted Elvis. "You okay, Elvis?"

Elvis looked out the patio door and howled.

"Elvis wants to be out there helping Sam." Honey walked to the pantry to get Elvis a treat, thinking it might settle them down for a few minutes. "Sam told Preston he thought someone was shooting at Elvis. Hap is already on his way to the back road."

Woodrow took a seat at the counter. "Good. I'm going to call the security firm that oversees the security at the distillery and have them send some men out here in the morning. I should have done that when someone left that note on the patio."

"Why would anyone want to hurt Elvis?" Honey asked.

Hap turned his headlights off before he turned onto the road leading to the back of Woodrow's property. Though he knew the road well, it was a cloudy night with fog settling in, making visibility difficult. When he reached the area he thought was directly in line with Honey's cottage, he spotted a flash of something shiny in the weeds. Pulling his car off the road, he parked behind a large tree and walked back to the area, where he found a car hidden in the brush. Reaching the front of the car, he placed his hand on the hood. Warm. Circling the car, he pulled a penlight from his pocket and directed it on the license plate. Quickly walking back to his cruiser, he radioed the night-shift dispatcher to run a check on the license number. Within minutes, he had the owner's name, address, and a condensed version of his long rap sheet.

Trying to be as quiet as possible, Hap hurried back to the car, intending to disable the vehicle. If the perpetrator was able to evade him, he'd have no means of escape. Raising the hood would be noisy, so Hap decided he'd release air from the tires. Once two tires were deflated, he searched for a good hiding spot near the shooter's vehicle. He felt his cell phone vibrate in his pocket.

"I'm here. I found the car he's driving and I'm waiting," Hap whispered. He gave Sam his location by the huge oak tree.

Fortunately, Sam remembered the tree. He told Hap they were headed in that general direction. "I don't think I'm too far behind him, but we're still a good distance from you."

"Only one person?" Hap asked.

"Yeah. We can handle this."

"I can't believe you don't even sound out of breath," Hap joked before he clicked off. Shoving his cell phone in his pocket, he pulled his pistol and settled in to wait. He didn't know how much time had passed, but he'd almost fallen asleep twice. He stood, holstered his gun and stretched. He thought about calling Sam, but he didn't want to chance that Sam forgot to turn off his ringer. Suddenly he heard noises coming from the brush not far from his hiding spot. He saw a man bolt from the dense foliage and run in the direction of the vehicle hidden off the road. Pulling his weapon, Hap kneeled down and crab-walked to the driver's side of the vehicle.

A second later, Sam ran from the brush. "Hold it right there," Sam directed in a clear voice.

The shooter kept running, and when he was a few feet from the vehicle, Hap stood up and pointed his pistol at the man's head. "Calvin, I think you were told to stop."

Calvin screeched to a halt and threw his hands in the air. "Who are you?"

Hap walked forward as Sam approached from behind the shooter. "I'm your ride to jail, Calvin."

Sam pulled Calvin's arms behind his back and slapped handcuffs on him. "What did you do with your gun?"

"What gun?" Calvin asked.

Sam looked at Hap. "Does Calvin have a last name?"

"Tibbs. And he also has a rap sheet longer than my arm," Hap responded.

"Anyone with you, Calvin?" Sam asked.

"No."

"Why are you out here at night shooting at an officer?"

"What officer? I didn't shoot at any officer."

Sam started frisking Calvin. "You're just out here doing a little nighttime target practicing?"

"I was just out for a walk," Calvin muttered.

Hap laughed. "Yeah, I can see it's a great night for a walk. Funny you hid your car in the brush while you were walking." He read Calvin his rights. "I'm arresting you for the attempted murder of Detective Gentry."

"I didn't try to kill no detective," Calvin blurted out. "I didn't know there was any officer there. I was told to kill that dog. That's what I was aiming at."

"Who told you to kill the dog?" Sam asked.

"I don't know."

Sam wrapped his hand around Calvin's arm. "Let's go. I think you were shooting at me, Calvin."

"Wait! I swear I don't know the guy who called me. He got my phone number from a guy I know. But he didn't give a name."

Sam stopped walking and looked at Calvin. "Did he pay you?"

"There was five hundred left on my car seat this morning. He said when I did the job I'd get another five hundred."

"When did he call you?" Hap asked.

"Yesterday. If I did it tonight, he told me he'd give me an extra five. He told me where the woman worked, that she drove a red Jeep, and where they lived. That dog was always supposed to be with her. He told me I could get to the house from the back of the property."

Sam had shoved Calvin's phone in his pocket when he searched him. He pulled it out and scrolled through the numbers. "Did you erase his call?"

"No. He called early yesterday morning."

Once Sam confirmed that Calvin did have several calls early yesterday morning, he tucked the phone back in his pocket to check it out later. "Where did you ditch your weapon?"

Calvin didn't respond.

"Why did this caller say he wanted to kill a dog?" Hap asked.

"He didn't say. I needed the money."

"Did he provide the gun?" Sam asked.

"No, I told him I had one."

Sam grinned at Hap. "A felon with a gun." After Sam escorted Calvin to the back seat of Hap's cruiser, he walked to the passenger side. "Hap, would you mind driving me around to the cottage so I can pick up my car?"

"Sure thing." Hap turned on the interior lights to call for a wrecker to impound Calvin's vehicle, and he saw the blood on Sam's shirt. "How bad is that?"

"Not bad. Just a scratch on my shoulder." Sam looked back at Calvin. "But since Calvin doesn't want to help me find the person who set him up to shoot at an officer, it's going to start hurting a lot more. I may need to go to the hospital so I have proof of how bad it is."

Hap glanced at Calvin in the rearview mirror. "Attempted murder of a police officer is a serious charge."

"Honest, I didn't shoot at him. I was aiming at the dog," Calvin insisted.

"I read you your rights, Calvin. You want to wait for your attorney before you start talking?" Hap asked as he hit record on his phone.

"I don't need no attorney," Calvin stated.

"Give me the name and number of your friend who recommended you to the man who hired you," Hap said.

Calvin gave them his friend's name along with his phone number. "I think my friend works for the man who called me."

Turning around in his seat, Hap pointed his meaty finger at Calvin. "Just so you know, Calvin, several months ago I deputized that dog you were trying to kill. He still works for the police department, so either way, you were trying to kill an officer of the law."

"You're hurt!" Honey saw the blood on Sam's shirt as soon as he walked through the door.

"It's just a scratch." Sam rubbed Elvis's ears when he jumped on him. "You okay, buddy?"

"He's been waiting for you." Woodrow poured Sam a shot of bourbon and handed it to him. "Here, you probably need this."

"Thanks, Woodrow." Sam tossed the contents back.

"Come on, I need to have a look at your shoulder." Honey took him by the hand and pulled him to the bathroom.

Everyone followed them to the bathroom where Sam removed his shirt. Honey pulled out her first aid kit from the cabinet and pointed to her vanity chair. "Sit."

"The bullet just grazed me. It's nothing serious." Truth was, he sort of liked Honey fussing over him. But the bathroom was very crowded with everyone in there, and Elvis was trying to climb on his lap.

Honey opened the first aid kit. "It may not be serious, but it still needs to be cleaned."

"If you don't mind, I'll shower first. I have a change of clothes in the car."

"I don't mind. I'll disinfect your shoulder after you shower. Preston can get your clothes from your car." Honey guided everyone from the bathroom to give Sam some privacy. Preston lagged behind and told Sam that Troy Spencer was at home when he called.

"Thanks, Preston. I'd appreciate it if you would keep this conversation between us."

When Preston walked out, Sam looked around Honey's bathroom. He liked the way she had all sorts of girlie items lined up on the counter. He picked up a bottle of perfume and sniffed. Glancing down at Elvis, he held the bottle to his nose. "This smells really good. Is that why you're always sniffing her neck?" He set the bottle down and looked at the huge jetted tub at one end of the room. He was tempted to climb in there and relax for an hour, but he didn't have time.

After he showered, he found his clean clothes on Honey's bed. He pulled on his jeans, but he left the bedroom carrying his shirt. Honey was waiting for him with a fresh cup of coffee and her first aid kit.

While she worked on his shoulder, he told everyone about capturing Calvin. "Someone paid him to kill Elvis."

"Sounds like the killer is worried that Elvis will lead them straight to their door," Woodrow commented.

Sam glanced at Woodrow. "This is probably my fault. I mentioned to several people I've interviewed that Elvis could remember anyone or anything he smelled. I'm afraid I endangered both Elvis and Honey.

"The paper published an article about Elvis when he found that boy. You didn't say anything that people didn't already know," Woodrow assured him.

"No one had committed two murders then," Sam replied, feeling guilty that he'd put Elvis's life in danger.

Woodrow wanted to alleviate Sam's concern. "Starting tomorrow we will have six guards around the property. This isn't going to happen again."

"I'll be back in a few hours to search for the pistol Calvin used. Elvis will be a big help."

Honey added the last piece of tape to the gauze. "All done." She thought he was going to have another scar to add to his collection.

"Thank you." Sam smiled at her as he pulled his shirt on, tucked it inside his jeans and clipped his holster to his belt.

Honey watched his every move. "Thank you for protecting Elvis. Please be careful."

Elvis nudged Sam's hand, and Sam ruffled his fur. "Anything for my buddy." He then leaned over and kissed Honey. "Thanks for the coffee and the patch job. I'll be back in a few hours. Don't let anyone in the yard until I find that spent cartridge and the pistol."

CHAPTER TWENTY-FOUR

WOODROW STAYED AT THE COTTAGE all night, and the men he'd hired for surveillance arrived at the same time Sam returned to the cottage. Sam directed the men to the most vulnerable locations around the property. Sam walked out the door with Elvis on a leash when Officer Reed pulled into Honey's driveway.

Officer Reed joined Sam on the porch. "I thought you might need some help finding that weapon."

"Thanks. We have Elvis, so we might get lucky and get this done a lot faster," Sam replied.

They quickly found the spent cartridge, and once Sam held it to Elvis's nose, they took off into the woods.

"I've never seen anything like this dog," Officer Reed told Sam twenty minutes later as he snapped photos of the weapon that had been tossed in the brush.

"He makes our life a lot easier." Sam picked up the .38 pistol Elvis had discovered and tucked it inside an evidence bag. "It would have taken us several hours to find this thing."

Sam left Honey's to go to Bunny Spencer's house. He wanted to return the bottle he'd *borrowed* earlier, and he intended to ask her a few more questions. When he arrived at the Spencer home, he saw Lorraine's car in the driveway.

"I'm sorry, but Mrs. Spencer is indisposed," the housekeeper told Sam.

Sam glanced at his watch. Seeing it was just a few minutes past noon, he figured *indisposed* meant she was probably drunk. "I see Lorraine Howell's car in the driveway. Would you tell her I'm at the door?"

He didn't wait long before he saw Lorraine hurrying from the study. "I didn't expect to find you here."

"Sam, I don't think Bunny is in any condition to be interviewed. She's already had too much to drink today. I came over hoping I could convince her to go to a rehab facility."

"I'd like to try to talk to her. It's important," Sam replied.

"You can try. She's in the study."

Bunny was lying on the sofa when they entered the study. When she saw Sam, she raised her head from the cushion. "I'm surprised to see you again so soon." She then looked at Lorraine and frowned. "Lorraine, you shouldn't have called him. You know I'm not at my best."

"Lorraine didn't call me." Sam walked to the bar to pour a glass of water as he discreetly returned the bottle he had in his suit jacket.

He walked back to Bunny and handed her the glass of water.

Bunny took a sip. "I think you forgot the bourbon."

"You're not getting more bourbon," Lorraine stated firmly.

Bunny exhaled loudly. "Lorraine, you don't understand. How could you? You don't have to worry about your husband leaving you for another woman."

Lorraine took a seat beside Bunny and reached for her hand. "If your husband would leave you for another woman, he isn't worth drowning your sorrows in bourbon. Look at what you are doing to yourself. You didn't drink like this before you married Troy."

"Nobody understands," Bunny mumbled and closed her eyes.

"Then explain it to me."

Bunny waggled a finger in Sam's direction. "I can't talk with *him* here."

Sam sat in a chair across from her. "If you'll answer a couple of questions for me, I'll leave you alone."

Bunny turned her bloodshot eyes on him. "What do you want to know?"

"Do you know Calvin Tibbs?" Sam asked.

"Calvin Tibbs?" Bunny shook her head. "I don't think so. Should I?"

"How well did you know Alan Snyder?"

Closing her eyes, Bunny covered her face with her arm. "Well enough to know he was no good."

"Why did you meet him in that parking lot across from Randy's Drive-In?" It took her so long to respond that Sam thought she had fallen asleep.

"He wanted money," Bunny mumbled softly.

Lorraine glanced at Sam before asking Bunny, "Why would Alan want to borrow money from you?"

"I didn't say he wanted to borrow money."

Sam leaned forward in his seat, bracing his forearms on his thighs. "Was Alan blackmailing you?"

This time when she didn't respond Lorraine shook her. "She's out cold." Lorraine stood and walked to a chair near Sam. "Bunny has changed since she married Troy. She was always worried about being alone, but now it's worse than ever. She believes Troy is seeing Eugenie."

"Is Troy having an affair with Eugenie?"

"Honestly, I don't know. I can't see Eugenie having an interest in Troy."

Sam didn't tell her that Honey agreed with her. He stood to leave. "I want you to get out of here before Troy comes home. I don't trust him."

Lorraine knew Sam wasn't a man to overreact. "You think Troy is involved in these murders, don't you?"

Sam saw no reason to lie to her. "Yes, and he may be desperate enough to do something stupid."

Glancing down at Bunny, Lorraine whispered, "I don't want to leave Bunny here. I'll wait until she comes around and we'll leave together."

Sam agreed with Lorraine that Bunny needed to be in a rehab facility. And it probably wasn't wise to leave her alone with Troy. "I can carry her to your car now."

Lorraine smiled at him. "Thank you. I'll ask Woodrow if I can take her to his home. Troy would never look for her there." She pointed to a large tote by the door. "I packed her a bag before you arrived. I was hoping I could get her to check into a facility today, but this will give me time to gain her cooperation." Lorraine grabbed the overnight bag and Bunny's purse.

"I hope she listens to you, and appreciates your friendship." Sam lifted Bunny in his arms and carried her out the door.

Sam's phone rang when he jumped in his car. "Yeah."

"I've arranged an appointment with the judge so we can try to get that search warrant you want. Meet me at the courthouse in fifteen minutes," Hap told him.

"On my way." After he clicked off from Hap, he called Honey to tell her that Lorraine was on the way to Woodrow's with Bunny.

"I'll call Mom and tell her to bring Bunny here. Gramps is still here."

"Am I ever going to be alone with you again?"

"If you're lucky," Honey teased.

Sam chuckled. "Tell Elvis I'll see him later."

Pulling into the courthouse parking lot, Sam's phone rang again. He wasn't going to answer, but seeing it was the medical examiner, he quickly changed his mind. He turned his engine off and listened to what Mitch had to say. "I didn't think the knife killed him. Can you put a rush on the results?"

"I thought Judge Abbott was going to have a coronary when you told him Elvis was a corroborating witness," Hap commented as they walked from the courtroom.

Sam left the door to the courthouse rattling on its hinges as he stormed out. "I can't believe he turned me down."

Hap had to jog to keep up with him. "You have to admit, most of our case is circumstantial at this point."

"Hap, I pulled the records from the sale of Pickett's Distillery. You saw in black and white that at the time of the sale, Pickett's Distillery didn't have the inventory to be able to distribute so much bourbon so quickly. I know this has something to do with Alan Snyder. But I need to get inside that building and see what is going on."

"But did you have to tell the judge that Elvis would sniff out the truth?" Hap was laughing and wheezing from exertion at the same time. "That was when he slammed his gavel down so hard I thought the darn thing would break his century-old desk."

Sam threw his hands in the air. "The judge was acting like a jerk. I told him I could bring Elvis into his courtroom to demonstrate his abilities if he didn't believe me."

"The expression on his face was priceless. I swear his face was candy apple red." Hap laughed harder. He grasped the back of Sam's shirt, forcing him to slow his stride.

Sam came to a halt and glared at Hap. "Go ahead and laugh. Wait until you see it for yourself. I can't explain it, but Elvis couldn't distinguish between Pickett's bourbon and Woodrow's. They are one and the same. And that bottle of the unlabeled bourbon I found at the Spencers' home was Woodrow's newest bourbon. Woodrow didn't give them a bottle, and it's not available for sale yet."

Hap held his hand in the air, indicating Sam should give him a minute to catch his breath. When he could finally breathe and talk at the same time, he said, "That's one of the problems. We couldn't tell the judge you lifted that bourbon without a warrant from a suspect's home. That's all we need is for him to find out that piece of information. He's so hard-nosed that he'd have us cooling our heels with the people we arrest. And who could blame him? We need hard evidence to convince Judge Abbott."

"I don't need that bottle of bourbon to know that Troy is our man, and somehow Eugenie Grayson is wrapped up in this to her diamond-studded neck," Sam muttered.

"Surely you understand that the judge can't wrap his brain around the idea that the town's wealthiest citizen could be involved with a murder, much less two murders," Hap countered. "Particularly when Eugenie doesn't have as much as a traffic ticket on her record. Not to mention that Eugenie and Jefferson are the benefactors of almost every worthwhile cause in Kentucky. And he probably donates a hefty sum to all of the politicians!" Hap took another deep breath. "I know what a fine detective you are, but I think we're stretching on this one. What does Eugenie have to gain? Do you think she's having an affair with Troy and committing murder for him?"

Sam pulled his sunglasses from his pocket and put them on. "I think Troy wants me to think he's having an affair with Eugenie. I'm not convinced they are, but I know she's involved in some way. And just today, Bunny Spencer said Alan wanted money from her."

"You mean he was blackmailing her for some reason? Did the money we found in Alan's home come from Bunny?" Hap asked.

Sam told him Bunny wasn't in any condition to be questioned at that time. "I imagine Bunny is sleeping it off at Honey's right now."

"Sam, are you positive Troy is the murderer?" Hap asked.

Sam didn't need time to consider his response. "Yes."

"Then we'll take another shot at the judge tomorrow, but you need to try to come up with something more than Elvis's nose."

Sam was beginning to understand how small towns worked. He wasn't holding out a lot of hope that the judge would see things their way. In the meantime, he'd find more proof of Troy's involvement.

Elvis jumped up and ran to the door with tail wagging, and Honey knew Sam had arrived. When she opened the door, Elvis leaped into his arms, and Honey issued a warning. "Come in if you dare face all of the estrogen in here."

"And I thought Elvis was just glad to see me. Now I know he's trying to escape." Sam laughed as Elvis covered his face with sloppy kisses.

Honey smiled at his comment. "You look tired."

"It's been a long day."

"How's your shoulder?" Honey had worried all day about him.

He smiled at her. "Just a scratch. I had some beautiful woman patch me up."

"I hope that doesn't happen often," Honey remarked.

"What? Having beautiful women patching me up?" Sam asked trying to look innocent, but his blue eyes were twinkling.

"No, getting shot!"

Sam didn't want to make any promises. "Is Bunny here?"

"Yes. She's in the extra bedroom sleeping. She talked to Mom for a while before she fell back to sleep."

"She hasn't had more to drink, has she?" Sam wanted her sober when he talked to her.

"No. Mom said she's mentally exhausted. We thought we should let her sleep," Honey replied. "Come on in and have some dinner. I made a chicken broccoli casserole, real mashed potatoes, and even baked a loaf of bread."

The thought of a good meal made Sam forget how tired he was. He sniffed the air, much like Elvis. "It smells wonderful in here."

Honey laughed at him. "Have you eaten today?"

Sam shook his head. "No time." They reached the kitchen and Sam greeted Lorraine and Georgia.

Lorraine reached over and patted Sam on the forearm. "Thank you again for your help today, Sam."

"No problem. Is she going to be okay?"

"I think so. She was more lucid when she woke earlier. I think she will go to rehab now."

"Sit down, Sam," Honey instructed.

Sam pulled out a chair at the counter as Honey placed a plate of food piled high with a glass of iced tea in front of him. "This smells delicious." When Honey set the basket of warm bread beside his plate, he smothered a piece with the softened butter.

Georgia started grilling him about his investigation. "Do you know who paid the guy to shoot Elvis?"

"I think I do." Sam stuffed a big bite of mashed potatoes in his mouth.

"So did you arrest them?" Georgia asked.

Sam shook his head. He really didn't want to discuss the investigation.

A phone rang, interrupting Georgia's questioning.

Lorraine held the phone in the air. "It's Bunny's phone."

Sam read the screen. "Troy." Sam wasn't surprised. "Has she spoken to him yet?"

"No, and I'm not telling her he's calling. She needs to stay away from him."

"I can't disagree with that," Sam responded.

Before Georgia could commence with her questions again, Honey picked up Sam's glass and added more tea. "I need to take Elvis out.

Would you like to sit on the patio and finish your dinner? I'm sure you're tired of talking about all of this."

Sam smiled at her, grateful she'd read his mind. "Sounds good."

Once they were on the patio and Sam finished his dinner, Honey fluffed a cushion on one of the lounge chairs. "Sit here and relax." She walked back inside and poured him a bourbon.

Sam was sitting on the lounge chair when she returned and she handed him the bourbon. "I'll walk around for a few minutes with Elvis and give you some time to relax."

"Stay where I can see you."

"Don't worry. Gramps has this place surrounded like Fort Knox."

He watched Honey and Elvis as he sipped his bourbon and thought about his meeting with the judge. He didn't know what it would take to convince the judge, but he knew he was right. Everything hinged around getting a search warrant for the property on Old Honeysuckle Road. The only piece of the puzzle that wasn't sliding into place was Eugenie. What was her part in the murder or murders? What possible reason could she have to want K.C. dead? Did he threaten to tell her husband about their affair? From what everyone said about K.C., he was a great guy. Great guys wouldn't blackmail a woman. And K.C. clearly didn't need money. Honey knew K.C. well, and she didn't believe he had been dating a married woman, even though Sam knew it was a fact. Did she just not want to believe anything negative about him? He had to admit, from what he'd learned about K.C., it was out of his character to date a married woman. But sometimes, even the best people made mistakes.

Honey and Elvis walked back to Sam. He was sound asleep, clutching his glass that was resting on his stomach. Honey gently removed the glass from his grasp as Elvis sniffed his neck. Sitting in the lounge chair beside Sam, Honey motioned for Elvis to climb up beside her. When he snuggled up next to her, she whispered in his ear, "Be very quiet and let him sleep."

CHAPTER TWENTY-FIVE

"Is Detective Gorgeous awake?" Georgia asked when she stepped out on the patio.

Sam's eyes were closed, but he grinned as he stretched. "Yep, Detective Gorgeous is on the job. What do you need, Georgia?"

Honey turned to Sam and smiled at his response. "We thought you were asleep."

Elvis jumped from Honey's chair and made himself comfortable on top of Sam's chest.

Sam looked at Honey and chuckled. "Why don't you call me that?"

"You might get a big head."

"Honey prefers Sleeping Beauty," Georgia told him.

Sam locked eyes with Honey. "Sleeping Beauty?"

"Long story." Honey glanced at Georgia. "Did you want Sam for a specific reason?"

Georgia slapped her forehead with her hand. "Oh yeah! Bunny is awake and sober. Lorraine told her you wanted to talk to her."

Sam scratched Elvis behind the ears. "Buddy, let's go see what she'll tell us."

"I'll get Mom and we'll sit outside while you talk to her."

They walked back inside to see Lorraine and Bunny sitting at the counter.

Bunny greeted Sam when he walked to the opposite side of the counter. "Thank you for your help today, Sam."

"No thanks necessary."

"I can answer some of your questions now." Bunny smiled at Lorraine, and added, "Thanks to my friend, I'm getting myself together. She's the only person who ever stood beside me."

Lorraine started to reply, but Bunny's phone rang. She glanced at the screen and slid the phone to Bunny. "It's Eugenie."

"We'll give you some privacy, Bunny," Honey said.

"No need. We all know what's going on."

"Don't tell Eugenie where you are," Sam advised.

Nodding her understanding to Sam, Bunny answered her phone. She listened for a few minutes and then replied, "Eugenie, it's none of your business where I am. I think you have a lot of nerve calling me when you are having an affair with my husband." She listened again to what Eugenie had to say, and then responded, "No, the detective didn't give me that information. I'm just not as dumb as you think."

Honey and Sam exchanged a look. Sam was impressed that Bunny was maintaining her composure. She wasn't even yelling, and Sam thought that took some self-control, considering she thought Eugenie was having an affair with her husband.

"Eugenie, I may flirt with men, but I've never cheated like you," Bunny snapped. "Since Troy called you so concerned about my whereabouts, you can give him a message from me. Tell him my attorney will be in touch, and as of ten minutes ago, he no longer has access to any of *my* money. As for you, *my friend*, you will be named in my divorce papers as the *other* woman. Jefferson will know your part in this." Bunny clicked off her phone and looked at Sam. "Now, let me tell you about Alan."

"Are you certain you don't want privacy? We can sit on the patio until you're finished," Honey offered again.

"It's not necessary, Honey. I have nothing to say that all of you can't hear. Would you please make some coffee? I think I'm going to need a gallon." Bunny jumped up from the counter and walked toward the living room. "Why don't we get comfortable?"

Honey and her mother served the coffee in the living room. Honey took a seat on the sofa beside Sam, with Elvis on his other side.

Bunny started by saying, "I gather you all know that Eugenie is having an affair with Troy."

"I know that's what Troy wants everyone to think," Sam answered.

Bunny arched her brows at Sam. "You don't think he is? Eugenie didn't say it wasn't true."

"I think Troy has something he is holding over Eugenie," Sam replied. "I also believe Eugenie is involved in some way with the two murders, but I'm not convinced she is having an affair with your husband."

"What about Troy? Do you think he's involved in murder?" Bunny asked.

"I'll be honest with you. Troy is my number-one suspect. As a matter of fact, I'm trying to get a search warrant for your property on Old Honeysuckle Road." Sam saw no reason to hold back. He didn't suspect Bunny was involved in murder, and since she was in a cooperative mood, he thought he might finally get some answers. "What were you going to tell me about Alan?"

"Alan called me and asked me to meet him that morning at Randy's. He told me about Troy and Eugenie meeting at the Tucker property. He also said Troy was involved in something much more serious. That's why he was asking for money. He told me if I paid him two hundred thousand, he'd destroy the pictures he had of Troy and Eugenie."

"Did he show you the photos?" Sam asked.

"He showed me one photograph that morning. He told me I would get all of them when I paid him."

"And you were certain it was Troy?"

Bunny was silent for a moment as she tried to recall the photo. "It was definitely Eugenie. All I saw of Troy was his back. I thought it was him. It was taken in the upstairs bedroom at the Tucker farm."

"Did you pay Alan?"

"No. I told him I needed time to get that much cash together. He tried to call me again, but I didn't return his call." Bunny looked Sam in the eye. "I guess I could be a suspect in Alan's murder, but I didn't kill him. I had actually made a decision to pay him to keep the affair a secret. I was going to tell him the night of the party on the train."

"Did you see Alan at all that night?" Sam asked.

"No. Even though I didn't want to face it, I knew Troy was involved in something more serious than an affair. I didn't want to believe what I was thinking, so I...drank to keep from thinking."

"Did you think Troy killed K.C.?" Sam guessed that was what she'd thought all along.

She looked at Sam and nodded. Tears slid over her cheeks, leaving trails of black mascara. "I didn't want to think he did. I thought if he did commit murder, then I was to blame because I flirted with K.C."

Honey walked to the bathroom and came back with a box of tissues and placed them beside Bunny.

Bunny wiped her eyes and continued her story. "I asked Troy if he killed K.C. He said he would never kill a man over me. He told me I wasn't worth it."

Not wanting to interfere with Sam's questioning, no one uttered a sound. Even Elvis sat quietly as though he knew the conversation was important.

It was Bunny who broke the silence. "Sam, why do you think Troy killed K.C.?"

All eyes turned to Sam to see how he would answer that question, but a knock on the front door drew their attention. Sam motioned for Honey to keep her seat. "I'll get it." He stood, but the door opened and Woodrow walked in.

Seeing everyone seated in the living room, Woodrow hesitated to join them. "Am I intruding?"

Bunny shook her head. "No, please join us. You'll want to hear this. Sam was just about to tell us why he thought Troy killed K.C."

Sam debated his response, but he thought he would lay his circumstantial case on the table. "Before I answer that question, let me start at the beginning. I think Alan was supplying Woodrow's bourbon to Troy."

Bunny interrupted with a question. "Why would he do that? There was some inventory when we bought Pickett's."

"I know. I researched the sale and spoke to the banker. There was some inventory, but certainly not on the scale supporting the recent distribution. I think that was why he pressured you to buy the property on Old Honeysuckle Way. I think Alan found a way to cook the numbers at Woodrow's distillery so no one would notice that he was stealing bourbon." Sam glanced at Woodrow. "I think that was the real reason he was so upset with you for hiring Cullen. He thought Cullen would eventually figure out what was going on."

"But Troy didn't need the money. I assumed all of the money I was giving him was going into the business. Why didn't he just wait and do things the right way?" Bunny asked.

Sam thought of his conversation with Hap. The three reasons for premediated murder. Greed—Sex—Power. "Greed." Sam thought Troy probably didn't want to be married to Bunny, but he wanted her money.

"Troy asked me a few months ago why I hadn't changed my will yet. I really don't know how he knew what was in my will. We never discussed it, but I guess he found a copy at home. He knew I hadn't changed it to include him." Bunny glanced at Sam. "I guess we now know why he was asking."

Realizing what Bunny was implying, Lorraine shuddered. "Thank goodness you didn't change it."

"But what does K.C. have to do with this? Why was he murdered?" Honey asked.

"K.C. and Eugenie met at the Tucker farm. I think the day he waited for the tow truck after Eugenie rammed his car, he nosed around and he figured out what was going on in that warehouse."

"But what's in the warehouse?" Georgia asked.

"It's my guess that we'll find stolen bourbon inside."

"I always thought K.C. was at the wrong place at the wrong time. But I never expected he would know his killer or killers," Woodrow said.

"And what about Eugenie? What's her roll in all of this? Georgia asked.

"Troy figured out her relationship with K.C. and he saw easy money. I don't know if they planned K.C.'s murder together, but I think she knew about it. I think Troy was blackmailing Eugenie."

"But why would Alan sell my bourbon to Troy?" Woodrow asked. "I paid him very well. There was nothing to indicate he needed money."

Sam couldn't explain Alan's behavior. "I don't know why he did it, but I'm confident he did. And you saw for yourself that Elvis pretty much confirmed my theory when he couldn't tell the difference between the bourbons." Sam rubbed Elvis's head when he looked at him. "He has the greatest nose I've ever seen." He looked at Bunny and explained the taste testing they'd conducted.

"I told Troy the two bourbons tasted exactly the same. He laughed at me. He said I drank so much bourbon that I didn't have a discriminating palate," Bunny told them. "Sam, you mentioned you tried to get a search warrant for the farm on Old Honeysuckle Road. Do you still need that?"

"Yes, Judge Abbott wants more evidence. He doesn't have as much faith in Elvis's nose as I do," Sam admitted.

"You mean Theodore Abbott?" Bunny asked.

"Yeah, that's the judge. Hap and I couldn't convince him and he rejected our request. Hap said it would take a lot more evidence for him to allow suspicion to be cast on our most prominent citizens."

Bunny picked up her phone and scrolled her contact list. She made a call and put the phone on speaker. When a man answered, she said, "Teddy, this is Bunny. Sorry for disturbing you so late, but I wanted you to hear this from me. I am giving Detective Gentry permission to search my property on Old Honeysuckle Road any time he so chooses." She listened to his comments. "I'll put it in writing right now. And if he wants anything else involving any of my properties, he has my permission to do what needs to be done. I just wanted you to hear it from me. Thanks, Teddy." Seeing the surprise on Sam's face, she explained her relationship to the judge. "Lorraine, Teddy and I went to high school together."

"Thank you for that." Sam was beginning to soften his opinion of Bunny.

"Do you want to go tonight and have a look around?"

Sam thought he should have a look at that warehouse before Troy had time to clean it out. He glanced at Honey. "I'd like to take Elvis with me."

Honey nodded her approval.

"I'll call Hap and see if we have the people we need to do this tonight." Sam left the room to make his call. When he came back, he told them it was going to take a few hours to get everyone together. "I suggest everyone get some sleep."

Woodrow stood to leave. "Lorraine, if you and Bunny want to stay at the house, you know you are welcome."

"We'll come to your house if Sam will stay with Honey and Georgia tonight. Preston had to leave town to pick up a horse," Lorraine replied.

Sam's eyes landed on Honey. "I'm staying."

Before Bunny left with Woodrow, she handed Sam the keys to the home on Old Honeysuckle Road, along with her written consent to search the property. "If you need anything else, give me a call."

After everyone left, Sam, Honey and Georgia sat in the living room discussing the case.

"I'm still surprised a man used a knife as his weapon," Georgia mused. "If it was Troy, he has so many muscles, he could simply strangle someone."

"I still have a difficult time believing a woman could kill a man with a knife unless he was incapacitated in some way," Honey responded.

"You're on the right track, Honey," Sam stated. "A knife didn't kill K.C. or Alan."

Honey and Georgia sat wide-eyed, waiting for Sam to explain further.

Sam shrugged. "I can't tell you what killed them right now, but it wasn't a knife."

"I'm going to stop calling you Detective Gorgeous," Georgia threatened.

Honey laughed. "We don't want to know something if Sam can't tell us, Georgia."

"Yes, we do! I want to know every detail," Georgia countered.

Sam stood and pulled a lock of Georgia's red-streaked hair. "After tomorrow I'll tell you everything." He reached for Honey's hand and pulled her from the sofa and gave her a lecherous grin. "Now, do I get to sleep in your room since Georgia gets the extra bedroom?"

"I'll get you a blanket and a pillow, Detective."

CHAPTER TWENTY-SIX

S AM AND ELVIS ARRIVED AT the property on Old Honeysuckle Road before Hap and the other officers. After he batted away a few cobwebs at the front door, he pulled out the key Bunny had given him. The last time he'd been out here, he'd looked in the windows, but he couldn't see much. Before he walked inside, he opened the plastic bag in his hand, and held it to Elvis's nose. One of K.C.'s shirts was inside the bag. It was his belief that K.C. was murdered in this house. Sadly, he thought K.C. paid with his life for his mistake of dating a married woman. If Sam was right, K.C. saw something he shouldn't have, which resulted in his murder. It all revolved around this property.

Once he'd walked inside with Elvis beside him, the first thing he noticed was the dust on the expensive furnishings. No one had been out here to clean in a few weeks. He watched Elvis methodically sniff his way through the house. Elvis sat down at a closed door and turned his big brown eyes on Sam. Pulling his handkerchief out of his back pocket, Sam used it to open the door. Elvis bolted into the room and immediately ran to a leather wingback chair in front of a large walnut desk. After Elvis sniffed the chair, he barked. Sam knew that he'd found what he was looking for. Sam wasn't surprised K.C.'s scent was in the room, he'd expected it. Stroking Elvis's head, Sam praised him. "Good boy."

A bar at the back of the room caught Sam's attention. Bottles of Pickett's bourbon were lined up alongside Woodrow's bourbon. He noticed some glasses sitting on the counter that had obviously been used, but not washed. In one cabinet, he saw a small clear container sitting at the very back of the top shelf. Once he opened the jar with his handkerchief, he saw a small amount of a white, powdery substance. He realized that he could be looking at what really killed K.C. and Alan.

Elvis barked just before someone opened the front door.

"Sam, are you in here?" Hap called out from the foyer.

Sam walked to the hallway and motioned for Hap to join him in the study. "You need to see this."

Hap whistled as he walked into the study. "Boy, Eugenie spent a lot of money decorating this place."

"Yeah, she spared no expense for her lair to meet her lover or lovers." Sam pointed to the bar at the back of the room. "In that cabinet I think we are going to find what's left of our murder weapon."

"Well, I won't taste it," Hap replied.

Sam chuckled. "Considering what the coroner told me, I think that's wise."

"The boys will be here in a minute. I also have a bit of good news and bad news for you."

Sam arched his brow in question.

"There was a fingerprint lifted from that knife in Alan's back. The bad news is it didn't match any known criminal," Hap told him.

"And the good news?"

Hap waggled his bushy eyebrows. "The fingerprint matched the one lifted from the glass you took to the lab."

Sam grinned. "I thought it might."

"I know the person didn't realize you were lifting their fingerprints, but now do you want to tell me whose prints we were comparing? Was it Troy Spencer's?" Hap asked.

Sam shook his head. "Eugenie Grayson's."

"When did you lift that glass without her noticing?"

"When I was interviewing her that night on the train," Sam replied.

"So she offed both men?" Hap asked, still skeptical that a woman like Eugenie Grayson would commit murder.

"No, I think Troy killed both of them, but somehow he's involved Eugenie, and found a way to incriminate her. Let's go upstairs and see what we can find."

Upstairs, Sam and Hap searched drawers in the master bedroom, looking for anything that would give them evidence of a relationship between Eugenie and Troy. Sam opened the double doors at the back of the room and walked inside the expansive closet. Some dresses and shoes were still in the closet. Sam wondered who used the bedroom now, since Eugenie had sold the place to Bunny. He didn't see anything out of the ordinary until he started to walk out the door. Elvis was standing by the door and he nudged it with his nose, closing it just enough for Sam to see the small safe mounted in the wall behind the door. The safe had a combination lock, and though he didn't expect it to open, he pulled the handle.

When the door opened, Sam patted Elvis on the head. "What do we have here, Elvis?" He peeked inside and saw a manila envelope. Using his handkerchief again, he pulled the envelope from the safe. Seeing it wasn't sealed, he peeked inside and saw at least a dozen photographs of K.C. and Eugenie. The photographs had been taken in the bedroom. Sam knew from the angle that the photographs had to have been taken from the closet. He noticed a small hole at the back of the safe, so he leaned in and peered through the hole. There was a perfect view of the bed from that vantage point. "Troy, you dirty rotten scoundrel."

"What'd you say?" Hap yelled.

"See that Gustav Klimt painting on the wall?" Sam asked.

"The what?" Hap looked around the room and saw several paintings on the walls.

"The one with the man kissing the woman. The one beside the closet door," Sam clarified.

"Oh, yeah, I see it."

"Walk over and see if you see anything unusual about it."

"It's pretty." Hap inspected the painting and he saw the small hole in the crown of flowers on the woman's head. He looked through the hole and saw Sam's eyeball staring back at him. "Well, I'll be." He turned around to look at the room. The hole was in line with the bed. "Well, I'll be," he repeated. "Seems like we have a peeping Tom."

Sam walked from the closet. "I'd say we have a peeping Troy and a blackmailer."

Hap rubbed his jaw. "So, you're thinking that's what Troy was holding over Eugenie's head."

"Can't think of a better way to keep a woman like Eugenie quiet." Sam held the envelope so Hap could see the photos inside. "Nothing like catching unsuspecting folks in compromising positions to earn a buck. Troy was probably threatening to share the photos with Jefferson if she told anyone about his illegal business."

"That boy is a real piece of work."

Sam turned around and looked at the painting. "Yeah, and he ruined a beautiful painting."

Hap braced his arm against the doorjamb. "Let me get this straight. You think Eugenie found out Troy and Alan were stealing from Woodrow. Troy took pictures of her with K.C. and used that to keep her quiet about the theft."

"Yes, and I think Troy told Alan what he had on Eugenie. Alan wasn't about to miss out on the action, so I think he took it a step further. I think Eugenie was the source of all that money we found in Alan's house. Eugenie was on the losing end with both Troy and Alan."

"What I can't figure out is why you think Troy is the murderer. I think it's more likely Eugenie poisoned them. Women are known to use poison," Hap reminded him.

Sam grinned at him. "You sound like Georgia. She watches those true crime shows and says women use knives more than men."

"She's right," Hap agreed.

"Here's another puzzle for you. Why poison them, and then stick a knife in them after they were dead?" Sam questioned.

"Now that is something I can't figure out."

"That's why I think Troy is our killer. He killed K.C., and wanted to incriminate Eugenie if we got too close to him. Somehow, she watched him commit murder, or was involved in the planning. He wanted us to think a woman did it."

"I still think Eugenie poisoned them." Hap cocked his head at Sam. "If you are so certain it was Troy, would you drink a bourbon if Eugenie gave it to you?"

Before Sam responded, they heard the officers walking through the front door. "While they are going through the house, let's go see what's in that building out back."

Sam told the men about the items in the bar he wanted dusted for prints, and the contents of the glass container he wanted analyzed immediately.

"Hang on a second, Hap." Sam made a detour to his car, opened his trunk and pulled out his bolt cutters.

"I thought you had the keys."

"Bunny wasn't aware the building was padlocked." He easily cut off the lock and as soon as he pulled the door open, Elvis ran in. As Sam expected, the building was being used as a rickhouse. The walls were lined with racks filled with barrels of bourbon. Hap and Sam inspected the barrels along the right side of the rickhouse and they saw Woodrow's iconic horse with its flowing mane insignia branded on the barrels.

Sam noticed a large area walled off at the back of the building. He never expected to find a bottling facility inside the warehouse. Empty Pickett's Reserve bottles lined the shelves, ready to be filled. Sam and Elvis walked to the barrels lining the left side of the warehouse. On a row of barrels, there was Woodrow's newest label stamped on each barrel. "Hap, we have a row of Woodrow's new bourbon on this side."

Hap walked over and examined the barrels. "Bluegrass Devil's Due Bourbon." His eyes bounced over all of the barrels in the rickhouse. "It's hard to believe that Alan stole all of this bourbon from Woodrow."

"Yeah, they'd worked together for a long time. But I'd bet before the day is over, Woodrow will figure out how Alan managed to steal from him without anyone catching on before now."

"Fortunately, Woodrow will get these barrels back," Hap replied. "We'll have to post a man out here to see who comes to bottle the bourbon. Troy wasn't doing this alone."

Sam's phone rang, and when he glanced at the screen, he looked at Hap. "It's Chance McComb." Thinking it odd that Chance would be calling him, he put the call on speaker when he answered.

"Sam, I think you better get over to the Grayson estate in a hurry," Chance said.

"What's going on?" Hearing the urgency in Chance's voice, Sam started walking toward the door with Elvis on one side and Hap on the other.

"I'm here working at their pool house. I had some equipment running, but I think I heard a gunshot coming from the house. I knocked on the back door and tried the patio doors, but everything is locked," Chance explained. "Sam, I know Troy Spencer is in there with Eugenie."

Sam held the car door for Elvis to jump in the back seat as Hap slid in the passenger side. "Chance, hang tight, we're on the way. If someone has a gun, I want you to stay out of sight."

"I'm behind a bush where no one can see me. I thought I'd wait and see if someone came through the front door."

"Did you see Eugenie earlier? Are you sure she's there?" Sam asked as he drove down Old Honeysuckle Road doing one-hundred-twenty miles an hour.

"The garage was open and I saw her Bentley inside. She'd told me Jefferson would be out of town this week and that's why she wanted me to do the work now."

Sam thought if Troy had shot Eugenie, he would be in a hurry to leave the home. In the event something else was going on, he wasn't willing to risk Chance's life by having him break down the door.

Hap pulled out his cell phone and dialed the Graysons' home while Sam stayed on the phone with Chance. No one answered.

Skidding to a halt on the circular driveway in front of the Grayson estate, Sam told Elvis to stay in the car. He wasn't going to take a chance someone would shoot at him again. Sam and Hap ran from the car, drew their weapons and raced up the stone staircase. Sam scanned the side of the house for Chance and spotted him waving from behind a tree.

"Go around to the back, but stay out of sight. If someone goes out that way, call my cell," Sam instructed.

Sam gave Chance time to make it to the back of the house before he rapped loudly on the door. They listened, but heard nothing. He glanced at Hap. "Want me to kick it in?"

Hap peered through the oval beveled glass on the door. "Wait. I think I see Eugenie walking to the door."

Eugenie opened the door, but she didn't say a word. She turned around and walked away.

"Eugenie, what's going on here?" Hap asked.

When she didn't respond, Hap and Sam followed her down the

hallway. They glanced inside each doorway they passed to make certain the room was empty. Eugenie walked inside the study with Sam and Hap right behind her. Sam immediately spotted Troy lying on the floor in front of the desk. Holstering his weapon, he ran to Troy, kneeled down and felt for a pulse at his neck.

Sam met Hap's eyes and shook his head. "He's dead."

"Eugenie, what happened here?" Hap asked.

Eugenie stared down at Troy.

"Eugenie?" Hap looked at Sam and mouthed, *Shock?*

Sam shrugged, and pointed to a pistol on the desk.

Hap walked closer to Eugenie and spoke softly. "Why don't you tell me what happened?"

She finally looked up at Hap. "I shot him."

Sam picked up the pistol with his handkerchief and smelled the barrel. He nodded to Hap.

"Why did you shoot Troy?" Hap asked.

Eugenie stared off into space, then abruptly turned and walked to the bar across the room. "Can I get you something to drink?"

"No!" Sam and Hap said in unison.

CHAPTER TWENTY-SEVEN

THE EVENING BEFORE THE GRAND opening of the café, Honey invited her family and a few friends for a private dinner at the distillery. She hadn't seen much of Sam since he'd brought Elvis home the day of Troy's murder. They'd talked on the phone, but their conversations had been brief. Both Sam and Hap promised they would be able to make it tonight. If they didn't arrive soon, she thought she'd have to drive Elvis to the station to see Sam. Every time someone walked into the café, Elvis whined if it wasn't Sam. She told Georgia she expected Elvis to run away from home and find Sam if he didn't show up soon.

Elvis was in the kitchen with her while she was putting the finishing touches on dinner. Instead of begging for treats, Elvis's eyes remained fixed on the entrance to the kitchen.

"He will be here soon, Elvis. He promised," Honey told him.

Elvis turned his large brown eyes on her and groaned before he turned his gaze back to the entryway leading to the dining room.

Several minutes later Elvis lurched to his feet and howled. Honey knew Sam had arrived. As soon as Sam walked into the kitchen, Elvis jumped on him. Sam sat in a chair with Elvis in his lap. Elvis was sniffing his neck and covering his face with sloppy kisses.

"Why don't you greet me like Elvis?" Sam asked Honey.

Honey laughed. "I don't think you can hold both of us."

"I'll lift more weights," Sam teased. He stood and walked to Honey, wrapped his arms around her waist and kissed her neck. "You smell good."

"Me or the food?" Honey asked.

"Hmm. Do I have to choose?" Instead of giving her a chance to respond, he kissed her. As he'd envisioned in his mind a thousand times over the last few days, he backed her to the counter and kissed every inch of skin available to him. "I've missed you and our baby boy."

Honey smiled. "I take it you're referring to Elvis."

"Good guess."

"He's missed you terribly. I think he worries about you," Honey told him.

"We need to do something about this situation. I don't like being away from you two."

Before Honey could comment, Georgia walked into the room. "Hello, Detective Gorgeous. Hap said you were in here."

Sam stopped nibbling on Honey's neck. "Hi, Georgia, how are you doing?"

"Great. I guess you know we have been waiting for you and Hap to answer all of our questions."

"I expected as much. Thanks to a cooperative witness and accomplice, I think we have all of the answers," Sam replied.

"Chance and Cullen have arrived, so everyone is here," Georgia announced.

"Perfect. Dinner is ready." She grinned at Sam. "Guess what you're having for dessert."

"You in a pink silky robe?" He whispered in her ear.

Elvis stretched out on the floor between Sam and Honey's chairs, strategically positioning himself to receive tasty morsels from his favorite humans.

Woodrow had insisted they allow Sam and Hap time to enjoy a nice dinner without discussing murder. But after dessert was served, Woodrow relented and told Hap and Sam they'd waited patiently to hear the details of their case.

"Sam can explain it all. He had it figured out early on," Hap remarked.

Sam leaned back in his chair and glanced around the table at their questioning faces. "I can't say I had all of the pieces of the puzzle together, but Eugenie filled in the blank spaces. As all of you know by now, Alan was stealing bourbon from Woodrow and selling the barrels to Troy. Troy needed an isolated place to store the barrels so no one would notice what was going on. That's when he happened on the property on Old Honeysuckle Road. Eugenie had purchased the place specifically to have her illicit affairs. We don't think K.C. was the first. Troy discovered the farm was owned by Eugenie, and he called her to work out a lease for the barn and he paid, or I guess it would be more accurate to say, Bunny paid for a new warehouse to be built. At first, Eugenie wasn't aware that Troy was storing stolen bourbon.

"According to Eugenie, one morning she was with K.C. at the farm, they accidentally left the door unlocked on the house. Troy later told her he snuck inside the house that day and saw them in the bedroom. Apparently after that, Troy managed to install a camera in the bedroom closet. He used the photographs to blackmail Eugenie. She gave him a substantial amount of money to keep him quiet.

"The day K.C. broke off the relationship with Eugenie, she was so angry that she rammed his car. While K.C. waited for a tow truck, I think he must have looked around the property. K.C.'s mother told me he was interested in purchasing the property from Eugenie. According to Eugenie, K.C. had an attorney call her about buying the property. Troy told Eugenie that he saw K.C. at the property one day when they were moving barrels to the rickhouse. Troy explained to K.C. that he was leasing the property from Eugenie.

Eugenie said Troy became paranoid, afraid that K.C. had seen Woodrow's brand on the barrels. He convinced Eugenie to call K.C. and agree to sell him the farm to lure him out there. She told K.C. he could inspect all of the buildings, and Troy would join them to work out their lease agreement on the rickhouse. Eugenie said that K.C. wanted to see the inside of the rickhouse before he signed the contract. Troy insisted they have a drink before they inspected it. That's when Troy poured the bourbon and put cyanide in K.C.'s glass."

"So that's what really killed them?" Georgia asked.

Sam nodded.

"Where did Troy get cyanide?" Woodrow asked.

"Troy told Eugenie that Alan supplied the cyanide. Alan told Troy he used it to get rid of rats. Unfortunately, the dose was enough to kill K.C. instantly."

"Too bad Troy didn't drink it himself. He was the biggest rat of all," Georgia commented.

"You can say that again," Hap agreed.

"Troy forced Eugenie to stab K.C. after he was dead. He told her he wanted to make sure she didn't lose her nerve and go to the authorities. If he was going down for K.C.'s murder, he was taking her with him. They took K.C.'s body to the park late one night. Eugenie said that's when Troy made her stab him in the chest. She watched him remove the knife from K.C.'s chest and replace it with another knife without her fingerprints. He told her he was keeping the murder weapon as a safeguard."

"Not very original of Troy," Lorraine stated.

At her comment, everyone turned to her, and Honey asked, "What do you mean?"

"Your father and I invited Bunny and Troy to dinner on the train when they first started dating. It was murder mystery night and the play performed was *Murder on the Orient Express*. I guess that's where Troy got the idea for the knife."

"Why did they kill Alan?" Honey asked.

"Alan told Troy he wanted more money if he was going to continue supplying the bourbon. Alan made the mistake of telling Troy he was going to confess to Woodrow if he didn't give him more money. The day of the party, Alan called Troy and threatened him again. Troy knew Alan had been drinking, so he agreed to meet him on the train. By the time they met, Alan was drunk and saying all kinds of crazy things."

"But why kill him on the train?" Woodrow asked.

"Troy told Eugenie that Alan was going to confess that night. Troy poisoned him to keep him from talking," Sam explained. "I think he met Alan on the train with the intention of killing him. Otherwise, why did he bring the knife with Eugenie's fingerprints with him, and the cyanide? He met Eugenie in that private compartment and told her what he'd done. Apparently, Troy went back to the compartment later to make certain no one found Alan. That's when he found him in the cooler." Sam stopped talking and glanced at Honey, Georgia, and Cullen. "He didn't know if someone saw him leave the compartment when he killed Alan, or if the police had been contacted. He knew he had to come up with a new plan. He made the decision to push the cooler into the lake. He told Eugenie he still had the knife with her fingerprints. That's what kept her quiet. But in truth, he'd left the knife with her fingerprints in Alan's body."

"I guess Alan thought it would be safe to meet Troy on the train during a party," Woodrow said.

Honey couldn't believe stolen bourbon was the reason K.C. had been killed. "Alan had to know what Troy was capable of doing. If he went to the authorities he would be in jail, but he would be alive."

"Sam has the police department in Troy's hometown looking at their unsolved crimes. We don't think this is Troy's first time at murder," Hap told them.

"Are you saying you think Bunny married a murderer?" Lorraine asked.

"I wouldn't be surprised," Sam replied.

"I just wish I knew why Alan did this," Woodrow said.

"Woodrow, I doubt we will ever know the answer to that question. Sometimes there's no explaining greed. It didn't look like he needed money. He didn't have a gambling or drug habit that we could find," Hap replied.

"Sam, how did you know this was about bourbon in the first place?" Thomas asked.

"I suspected it had something to do with bourbon when I saw that huge warehouse on the Tucker farm. That's when I did some investigating on the sale of Pickett's Distillery. I found out Troy didn't have that much inventory to sell immediately. Proving my theory was a different story. To be honest, I thought I might be wrong until I tested the bourbon on everyone. But Elvis was the real hero. When he sniffed both bourbons and he couldn't tell the difference, I knew my theory was right."

Hearing his name, Elvis stood, put his head on Sam's lap waiting for an ear rub. "Yep, you solved the crime, buddy."

"I'd say it was a lot of good detective work that solved this crime," Thomas responded. "Hap speaks highly of you, Sam, and I can see his praise is warranted. I haven't had the opportunity to thank you for protecting my daughter and Elvis. I appreciate what you've done." Thomas stood and stuck his hand out to Sam.

Sam shook his hand. "You're welcome. But I really couldn't have solved this case without Elvis."

Honey was thrilled her father was finally able to spend some time with Sam. She wanted him to know what a great guy he was.

"I was totally convinced Eugenie committed the murders," Georgia confessed.

Hap smiled at her. "Don't feel bad, I thought she was the murderer too. I was confident she was the one who used the poison. Of course, we are taking her word that Troy was the one who used the cyanide, and Troy is no longer here to say otherwise."

"But why did Eugenie shoot Troy? She'd already paid so much money to keep everything quiet," Honey asked.

"I think she should have poisoned him. Give him a taste of his own medicine," Georgia replied.

"Preston, I would advise you never to make Georgia angry," Hap teased.

Preston leaned over and hugged Georgia. "I don't plan on making her mad. She watches so many crimes shows, she'd know how to dispose of my body without anyone knowing."

"And she knows how to make you look good after your demise," Honey added.

Everyone laughed, appreciating the moment of levity.

"Eugenie told us Jefferson was questioning the money she was spending, and Troy was asking for more. She told me she was glad she shot him. She was tired of being blackmailed," Hap told them.

"Didn't her attorney advise her against admitting her guilt?" Honey asked.

"He did. But you know Eugenie. She was going to do what she wanted to do," Hap replied.

"I'll say this for Jefferson, he hired the best attorney to defend her," Woodrow said.

Hap nodded his agreement. "I think she's going to plead insanity as her defense."

"But who hired the guy to kill Elvis?" Honey asked.

"Troy hired the guy. Eugenie said the night Troy saw Elvis at the restaurant in Lexington, he became even more paranoid. He thought Elvis smelled his scent at the park where he'd found K.C.'s body." Sam paused and looked at Honey. "I'm afraid when I told Troy that Elvis could remember scents, he became even more convinced Elvis knew he was the murderer."

"I think Elvis knew Troy was the killer and that explains why he was so agitated that night at the restaurant," Honey replied. She told her family how Elvis kept her away from Troy that night.

"He definitely knew," Sam agreed.

When the questions stopped, Woodrow told them how Alan stole the bourbon. "Alan and Troy started stealing right after Troy bought Pickett's Distillery. Alan managed to have trucks pick up the barrels after hours, right under our noses. He met the trucks at the distillery, so the security team didn't question what was going on. Troy even had the trucks painted to look like one of our distributors to avoid suspicion. Troy supplied the men to load the trucks."

"No one expected Alan would steal from Woodrow. Alan wasn't the easiest person to get along with, but no one at the distillery thought he was a thief," Cullen added.

"With nearly a million barrels in the warehouses, it was easy enough for Alan to do. But Cullen and I are taking steps to make certain something like this can never happen again."

"I'm sure you heard about the two bodies that washed ashore under Bootleggers Bridge yesterday," Hap said.

"Have they been identified?" Woodrow asked.

Sam hadn't confirmed the identity of the men to the reporters. "Both men were from New York, and they worked at Pickett's. The coroner thinks their bodies were dumped into the lake before Troy was killed. We have a man in custody who was involved in the whole scheme with Troy, and he swears Troy murdered those men. He's given us information on everyone involved. Three men left town when they heard two of their partners in crime were murdered. Apparently, there were six men working for Troy. They drove the trucks, loaded the barrels and handled the bottling at Tucker's farm. We also learned that they were selling bourbon on the black market."

Woodrow shook his head. "You're saying Troy was bootlegging my bourbon?"

Hap nodded. "Yep. They were more sophisticated than they were in the old days when they sold bourbon under Bootleggers Bridge."

"It's all so sad," Lorraine commented.

"Crime usually is," Sam responded. "No one ever wins."

Lorraine nodded. "Poor Bunny. But Sam, you didn't tell us if Alan really had incriminating photographs of Eugenie with Troy. Did they really have an affair?"

"Eugenie denies it. We found some photographs at Alan's home, but it's difficult to tell the identity of the man. Eugenie swears it's K.C. and not Troy."

Honey left her Jeep at the distillery and rode home with Sam. On the way to the cottage, Sam told her his grandmother had invited her and Elvis for Sunday dinner. "Can you two make it?"

"She invited Elvis too?" Honey was surprised that Sam had told his grandmother about them.

"Yes, the invitation includes Elvis. Where we go, Elvis goes. She's excited to meet you both."

"That was very nice of her. We'd love to join you."

Sam glanced her way. "I'm thinking we should also invite Woodrow."

"Did your grandmother invite him?"

"No, but she wouldn't mind. She speaks fondly of Woodrow. I have a feeling they might enjoy renewing their acquaintance."

Honey laughed. "Sam, are you playing Cupid?"

Sam grinned. "Could be. Woodrow's single, she's single. Could be a sign."

Honey rolled her eyes at him. "Oh no! Georgia is rubbing off on you."

Sam reached Woodrow's estate and punched in the code to the gate. When he pulled up to the cottage, he turned off the engine. Before he opened his car door, he turned to look at Honey. "I guess I'll have to get used to Cullen and Chance always being around."

Honey turned in her seat and studied him, thinking he was teasing, but he wasn't smiling. "Why do you say that? Are you jealous?"

He'd noticed how both men looked at Honey throughout dinner tonight. He figured both of them were half in love with her. "I could be." Elvis stuck his head between them, anxious to get out of the car. Sam rubbed his head. "Just a minute, Elvis." He removed his seat belt and swiveled in his seat to face Honey. "You had three men interested in you the first night I had dinner at your house."

Honey thought about seeing him at her door the first time, standing behind Hap, wearing his aviator sunglasses and a killer smile. At the time, she thought he was a handsome man with the most beautiful blue eyes she'd ever seen. After spending more time with him, she realized he was much more than a handsome face. He was intelligent, loyal, kind, and he loved Elvis. "I liked you."

Sam stroked Elvis's ears, and Elvis leaned over and sniffed his neck. "You liked Cullen and Chance too."

"That's true. But there was one thing that definitely swayed me in your favor—besides your Sleeping Beauty blue eyes," Honey teased.

Chuckling, Sam asked, "Will you please tell why you say my eyes are Sleeping Beauty blue? Did Sleeping Beauty have blue eyes?"

Honey told him about the Sleeping Beauty mine. "Georgia says your eyes are the exact turquoise color. She dubbed you with that nickname the night she met you. Then she came up with Detective Gorgeous."

Sam just shook his head, but he was smiling. "So what was the other thing that swayed you in my direction?"

"You paid attention to Elvis."

Sam was surprised by her response. "How could anyone not pay attention to him? He's a great dog."

"Yes, but it was obvious you really liked him. And Elvis was crazy about you from his first sniff. Then I saw him do something he doesn't do to anyone other than me."

"What was that?"

Honey flashed him a smile. "He sniffs your neck, just like he does mine. He doesn't do that with anyone else, and Elvis is a great judge of character. As Georgia would say—that's a sign."

Reaching for Honey's hand, Sam linked his fingers though hers. "It's a sign he knows I'm crazy about him, like I am his owner."

As if Elvis understood what Sam said, he nuzzled his neck and licked him on the cheek.

Honey watched the two of them. "I think Elvis fell in love with you at first sight."

Sam's gaze slowly slid to Honey's. "I think I did too."

With the exception of the first time Honey saw Elvis, she wasn't certain she believed in love at first sight. But like Elvis, her heart was lost the first time she saw Sam. "I think it was mutual."

Sam brought her hand to his lips. "Like I said, we've got to do something about this situation. I miss you guys when I don't see you."

"I think you miss Elvis's licks," Honey replied.

Sam grinned. "There is that. What about you? Do you miss me a little?"

Honey looked up at him. "Well, Detective Gorgeous, I might miss you a little."

Sam lifted Elvis's long, droopy ear and whispered, "Did you hear that, Elvis? She finally called me Detective Gorgeous. I think we're making progress."

Elvis sniffed his neck again and left behind a stream of drool, but Sam just laughed. Honey pulled a towel from her purse and dabbed at Sam's neck and shirt. "There's another reason I liked you from the start."

Sam gave her a quizzical look. "What's that?"

"A little drool doesn't seem to faze you."

"Actually, I've been wondering why you don't drool over me like that."

Honey shook her head at him, but she was smiling. "I only drool in my sleep."

"Your point?" Sam's blue eyes were twinkling when he asked, "Are you asking me to spend the night with you?"

Honey arched her brow. "You're the detective. Can't you figure that out?"

Sam leaned over, unbuckled her seat belt, and brushed his lips over hers. "Please tell me we're going to be alone tonight."

"I think so, but knowing my family, I can't make any promises."

His lips moved to her neck. "Of course, if I didn't stay in the extra bedroom, we'd have to make it legal. I wouldn't want Woodrow to challenge me to a duel."

Honey tried to focus on what he was saying instead of what his lips were doing on her neck. "He is...a...good...shot."

Sam's nibbled his way back to her lips and they shared a long, intimate kiss. When he finally pulled his lips from hers, he gazed into her smoldering eyes. Suddenly, he turned from her, opened his glove compartment, pulled out his handcuffs and handed them to her.

Honey held the handcuffs in the air. "What do you want me to do with these?"

"You'll need those for me in case you wear that little pink robe tonight."

Honey laughed. "I'll keep that in mind."

Sam touched Honey's cheek and he looked into her eyes. "I think we need to spend a lot more time together to see where this is going. What do you think about that?"

Before Honey could even form a reply, Elvis nudged his nose between them, dropped his head on their shoulders and sighed contentedly.

Definitely a sign.

I hope you enjoyed reading *Murder on The Bluegrass Bourbon Train*. I love hearing from my readers, so please leave a review with your favorite retailer and tell me what you think!

ACCLAIM FOR SCARLETT DUNN

Dunn is a talented author who gives fans what they expect in historical romance."

—*RT Book Reviews*
Finding Promise

"Fans of both ethical dramas and historical romances will find much to enjoy."

—*Publishers Weekly*
Whispering Pines

"It is bittersweet when a series ends; questions are answered, readers are reunited with beloved characters. Mary Ann was a favorite; she defied her family and society to explore the Wild West and to prove she could take care of herself. Dunn in a talented author who has brought new and refreshing ideas to the historical romance genre."

—*RT Book Reviews,* 4 Stars
Last Promise

"A Textured, uplifting, inspirational love story."

—*Kirkus Reviews*
Christmas in Whispering Pines

"Marshal Jake McBride is the quintessential romance hero: strong, fiercely loyal to his family and dedicated to justice."

—*Publishers Weekly*
Finding Promise

"The banter between these two free-spirited characters had me smiling bigger and bigger as I turned each page. I didn't want it to end!"

—Carey Ostergard, *First for Women* magazine
Last Promise

"This one swept me off my feet...I didn't want it to end!"

"For those who want a little historical romance and bad boy cowboys, this is the perfect read."

SCARLETT DUNN BOOKS

ABOUT THE AUTHOR

Before becoming a published author, Scarlett Dunn was an entrepreneur. In addition to writing cozy mysteries, Scarlett has several historical inspirational romance novels published. She lives in Kentucky, and as an avid outdoorswoman she enjoys any activity under the sun where she develops her characters and plots. When not writing, her favorite days are spent with those she loves. She has many hobbies, including making bourbon balls. She would tell you her closely guarded recipe, but then she'd have to throw you off the train!

Visit her website: www.scarlettdunn.com

CPSIA information can be obtained
at www.ICGtesting.com
Printed in the USA
BVHW032107250520
580292BV00001B/173